Recipe for Joy

Recipe for Joy

a novel

MONICA COMAS

LAKE UNION
PUBLISHING

This is a work of fiction. Names, characters, organizations, places, events, and incidents are either products of the author's imagination or are used fictitiously. Otherwise, any resemblance to actual persons, living or dead, is purely coincidental.

Published by Lake Union Publishing, Seattle
www.apub.com

EU product safety contact:
Amazon Media EU S. à r.l.
38, avenue John F. Kennedy, L-1855 Luxembourg
amazonpublishing-gpsr@amazon.com

ISBN-13: 9781662532412 (paperback)
ISBN-13: 9781662532429 (digital)

Cover design by Sarah Horgan
Cover image: © Edge Creative, © venski, © Cat_arch_angel / Shutterstock

Printed in the United States of America

For

My mother, Patty

My sister, Kristie

My husband, John

The three who mean the world to me

Sour

Part 1

A clean house is a sign of a misspent life.

Chapter 1

The circular nature of returning to one's childhood home carries an inescapable rhythm—but the precise beat depends on the type of circle being followed.

"Where you in from?"

The Uber driver's voice interrupted my appreciation of the landscape whizzing by. Every mile of highway from the airport felt like I had ownership of it, even though I had no idea what lay beyond the three pink silos labeled *Cocoa*, *Milk*, and *Sugar* at Malley's chocolate factory, or where the Brook Park exit led. Still, these signposts, they were all mine.

"New York." I liked how that landed on people, how it set me apart, as if I'd somehow made it because I lived there instead of here in Cleveland. But this smug delivery, this reply I always had at the ready, felt particularly shameful right now. The bills I'd barely paid off, the checking account I'd drained in the process, the spare key I'd slipped into an envelope and mailed before leaving town, it all felt acidic. Like failure. I leaned back so the driver couldn't meet my eyes in the rearview mirror.

"The Fourth is a good day to travel."

I agreed and lowered the window to feel the breeze, but a hot blast flooded in. I put the window back up.

Silence filled the car for many miles.

"Your parents must be happy to have you home."

I sighed inwardly, preferring the silence. "Actually, my grandmother."

"Aw." He slowed the car and exited the highway. "I'll bet she's looking forward to the help."

I chewed my cheek.

He sat taller to see me in the rearview mirror when I didn't reply.

I nodded. "For sure."

The highway dumped us onto a thoroughfare crammed with suburban retail mainstays. But as we left the business district and entered the village of Gates Mills, the road quieted and narrowed, meandered down a grand verdant hill. Trees grew tall and thick here, rose on the horizon tight like broccoli crowns. The vista felt like an exhale.

The driver hung a right onto Chagrin River Road, which wound through the historic village's white clapboard houses and colonial brick buildings. Trees towered in between homes, near the post office and town hall, all around the library. The village prided itself on a love of nature. Such altruism made for a beautiful hometown.

We passed over a bridge and turned onto Old Mill Road, with its red brick sidewalk that was as familiar as the back of my hand. The houses here were fronted by a long white picket fence, which undulated over short entry gates like tiny waves cresting in front of each home.

The driver stopped in front of Gran's house, a white clapboard cottage with black shutters. It shared features with the neighboring homes—same historic construction, same striking shutters. But like the rest, Gran's house had subtle variations. The windows were in different spots, much like the stubby driveway, and the chimney's masonry was slightly askew in its own way. Some homes had sitting porches. Others, flower boxes. But all the houses stood close like a family, gathered near the road in a companionable line, the way villages were built more than 150 years ago.

I stared at the home I'd called my own since childhood, feeling overwhelmed that someplace so small and neat could hold such complicated enormity within.

The front door opened and Gran stepped out, threw her hands in the air, and twisted her hips back and forth. The way no eighty-seven-year-old did.

"That's your grandmother?" The driver leaned toward the window to take in her exuberance.

Agreeing that I was here to help Gran was an obvious fiction—made even more evident now that she was descending the front steps with ease. Clapping in celebration. Now waving jazz hands. Demonstrating with crystalline clarity that she required help with nothing. The shame of pretending otherwise echoed in my head, and with it, the unmistakable clang of my crashing return.

I muttered thanks to the driver, yanked my bag from the trunk, and rolled it through the waist-high gate.

"Here's my dolly!" Gran wore the dark Sansabelt pants she gardened in, a pink short-sleeved smock top, and thick rubber-soled slip-ons the color of dirt. She beamed, held her arms wide, eyes squinty with cheer like a garden gnome.

I wrapped my arms around my grandmother, Annabelle Bennett, my namesake, and held her roly-poly softness close. Since I was little, Gran had hugged with her whole heart, like she was trying to squeeze love right into you, her presence never a question. Her familiar scent of rose water and Aqua Net wafted up. Even though the top bun of her gray hair didn't reach my shoulder, the energy Gran exuded towered over me. Today, her greeting felt particularly poignant. I blinked to contain the swell of emotion. "I missed you."

"Let me look at you, my beauty!" She leaned back, then held my face and pursed her lips. "Oh, Belle."

"No pinching, Gran."

She pinched me anyway.

"Mrs. B.," a man's voice called from across the street. "I didn't know you had an older sister."

I looked over. "Jeremy, you grew!" Jeremy Watson, who lived in the next town, was the grandson of the neighbors a couple of doors down, and had, since December, sprouted into a stunner of a young man. He bounced a basketball while walking down the sidewalk, had a lightness to his step that you only have at seventeen. A tank top hung from the waistband of his shorts.

"Jeremy, you put your shirt on when you're walking through the village," Gran yelled back. "Now, come here, I have something to give you."

He grinned, slipped the tank over his head in between dribbles, and crossed the street.

I hugged him hello. "You're legit good looking. How'd that happen?"

He shrugged, his grin turning self-conscious.

"He's now the town nudist," Gran quipped. "Carry Belle's suitcase in, would you, dear?"

"Gates Mills needed a nudist," I said to him.

He laughed and took hold of my roller bag.

"How are your parents?" Jeremy's dad, Nate, was a couple of grades ahead of me growing up.

"They're good—you staying a bit?"

"A bit." I paused, then tried to smile away my discomfort. "Yeah."

"We'll do the sparklers later." His eyes were clear, not a hint of anything jaded behind them. He was a young man still enchanted by our tradition of lighting sparklers on the Fourth.

"You know it."

Jeremy followed Gran into the house like a big-pawed puppy, all loose-limbed and eager. His life hadn't even started yet, and he found everything a delight. I was old enough to be his mother, old enough to have perspective on a life lived . . . or not lived, to its fullest. This was a boy—a young man—whom I adored, yet his youthful vim cast a shadow upon me now and drained my energy.

Gran showed Jeremy which bedroom to put my suitcase in, then led him to the kitchen, the two of them chatting away.

I stood inside the front door, savoring the most familiar place on earth. Wide plank floors worn smooth from decades of crisscrossing.

Dollhouse-sized rooms. Brass candle sconces flanking the fireplace mantel. Although the house looked small from the street, it actually extended back from the road to allow for two bedrooms, a bathroom, a sewing room, a living room, a dining room, and a kitchen. All sparsely decorated and reliably neat, with the exception of the sewing room, which was crammed full and had never in all my forty-five years seen any order whatsoever.

My grandparents had moved here when they were newlyweds, before the town got prohibitively expensive for newlyweds. Over the years, bigger, newer homes were built within the town's limits—and then even more massive ones. But the diminutive houses in the village center retained their historical charm, as if cast in amber by Currier and Ives.

I basked in the relief of being here and, at the same time, hated the fragile gloom I'd brought with me.

I'd been alone for so long. Cocooned in solitude, pandemic imposed, then self-imposed. Arriving here felt like a lot suddenly. Too much. Here it was 2022, and the world seemed to be spinning so much faster, or maybe that was how everything normally felt to people. But long ago, normal had morphed into something abnormal for me.

Gran and Jeremy came back into the living room. She carried a plate and a ziplock swollen with dirt.

"When your uncle moves back," she said to Jeremy, "you tell him I want to see him."

"Will do."

"Now, take this." She handed the plate to Jeremy. "Those are cookies for your nana, so don't eat them all. And these," she handed him the baggie, "are night crawlers for your pop pop." She put a hand on Jeremy's arm. "Don't eat the night crawlers."

"Got it." He glanced back as he walked out the door, holding the ziplock aloft. "So, eat these, give the plate to Pop Pop."

Gran smirked and waved him out. "Go, you."

She was always in charge, no matter the situation. I thought back to forty years ago, in the Murray & Sons Funeral Home parking lot.

My dad, his words rushed, told Alexis and me to wait in the back seat of the car while he went inside.

Wearing ruffled dresses and shiny Mary Janes, we sat like dolls in uncertain silence as steamy heat shimmered off the blacktop. Then Lexie, her dark hair damp at the temples, turned to me. "Belle, are we going to see Mommy?"

I looked into her three-year-old eyes and nodded, urging her to understand. "We're going to say *goodbye* to Mommy, Lex." I was only five, but at that moment in the frying-pan-hot car, I felt decades older.

It was all I could get out because then I started crying. Lexie, now scared, began wailing, even though she wasn't entirely clear on why.

That was when Gran marched over to the car—I didn't even know where she'd come from, such are the hazy memories of childhood, especially at that time. Then my father strolled out of the funeral home.

"You left your daughters in the car alone?" Gran hissed at him over the hood. "Shame on you."

He started to protest.

Gran held her hand up, cut him off. "Shameful."

She opened the car door and crouched down to be eye level with us. "My dollies, come here."

We clambered out of the car into her lap, where she gathered us up. Let us cry and cry. She rocked back and forth on her haunches. Her knees must've fallen asleep, but she kept hugging us close. At the wake for our sweet mom, Gran, grieving mightily herself, focused on being a mother to her daughter's daughters.

Eventually, she picked up Lexie and held my hand. As the three of us walked into the funeral home, I caught only a glimpse of my father, a shadowy figure standing off to the side in the distance. And in the proceeding years, that was where he remained.

Even now, decades removed from that moment, I could still recall Gran's close comfort, feeling squished and secure with her and Lex.

"Are you hungry?"

Gran's question pulled me from the memory. "I love how you always want to feed me."

She reached for my hand. "I have fresh raspberries."

The kitchen had been the same daffodil yellow since I was a kid. Morning light streamed through the window, glinting off the porcelain sink and stainless-steel faucet, filling the room with a brightness that had never found my studio back in New York. On the windowsill, a tiny cross-stitch sampler, red floss against a white background, read *A Clean House Is a Sign of a Misspent Life.*

The oak table was the same one I'd sat at my whole life. A glass butter dish, salt and pepper shakers, and a squat cup holding a clutch of pencils (a throwback to when my grandfather was alive) sat on a white doily in the middle of the table. The home's reliable heart thrummed strongest in this room.

Gran set a small, shallow bowl of raspberries in front of me, and one for herself opposite my chair. She drizzled cream over the berries, then sprinkled sugar on top.

"This is perfect, thank you."

Gran stirred her berries, took a bite, and moved her shoulders right and left the way she did. "Good, good, good. You know, my mama used to make this in the summer after morning chores."

The way the story went, my great-grandmother made this for Gran and her sister, Grace, who was three years younger. But I knew better than to ask about the two of them.

"Have you talked to Lexie recently?" Gran said.

I nudged a raspberry through the cream, rolled it over and over.

"Belle?"

I rested the back of my spoon atop the berry and smooshed it. The red juice swirled in the cream. "Not recently."

I could feel Gran's gaze, awaiting more. As usual, there wasn't any. The delicate tapping of our spoons in the berry bowls stood in for conversation in the stilted silence.

"We'll call her while you're here this weekend," Gran said as I cleared our dishes.

She sounded so upbeat at the prospect. I rinsed everything in the sink and thought about how I didn't want to disappoint her. "Sure."

My suitcase belched out a crumpled wad of clothes when I unzipped it. I fished out a pair of khaki shorts and a worn black T-shirt to change into, then sat on my bed near the window, hunched over, head in my hands. A drum mallet beat on a nerve behind my left eye. All I wanted to do was take an Ambien and sleep for ten hours.

Which wasn't an option. I sat up, let the lightheaded woosh settle, and stared at Lexie's bed. It had been decades since we'd shared this room, yet I still thought of that other bed as hers. Whenever I was home, I never set anything on it or used any of the dresser drawers that had been hers, which made no sense. We barely talked anymore, hadn't maintained so much as a toehold in one another's lives. The seam of us had started splitting decades ago. It was the kind of gradual pulling apart that goes unnoticed when you're a teenager and mired in your own self-centered world. But the years pass, and things happen that you notice, things that you absolutely can't ignore. Then other things happen that you can't forgive.

"You decent, Belle?" Gran called through the door.

I opened it. "Define *decent*."

She snickered, looped her arm through mine. "I want to show you what I need help with outside."

We walked down the hallway, but I stopped at the sewing room and marveled at the mess.

The sewing machine sat in the center of the room, a wide dresser just behind it. Boxes stood here and there, some stacked three high, all filled with fabric. Scraps, substantial yardage, all manner of cloth. Cotton, corduroy, silk, linen, chambray. Entire bolts were propped against the walls. Skeins of wool spilled out of one plastic tub. An open box in one corner held pieces that had been cut from patterns, bits big enough that Gran never threw them away. Four more cardboard boxes, corners soft with age, held similar remnants.

"Why did you save this stuff?" I shook my head. "What possible need could you have for all this?"

Gran's smile was cheeky. "She who dies with the most fabric wins."

Just as we neared the kitchen door to the backyard, a pair of voices trilled in the living room. "Knock, knock."

"Come on out back," Gran called as we stepped outside.

Her petite backyard was a verdant oasis. A narrow gravel path meandered through hydrangea bushes with pink and blue pompom blooms, clusters of glossy-leafed hostas, and beds of perennials with vibrant azaleas.

Over the decades, Gran had nurtured every inch of this garden, her beloved outdoor room. A small wrought iron café table and three chairs stood under a sugar maple in full view of two shepherd's hooks—one held a cylindrical bird feeder with a fat column of seed, the other, a milky-white cake of suet. A stone birdbath sat between the two feeders.

"You know the corner." Gran pointed to a sole patch of overgrowth.

"Time to tame this, huh?"

Gran stared at the last wild bit of her plot, which had been shaggy with anemic bushes and weeds for as long as I could remember. This was the corner left undone, or to be done. One last garden delight forever put off for another day. Until now. I wasn't sure if Gran's gaze was limned with anticipation or resignation. She seemed oddly placid about finally tending to this corner of her yard.

She patted my arm. "It's time."

"There you are!" a voice called behind us.

We turned to see Sophia Peroni and Faye Harrison walking toward us. Gran's dearest friends, also widows, neighbors on either side. Mama P, as everyone called Sophia, was short and wide. She kicked off her shoes when she hit the grass. Faye stood tall, impeccably dressed in capris and a blouse, an Hermès scarf draped just so.

"Look at you," Faye groused. "Scampering around like a child in bare feet. You're going to get filthy."

"And you wear silly fancy shoes—gilded channel slippers that you can't actually walk anywhere in for fear they'll get dirty!"

"Chanel. They're Chanel flats. Not something worn in a waterway."

"Look!" Mama P stomped. "I can walk everywhere like this. And my feet are cheaper to clean."

Gran smirked. This is what the two of them did—faux bicker. Faye, imperious village richie, Mama P, gardener extraordinaire, earth mother.

"Hi, honey." Mama P squished me in her embrace. "Your gran said you were coming today! Faye put on her prettiest shoes for you."

"All right, don't squeeze the air out of her now," Faye said. "How's the city that doesn't sleep?"

"It needs a nap." I leaned in for Faye's stiff hug, which she routinely brought to a quick close with two succinct pats on the back.

They sat down with Gran around the café table. Extra lawn chairs were kept in a big outdoor container by the fence. I pulled one out and joined them.

"Oh, this is nice." Mama P looked up at the tree canopy before focusing on me. "It's so good to see you! Are you staying a few days?"

"Yeah." I nodded. Smiled. Did everything I could to sell normal. This was normal, my response. My plans. Everything about me right now. All normal.

Faye eyed me with the faintest knowing smirk.

I swallowed, forced myself not to react. She knew my answer wasn't forthright, and if she knew, they'd all know soon. Gran would know.

They chatted away, about how nice it was to have good weather for the holiday and to have me visit for a few days. I contributed nothing to the conversation.

Gran cupped the side of my face. "Tired? Traveling can take it out of you."

"Maybe . . . yeah." The obfuscation immediately sat wrong, filled me with guilt.

And there was Faye, staring at me across the table with her hawk eyes.

"How about I put a pot of coffee on for all of us?" Gran said.

"None for me, thanks. I have things to tend to before the parade, so I'm going to leave." Faye stood and tapped Mama P on the shoulder.

"I should go too, let you both catch up." Mama P squeezed my arm. "I'm so happy you're home!"

"I'll walk you out," Gran said. "Bellie, you relax. I'll make us some coffee."

I maintained a smile until they were all inside the house, then closed my eyes.

I hadn't been honest. By omission—but still.

This wasn't me.

That afternoon, the village was abuzz.

Neighbors came out in force for the parade. They unfolded lawn chairs on the sidewalk, unfurled blankets on lawns. Red, white, and blue bunting popped against the pristine rails of the picket fence. I always came home for the Fourth of July, but lately I found myself longing for the homespun familiarity of Gates Mills. I missed Gran, but also the fabric of neighbors and friends woven into her life, and, by extension, into mine.

Jeremy, his parents, Nate and Jenny, and his grandparents headed down the street toward Gran's house. I waved hello as they set up lawn chairs next to Gran, Faye, and Mama P.

"I got 'em, Belle." Jeremy came over holding two unlit sparklers and a lighter.

"What do you mean? We don't do these until later. It has to be dark."

"I know." He glanced at his sneakers before looking up. "I have a party to go to later."

"You're cheating on me?" My mouth dropped open. "On the Fourth? This is our day!"

Worry flashed behind his eyes.

"Oh my gosh, no, no, no." I smiled wide so there'd be no uncertainty and rubbed his arm like he was still a young boy. "I'm totally kidding!"

Relief washed over him.

"Sorry, my deadpan is Olympic-level stuff."

He barked out a laugh. "Man, gold medal all the way."

"It's my one talent. C'mon, let's light these babies up."

With a flick of his thumb, Jeremy lit the powder-coated sticks. They immediately spit white sparkly light that sent a jolt through me. This was something we'd done since he was a child, so it wasn't unfamiliar. What felt foreign was embracing this sliver of a moment—it had been so long since anything happy had been ignited within me. Jeremy started running around Gran's front yard, twirling his sparkler overhead, the way we always did.

"Sparkle, Belle!" He grinned as he called out what I used to yell at him when he was a kid.

My feet felt leaden, but I moved them, keeping my eyes on Jeremy, his unadulterated happiness to be doing this silly thing we did. Jeremy was a blur, laughing. Over the years, this ritual had become increasingly funnier as we'd gotten older. I leaned into the happy, but it felt forced, fake, even. And right then, nothing in my long list of disappointments disappointed me more.

But I kept at it, zigging to Jeremy's zag. His laughter eventually loosened something within me. We ran around the yard. I whooped—literally didn't know I had a whoop in me. But there it was, full-throated and foreign all at once.

By the time we'd done a couple of laps and interlinked the crooks of our arms, still holding the sparklers aloft, I felt drunk. Or unmoored.

The whole thing ended with us spinning each other, then collapsing on the grass, laughing. The way it always did.

"Good show!" some passerby yelled.

I waved in acknowledgment without looking up.

Jeremy rolled onto his side. "That might've been our best one yet."

I scrunched my face. "You think?"

"Yeah." He sat up. "You brought something to it."

I closed my eyes, not wanting to break the sweet spell.

"Jeremy, c'mon," Nate called from the sidewalk.

"'Kay, I'm going with my dad and Pop Pop to the driving range, so I gotta bounce." He got up.

I propped myself up on my elbows. "Nate, you just got here!"

"Shhhh!" he mocked. "Jenny and my mom will never know we're gone."

I smiled. "Stellar golfer's rationale."

Jeremy held out a fist to me. "When you staying until?"

I bumped his fist goodbye. "You know, a little bit." It wasn't a lie. Wasn't the whole truth either.

As Jeremy strode off, I lay back down to watch the clouds. My breath slowed. I closed my eyes, enjoying the sun on my face. Jeremy and I could've abandoned our sparkler romp years ago when he was no longer a child who required entertainment. But we didn't. Maybe because childlike fun after you've aged out of it is freeing. Profoundly absurd, but freeing. What snagged me mentally was how difficult it was to tap into this year. And something else: Running around, acting like kids, flopping down on the lawn, left me unbalanced, but in that short burst of silliness, I'd felt more like myself than I had in a long time.

After the barbecues and fireworks, after kids traipsed off to parties, Gran and I sat in the backyard taking in the evening air, as she called it. Boisterous afternoon festivities had given way to a gentle twilight. Firefly bottoms winked at us.

"I can't believe I only get you a few more days." Gran closed her hand over mine and squeezed it. "I do love having you here."

I sandwiched her hand with mine, knew it was time to tell her everything. "I love being here."

But left it at that. Sullying the moment didn't feel right.

Shame crawled up my spine.

Gran slapped her arm. "I think the bugs are coming out."

"Why don't we go in? I'll make us some tea."

"You put the kettle on." Gran got up. "I want to change into my nightie."

Inside, I put the kettle on the stove. Unwrapped the tea bags. Got the pot of honey from the cupboard. Focused on simple tasks. Ignored how fragile I felt. The kettle whistled. I filled two mugs and bobbed the tea bags to get the steep going.

Gran's slippers slapped against the floor as she walked into the kitchen. "Let's have some cookies too."

I opened the pantry door, peered inside. "Which ones do you want?"

"Do we have shortbread?"

The way she phrased her question, as if the cupboard's contents were ours, warmed me. "Yep."

I put six on a dessert plate and set it in the middle of the table.

Gran fixed her cup with some honey, then dunked a shortbread and bit off the soggy end. Did her little shoulder shimmy. "Good, good, good."

There was no putting this off any longer. It felt like I'd been lying to Gran. I'd never lied to her. Here I was, middle aged, aching with embarrassment, becoming a paler version of myself with each passing day.

"I have to ask you something." My voice faltered.

Gran raised her eyebrows in assent while she chewed.

I swallowed. "Would it be okay if I stayed a little longer?"

"Of course! You know I'd love that." She looked more closely at me, saw me blinking so I wouldn't cry. "What is it?"

I stared at the table.

"Here." Gran slid the honey pot toward me. "Fix your tea. Eat a cookie."

I drizzled honey in my cup. Bit into a shortbread. Took a sip of tea.

"I lost my job . . . some time ago." I paused before looking up. "I got laid off, so I started freelancing. But . . ." The sentence hung unfinished as every wrongheaded decision avalanched in my head.

"It's been a difficult time for so many."

Gran was right: Millions had faced hardship and heartbreak far eclipsing my own. I'd gotten through, but difficulties lingered. Here I was without an apartment that I could afford, without any savings, with only the smallest of retirement nest eggs, without health insurance, without a job . . . the list went on.

Underpinning it all throbbed a deep disappointment, the kind that lingered under the skin, felt impossible to scratch out. Was it due to the long months of isolation? Doing something I didn't particularly enjoy . . . until I was laid off? Was it from feeling defeated at having all my freelance work dry up? Watching my bank account drain away? Or was it because I had no clue how to restart my life and felt overwhelmed by the prospect? Whatever the underlying anxiety, it dragged me low, made it hard to see a way through to something better. I'd slid down the rope of my life. My hands, raw from gripping tightly to what was, couldn't begin to fathom what could be.

"I know so many had it far worse than me." I focused again on my tea. "But I'm in a place now that . . . I'm embarrassed to admit I don't know how to get out of. I sublet my apartment to a friend who needs to be in the city for business. So, that helps. But . . . I literally don't have a place to live, or any idea what I'm going to do next."

What went unspoken was my stubborn insistence on staying in New York for so long, barely eking out a living from a string of marketing jobs haphazardly tied together. I'd wasted years of earning—and living—fully subservient to a studio apartment's exorbitant rent. All so I could live in the city. Although how much living had there been? The bills, the stupid cost of everything . . . it had been too much for years now. But I think what was worse was the realization that living there had stood in for actually accomplishing anything. *I live in New York.* Now here I was, mid-career without a career. Middle aged without the backstop of a professional track record I could be proud of. And without so much as that precious zip code.

I finally met Gran's eyes, which showed only compassion. She reached across the table and took my hand. "You know you're welcome to live here. This is your home."

I scrunched my face to stop from tearing up, but her tenderness broke me. "Thank you."

"Stay as long as you like." Gran held my eyes. "But dolly, don't hide here. Taking time for yourself is one thing. Hiding never does any good. I want you to live a vibrant life, one that fulfills you . . . one you enjoy."

I nodded, wiped my cheeks.

"Good." She released my hand. Took a bite of shortbread. "Good, good, good."

Chapter 2

Dread always found me as soon as I awoke, like it had been biding its time until my eyes opened, stalking me all night. What wouldn't I manage today, what wouldn't I get together, what wouldn't I fill the day with and then feel guilty about? It was the usual existential stuff—I knew I wasn't special—along with a smattering of real-world fears that would send me into a panicked tailspin before my feet hit the floor.

That heaviness slunk back to its place in the center of my chest for half a breath—but only that. Because sunlight was streaming through the window, warming my pillow, kissing my face the way it never did in New York. My studio had a sleeping loft. I used a ladder to climb up to its cave-like enclosure every night. A delightful prospect if you were eight years old. Markedly less so at forty-five. No light reached the loft. No natural light, anyway.

But I wasn't there. I was here, at Gran's . . . I was home. My entire body relaxed. I knew it wasn't the answer to anything—it just felt so good I didn't even care.

The aroma of Maxwell House beckoned. I pulled my hair back and padded into the kitchen.

"Mornin'."

"Hello, my dolly." Gran turned from the canisters of flour and sugar on the counter and gave me a hug.

I eyed the array of baking stuff. "Whatever do we have going on here?"

She smiled. "I felt like peanut butter cookies."

"I always feel like your peanut butter cookies."

"Good." She set a mixing bowl on the table. "Pour yourself a cup of coffee and get the peanut butter. You'll help me."

It felt surreal, Gran's cookie-making come hither, coffee already brewed, and my gosh, again, that sunlight. That gorgeous honey tint that illuminated every room inside this house, as if light fractured differently here. Laws of science would say otherwise. Philosophers would point to the happy . . . the peace. Standing barefoot in the kitchen as Gran tied an apron around my waist, it all seemed a little too perfect. I'd been blue for so long, having lingered in the swampy ennui end of the pool until my skin pruned, that right now in this kitchen, I didn't care how strangely idyllic the moment felt. Maybe I had a little relief due to me—a thought that was immediately followed with, *Do I, though . . . honestly?* You couldn't really lose the thread of your life to the point that you were a professional self-saboteur and then think, *Oh, but surely I have some easy coming to me.* I was well aware of my faults.

I was also abundantly grateful for Gran's conversation, her voice funneling through my ears like happy chirps, lighting up the folds of my brain. I was relieved to not dwell on all the ugly parts of me, the unsightly characteristics I'd honed over the years, then polished to a fine shine like obsidian tchotchkes that were good for nothing and just looked bleak.

Like Gran asked, I took a jar of Skippy out of the pantry.

She shook her head. "Not that one. Get the dark roasted."

I found the right jar. "Why this one?"

"If you use anything else, the cookies won't taste like peanut butter." Gran scooped the entire jar of peanut butter into the bowl, then looked at me with all seriousness. "Your great-grandmama knew her way around a cookie."

"We get our cookie gene from her."

Certain exchanges with Gran had the well-worn comfort of slippers. Great-grandmother giving us the cookie gene was one of them.

"When Mama would make these"—here Gran raised a finger—"and we only had them on very special occasions, she'd get the peanuts from the general store and roast them before grinding them into butter."

I knew that Gran's peanut butter cookie recipe had come from her mom, but like all her stories, a fresh detail emerged with each telling.

"That's the secret." Gran handed me a canister of sugar and a wooden spoon. "You mix."

I knew the basics of the recipe, but Gran walked me through each step. Being guided and supported in the effort . . . I'd longed for that so much of late, but time and time again had come up short.

I portioned out the cookies onto baking sheets and slid them into the oven while Gran changed.

Moments later, she marched back into the kitchen and announced, "While the cookies bake, let's call Lexie!" She saw how little enthusiasm I mustered up. "You and Lex should talk all the time. I call her every week."

And that was what got me: Yes, Gran called Lex every week, but I was sure my sister never called her back. The difference between us was striking. I came home to Gates Mills at least four times a year. And when I wasn't here, Gran and I had a standing phone dinner date on Tuesdays. Ever since I moved to the city more than two decades ago, we'd chat for at least an hour while eating dinner together—it was time that I cherished.

Lexie, meanwhile, cherished little. Time after time, she canceled plans to visit or made excuses why she couldn't come. At her wedding, she prioritized the old-money family of her husband, Jeffrey, and their equally affluent and impressive friends, to the point that she had me share maid of honor duties with some richie she'd met a year earlier in law school. There was more, but the point was Lexie had relegated Gran and me to the background of her life a long time ago and that was where we'd stayed. Gran, bless her, always thought the best of Lexie, always held out hope. There was a time when I thought it would get better. Gran tried to smooth over moments by saying "She's so busy" or "She's balancing so much" or "It's not easy raising two girls with a high-powered career." But nothing ever got better. It got worse.

So, it was times like this when Gran was all excited to talk to Lexie that I had to bear witness to my sister disappointing our beloved grandmother. Again.

Four years ago, we were all set to spend Christmas together—Lexie; Jeffrey; their kids, Violet and Gwen; Gran; and me. I came a week ahead of time to decorate the house with Gran. We trimmed the tree, hung stockings and garlands. I draped strings of white lights everywhere, around doorways, threaded through plants, tacked on top of windows so they'd dangle down. The entire house twinkled. I cleared a corner of the sewing room and made an Aerobed fort with bolts of material where the kids would sleep. Lexie and Jeffrey would sleep in our old bedroom, and I'd crash on the couch.

Gran and I worked like cheery elves that week, baking cookies in the morning, wrapping presents in front of the fire in the evening. We crackled with excitement. Violet was six and Gwen was four—prime Santa Claus ages. Gran hung the felt Advent calendar she'd made for Lexie and me when we were young. We thought up activities for the kids—a scavenger hunt! Homemade candy canes! They were finally old enough to remember our connection and to delight at being at Gran's. The special love she'd enveloped us in after our mom had passed away, now here we were widening the love bubble for the next generation, to make formative memories. Maybe this would finally make us feel like we were becoming a larger family together. I hoped, anyway, and I think Gran must've too, although neither of us said as much. I shoveled snow every day, giddy it was going to be a white Christmas.

The evening before they were coming, Gran and I rushed in from the backyard—we'd just positioned ceramic lanterns along the gravel path. She was so excited about how they'd look at night. We shook off our coats, laughing at how hard the snow was coming down. Gran announced, "Oh, we got a message!" She looked at me, eyes wide, pressed play on the answering machine. Lexie, her voice clipped and quiet, said they weren't coming. She was sorry, but something came up with work. The answering machine beeped.

Gran frowned at the antiquated box, just stared at it for the longest time. She pushed a button to replay the message, but the machine erased it, stating in its mechanical monotone, "No new messages." Again, she pushed it. "No new messages." Gran swallowed, smoothed her red sweater, which wasn't wrinkled. The air grew thick.

"I guess . . ." Gran swallowed, still staring at the machine. "I guess we can ship the presents." She looked up, her eyes moist, and nodded. Her smile, so small and hollow, broke my heart. "Yes, we'll do that. Okay then."

She shuffled out of the room. I stayed behind, stung by the way Lexie had disappointed Gran—both of us—so piercingly.

Lexie had promised to call back. She hadn't. Not even on Christmas.

In the days leading up to her message, I'd foolishly viewed everything through Hallmark glasses, which didn't reflect reality at all. I also never confronted Lex about what she'd done. I was too hurt and, I think, embarrassed at how bruised my feelings were, at how tightly I'd clung to this idealized version of what that holiday would mean to all of us . . . to me and Gran, especially when it obviously didn't register as a loss to Lexie.

We cleaved further from one another after that. What went unspoken turned frosty, then froze over. The kids were now ten and eight—I really hadn't been in either of their lives, which gnawed at me. But then I'd get angry all over again.

Lexie brought the kids to see Gran in the winter of 2019, but hadn't been back since.

I visited Gran even when the world got tricky—it was possible if you took the right steps. So, Lexie had no excuse. She'd grown to be selfish and practically dismissive of our grandmother, which was unforgivable to me.

But, as usual, I didn't say any of this to Gran. It would've been too hurtful. So, I went along, summoned some lukewarm cheer every time the subject of Lexie was raised. Was I being honest with Gran? No. But it felt merciful and loving somehow.

And so, this was me: "No, you're right, let's call her."

"That's my girl. Good!"

Gran settled herself into a chair at the kitchen table while I dialed. That right there was heartbreaking, how she always expected to talk to Lexie, how she always expected the best from her. I hated my sister right then.

The call rang and rang. "It's going to voicemail."

"Oh, okay, give me." She held her hand out for the phone and, my gosh, looked so happy. Her eyes sparkled in anticipation of leaving a message. "Hello, Alexis, love, it's your grandmother. I'm here with Belle and we're having such a nice time together. I wish you were here too! I hope you and Jeffrey and the kids are all well in DC! Call me back when you can. I'd love to hear how you and my sweet great-grandbabies are! Okay, bye-bye, dolly!"

Every utterance was punctuated with so much cheer, I wanted to cry. But I smiled and hung up the receiver.

"She'll call back," Gran said.

I knew she wouldn't, and couldn't muster the lie to assure Gran otherwise.

Whenever I came back to Cleveland, it was to Gran's. Not even to my father's, when he still lived in the area. Lexie and I moved in with Gran shortly after Mom passed away. When we were older, Gran would only say that Dad didn't have the necessary tools to be a father. Which seemed abundantly gracious. The truth was he simply wasn't interested. Which never registered as a loss, because we had Gran, and she was everything. It was how she remained to this day. For me, at least.

And it was here, on this one sacred point, I'd assumed Lexie and I would've remained the same: cherishing our tether with Gran. Assuming morphed into hoping. That hope had asserted itself within me and shattered so many times over the years that now, broken felt normal. And hope felt foolish.

Gran brushed some flour into a pile with the side of her palm and didn't say anything for a bit. Maybe she knew Lexie wouldn't be calling back anytime soon, that there was no reason to stay at the kitchen table waiting for the phone to ring. Maybe rolling onward with the day in happy fashion wasn't so easy when the roll had been arrested by disappointment. I was all too familiar with the way sadness rode with a sidecar of inertia.

But true to form, Gran's moment didn't last long. Wallowing never did any good, she was fond of saying. She looked up and smiled at me. "I thought you might help me with a bit of planting today."

I gasped exaggeratedly. "You know I'd love to."

The timer dinged and I pulled the cookies out of the oven. An aroma of peanut butter filled the kitchen. "Oh, Gran, we outdid ourselves here. Come look."

"Let's have one now while they're warm." She picked up a cookie and handed me half.

I took a bite. "Oh my gosh." I wrapped my arm around her shoulders. "You make the best breakfasts."

She smiled, leaned her head on me briefly, then said, "Okay, we have work to do. Go get dressed."

I changed into gardening clothes, and we headed out to the garden shed. The double doors creaked when Gran threw them open. The musty scent that I loved wafted out. Pots stood on one shelf, stacked by size. Tools hung in neat alignment on the opposite wall. I rolled the wheelbarrow out.

Gran handed me a pair of gardening gloves. "Take the tool bucket, the chairs, the foam kneelers, and let's bring that peat moss. Oh, and these." She pointed to a couple of marigold flats on the ground outside the shed. "That's what we're planting by the steps."

With everything loaded in the wheelbarrow, we set off to the front yard, which was awash in sunlight.

I opened a lawn chair for Gran. She set the tool bucket on the ground. I took a three-prong rake whose wooden handle fit perfectly into my palm and dragged it through the soil.

"That's right, work that dirt up real nice. And let's give the area a drink. Goodness, it's been dry."

I watered the beds, then turned off the sprinkler head.

"Okay, you've got two flats, so let's arrange one on each side of the steps." I eyed the space. "I'm thinking of an oval of marigolds, and then what about allium in a crescent behind it for height variation, and then . . . maybe something on the left and right of the marigolds."

Gran's brow furrowed.

"You don't like that?"

"No, I like that very much." She got up from her chair. "What if, since we get such nice morning sun here, we plant creeping thyme on either side of the marigolds, and then, picture this." She pointed. "The lilac bushes there and there will bookend a beautiful array of color."

Gran raised her eyebrows at me.

"I think I love that."

With a trowel, I made indents in the left bed, redid a couple that weren't even, then looked back at Gran. "How's that?"

"Good. Give me a square of plugs."

I handed her four tiny pots that were connected, then positioned a foam kneeler under my knees and started at the back of the bed.

"I've been thinking about everything you told me last night." Gran paused as she squeezed the bottom of a nursery pot to coax out the flower. "Have you thought about what it is you want to do?"

There it was. The day had been a little too on the nose—here was the question I'd dreaded, the one I'd rolled over and over in my head until I was nauseous with the not knowing. But of course, reality wasn't going to be suspended at Gran's. It couldn't be. That wasn't how she lived—nor, it was worth noting, how she'd raised us. I'd drifted so far off course.

I pushed the trowel into the ground, then worked it deeper and deeper until the hole was entirely too large. I shoveled some dirt back in. Gran handed me a marigold. I nestled it into its new home, backfilled the hole, and pressed on the soil to ensure there weren't any air pockets.

I rose to my haunches and started digging another hole.

"How about this . . ." Gran continued, handing me another marigold. "What do you enjoy doing? I ask because maybe this is a time to do something new."

I sat fully on the ground, surrounded by the loamy soil. The sun was higher now. I could smell the lilac bush. A chicka-dee-dee-dee symphony carried in the warm breeze. It was so clear, but obviously, not an answer either. "I love doing this."

Gran smiled, put her hand atop mine. "Me too."

July rolled along in luxurious fashion.

Each day, Gran and I worked in the yard, pulling weeds or trimming a bush that she announced needed tending. We drank coffee in the mornings and cooked dinner every night. I automated her bills so she wouldn't have to think about them. She added my name to her accounts so if anything needed to be ironed out, I could handle it. Mostly, we did a lot of enjoying one another's company.

One morning in the first week of August, I awoke so early the sky still clung to its midnight-blue tint. I brewed a small pot of coffee for myself. Gran wouldn't be up for a while, and I didn't want her coffee to taste old. I carried a mug to the backyard to watch everything awaken.

The sky shed its slumberous hue and two cardinals—a male and a female—landed on the bird feeder. Several bossy goldfinches soon jockeyed for perch position. Sunbeams, young and strong, shimmered across the grass and broad hydrangea leaves. A warm breeze danced through the maple.

Daybreak washed over me, worked a soothing magic that settled me into the chair, my bare feet in the damp grass. Such peace unfolded in this simple rousing every morning. How had I not noticed this before?

I'd been here a month. Soaking in the morning's magnificence signaled something. Moments that tread so softly they were usually missed by my mind twirling with its dance partners of anxiety and shame for once hadn't gone unnoticed at all. The thought hit with resounding clarity, pure and right: I needed to revive my freelance work.

I got my laptop and brought it outside. Over the years, I'd held marketing positions for financial institutions—ghostwriting for economists, rewriting equity strategists' missives into something coherent. I knew the lingo, the material. It was a specialized form of writing, translating financial concepts for investors, certainly nothing I was passionate about, but it paid. I sent emails inquiring about freelance work to ten different contacts, hoping someone would remember me. If I threw enough darts, maybe something would hit.

As I closed my laptop, someone moving around in the kitchen caught my eye—someone who wasn't Gran. A bolt of alarm shot through me. I rushed through the back door.

"Oh, hey!" A perky young woman with skin like a baby and her brown hair in a high pony smiled at me like nothing was wrong in the world. "Annabelle's still sleeping." She made an *awwww* face.

"What?" I set my laptop on the table harder than I should've. "You . . . you looked in on my grandmother? Who are you? Why are you in our house?"

She smiled, made a shush noise with her finger.

"Don't shush me." Then I noticed her bare feet. She'd taken off her shoes at the door like we always did. Alarm receded. Confusion took root. "What's going on?"

"It's okay, you're Belle, right?" She cocked her head, wide-eyed, inexplicably still smiling. "It's so nice to meet you! I'm Sydney. I help your grandmother and her friends every few weeks with odds and ends—sometimes cleaning, or shopping. I cook too." She looked at her watch. "I was going to put Annabelle's coffee on now, would you like some? Or I could make you some breakfast?"

"No." I didn't know what to make of this child who was treating me as if *I* were a child. "My grandmother can make her own coffee."

Sydney's smile faded into something that was knowing . . . older, even. She loosely clasped her hands in front of her—the ultimate sign of nonconfrontation. "Of course she can. Annabelle can do most everything, but it's a treat to have someone do things for her every now and again. That's all."

I swallowed, feeling like I was being handled and at the same time displaced. Emotional static frizzed off me.

Sydney smiled and nodded, her cheer renewed. "Okay." Which was a response to nothing I'd said or acquiesced to. She set about cleaning the coffee percolator and setting it up for a fresh pot. "Sure you don't want some?"

I murmured, "No."

She turned on the burner, then went to the skinny cupboard, pulled out one of Gran's aprons, tied it around her waist, and proceeded to wipe down the kitchen counters. I never thought I'd feel protective of Gran's aprons, but here I was. Sydney's well-practiced comfort in the house I grew up in jarred me.

"Sydney, you're here!" Gran shuffled into the kitchen in her slippers and housecoat. "Did you meet Belle?"

Sydney's thousand-watt smile flashed at Gran, then at me, then back to Gran. "I sure did." She enveloped Gran in a hug. "How'd you sleep?"

"Good, good, good." She saw the percolator on the stove. "Oh, thank you for starting the coffee."

"Of course." Sydney set a small pitcher of cream on the table and pulled out Gran's chair for her. "Want me to go grocery shopping today?"

"Oh, yes. I have a list all ready."

As they chatted, as Sydney poured Gran a cup of coffee and set it before her, as she made Gran toast with butter and raspberry preserves, I felt myself receding into the background of the Sydney and Gran show.

"I think . . ." My voice didn't cut through their conversation, so I cleared my throat. "I think I might go for a run."

"Oh, you should, that's a great idea." Sydney's smile patronized. Her voice patronized. "Enjoy that!" Her poreless, unlined face patronized.

Gran seconded everything Sydney had said, and they immediately fell back into their conversation.

I forced a smile, went to my room to change, then walked out the front door. Ran all the way down the brick sidewalk to the corner and turned onto Epping, a grand tree-lined lane that wound lazily past big-lawned estates. Normally, this picturesque road, quiet and wide, held peace in its pavement, but I was running too fast out of the gate, jangly and agitated.

Why hadn't Gran mentioned Sydney? Or that she obviously had a key to the house? My feet pounded the ground. Did Gran think I couldn't handle whatever she needed done?

I wiped my face. A gnawing thought ate through my middle. Look how I'd reacted to someone saying they were there to help. Weird. Fearful. Jealous and overly protective. Sydney was a young woman *helping*—that was it. I'd behaved poorly in Gran's kitchen, showed no grace, had my feelings bruised too easily. I replayed everything in my head until it carved an embarrassed groove in my brain.

My heart banged against my chest wall with this stupid-fast pace, but I kept running, thoughts slamming into one another, piling up in an ugly sandwich.

The road forked up a hill. My chest and thighs burned with effort. I pumped my arms to help propel myself up to—*finally*—a flat straightaway.

I eased up on the pace and a sense of calm found me—maybe because my heart and lungs got a break, or maybe because I'd managed to shed some shame in the miles behind me. I would do better. Be better. I hung another right and jogged down the giant hill that led me back to Gran's.

As I neared the house, my GPS watch showed that a few more minutes would make this my longest run in years. The milestone was irresistible. I continued past Gran's, over the bridge, and turned left. When my watch beeped, I stopped in front of The Cardinal, the upscale restaurant in town. I walked home, endorphins bouncing off my insides. Everything was beautiful. The sun-dappled tree canopies, the bright glow enveloping the town. It all left me in awe.

Back at the house, I kicked off my running shoes, ready to start fresh with Sydney. Gran's happy lilt carried all the way to the front door. I mean, anyone who made her laugh like that couldn't be bad. Gran had the best laugh, the kind that was infectious. After a few minutes, she called out, "Belle . . . Belle, come here."

I followed her cheery beckon and found her at the kitchen table, not with Sydney, but alone, talking on the phone. She was holding a carrot above a pile of peels and laughed again, which made me smile.

"Oh, I know!" Laughter. "I know!" She nodded at me, her eyes crinkly, she smiled so wide. "That's wonderful to hear, just wonderful. Okay, you be good now . . . I love you too. Here's Belle."

Gran held the phone out to me. "It's Lexie."

I froze at my sister's name. Forced myself not to recoil, because I didn't want to hurt Gran's feelings. But I also didn't want to take the phone. Every endorphin drained from me. Gran gave a playful shake of the receiver, not noticing my hesitation. Maybe she was overcome with happiness at having been able to finally talk to Lexie. I hoped so.

I reached for the phone. "Hi."

"You're staying with Gran?" Lex led with imperiousness. All sharp elbows and edge.

Not *How are you* or *How've you been* . . . none of the conversational starters you'd expect from someone you hadn't spoken to in more than six months.

I cleared my throat. "Yeah . . . for a bit."

She made a *huh* sound. "How long is a bit?"

It was the windup, lobbing an easy question over the plate before she unleashed a barrage of judgmental heaters. Lexie didn't have a conversation with me as much as she led an inquisition. Perched on her throne of career achievement, in her five-thousand-square-foot home in some moneyed enclave of Washington, DC, that was professionally decorated and cleaned. That had curated objets d'art and bric-a-brac and whatever other stupid thing looked good on styled bookshelves. Stuff stacked and arranged just so, magazine perfect, with no sentimental value whatsoever.

"Belle?"

"Sorry . . . what did you say?"

Lexie sighed. "Never mind. Look, I have to hop on a conference call. Talk to you later."

The line went dead.

Gran looked up from the carrot she was peeling and smiled, as if entreating me to think the best of the phone call and of Lexie. I managed a wan smile. Rested the handset back in the cradle.

"She had a conference call." I felt numb at how abruptly Lexie had hung up. "She . . . had to go."

"She's so busy." Gran's cheer revved up again. "Oh, it was good to talk to her."

She went on, telling me all about what they'd talked about, but I didn't hear any of it. I nodded and smiled an empty smile, sat down feeling hollow and angry.

"I can't believe how those girls are growing up." Gran was still talking, peeling another carrot. "When I think about . . ."

Where was Lexie when I called her last winter? When I was in such a desperate state after losing my job and after all my freelance work had dried up? When I wanted to feel like I was tethered to someone, like I had support that had blood running through it, but didn't want to worry Gran with my panic? Lexie was in Aspen. She answered the call, announced she was on top of whatever mountain about to eat lunch and she'd call back. Then she hung up. I hadn't said a single word. It had taken a lot for me to make that call—I'd reached such a dark low. Lexie hadn't asked one thing about me, why I was calling, or how I was. She also never called back.

"Belle?" Gran's voice interrupted my thought ramble.

I met her eyes.

"You all right?"

The cheeriness that had risen high in her cheeks only moments before was now gone. God, I'd done that.

"Yeah, yeah, I'm good." I smiled. "Sorry." I screwed my face into an *I'm so silly* visage. "I was just lost in my head there for a second. Too hot from my run. So!" I clapped my hands together. "What are we making here?"

Gran's eyes regained their twinkle. Inwardly, I relaxed.

"Vegetable stock." She told me to get the big pot from the pantry.

"First, coat the bottom with oil." Gran set a mound of vegetables and herbs next to the stove for me. She told me how to cut the onions, carrots, and celery, how big to leave the potato chunks. Then she handed me fat fistfuls of parsley and dill.

"All of these?"

"That's right, toss 'em in." She handed me more big fistfuls of thyme, sage, and rosemary.

"You don't just use a little dill, a little parsley? Really, you put all this in?"

"If you don't want your stock to have much taste, you use a few sprigs, but if you want a vegetable stock with some"—here she stretched her arms wide and shimmied her chest—"va-va-voom, you put all these herbs in."

I laughed. "You saucy thing, you."

"Now, cover everything with water, put the lid on, and we're going to boil her till she's nice and flavorful."

"Should I put salt in?"

"Just a little, we'll wait to really season her good." Gran took two small-footed dessert bowls from the cabinet, portioned blueberry cobbler in them, and nestled a scoop of vanilla ice cream atop each. "Let's sit down and relax. Get two spoons."

"Oh, Gran, I just ran, I don't know—"

"Well, then get a glass of water to wash this down." She strode into the living room carrying both dishes, called over her shoulder. "It'll be refreshing!"

I checked the flame under the stockpot, grabbed the spoons, then joined Gran on the couch. She'd propped her feet on the tufted footstool she kept nearby.

"This is beyond delicious." In one bite, I'd gone from being reluctant to follow a good run with dessert to seriously considering another bowlful.

"It's a nice treat." She licked her spoon. "How was your jog?"

"Good. I missed running here."

An odd silence bloomed between us as we finished the cobbler.

"You cannot let distance and issues push you and your sister apart." Gran kept her voice quiet, but its severity screamed. She looked me straight in the eye. "Trust me, you do not want to carry that heartache through life."

I let her words settle but then couldn't help myself. "When was the last time—"

"That's all I'm going to say about that." Gran got up from the couch slowly, the way she did after her hips got stiff from sitting too long. I followed her into the kitchen and set our dishes on the table because she'd gone to the sink. In the moment, it didn't feel right to crowd her.

She picked up a bud vase with a single pink rose in it from the windowsill and changed the water.

Five times, she changed that bud vase's water.

It was as close as Gran ever got to the topic of Grace. Her sister, who was three years younger. Her sister, who lived on a farm in Southern Ohio. And who, in all my forty-five years on this earth, Gran had never talked to . . . or talked about.

Chapter 3

In the early days of my career, I got ensnared in New York's hustle, in the going and doing. It was a rushed existence, a propulsion of life at a sprinter's pace.

But the city's frenetic momentum doesn't carry you if you fail or lose a gear. You sink to the muddy bottom while urban waves roll above, lodging you deeper into the muck beneath the doer class.

You fall off radars, off email invites, off text strings. You become forgotten.

The pace of youth no longer within reach, the possibility of what might be with reinvention drifts further from your grasp with each passing day. And the longer you remain in that limbo of forgotten, the more you become comfortable being alone. You prefer it.

Humans are supposed to be social creatures. But that's only until you stumble so spectacularly that being alone is easier than putting yourself out there—having to explain your absence . . . how you have failed. You hide. Fear takes root. The way through becomes cloudier and cloudier.

But the skies were clearing here in Gates Mills. My jelly insides firmed up just feeling like I belonged somewhere. Which, of course, I always did at Gran's. But after being isolated for so long, you start to feel like a foreigner in your own life. You forget you have any place at all.

Gran came out to the backyard where I was sitting, a hand raised to shield her eyes. "Oh, goodness, it's hot already! August always ends in a steam bath."

"That she does." I finished typing a sentence on my laptop.

"What's this you're doing?"

I saved the document and closed the computer. "I drummed up some freelance work."

"Bellie, good for you!"

"Well, it's just a start, but a start was . . . overdue."

"You wait here, I'll get us breakfast." She waved off my offer to help.

The air felt heavy, laden with humidity. Today was going to be a scorcher. A haze hung above the daylilies. A ruby-throated hummingbird buzzed by, its wings a blur.

Gran marched out of the house carrying a half-gallon carton of Pierre's coffee ice cream and two spoons.

I laughed. "This is breakfast?"

She sat down, peeled back the lid, and handed me a spoon. "Coffee is a morning flavor."

We ate our ice cream breakfast and watched the birds.

"Sydney will be by later," Gran said. "She'll do a bit of cleaning while we work outside."

I ate a spoonful.

"You never mentioned her before. I was . . ." I managed a chuckle. "Well, surprised to find her in the kitchen last time she was here."

"She started coming not too long ago. She goes to Ohio State and does this during the summer—she heads back to school in a couple days." Gran licked her spoon. "She wants to be a nurse or work in a residential living facility, so this is nice practice."

"You know . . . I can do whatever you need, right?"

"I do, but she was wonderful help to have when you weren't here." Gran looked pointedly at me. "Getting old isn't easy. Sometimes we need help."

Never had I thought of Gran as needing help. There was a reality here that Sydney had done a better job of recognizing—or admitting—it than I had.

Despite the heat, Gran announced that today was the day we'd tackle the corner. She looked serious, like she really wanted to get at it. Like there would be no waiting for a cooler day.

"I'm ready, Gran."

I carried the ice cream breakfast remnants into the kitchen, then changed into cargo pants and the lightest long-sleeved shirt I had. On the dresser, my cell phone glowed with a text message notification.

A tiny hand gripped my chest the way it did every time one of these came in.

Good morning! Drinks tomorrow? Who's in?

Four were on this string, including me.

These were the only friends who still considered and included me. We'd been in one another's lives for two decades. Others had drifted away after I'd passed on enough invitations to social Zooms, which, to be honest, I didn't mind. It was one less source of anxiety. But these women on this text string right now . . . they were different. I had at least stayed in touch with them—barely, really. It was arm's length, reliably noncommittal, sometimes after the fact, but enough still to eke out inclusion. I didn't want to lose these women from my life. But I also knew that, at some point, the consideration they'd extended to me would wear thin as it had with others.

We called ourselves the four women of the Herpocalypse.

We met in Citigroup's marketing department, writing copy for pamphlets, tear sheets, letters, and whatever else private-banking higher-ups deemed necessary.

Bridgette always pushed her points hard, fought for her edits. She hailed from Rye, a wealthy enclave north of the city. On her first day, she strode in, set her Gucci bag on a desk in the middle of the bullpen, as it was called, and told the managing director that she was going to need a better chair. A better chair was brought. And then we learned that her mother was on the board of directors. Bridgette held herself above most others, the way children of means and entitlement do, but the more you got to know her, the more you realized she had a self-deprecating side that was fierce and funny. She didn't show it to everyone, only those she held close.

Julianne was a yoga devotee with a wide face and long hair that she twisted in a topknot. Nothing ever rattled her. Nothing shocked. She was preternaturally calm. Except when it came to serial commas. Or when people didn't use the right possessive pronoun. Or when they butchered the subjunctive tense. The only buttons that set her off were copyediting ones.

Lannie was from Georgia and perpetually felt like a fish out of water in New York. She had big brown eyes and an easy smile. Her upbringing was the opposite of Bridgette's, her family struggling to make ends meet. They'd buy odd cuts of meat past their prime or Lannie would go without dinner so her younger sister could have a bigger portion. She told us this one day over lunch like it was no big deal, just how it was. Nothing to lament or feel wounded about. It was the split pea soup she was eating at the time that she couldn't stop going on about. But for all her quiet and golly gee, she spun out sterling copy faster than anyone else. I once asked how she wrote so quickly, tossing lyrical phrases off the cuff. She shrugged like it had never occurred to her she was any different, said maybe because she spent a lot of time at the library growing up. "Libraries"—she grinned—"are free."

It was the first real job for all of us, so we banded together, a fast friendship forged in the fiery pits of the daily grind. I couldn't even remember why we started calling ourselves by that silly name. We were word people given to hyperbole. At the time it was hilarious and binding.

We only worked together for a few years, but it was a formative time, when we'd all come to the city from different places, different walks of life. Those first steps into new careers came with camaraderie. After we moved on to other jobs, our foursome remained tight. We'd grown up together and were now two decades into our friendship.

When the world tilted, all of us in the city lived like bees in our honeycomb apartments, right next to one another but separate. Instead of meeting for drinks, we had a standing Zoom cocktail hour every Wednesday. It felt like such a lifeline at first. But then things got bumpy for me on the work front, and I started making excuses why I couldn't join—an impending deadline for a freelance project, a conflicting call with a new client (all lies). When my excuses ran out, I often simply didn't respond.

When things started opening up, weekly Zooms became monthly drinks at places with outdoor seating. I didn't respond to more invites than I care to admit. Still, in their eyes, I guess I remained one of the Herpocalypse.

I exhaled and began to type.

> Sorry it's been so long since I've chimed in here. I'm home at my grandmother's for a visit. Looking forward to seeing you when I'm back. Xo

Was I honestly looking forward to seeing them? No. At least not to seeing how they viewed me now. My reluctance to admit how much I'd struggled muddled everything. Far easier to avoid and close off. I powered down the phone and shoved it in the top dresser drawer.

Gran was waiting in the backyard with all the tools. She handed me a shovel and carried two weeders to the overgrown corner. She traipsed through the snarl of low weeds that had spread netlike over the ground.

"I don't know how to tell you this"—I cast my gaze around us—"but we're surrounded."

She handed me a weeder. "We'll have to weed our way out."

Gran bent down and worked the tool into the ground, loosened a thicket of dandelions, beat the dirt off the bottom, and pitched the battered bit over her shoulder. "First we'll get all these out." She pulled up three tall stalks, jiggled the dirt from the bottom and lobbed them onto the pile of debris. She stood, put her hands on her hips, her face red. "Then, we'll use the shovel to break up all the dirt."

I followed her lead: ripped weeds from the ground, salvaged what dirt I could from the root clumps. We weeded together for a good forty-five minutes. The sun ascended higher in the sky. The entire backyard was steaming up.

"Okay." Gran's breathing was labored as she picked up the shovel and thrust it into the ground. "Now for the real work." She shoveled up a heap, turned it over, and used the blade to slice through it, mincing the soil, aerating it. "Go get another shovel from the shed."

I needed to tread carefully here. "How about I do some shoveling while you sit in the shade for a bit? Just take a tiny break." I knew how much Gran loved working in the yard, how suggesting she stop and let me do the heavy lifting had to be handled delicately. I probably should've suggested this a half hour ago, but she had been enjoying it too much.

She leaned on the shovel. Damp tendrils fell loose from her pinned bun. She swept the hair off her forehead, considering. Finally, she exhaled. "Maybe I will, just for a bit."

"Good." I looked across the area, assessing all the work that still had to be done. "Why didn't you have someone come in and rototill this for you?"

"Because I wanted us to work the land." Gran handed me the shovel. "I don't want any machinery messing up my geranium beds, or my hydrangeas. And you know they'd knock over all the boxwoods. No." She was quiet for a moment. "This ground needs to be brought back slowly, and with care."

"You're right, of course." My comment had been thoughtless. Yard work was Gran's joy. She'd never hired anyone to do anything and wasn't about to start now. Besides, Gran had saved this last project for years.

She hadn't done that for some company to tear through it slapdash. She wanted to savor it.

I stepped on the shovel, forced it into the ground, then levered up a hunk and chopped it with the blade.

"That's it." Gran sat down at the table under the maple. "Look at you!" she called while patting her neck with a hanky. "You're a natural with a shovel. This corner is going to be in shape in no time."

It was silly, but a giddiness rushed through me. For so long, I hadn't felt capable of anything.

Gran sat in the shade, replanting herbs in terra-cotta pots while I kept at the spading. After a while, my arms felt the weight of the packed earth I was turning over. My shoulders registered every thwack of the mounds I broke up. But it was a good strain, a fatigue that built slowly, like, finally, it had been earned.

As I dug deeper, the soil became clay: tan colored and more compact. This layer was the heaviest. Each squatted lift of dense clay started to strain my back and hamstrings. As I turned the weighty lumps over and chopped at them, my muscles burned. I knew this work, had done it my entire life with Gran. But the surprising thing about the fatigue and muscle ache now: how invigorating it felt.

The next time I looked up, Mama P and Faye were sitting with Gran. They waved hello. I waved and kept digging. Dug deep and mixed all the dirt with slices and thwacks of the shovel.

The next time I looked up, the terra-cotta pots were gone. A pitcher of lemonade and five glasses were set on the table. Sydney was sitting with them.

"Bellie, dear, come join us," Gran called. "Have a rest."

"I'll join in a bit!" I waved. "Hey, Sydney!"

She gave a cheery wave, then went back to whatever she was saying, and everyone laughed, which was good to see. It said something that she fit so well with all of them.

I thrust the shovel into the ground again and again. Turned over clump after clump of dirt. The sun rose high in the sky, blazing white.

Hot. My heart pounded at the exertion. It exhilarated and exhausted. Absolutely intoxicated. I stopped to catch my breath, leaned on the shovel to stretch my back. I wiped my forearm against my forehead, no doubt smearing dirt on my face, and set to digging some more.

Gran called over again to me, telling me to come rest. Sydney must've gone inside to clean. I waved Gran off with a smile. I hadn't realized how restless I'd become in recent months, how hungry for movement and purpose. I kept digging. I was so close to turning over this entire patch of yard. Just a little more. The sun bore down. My shirt was soaked. Only a few more shovelfuls. I felt the strain in my shoulders, my neck, the joints of my hands. Every muscle talked back to me. Sweaty with exertion, thirsty from hard labor, it became clear how sitting in my apartment not working, spiraling deeper into my insecurities, I had slid into a funk.

Mama P and Faye waved goodbye, and I waved back, smiling in a way I hadn't in so long.

Finally . . . I was doing something. Feeling something that wasn't rooted in self-defeatism. Or depression. Something that felt virtuous.

I picked up the tools and carried everything to where Gran was sitting. The lemonade was gone. In its place: two bottles of beer.

"Those look good." I sat down and Gran handed me a bottle slick with delicate condensation.

"Nothing better after a day of yard work."

I clinked my bottle against Gran's and took a deep sip. The hoppy effervescence danced across my tongue. "This might be the most perfect drink ever." I pedaled out of my tennis shoes, peeled off my socks. My feet were so hot they looked puckered. The grass felt cool, luxurious. I sank lower into the chair, stretched out my legs. My body thrummed, yet a pillow of contentment supported me.

I gazed at the area I'd cleaned up. "Do you want me to mix some compost and topsoil into that bed?" It would add a revitalizing finishing touch.

"That would be lovely. But not today."

That corner had never looked so neat, ready for planned growth. I kept staring at it as if watching a riveting show on television.

"Thank you," I murmured. "For letting me do all that."

Gran smiled softly. "Good, hard physical work does wonders."

She spoke from experience, of course. But I sensed something else in her tone: calculation.

The Chagrin River Valley absolutely dazzled in autumn.

New England got all the leaf-peeping accolades, but those singing its praises obviously hadn't spent a single fall in Northeast Ohio. I never saw autumnal vistas anywhere match the majesty of the ones I grew up with. The season's first cold snap transformed the hills surrounding Gran's house into a mosaic of vibrant oranges, yellows, and fiery reds that transfixed, wouldn't let go.

The air crisped. Days grew shorter. And, eventually, nature's spectacular color show faded. Leaves browned and turned brittle, then fell, imbuing the breeze with a sweet scent of vegetal decay.

Here we were, two days from Thanksgiving. Gran and I were about to make her stuffing. I'd gathered most everything we needed on the kitchen table: celery, onions, cutting boards, knives, and a loaf of bread.

"Before we start, let's call Lexie!" Gran picked up the receiver and dialed her number. "It's ringing!"

There was a knock at the front door.

Gran shoved the phone at me and held on to the table as she got up. "Here, you talk first. I'll get the door."

I stood speechless, holding the phone.

"Hello?"

Lexie answering shocked me.

"Hey . . ." I literally didn't have anything to say to her. "Gran wanted to call you."

"Still there, I see."

I said nothing.

"What's your deal? Do you . . . have a job?" She paused. "Or is Gran fully supporting you?"

I bit the side of my cheek, unable to even be angry about what she'd said. What she'd described was embarrassing and pathetic. What she'd described was me.

"I'm . . . freelancing." My voice was soft, an apology.

"So, you're not on staff anywhere? Nothing regular?" Her exhale was full of annoyance. "Do you even have health insurance? You're literally a middle-aged woman. You need health insurance."

Acid pushed up my throat. I stayed silent. She wasn't wrong. I'd been enjoying the time with Gran, finding my footing, and above all, loving being back home. All I'd done was drum up a little freelance work, which didn't answer any pressing questions in my life: what I would do for a steady job, where I'd live, how I'd support myself. And yes, health insurance. Things people managed to handle every day.

"Belle?" Her voice stabbed at my ear.

"Ooo, did you get her?" Gran came in with her hand outstretched, and I handed off the phone like it was hot. "Hi, Lexie!"

Gran sat down and talked to Lexie in the cheeriest of tones. She laughed, which meant Lexie was actually making her happy. Gran listened for long stretches, which meant Lexie was actually telling her things about her life, about the kids, who knew. She was a stranger to me—that wasn't exactly right, because I wouldn't have the same reaction to some stranger. I wouldn't be staring into the middle distance right now with my head ringing. Listening to Gran's side of a conversation with a stranger wouldn't stir up anger inside me . . . along with something else far more uncomfortable, something wobbly that I couldn't quite put a finger on.

I moved away from the table where I'd been standing slack jawed and got the big bowl from the top of the fridge that I knew we'd use. I needed to feel like I was doing something.

The conversation eventually ended. Gran returned the phone to its cradle. "Oh, it was good to talk to her! Wasn't it good to talk to her?"

"Yeah." I managed to sound fine.

I sat back down at the table, forced myself to be in the moment.

"I invited Lexie to come, but they're doing Thanksgiving with Jeffrey's family," Gran said.

I kept my face placid. "That's too bad."

But of course, all I could think was *When was the last time Lexie came for a holiday?* It had been at least a decade. Well before her kids were born. All her excuses were tissue paper thin. How little Lexie seemed to care about Gran, how precious few moments she deigned to give her, made me irate.

I tended to this silent fury, my angry garden. What I wanted to say was *You know what, Gran? Forget her.*

"You know what, Gran?" I leaned over the table, my eyes narrowed. "More stuffing for us."

Which made her laugh.

I let myself get swept up in the business of stuffing making, listening intently to Gran's every direction. We were making it early because stuffing, through some magical alchemy, always tastes better at least a day after it's made—there's no explanation why. It's simply fact.

I started pinching white bread into the big bowl.

"And remember, don't use any of the tops," Gran said.

"Right."

I followed her every word. She admonished me to not pinch the bread too tightly, to use a light touch. To use some sides of bread slices, but only some. Like, five times she reminded me not to use the shiny tops.

"We'll throw all those out to the raccoons." Gran took out dried sage and salt from the cupboard. "Remember, not too much sage—you need to taste it, but you don't want it to overpower."

I made my way through a loaf of white bread, pinching (not too tightly! not making pieces that were too big!). The task's slow repetition calmed me. I sprinkled sage and salt over top, fluffed the soft pinched bits with both hands, then added a little more before tasting a piece. "How's this?" I held a piece out to Gran.

She ate it, shaking her head. "More sage, and more salt."

I remixed.

"Add a tiny bit more," Gran said before I even offered her a piece. "It's good that you didn't add too much at first. You can build up to the right amount of sage."

I did as she said. "Okay, how about now?"

Gran took a bite, then pointed at the bowl. "That's it! That's perfect. You see how you can taste the sage and it's a little salty—but not too much of both? Good, good, good! Now we'll let it dry out."

Next, I chopped the celery and onion into fine slivers, kept them in separate piles like Gran did, then sautéed them in butter and oil. Added salt and sprinkled sage on top. The sauté took three batches. Every time I thought I had the seasoning mix right, I asked Gran's opinion. It usually needed more of something. Each batch went this way.

Finally, when Gran declared "That's it! Oh, that's delicious," I felt like I'd won an award.

"Now, try it so you know exactly how it should taste," she said. "And eat enough so the flavor stays with you."

I ate a spoonful and looked at Gran, wide-eyed. She grinned. I ate another—it tasted exactly like hers. A sense of pride surged through me.

"This is how you learn." Her smile was serene. "Now you'll always know."

Winter arrived early—precisely the day after Thanksgiving.

The wind howled, rushed down the chimney, and set the logs' embers dancing. Snow came down in peaceful flakes that sparkled in the porch light. Big drifts hugged the fence.

It was after dinner, and Gran and I were in the living room, heat rolling off the fire. She'd set a dish of candied spiced nuts on the coffee table. I sat cross-legged on the couch in sweats and thick socks. Gran was in her robe and slippers, her feet propped up on the hassock. We shared a blanket draped over our laps. The wind constantly found its way through the boards of this old house, so come November, you needed to curl up with a blanket.

I'd been telling Gran about how I'd struggled in the city. I think she'd already gleaned a lot of what I was sharing, but I'd never articulated it, the cocooning in my own anxieties, the fearful unknown.

Gran patted my knee. "I'm glad you're okay now."

All I could think was *Am I?*

She held my eyes for a moment, then nodded. Eased her feet to the floor, scooched to the edge of the couch, and got up.

"Sometimes life feels like a long winter." Gran shuffled over to the basket with her sewing things. "A winter where you have to hunker down, get cozy, and find something to occupy yourself with."

She brought a quilted carryall back to the couch, handed me a crimson hank of embroidery floss, a needle, and a tiny pair of gold scissors.

"It's all about finding the good in a situation." Gran stretched a square of cross-stitch canvas into a small spring-tension hoop and handed that to me as well.

Then, seeming to remember something else, she walked to the tiny brass bar cart in the corner and proceeded to pour several amber-colored liquors into a shaker filled with ice. She tilted the canister back and forth a few times, then poured the cocktail into two glasses.

"Do you know what my girlfriends and I would do during a big snow like this one?"

I took the drink Gran offered me. "Get blotto?"

"No." She sat down and looked at me with a seriousness that erased the bemused look from my face. "We'd embroider."

Her serious facade cracked, and she giggled, shoulders bobbing up and down impishly. "We'd get a little blotto too!"

I laughed with her.

"But my point is, we didn't bemoan the snow, or the circumstance," Gran continued. "One must carry on in cheery fashion."

I smiled, took a sip of my cocktail, and coughed at the burn. "Oh my gosh, what is this?"

"This is called a Manhattan!"

My eyes watered. I choked out a laugh. "Okay, I live in Manhattan—I don't think anyone there drinks anything like this."

Gran took an easy gulp. "Keeps you young."

A self-conscious moment reared up on me as my smile faded. I wasn't sure why—maybe it was a reframing of my life working out in my subconscious, but it left me pensive. Gran patted my lap.

"You'll find your way." Her voice was tender. "I think this could be an opportunity for you to do something that you love, something that feeds your soul."

I looked into her eyes, a needy lilt underpinning my voice. "You think?"

Gran leaned closer. "I think I know."

We spent the evening doing cross-stitch. Watching neat rows of tight stitches take up more and more of the canvas plucked a satisfying chord within me. The snow piled up outside in fluffy mounds that grew girthier. Every now and again, we'd hear the snowplow's soft *shush* as it went past.

Gran drank two Manhattans to my one—an inexplicable feat I had no words for, nor any understanding of how, at her age, she was capable of it. As the time wound later, Gran leaned her head back, nestled into the couch, and closed her eyes. She had a peaceful smile of contentment while she dozed.

An evening that had begun with me enumerating every panic pulse point I'd experienced in the last two years ended with me feeling entirely whole, sitting there with Gran—for an evening, no longer a wayward soul at the mercy of life's circumstances. I wasn't sure when it happened, but sometime after emerging from that Uber in July, my shoulders and chest had slowly, mercifully, unclenched.

For the first time in so long, I went to bed with a sturdier sense of self.

And that was a start.

Chapter 4

It was the week before Christmas.

I wiped the last of the powdered sugar from the table. Gran looked at the clock, then turned on the AM radio that she kept on the counter. A jubilant accordion tune filled the kitchen.

"It's time!" Gran, a gleam in her eyes, arms at a jaunty angle, two-stepped around the table. "You know, when your grandfather was courting me, we'd go polka dancing twice a week."

I turned up the music and clapped my hands.

"That's my girl!" Gran yelled over the music. "Oh, Grandpa and I had so much fun."

The doorbell rang. Gran did her tiny polka to the front door, opened it to find Mama P moving her hips side to side on the doorstep.

"I heard the music!" Mama P grinned.

Gran took her friend's hand and they polka danced around the living room, ever so slowly, and into the kitchen.

"Bravo!" I clapped.

"Okay, the old lady has to sit now." Mama P chuckled as Gran lowered the volume. "I love to polka in the afternoon! Makes me hot, though."

"Let's have a drink." Gran poured three small glasses of ginger ale.

Mama P took a big sip, wiped her mouth with the back of her hand. "Oh, that's good, thank you." She fixed her gaze on me. "You should polka."

"Honestly, it's been so long," I said.

"You need the polka." Mama P raised a finger in emphasis of her edict. "I see this. I do."

Then she slapped her hands on the table. "I must go. I need a nap before tonight."

"All right, take these." Gran handed her a tin of tassies.

"Oh, I love your tiny pecan pies!" Mama P bit into one as she made her way to the front door. "Delicious!" Then she called out, "Belle, wear your polka shoes!"

The Gates Mills holiday dance was one of those small-town events that everyone looked forward to. And for someone who'd lived in New York for as long as I had, and who, at one time, anyway, went to loud, crowded parties and waited endlessly on dinner reservations, attending a dance at the village historical society with Gran was a welcome respite from the city's brand of high-strung holiday cheer.

Gran looped her arm through mine as we walked in. The doors to the party room were draped with fresh evergreen garlands. A Christmas tree trimmed with red ribbons and strings of popcorn stood in one corner. A striking menorah stood in another. The lights were dimmed and refreshments—punch (fruit, for the kids, and a larger bowl, spiked, for the adults), along with all manner of finger food (pigs in a blanket, a perennial favorite)—filled two tables to the side of the parquet dance floor. On the opposite side of the room stood a stage where musicians, decked out in gray suits with red carnations, played swingy big band numbers and holiday classics.

"They really did a nice job this year!" Gran looked up at me, happiness radiating off her.

She'd put on makeup for tonight: pink rouge and a berry-colored lipstick. Earlier, when I asked if she wanted me to do her eyes, she'd hesitated only a second before agreeing. I removed her glasses, swiped a little fawn-colored eyeshadow across her lids, and carefully wanded mascara through her lashes.

"Gran, you have the most beautiful eyes." I slid her glasses back on so she could see herself in the mirror.

She stared, uncharacteristically lost in her reflection. I couldn't tell if she was shocked by her appearance or unhappy with the eye makeup. I'd used a light touch, but she was unreadable, almost far away.

Then she looked up at me and whispered, "Is it too much?"

"You look beautiful." I wrapped my arm around her shoulders, brought my face close to hers, and shifted my gaze to the mirror. Had she thought back to another time when she'd gotten all dolled up to go dancing . . . maybe with Grandpa? In that moment of her looking in the mirror, it felt like I'd retreated and a flood of memories had overwhelmed her. "Look at us, a couple of pretty ladies going to a dance," I said gently. "The only people luckier than us are the gentlemen we're going to dance with."

She swallowed, looked nervous, so unlike herself.

"It's going to be so much fun." I held her eyes in the mirror.

After a moment, her face scrunched up in a smile, and just like that, she was back, my Gran. The moment of reflection, whatever swirl she had been caught in—I'd never seen her like that before. We'd been to this dance every year, and this was the first time she'd seemed hesitant. But it was fleeting, and by the time we walked out the door, down the street, and into the village historical society, she seemed plucky and looking forward to the evening ahead.

Now the warmth of the historical society all gussied up enveloped us like a hug.

"Annabelle!" Mama P, standing near the refreshment table, waved a triangle of cheese high in the air so Gran would see her.

Gran grinned, raised both hands above her head, opened and closed her hands in a hello of fingers.

"Here, give me your coat," I said. "You go on in. I'll be right there."

She wiggled out of her wool coat and rushed over to Mama P.

I shrugged off my own and carried both to the coat check area.

"Hey, Belle." Jeremy walked up just as I collected our tickets.

"Happy holidays!" I kissed his cheek, gave him a once-over. "How spiffy you look. Nicely done."

A young woman wearing a black cocktail dress slipped her hand in his.

"This is Marie," he said to me. "Marie, this is Belle."

Marie's smile reached her eyes. She stretched out a hand, her nails lacquered a deep, shiny red. "Pleasure to meet you."

"Nice to meet you as well."

"Babe, I'm going to run to the restroom real quick, okay?" She touched his arm, then looked at me. "I'll see you in there!"

Jeremy watched Marie walk away from us. He turned back, all smiles.

"Babe?" I fanned my face with my hand. "Oh my, Jeremy, what have I missed here?"

He laughed. "Stop. She's just a good friend."

"Of course." I nodded. "I call all my good friends *babe*."

"All right. She's . . . good friend–adjacent."

"I'm just kidding. Don't get caught up in labels. Enjoy each other's company."

He didn't say anything for a beat, then smiled shyly. "Okay, I will."

"And don't drink and drive," I said. "You know what that one bowl of punch is like."

"Belle, we walked here."

"We did." A man who I'd never seen inserted himself in our conversation. "But the admonishment is always relevant."

He was tall, had to be at least six feet, a little older than me, dressed in a tweed jacket, white shirt and red tie, dark pants, respectable village holiday attire.

"I'm Simon." He held out a hand, and at the same time looked straight into my eyes in a piercingly intimate way that made the foyer feel overbearingly warm.

"Belle." I shook his hand.

"My uncle," Jeremy said, by way of explanation.

"Seriously?" I said. "Simon? Nate's brother? I literally haven't seen you since, what? You were in high school? Where've you been?"

"He's been living in Seattle forever," Jeremy said.

Simon, still looking at me, nodded toward his nephew. "What he said."

His eyes, an arresting green, struck me as so open and earnest. His face had that healthy, taut appearance of someone who worked out, took care of himself. Dark hair, thick, a little body on top and cut short on the sides—business, but also fun. Sexy. I was still shaking his hand. Now this was weird. I was weird.

"So"—Jeremy patted Simon's back—"we'll see you in there." As soon as he stood safely out of his uncle's view, Jeremy raised his eyebrows in an exaggerated way at me and fanned his face like he was going to faint.

I ignored him.

"This is probably the longest I've ever shaken anyone's hand," I said.

"It's been memorable."

He laughed, which made me laugh.

We let go of one another's grasp and stood there. If we'd shared that connective handshake and then I'd run off flapping my arms like a chicken, it would've felt more organic than this awkward pause right now. The one that was unending. Interminable. Making conversation was too enormous an undertaking. I glanced at my shoes, then into the room with the dance floor and saw Jeremy talking to his parents, to his grandparents, to Gran, pointing at us. My cheeks flushed. Good lord. I was fourteen.

I returned my attention to Simon. "So, what brings you to little ol' Gates Mills after all this time?"

"I actually just moved back." He paused. "I mean, not to Gates Mills, to Pepper Pike."

"Right next door."

I glanced again at the dance floor. Jack Harmon, the dapper gentleman from down the street who'd been sweet on Gran for years, walked over to her, held out his hand, and said something. She tilted her head, smiled in a coquettish way, and handed her purse to Mama P. Jack, dressed in a red sweater-vest, white shirt, gray tie, and tan khakis, led Gran away like she was a queen. I rarely got to observe Gran not as my grandmother but as her own adult self, separate and whole and joyous, tickled to be asked to dance, looking flirty and happy in a way that didn't involve love for a granddaughter, or grandmotherly concern. There she was, delighted in her deep friendship with a soft-spoken widower who'd occasionally take her to dinner, or for a stroll around the village, and who always, every year since Grandpa passed away, danced with Gran at the holiday dance. For a moment, I was apart from my grandmother, and overwhelmed by how touching it was to stand at a remove and see how deeply she cared for this lovely white-haired man three years her junior.

"Mrs. Bennett looks well, I'm happy to see."

Simon said this gently, like he understood the tender moment I was having watching her.

I nodded, blinked my eyes to tamp down the unexpected swell of emotion that had rushed up, but couldn't manage to say anything.

"Can I buy you a cup of punch?" He extended his elbow like they did in the olden days, a little jaunty, a little bit funny, which helped me regain my social footing.

"I'd love that." I looped a hand through the crook of his arm, and we walked into the next room. The band was playing a slow melody that sounded sweet and uplifting. I watched Jack and Gran dancing together. They were talking and laughing, their swaying to the music perfectly timed.

At the refreshment table, Simon dipped the ladle into the spiked punch bowl, filled two cups, and handed me one. We clinked cheers and watched everyone on the dance floor. The room felt full and merry.

I sipped my punch—the spirited spike cut a sharp line through the fruitiness. Thank goodness. I took a big swig to steady myself. "So . . . you're back. How'd you end up in Seattle, anyway?"

"I moved there after college to do the tech thing. Got married." He shrugged. "Got divorced."

"What does 'the tech thing' mean, exactly?"

He chuckled. "What doesn't it mean? I've done software development, managed entire product divisions, handled sales for big corporations. I did a tour at all of them . . . Microsoft, Amazon, Google, and boomeranged back to Microsoft—it's kind of how it goes out there. Now I run cloud computing sales—the way work has changed, I can do my job from anywhere. And I wanted to be back here. It was time."

"Do you have kids?"

"No." His gaze drifted to the dance floor. "My ex and I were too career focused. Jobs were the priority, not kids."

"Do you regret that?"

He didn't answer.

"Which is absolutely none of my business. I'm sorry." I paused. "That was the punch talking, not me."

He chuckled and refilled both our cups. "It's okay. Being asked a real question, something meaty, is . . . refreshing."

Neither of us said anything for a beat.

"So, the answer is, sometimes, yeah . . . I do regret not having kids." He seemed lost in a thought. "But there's no way my ex and I would've stayed married, and I can't imagine a functional coparenting situation, so maybe things work out for a reason."

I agreed, said maybe so, which didn't further the conversation in the least.

We stood watching the dance floor. Drank our punch side by side.

Then Simon leaned closer. "I've been thinking about getting a dog."

"Yeah?" Him keeping the conversation going sent a fizzy wave through me. "Tell me more."

He set his cup on the table and held out a hand. "Can I tell you while we dance?"

I smiled, said "Yes."

He set my cup beside his, then held my hand as we walked to the dance floor. We assumed a proper getting-to-know-one-another form: one of my hands on his shoulder, the other holding his, which was slightly outstretched. His other hand rested ever so lightly on my back.

Nate and Jenny danced our way.

"Look who's back in town," Nate said to me.

I laughed. "I literally didn't know who he was."

"Wasting little time, huh, Simon," Jenny said.

Simon's smile was gracious. "Okay, I expect that from my little brother, but my sister-in-law? C'mon!"

"She plays for Team Nate," Nate said.

Jenny cocked her head, her tone playful. "*What* team do I play for?"

Nate bowed his head in mock apology. "Team Jenny, dear. You play for Team Jenny."

Simon and I laughed at this bit that they'd obviously done before.

"C'mon, let's give these two some space," Nate said to Jenny, who winked at Simon as they waltzed away.

We danced silently.

"She's a Frenchie," Simon whispered in my ear.

The timbre of his voice sent a ripple down my spine. Then I realized he was talking about the dog he wanted. "French bulldogs are the cutest. They're like happy dumplings."

"That would be a great name: Dumpling!"

He laughed, and in a shift that was smooth, drew me closer. He set my hand he'd been holding on his shoulder, then wrapped both arms around my waist, his hold subtly firmer. My fingers encircled the back of his neck, which felt muscular, solid, like the entire front of his body, which was now pressed against mine. It had been so long since I'd been this close to someone new, anyone, really. So long since I'd flirted—or whatever this was I was doing. Ages since I'd felt even remotely interested in someone, much less felt a bolt of arousal zigzagging through me. Dancing with Simon, close enough to feel his rhythm, his vibration, made everything feel warm, like fresh blood was coursing through my veins, livening bits of me that had languished. I'd become such a foreigner to . . . life. And now, in this drafty room, with winter whistling through 175-year-old crevices in the historical society's walls, I worried about sweating.

I'd had a serious boyfriend in my early thirties that fizzled out because neither of us were ready to take the next step—either moving in together or getting engaged. But a year after we broke up, when I heard save-the-date cards had gone out for him and his fiancée, I was forced to reevaluate more than a few things about our relationship. The point was, even when I seriously dated someone, it was a barhopping, "grab a slice while walking home" kind of relationship. Nothing about it was adult.

My late thirties marked a time of exuberant dating—dinners out, meeting for drinks. But it was surface fun, nothing that sparked a lasting, meaningful connection.

For the last few years, Gran had had the good sense not to ask if I was seeing anyone. Of course, her not asking spoke directly to how much of a sad-sack figure I must've cut. Anyone holding their shoulders back, chin up, eyes atwinkle would welcome such inquiries, the conversation bouncing from delightful love interest to future plans to career advancements, maybe even upcoming travel. However, for me—barely taking up space, eyes cast downward, hair in need of a wash, shoulders rolled forward, picking at my cuticles—Gran knew love life inquiries weren't merited.

But recently I'd felt differently. More sure . . . maybe even secure.

And now here I was dancing with this man, my insides stirring in a way that felt both foreign and exciting.

"And what about you?" Simon's voice pulled me from my thoughts. "Are you married, divorced, betrothed? Kids?"

"None of the above."

He inhaled, his chest expanding against mine, and smiled on the exhale.

I was so lost in the intensity of the moment that it took a beat to notice that Simon had stopped his slow sway. The band had struck up a jubilant song led by accordions. Someone grabbed my arm.

"You must polka!" Mama P tugged at me, then turned to Simon. "Belle must polka!"

"I would never stand in the way of a polka," he said, then to me, "I hope to see you later."

His smile electrified me, short-circuited my words. All I could do was wave as Mama P led me to the other side of the dance floor.

Gran was doing her tiny two-step, arms akimbo.

"I've come to polka!" I opened my arms.

Gran beamed.

I led us around the dance floor, but without the dizzying turns that Gran used to take when she was younger. Ours was a more subdued polka. We danced along one side of the floor, then made a turn, nice and easy, and danced up the other side. Gran was chatty, bubbling over with tidbits she had to tell me about everyone in the room. I hadn't polkaed with her in so long—the holiday dance had been canceled the last two years. But on this cold night, in this room that felt warm and welcoming, while dancing with Gran, an easiness settled into my movements. I wasn't in my head, worrying or feeling less than. Doing a polka made it impossible for darker thoughts to plant themselves and take root. Maybe Mama P knew that.

The song ended and everyone clapped.

"Oh, dolly, that was fun!" Gran took my arm and laughed. "I need to sit down now."

We walked to the table where Mama P and Faye were sitting. I pulled out a chair for Gran.

"You looked grand out there." Faye took out a cigarette case and a silver lighter from her clutch, then snapped it shut. She scooted her chair back from the table and stood. "I'm going to have a quick smoke."

"In this cold you're going to go suck on some death?" Mama P said. "Oh no, you're not. Sit back down."

Faye stared for a beat. Then did as she was told.

I looked back and forth between the two. Faye still held the cigarette.

Mama P pointed at it. "And you can put that away."

A hint of amusement played across Faye's face. She put the cigarette and lighter back in her clutch, closed it with a snap.

I broke the silence. "How about I get us some punch?"

"Make mine spiked," Faye said, then twirled a finger in the air. "Make 'em all spiked."

The three of them laughed.

I threaded my way through the crowd to the refreshment table, set out four cups, and started ladling punch into each.

"You are getting serious about your party."

I looked up. Simon grinned at me. His eyes captivated—was it because his gaze was vibrant or warm . . . maybe spellbinding?

"Belle?"

"Huh?"

He pointed at the four glasses I'd set out. "Your party. That's looking serious there."

"Oh, no!" I laughed. "They're not all for me."

"Hey, I make no judgments."

His eyes had a dancy feel to them. That was it. Dancy. Movement. Verve. Something in my center fluttered.

I picked up a fifth plastic cup to calm myself. "I'm pouring you a glass so you can join the party with those ladies over there who are leveling up."

His eyes grew wide. "They look like heavyweights . . . I don't know if I have the stamina."

"Trust me: You don't. Join us anyway."

Gran beamed when she saw Simon with me.

"Simon Watson, I haven't seen you in ages!" She stood up. "You come give me a hug."

"Careful," I said. "She pinches."

Gran's eyes scrunched she smiled so wide. "I do!"

"Aw, Mrs. Bennett, it's good to see you again." Simon enveloped Gran in a hug, then lowered his head so she could pinch his cheeks.

"You're a good boy," she said as he helped her sit back down. He made his way around the table, hugged Faye and Mama P.

"Your mom told us you were coming back to town," Mama P said as she gave a wave to the table where Simon's parents, Nate, and Jenny were sitting.

Simon sat in between Gran and me. "Yep, all moved in, got a new driver's license and everything."

"How's it feel being back after all this time?" Faye asked.

"Really good . . . yeah." He paused. "The kind of good I feel here." He patted his chest.

"That's how you know something is right," Gran said. "It must be felt in your center."

Jeremy walked up to the table. "This is for you." He slapped down a slip of paper in front of me. "And that's for you." Slapped another sliver in front of Simon and opened his arms wide. "You're welcome."

Simon looked down at the paper and said in faux reprimand, "A gentleman likes to ask for a lady's number himself when the time is right."

"Yeah, well, no one's got time for you olds to get things done." He wrapped an arm around Marie's shoulders, raised a hand in a peace sign, and walked away.

The evening wound on festively. Before long, the first group of partygoers started making the rounds saying goodbye. I walked around with Gran as she bid good night to her neighbors but held back as she walked over to Jack. She took his hands and spoke to him, then reached for his face. He leaned down and Gran kissed him on the cheek. They held one another's gaze for a moment, then she walked back to me, lost in her own smile.

We made our way to the foyer, and I helped Gran into her coat.

"I'm going to walk home with Faye and Mama P," she stage-whispered to me, patting both my arms for emphasis. "You take your time."

"Gran, you're as bad as Jeremy."

Her cheeks were ruddy like a cherub's. "I know!" Then she linked arms with Faye and Mama P and strolled out the door.

"Here, allow me." Simon was suddenly next to me, reaching for my coat. Had he been waiting for the right moment? Or simply . . . apparated?

I handed him my coat and he held it open for me. The gesture charmed. The consideration, it felt like a throwback. Or at least like something I'd never experienced in my city dating life. Which, to be clear, was unremarkable and so far in the past it barely echoed.

"Can I walk you home?" Simon wrapped a gray cashmere scarf around his neck and smiled in a way that struck me as earnest. He radiated confidence but wasn't cocksure. It was something gentler, the way of someone who simply knew who they were.

"I'd love that."

As soon as we stepped outside, I gasped. "I didn't realize it was snowing so hard!"

Big flakes fell thick and dramatic. The snow sparkled under the soft light of the lampposts. It was like someone had frosted the village with a layer of fluffy icing.

"It's beautiful," I whispered. "I love walking in a big fresh snow."

"Really?"

"I think it's the most special thing." I looked down the street and saw that Gran, Faye, and Mama P were almost at their respective doors. "Would you . . . want to walk a little bit? Maybe not go straight home?"

"Let's walk across the bridge."

I grabbed his arm in excitement. "Yes!" Then released my grip. My enthusiasm for snow could be startling to others.

We set off. I didn't care that I was wearing kitten heels. Normally, I'd wear boots, but right now, I just wanted to feel the snow. Have it wake me up deep down.

The village was silent, like all the buildings were tucked into bed under a feather comforter.

"This is my favorite thing to do in the winter," I said. "I love the peacefulness . . . Thank you for joining me."

"It's my pleasure." He inhaled deeply. "Nothing smells like this where I lived in Seattle."

"It's like the purest, freshest air ever, right? You can't find it anywhere else."

The path narrowed at the walking bridge that cantilevered over the Chagrin River. Simon let me go first. Halfway across, we stopped to take it in. Snow drifted on the banks. Ice formed a ledge along the edges. When we got to the end of the bridge, the sidewalk widened enough for us to walk side by side again.

Simon took my hand and held it. I was glad for the cover of darkness so he wouldn't see me blush.

"I want you to know, I was going to ask for your phone number." He paused. "Jeremy beat me to it."

"Kids."

"I know the holidays are busy, but I'd love to see you in the New Year."

My insides flip-flopped. Such a strange sensation—there'd been so many tonight. This didn't feel like my life at all. "That . . . would be really nice."

I looked up to find him smiling. The snow was welcome on my hot cheeks.

The sidewalk stopped just as we passed the town hall.

"We're at the end," I said.

"Funny." His voice enveloped me in the darkness. "Doesn't feel like it."

Chapter 5

January was a blur of snowstorms, shoveling walkways, and building fires. If I'd poured maple syrup into the snow to make candy, one could've mistaken us for *Little House on the Prairie*.

The snow was coming down thick tonight. I watched it while washing the dishes, transfixed by the beauty. The back porch light caught the snowflakes' delicate angles, making them twinkle. This kind of snow reminded me of when I was a kid . . . when we were kids.

That notion froze me. The plate in my hand dripped sudsy water. Rarely did I think about Lexie and me as children. For too long, it had been easier not to.

Gran rested her hand on my back. "Belle?"

I was still holding the soapy plate. "Sorry." I rinsed it, mustered a weak smile, and handed it to Gran to dry.

We finished cleaning up from dinner, then sat on the couch by the fire.

Gran got out her knitting, and I was working on a cross-stitch sampler when I heard my phone vibrating. I hadn't realized I'd left it on.

"Someone wants to talk to you!" Gran trilled as I got up.

It hit me. The snow. I knew who it was before looking at the caller ID. "I had a feeling it might be you."

Simon laughed. "Happy New Year. I wanted to see if you felt like a walk."

I mouthed to Gran that it was Simon. She raised her eyebrows and smiled.

"Make some fresh tracks?" I said to him.

"Exactly."

I looked over at Gran, mouthed that he wanted to go for a walk. She silently shooed me with both hands and mouthed, *Go!*

I turned up my hands, as if to say, *I don't know.* Then pointed to the cross-stitch and did an absurd pantomime of sewing.

"Goodness." Gran marched over to me with a hand outstretched. "Give me the phone."

I ducked away from her, spoke quickly, "Okay, that sounds great, yeah."

"I'm at my parents' house," he said. "I'll be over in a few."

I raced through a goodbye and ended the call. Looked sheepishly at Gran.

"Good girl," she said.

Not five minutes later there was a knock at the door. I froze, which made no sense. I knew who it was. He'd just told me he was coming. I was a teenager.

Gran opened the door. "Simon, good to see you!"

He shook snow from his coat before walking in. "Hi, Mrs. Bennett." He bent down for a hug. Then he saw me and raised a hand hello, which seemed odd after the affection he'd just shown Gran.

"Hey."

Neither of us so much as inched closer to one another.

"You two have a nice time." Gran smoothed over the moment. "Stay warm out there."

I kissed Gran on her cheek and wrapped a scarf around my neck twice. Pulled a hat low on my head, shoved my hands in thick mittens, and led the way out.

As soon as my boots smooshed into the thick layer of snow that had blanketed what I'd shoveled earlier, my agitation at our awkward greeting fell away. The snowflakes captivated. Fluffy fairy-tale magic fell quietly, almost soulfully. It transported me to a different mindset from the one that had consumed me only moments ago. A good snow, quiet yet powerful in its majesty, was cleansing that way. It filtered out the unnecessary, the static, anything that wasn't pure or right.

"I'm glad you were home."

Simon's smile was warm, like it had depth of meaning.

"Me too."

We walked in companionable silence and turned up Epping. The quiet absorbing our footsteps was exquisite. Snow clung to the massive old trees. The road ambled up the hill, past the stately homes, making it feel like we were walking through a magical land.

Simon took my right hand in his.

"I was hoping that would've been a smoother move," he said.

"You got all mitten."

"Nuttin' but fleece!"

I stopped. Made a dramatic show of pulling my thick mitten off.

He stepped closer. "You'd risk frostbite for me?" His voice was low, like we were sharing secrets.

"Just for a minute." I barely breathed the words.

He peeled off his leather glove and took my hand.

The warmth of his skin touching mine in the frigid cold felt like such an intimate act. Heat rose to my cheeks. My scarf suddenly seemed like too much.

Fat flakes shaved from the thickest part of the lake-effect cloud layer fell quickly. Our boots compacted the snow in squeaky crunches, a deeply satisfying sound. Snow like this invited a profound sense of peace, the kind you wanted to fill your veins with. Never go inside. Ride out the snowstorm in the elements. Walk this contented road forever.

Simon inhaled deeply. "You miss how clean winter air is, living elsewhere."

Yes, the air.

We spoke in gauzy generalities about the snow, the air, whatever else. It didn't matter. It all felt small, like a placeholder for something more meaningful.

Simon stopped. Took my mitten and put it back on my hand. "As much as I want to keep holding your hand, I can't in good conscience let you get any colder." He put his glove on, then took both my hands in his. Stepped closer. Looked into my eyes before murmuring, almost to himself, "You've been a surprise."

Meaning engulfed me, arrested my breathing.

"I'd love to see more of you," he said. "I hope you're staying in town."

The snow stopped. All breath leaked out of me. Movement and magic ceased for the longest tiniest moment, as I thought, *Am I staying here?*

A flicker of something—confusion?—shadowed Simon's gaze. He cleared his throat. "At the very least, I'd love to take you to dinner."

The twinkle of the snow, the hopeful flakes, I noticed them again. The magical beauty of the moment returned. "Love that." It was all I could manage.

"Good." Simon's voice dropped low. He stared intently, then leaned down and kissed me with an arresting tenderness. Backstopped by hunger, but gentle and coaxing, not voracious or disrespectful. The exquisiteness matched the snow.

We stood on the edge of the road's embankment, our feet covered in the building drift. A deep silence enveloped us, bearing witness to something that felt powerful. Simon vibrated my cells, summoned a hotness and thirst in me that had been lying dormant. I wanted the moment to stretch for days. Years. An eternity.

He eased away, gently brushed a lock of hair from my face. "I couldn't wait any longer. I hope that wasn't too forward."

I shook my head, searched for my voice. Everything tangled. My insides played a symphony of assent. "Not too forward . . . not at all." My voice didn't sound like my own.

But I loved the timbre of joy that it carried.

February was much like January. Cleveland's lake-effect snow was like a family member who needed tending to.

At the end of the month—a rare evening that didn't require me to go out and shovel for a second time that day—I made a pot of Gran's white bean soup. She'd taught me how to make it a few weeks back with homemade vegetable stock that she always had in the freezer, and for the first time, I made it without any direction from her. We ate on the couch from mugs in front of the fire, a blanket draped across our laps. The logs snapped and popped in a comforting way. I watched as Gran spooned up her first taste.

"Good, good, good." She waved her spoon in triumph. "Oh, Bellie, this is so good!"

Relief and pride washed through me. After dinner, I cleaned up, then made tea, which we also had by the fire. When it was time for bed, Gran shuffled to her bedroom to change into her nightgown, while I washed the last of the dishes. I turned on the light above the sink that Gran kept lit at night and shut off the overhead. The kitchen had such warmth in this soft glow. I cast my eye over the clean sink, the cutting boards leaning just so against the cabinet, Gran's ivory curtains trimmed with a delicate lace edge. I smiled to myself, happy for it all, and walked toward my bedroom.

"Oh, I can't wait!" Gran murmured as I walked past her room.

I stopped. Listened.

"I love that," she whispered. Then after a few moments, "Good, good, good."

I turned and stood at Gran's door. Watched her sit on the edge of the bed, staring out the window. Then she lifted her arms up as if to hug someone.

"Heyyyy." I kept my voice gentle as I walked in, not wanting to startle her. "Are you okay?"

Eventually, Gran turned to me. Her face had a beatific look on it. She smiled from ear to ear as she waved me over to her. I leaned in for a hug. "Oh, Bellie, Clemmy's making crumb cake! I love her crumb cake!"

Gran's words froze me. She never said my mother's name, only referred to her as my mother. Ever since I was a child, she'd done this. When I got older, I realized it was a subtle way of aligning herself with Lexie and me—it was the three of us after my mother passed. Always the three of us.

But here she was saying my mom's name, Clementine. Her Clemmy. Holding on to Gran now, I felt a subtle shift. The solid security I'd felt only moments earlier in the kitchen gave way to a feathery weakness in my chest.

"Aw," Gran sighed happily, prompted by nothing I'd said. She nestled her head into my shoulder.

I held Gran, supporting her as she leaned her weight into me, and rubbed her back. We sat that way for some time.

"You sleepy?" I said quietly.

"Yes, dolly." She didn't shift at all.

I waited a moment. "You want to go to bed, Gran?"

She slowly leaned upright and smiled, her eyes closed and content. "Yes . . . I'm ready."

"Okay, let me help you in." I helped her scooch back onto the bed, took off her slippers, her feet tiny and warm in my hands, then lifted her legs onto the bed. I pulled up the sheet and tucked the comforter up around her shoulders.

"Oh, that's nice," she murmured, eyes still closed. "I love you, dolly."

"I love you too, Gran. So much."

I turned off the bedside lamp and walked soundlessly across the room.

"I love you . . . I love you," Gran whispered before I got to the door.

I whispered again that I loved her and shut the door behind me with a quiet click.

Then held the doorknob to steady myself.

The next morning, I didn't smell Maxwell House first thing. I stretched in bed, pleased that Gran had slept in. I'd get up, put the coffee on, and make us an omelet for breakfast. There was sourdough bread from that European bakery in Cleveland Heights that would be so good toasted.

I padded into the kitchen and measured out the coffee, put it on the stove to percolate. The house felt still. I took out eggs and a block of cheddar cheese from the fridge, set them on the counter, and unwrapped a couple of slices of bread from the freezer and put them in the toaster oven to thaw.

The sky wasn't overcast for the first time in weeks. No snow overnight. Actual sunlight streamed through the kitchen window. It felt so cheery. Gran was going to love it. At the first sun sighting, she'd said, we'd start planning our spring garden projects. I walked to her room, excited to tell her, and cracked open the door.

Gran always slept on her side, but she was on her back.

I walked over to the bed.

Something was wrong. Dread blew a hole in my chest.

"Gran?" I whispered.

She was still.

Too still.

I crouched down next to the bed, laid my hand on her chest. No rise or fall. Perfectly still.

"Gran?" I shook her shoulder a tiny bit, but she was unmovable. And she didn't rouse. She felt oddly solid, like all the softness had left her.

No no no no no no . . . The tears slipped down my face. Poured out of me. I put my head on her chest and held her, crying. Wishing for so much, wanting so much more . . . finding no air for either.

Salty

Part 2

A beginning undone.

Chapter 6

Southern Ohio, Summer of 1951

Annabelle raced up the hill after Grace, who'd grown leggy like a colt since last summer. A year ago, she would've run backwards ahead of Grace, cheering her twelve-year-old sister to catch up. Now, with sunshine blazing across the meadows, the scent of sweet grass wafting up as they ran barefoot, Annabelle was the one lagging, despite having three years on Grace.

Grace jumped up and down when she reached the summit. "I finally did it! I beat you!"

Annabelle laughed and walked the last ten feet up the hill, clapping.

"Were you really running your fastest?" Grace plopped on the ground, legs splayed in front of her.

"I promise." Annabelle sat beside Grace. "I couldn't catch you!"

Grace smiled as she lay back, face toward the sky. Annabelle did the same, closed her eyes and exhaled. She loved these languid summer mornings, this time after they'd finished their chores—fetched water from the well, fed the cows, and then, the best one, felt around nests in the chicken coop for eggs.

Mama always wanted them to play after that—they could do whatever they wanted for the rest of the day. Come evening, they'd set the table and help in the kitchen. But Mama said that after morning chores, they were to be playing. It wasn't usual for living on a farm, especially in the summer when there was so much to be done. They had another set of hands, Mr. Bernard, come help on occasion. Sometimes he'd bring his young son, Crocker. But the girls, they weren't involved in the daily work beyond their morning and evening chores. Whenever anyone questioned Mama about it or marveled at the way she let her daughters do whatever they wanted all day, she'd say with a knowing air, "The pressure of life is gonna come at them fast and early. No need to hasten its arrival." Her response left no room for further discussion.

And so, Grace and Annabelle lay on the top of the biggest hill, soaking up the sun. They talked about wading in the creek. Hammering together a bunch of wood planks and making a tree house. Picking strawberries. Making a fort in the barn's hayloft. Swinging on the tire swing. They'd decide what to do in the afternoon after lunch. They might do some of the things they'd thought up while peering into the cloudless sky. They might do all of it. They might decide on something else entirely.

Such was their freedom.

They clambered down the hill, made their way through the side field over to the creek, and raced down the muddy embankment. They walked, calves submerged in the cool water. The rocks were smooth underfoot, some slicked with the slimy fuzz of algae. The two caught minnows in their hands, cupping them with water to see them wiggling up close, then gently releasing them back into the creek. They lost themselves exploring their favorite watery world.

Summer of 1951

Mama rang the bell outside the kitchen door, clanged it for a good minute so her girls would hear it no matter where they were on the farm. "Lunch!"

She spotted them on the ridge, then squinted. Was Grace carrying a cat? That girl was forever bringing strays home. She shook her head in amusement, walked back into the kitchen, poured some cream from that morning's milking into a saucer, and set it out on the back stoop.

"What's the grub?" Papa said through the screen door.

"Don't you be coming in here with those mucky boots, mister."

"I know, I know." He kicked off his boots outside and stepped into the kitchen, a grin on his ruddy face.

Mama looked over at him. "No."

"Oh, yes." He circled his arms around her waist, nuzzled her neck, and playfully pinched her sides.

"There's no pinching!" Mama tried to sound stern through her laughter.

"They're love pinches." Now Papa was tickling her.

"No, no, no!" She swatted his arm with a wooden spoon. "Take your pinches and tickles and sit down. I got food to get together here."

He laughed and did as his wife said.

"Mr. Bernard and Crocker comin'?"

Papa peered out the kitchen window. "Yep, presently."

He watched his wife move about the kitchen in her overalls and bare feet. Her hair was tied back in a faded kerchief, her face bronzed from working outside. Laugh lines marked the happy in her, making it impossible for anyone to take her stern act seriously. He felt that familiar swell of love in his chest. They'd been together since they were sixteen—the same age as Annabelle, which scrambled his brain a little. Been married since they were eighteen. Twenty-two years and the blink of an eye all at the same time.

Their days started before dawn with strong coffee and toast at the kitchen table. Cows needed milking. Stalls needed mucked. They didn't talk in the morning. They let the awareness of the day settle easily around them, then got to work before the girls woke up and needed breakfast. The work was hard, but good together. They'd made a beautiful life on land they loved. It wasn't easy, but they did it side by side, and that was the only way he ever wanted to do anything. At the end of every day, after the girls had gone to bed, they'd sit quietly together again. In the winter, they'd sit on the couch under a blanket and watch the fire. In the summer, they'd sit out on the porch glider and listen to the night come alive.

No matter the season, his joy was being next to his wife.

Summer of 1952

When Mama saw where the sun was in the sky, she propped her pitchfork against the wall. "I'm gonna start breakfast."

Papa heaved an armload of hay over one of the stall walls. "I'll be in in a bit."

The girls would be up soon, might already be. Mama kicked her boots off and walked into the kitchen, the screen door slapping closed. She washed her hands, then set the big cast-iron skillet on the stove. She cracked eggs into a bowl, added a splash of cream and salt, whisked it all together. Then she diced onions, potatoes, and a green pepper. Put a healthy knob of butter into the skillet and heated it up until it was good and bubbly, added all the chopped bits and stirred to coat all the sides with the butter bath. Then she let it sit to brown.

"Mornin', Mama." Grace finished braiding her hair as she walked in.

"Hi, honey." Mama scraped a wooden spatula against the pan to move everything around. "Where's your sister?"

"Here." Annabelle walked straight to the cupboard and pulled out four plates. "You and Papa having more coffee?"

"I think so."

She took down two teacups, started setting the table.

Grace looked over at the stove, then took the loaf of bread from the bread box and set it on a wooden cutting board. At the table, she cut five pieces. Papa would have two.

"I'll fetch the water," Annabelle said after she put forks and knives next to the plates.

The rhythm of the morning carried a comfortable predictability. Everyone working toward something virtuous.

When breakfast was ready, Mama rang the bell.

Moments later they were all seated, the skillet in the middle of the table. Papa served.

"Mornin'," Mr. Bernard called through the screen door. "Apologies, we're a bit early. We'll meet you at the barn."

"You'll do no such thing," Mama retorted. "Both of you get in here and sit down, have something to eat."

Mr. Bernard chuckled and walked in with his son, Crocker, boots already off. They sat down at the table. "I do love your breakfast."

Grace got two more place settings and cut more bread. Crocker caught her eye and smiled. She blushed. They were the same age, in the same class at school. This summer Grace had started acting shy whenever he came to work with his pa.

"You're sweet on him," Annabelle said one day last month after Mr. Bernard and Crocker had arrived to help with the garden, after Crocker tipped his baseball cap at Grace and her face reddened.

Grace turned her back and walked away, then looked back over her shoulder at Annabelle and flashed a secret smile.

Now they all sat around the breakfast table, and Grace was staring down at her plate, smiling that same secret smile.

Summer of 1953

"Darlin', what are you doing up so early?"

Annabelle shuffled into the kitchen. "I don't know. Can't fall back to sleep." She sat down at the table and pulled her knees up to her chin, watched her father stir cream into his coffee. She loved the smell of morning. "Where's Mama?"

"She must've got up early too. Most likely in the barn. Go tell her coffee's ready."

Annabelle stepped out into the dark and started walking toward the barn. Every now and again, she'd wake up like this, too early. Mama said it was because she was eighteen now, that she was getting into a more adult rhythm of sleep. Annabelle didn't mind waking up early. The hours before the sun came up felt special, like she was getting more time in the day. It was a gift. Later, she'd probably fall asleep for a spell under the big sycamore on the hill, but that would be okay too. Even if Grace wouldn't like it.

The barn door was ajar, which wasn't like Mama, especially so early. Annabelle stepped in. "Mama, you didn't close the—"

Her mother lay face down on the ground.

"Mama!" Annabelle ran over, shook her, said her name over and over. Yelled it. She was crying now. Mama wouldn't budge. "Papa!" She shrieked his name over and over, upsetting the cows, who groaned the way they did when they were distressed. "Papa!" The horses whinnied, pawed at the boards of their stalls. "Papa!" Annabelle sobbed. She couldn't turn Mama, couldn't get her to move.

"What in the world—" Papa strode in, ready to give Annabelle a stern talking to, when he saw his wife. The color drained from his face. "Lillian!" He put his fingers to her neck, rolled her over, caressed her face. "Oh, Lillian . . . my Lillian." His voice grieved at how waxy she looked, how far away she was from her body. He kissed her cheek. "My sweet, sweet Lillian," he said over and over, tears pouring down his face, shoulders shuddering as he gasped for air.

Annabelle, who'd expected that her father would make Mama all better, looked on in horror. She watched him change nothing, accept Mama lying there like that. Annabelle felt removed from the barn, the dirt floor, unable to process finding her mother face down, smashed into the dirt. She stared in disbelief—this wasn't real, she told herself.

This couldn't be happening. Not to Mama. She was strong like a bull. Then reality rushed up on her out of nowhere, brutal and unyielding, like a speeding train. It ran Annabelle clear down. Leveled her. She sobbed anew, covered her eyes with her hands, and drew her knees up. Made herself as small as possible.

When the doctor come round, Grace was still asleep. He said Mama had a strong heart but weak valves.

He put a hand on Papa's shoulder, told him that she didn't suffer any.

Autumn of 1953

Annabelle pulled a pan of biscuits from the oven. She'd finally made a batch that didn't burn on the bottom. It had been three months since Mama had passed. Fifteen pans of burnt biscuits. This small success made her tear up.

Papa trudged into the kitchen, slumped in a chair. Poured himself a cup of coffee from the pot that Grace had set on the table just a few minutes earlier.

Grace came in from outside with a pitcher of water, set it next to the stove.

"Thanks." Annabelle smiled at her sister, hoping it reassured her. It was what Mama would've done.

"It's gonna be a pretty day, Papa." Grace put an extra gilding of cheer on her words.

He looked up, managed a sad smile. "Sure, darlin'."

Honey light streamed through the windows as they sat down to a quiet breakfast. Fall had crept in without any of them taking real notice. There was a slight chill in the air, and the sun hung lower in the sky these mornings.

They were all lower since Mama left them.

Summer of 1956

Annabelle closed the top of her suitcase, latched it, then belted it around the middle so it wouldn't pop open on the trip. She pulled the belt tighter, struggled to get it to the notch she wanted. Grace, who'd been watching her silently from the doorway, walked in and grasped the belt just beyond her sister's hands. They pulled together.

"Got it." Annabelle pushed the buckle prong through the hole and threaded the belt through. "Thank you."

Grace, eyes watering, nodded.

That got Annabelle. She scrunched her nose to fight back tears. "Crocker downstairs?"

"Yeah." Her voice, thick with emotion, came out in a whisper. She sat on the bed.

Annabelle sat beside her. "I'll be back before the wedding to help with everything."

Grace smiled, wiped her eyes.

"This . . . this is how it should be." Annabelle spoke tenderly. She felt the enormity of the shift too, but being older she had to keep her emotions in check. Do what was right. "It's time for you and Crocker to live here, fill this house with babies." She smiled. "Make Mama and Papa proud."

Grace rested her head on Annabelle's shoulder. "I'm gonna miss you."

Annabelle took Grace's hand and held it. Swallowed back the sadness, the change that seemed inevitable after Papa passed away two years ago in his sleep. He never was the same after Mama died. It was like she took his heart with her. Annabelle and Grace lived on in the house, kept up the farm. They'd assumed most of the work after Mama passed away anyway, Papa being a shell of himself. Then Crocker asked Grace for her hand in marriage. Annabelle knew it was time for her to take leave of the family home. "I'm going to miss you more than you know."

Grace wiped her eyes. "Wait here, I have something for you."

She left the room, and Annabelle exhaled a big breath to steady herself, wiped the tears from her cheeks. She needed to be strong for Grace. Just when she had gathered herself together, her sister walked back in carrying two booklets.

"I made you this." Grace sat on the bed and placed one of the thin books in Annabelle's lap.

Annabelle's eyes welled. "What did you do?" She opened the small clothbound cover and whimpered. Tears fell. "Oh my goodness."

"It's all the stuff we would make with Mama," Grace said, her voice tender as a whisper. "I made myself one too so we'd both have one. I know we don't need anything written down to recall Mama's recipes but . . ." She couldn't finish the sentence. Her face scrunched up and tears rolled down her face.

Annabelle slowly turned every page, savoring the words her sister had written down for them. This tether she'd created was precious. "This is beautiful," she finally said. "I'm going to look at it every single day and think of us. Thank you, Gracie . . . from the bottom of my heart, thank you."

She hugged her sister. Grace and Annabelle clung to one another.

They parted, chuckled at what a mess they were, and wiped their faces with hankies. Grace handed Annabelle an extra one.

Annabelle unlatched her suitcase, carefully placed the cookbook Grace had made on top, and gently closed and secured the case all over again. She exhaled and lay back on the bed. Grace lay beside her.

"Have you thought . . ." Grace paused. "Have you thought what you'll do up there?"

Nerves fluttered through Annabelle's middle. "There's a lot to do in Cleveland. I don't know what all yet, but I'm gonna stay in a respectable home where ladies like myself can have clean room and board while they find a job."

Grace sat up and looked at her, worry behind her eyes. "What kind of job? What do you know about a job?"

Annabelle sat up, willed herself to be strong, to not give in to the worry that kept her up late at night. She smiled her most confident smile. "That's the adventure, figuring it all out."

March 19, 1957
Annabelle,

I can't talk to you anymore, so I'm writing you a letter to please let this go. Please. This is taking a toll on me that you can't imagine.

I can't take any more pressure from you. I'm telling you the same thing I told that company that won't leave me alone: I won't change my mind. So drop it. Stop trying to convince me to do something I don't want. Crocker agrees with me and we're standing firm. I'm not going to address this anymore.

Grace

April 2, 1957
Grace,

You don't want to talk? Fine. But you need to know that I'm only looking out for you. I don't want to lose you. Can't you see that that's why I keep bringing this up? That life takes a toll—I think you know it but don't want to admit it because then you'd be forced to acknowledge that I'm right. Or that you'd have to face change, and I know you're not one for that. Whatever your reasoning, I'm begging you to set that aside and reconsider.

Annabelle

April 13, 1957

Grace,

I wish you'd answer your telephone, but you won't, so I'm going to keep writing to you. I'm praying that you're hearing my words and will see the reason in what I'm saying. I mean it, why not live an easier life? One that will put you and Crocker ahead as you look to start a family? I don't understand why you're reluctant to do something different. Don't be stubborn.

Annabelle

Crocker walked through the screen door in his work boots. Grace slouched at the kitchen table, a cup of lukewarm tea in front of her. She didn't look up. Didn't admonish him to kick off his muddy boots.

He cleared his throat. "Lovie . . . the mail came."

Grace knew by the way he was hovering close that he expected her to respond. She exhaled a weary breath, waited for what he'd say next.

"There's another one." He gripped the letter tighter. "I can throw it away if you want."

Grace was washed out. She hadn't brushed her hair in days.

Eventually, she held out a hand. "I'll take it."

Crocker didn't move. "You sure?"

She looked up at him, hand still outstretched. "I said I'll take it."

May 2, 1957
Grace,

Once again, I'm writing after calling you countless times and you never picking up the phone. I don't understand how you can never pick up your phone! We need to talk. This is no way to do anything. I'm so frustrated that you won't even consider what I'm trying to do for you, how it could help you! You're not seeing how things could be, how they could be better, easier. You're only stuck in what is. Doing what you know and nothing else. Don't be shortsighted and pass up this opportunity. I'm begging you.

Annabelle

Grace, eyes dulled with grief, showed no emotion. All the crying had wrung her out.

She slowly ripped the letter into pieces and pushed the torn bits of paper to the bottom of her teacup to drown Annabelle's words.

May 20, 1957
Annabelle,
Stop contacting me.

This is the last letter you'll ever get from me—the last words I'll ever write to you, because what you've stolen from me you can never make up for. You have no idea what you've done, and I'm sure you didn't think for one second what this campaign of yours could do, the devastating impact it would have. Now I'm telling you that you can never undo the damage you've caused me and Crocker and the life we envisioned for ourselves. Your stubbornness,

> your refusal to leave me be, to accept my decision, has stolen my joy. Has gutted me. And for that, for all of this, I will never forgive you. No sister would ever do this. You're certainly no sister to me.
>
> Goodbye,
>
> Grace

Annabelle saw the outline in the envelope and knew what Grace had sent her without even looking.

The cookbook, the one that matched her own.

Southern Ohio, March 2023

Grace shuffled to the mailbox, feeling her age in her bones. It was a climb up the hill, then a long walk down the gravel drive to the mailbox. But it was a trip she had done every week since Crocker passed five years ago. It was one more task that kept her going, kept her young. Youngish. As young as she could be at eighty-four. Lord knew there was plenty to do on the farm. Things still needed to be kept up. The mail needed to be got.

The air had a mighty chill to it. The calendar now said March, but that wind had a sharpness that still felt like winter. The mailbox door creaked when she opened it, like it was bone weary from the cold.

Three envelopes rested inside. Grace pulled them out, closed the mailbox, and started the journey back up the drive. She flipped through the mail.

Bill. Flier.

She stopped at the sight of the next letter.

Her breath caught.

The writing on the envelope—it had been too many decades to count, but she knew that writing anywhere.

Holding the flimsy letters made her arms feel weak. Energy drained from her entire body.

She opened the envelope with the familiar handwriting, her fingers working greedily at the seal. Her eyes raced over the words. One hand covered her mouth in disbelief. A sob caught in her throat. She lowered herself to the ground, unable to stand, tears disappearing into the gravel.

Bitter

Part 3

Welcome to the Grief Legion.

Chapter 7

The ambulance arrived.

I pointed to Gran's room.

Didn't think to close the front door.

Faye hurried into the house moments later, frantic. "Belle?"

I lurched toward her.

"Oh, my dear . . ." She held me close, one arm wrapped around me, the other cradling my head.

She held me until my sobs subsided, then guided me to the couch when the paramedics returned to the living room and gave their condolences. Faye told them we had a funeral home, and that we would call. There was more talk. I sat at a remove from it all. Mama P walked in, her brow furrowed. She sat down and pulled me close.

Faye walked into Gran's bedroom, stayed for a few minutes, then came back out, wiping her eyes. She went into the sewing room and returned with a folder. She nodded at Mama P, who kissed my head and went into Gran's room as Faye sat on the other side of me. I couldn't stop crying—and then I would, my brain not believing what was happening. After the cogs turned and reality came into horrible focus, I'd start again. Mama P came out of Gran's room, gently closed the door behind her, and blew her nose in a hanky. She sat on the couch and wrapped an arm around me.

"I don't know what I should be doing now," I whispered.

"We need to call the funeral home," Faye said in a gentle voice, one I never knew she had.

I hunched over, face in my hands. Then calmed down and sat zombie silent. I wasn't sure how long.

Faye placed a manila folder on my lap. "Everything you need to take care of is in here, everyone you need to call. It's all explained."

I shook my head, unable to wrap my mind around Gran's passing having action items. Then, "How . . . did you know? About this?" I patted the folder.

"Well, we're three elderly women living alone," Mama P said, wincing at the tense. "We decided years ago to look out for one another when we couldn't look out for ourselves. So . . . we each made folders with all the necessary information so our relatives would know our burial wishes and who to call—and so our financial lives could be easily unwound and taken care of." She nodded at Faye. "It was her idea."

"Too many women don't plan or aren't prepared for their last earthly adventure. I didn't want to be one of those women. And I didn't want my dearest friends to be in those circumstances either. So, we helped each other."

I looked up from the folder toward Gran's room. My throat felt gravelly and pinched. "I'm not strong enough for this."

Faye put her hand atop mine. "You're Annabelle's granddaughter, so you are." She paused. "Your gran might not be here, but she's with you . . . She is."

They stayed while I called the funeral home. A hearse arrived and the representatives suggested we wait in a room where we wouldn't see anything. The three of us sat in the kitchen. I heard the wheels of a gurney rattling over the floorboards.

Faye looked toward the doorway, nodded, and held up a finger.

"Belle, they've taken your gran out," she said softly to me. "Would you like to stand at the front door with us before the hearse drives away?"

I nodded.

A black hearse was parked in front of the house. One of the caretakers stood on the sidewalk, hands clasped in somber acknowledgment. I cracked open at the sight of the hearse. At the caretaker's silent gesture of respect. At the sun glinting off the car's ebony polish. The caretaker tipped her cap and got in the passenger seat, and the hearse drove slowly away.

The afternoon was a blur. I met with the funeral director, planned the wake and the burial, was in touch with the church, sat on a settee in the funeral home's lobby and wrote an obituary with a box of tissues by my side. Back at Gran's house, I made the call I'd been dreading. When Lexie answered the phone, my throat closed up.

"Belle? You there?"

All I could emit was a weird gasp.

"What's wrong with you?" She sounded impatient.

Which pissed me off enough to get a hold of myself. "Gran . . . passed away."

Silence from the other end.

"Lex? Did you hear me?"

"Yeah." Her voice was a whisper.

She didn't say anything else.

So, I told her what I'd arranged, gave her the dates and times.

Lexie cleared her throat. "Okay . . . I'll set up someplace to go after the cemetery."

She'd circumvented all emotion and dove headlong into planning, doing.

"Sorry . . . I've got to go," she said. "Thank you for calling me."

I hung up without saying goodbye.

The wave was so dark when it crashed, I thought I'd never emerge from the churn. Never sip peaceful air again. Seaweed tangled my ankles, dragged me down further. The murk was dark, swallowing.

Memories flashed as I sucked in water with each sobbing inhale. I was drowning. It would never not feel this crushing and empty. I succumbed to the churn on the bathroom floor. Gasped for air. My lungs hitched higher and higher in my chest cavity, searching for salvation. Just when it couldn't go on another second, something unknowable buoyed me . . . there was air. I bobbed up and down, found breath. Gulped it down, starved. Then lay there, my cheek against the cool tile floor. Tears rolled out silently, without drama. Everything in the world was still.

The house phone rang.

Like an explosion.

Gran always answered her phone. Whoever was calling didn't know.

I closed my eyes, willed the ringing to stop. After what seemed an eternity, it did, but the echo lingered.

I sat up and blew my nose.

The phone rang again.

God.

I walked to the kitchen and reached for the receiver.

"Hello?" My voice sounded raspy.

"Hello?"

"Yes?"

"I'm sorry . . . do I—hang on." It was an older woman calling. She sounded flustered. "May I please speak with Annabelle?"

I steadied myself. "I'm sorry . . . may I ask who's calling?"

"This is her sister, Grace."

The air went thin.

"Hello?" Her voice went up a notch. "Can you hear me?"

"I can." I forced strength into my voice. "This is her granddaughter, Belle."

"Granddaughter? Yes . . . of course."

I waited for her to say something else. She didn't. "I'm sorry . . . but my gran—" My throat tightened. "My gran passed away two days ago."

The great-aunt who I'd never met, who Gran would never speak of, the woman who Lexie and I knew even as children to never ask about, this woman on the other end of the line, Grace, choked out a sob.

Then the line went dead.

In the funeral parlor, a small sign with tight felt ridges and plastic letters spelling out "Annabelle Bennett" felt surreal. I moved as if in a dream, disconnected from everything around me.

I'd arrived at the wake early to have a moment alone with Gran. Looking at her wearing foundation and blush, lying in the casket I'd picked out, fuzzed my brain, like it couldn't do the computation. I softly put my hand across hers, feeling her chilled skin, her preternaturally plump fingers. A sternum-crushing clarity rushed at me. Tears poured out in a steady weep, like when Gran would lay the garden hose in the dirt to give the daylilies a slow drink.

I stood with my head bowed until voices in the lobby swallowed the moment whole. People were starting to arrive.

"Lexie, look at you! And these cuties! Oh!"

I wiped my face with the sleeves of my sweater and braced myself. She was here.

Most people sucked up to my sister, her beauty and success. Everyone who met Lexie was eager to count themselves among those she favored, the ones she bestowed her charismatic glow upon. And right now, all that obsequiousness felt more wrong than ever.

I turned to see Lexie commanding appreciative glances in the lobby, much like a star making her eagerly awaited appearance on stage. She hugged people hello, said something to the funeral director. Mundane movements—the hanging of coats, the fixing of children's hair—were as elegant as a ballerina's when Lexie performed them. Her dignified response to the too-loud greeting she'd received was as smooth as softened butter. Unable to muster the civility to face her, I headed to the bathroom.

Moments later, Lexie breezed through the restroom door, wearing a crisp black suit. "Hey, Belle."

Her hair was pulled back in a sleek ponytail at the nape of her neck, and she smelled of expensive perfume. Her makeup was flawless, as if she'd been airbrushed with a palette of soft desert tones. It was like we didn't come from the same gene pool. My hair was stringy and limp; my skin, blotchy. And my black sweater had bunched unevenly around the neckline of my collared blouse. I'd escaped to the bathroom to avoid her. Now that she was here, I did the only thing I could think of. I washed my hands.

"How are you holding up?"

I glanced at her in the mirror, shrugged, and turned off the water. "As best I can."

"I know, it's sad."

Sad.

I yanked a fistful of paper towels from the dispenser. "Shame you hadn't bothered to visit her in years."

She cocked her head. "You have no idea—"

"Spare me the 'I have kids and a demanding job' routine. Everyone's got challenges. They also have priorities. Yours have been a disappointment for years when it came to Gran."

"That is entirely unfair."

"Glad you didn't come to visit? Feeling good about that choice right now?"

Lexie's gaze flattened. She seemed to shrink.

"Didn't think so," I said. "You know, I don't care how successful you are, how much money you and your husband bank on an annual basis, your behavior is disgraceful. May your grandchildren—or your children, for that matter—never treat you the way you treated Gran."

Lexie steadied herself against the garbage can. She opened her mouth, then closed it again as if unsure what to say. Then, in a feeble voice, "That's not fair."

I had one hand on the door handle and didn't bother looking back. "*Fair* isn't the point."

My anger faded when I saw how the room had filled. I slowly moved through everyone who'd come to pay their respects, saying hello, thanking them for coming. The conversations weren't long, but I needed to thank Gran's friends who were true and special.

I spotted Jeremy on the far side of the room, standing beside a sofa where Nate and Jenny sat with his nana and pop pop. I had started to make my way toward them when someone touched my arm. I turned to see Simon, solemn in a charcoal suit.

"I'm so sorry, Belle."

"Thank you . . . It means a lot that you came." I leaned in to give him a quick hug, but he held on to me. Then kept holding me until I relaxed.

We released from our embrace in a way that felt like something had been truly shared.

"Your grandmother was dear. I'm going to miss her." He took both my hands in his. "The entire town will."

I squeezed his hands, my voice a whisper. "Thank you." Simon went and sat with his parents, Nate, Jenny, and Jeremy.

Jack Harmon, his face gaunt, caught my eye and walked over.

"Hi, Jack." I teared up. "It's so good of you to come."

His eyes welled, shone bright blue. "I loved your grandmother." He nodded, tried to contain his tears. "I loved her in the only way she'd let me, which was from afar and as a dear friend, nothing more. Her heart . . . it forever belonged to another. Even after your dear grandfather passed, she loved him. But . . . I loved her."

"I know." I hugged him. "She loved you too . . . She did. Trust me, I would know. And she loved dancing with you at the holiday dance . . . absolutely loved it."

Jack's chin wobbled with emotion. He took out a hanky. "I'll carry her here with me." He tapped his chest. "Always."

He gave me a peck on the cheek and left.

Someone squeezed my arm. I turned to see Sydney.

"Belle, I'm so sorry." She threw her arms around me in a hug. It surprised me how long she held on. "Faye called to let me know."

"My gosh . . . You came all the way home from school?"

She looked directly into my eyes. "Of course I did." Her voice was gentle.

As we spoke a bit more, I was lost in a thought swirl, touched by Sydney's gesture. Here she was at OSU, no doubt having the time of her life, returning to pay her respects. I finally understood how special Sydney was and that I'd never given her enough credit.

Sometime later, as I walked into the lobby, I saw Sydney speaking with Lexie and dreaded what my sister was saying to her. A tall older woman in a faded black dress was standing by herself. She was wiping her nose with a hanky, silently consumed by grief. There was something familiar about her.

She looked around, then approached the funeral director and spoke to him. He smiled, said something back, then cast his gaze across the room. He touched the woman's arm and pointed at me.

The woman caught my eye and started toward me. Her salt-and-pepper hair was pinned in a loose bun.

"Belle?" Eyes rimmed red, she smiled through her tears and held out her arms. "I'm . . . your Aunt Grace."

"You mean . . . ?"

"Your grandmother's sister, yes." She nodded a teary smile and embraced me. "I'm so sorry for your loss . . . for all our loss."

I stood stiffly, taken aback, then lightly wrapped my arms around her bony back before we parted.

"I'm mighty sorry to have hung up on you when I called . . . I was just . . ." Her sentence trailed off as she shook her head and wiped a hanky across her eyes. "I was overcome."

Grace's plainspoken way plucked a tender chord inside me.

"I know you're probably surprised to see me here." She wiped her eyes again. "My sister and I had our differences." She cleared her throat.

"But even with so many soured years between us . . . I needed to say my goodbyes."

To stop myself from numbly staring at this woman, I reached out and gave her hand a gentle squeeze.

"Thank you for coming."

Grace struck me as honest and direct in a way that few were. She must've known that I had some understanding about her and Gran's estrangement, so for her to come here and present herself in this unguarded, heartbroken way was . . . something.

She studied me, as if trying to see some of her sister. Much like I was searching for a hint of Gran. They had the same eyes, but the similarities ended there.

"I'm so sorry," she said. "So very sorry."

I murmured my thanks, unsure what else to say.

"Do you have a family?" She blew her nose.

"If . . . you mean a husband and kids, no." I swallowed. "My sister does, she has a family."

"Alexis, right?" Something lurked behind her expression of interest, something resigned and blue. "Is she here too?"

I pointed behind her. "That's Lexie . . . I call her Lexie . . . over there . . . Two kids, husband, family." I'd reached the point where forming sentences was too much.

Grace turned back to me but didn't say anything for a moment. Her eyes searched mine. Then, "Families come in all shapes now, don't they?"

I looked away.

"Well then." Grace exhaled in a way that seemed to bring our interaction to a close. "I wanted to pay my respects." She folded her handkerchief into a small square and stared at it. "It would mean quite a lot to me if I might call you sometime . . . I know this might seem . . ." She lost the thread or didn't have the courage to finish her sentence. She gave her head a subtle shake and looked up. "It sure would mean a lot."

What had happened between her and Gran? This encounter was surreal. But her gaze was beseeching, and her interest felt genuine.

She hadn't come wielding a grudge and seemed to feel far more than she admitted. Everything inside me was too tender today, and that extended to Grace.

"Of course."

Her face brightened. "Oh, good . . . good." She opened up the clasp on her black pocketbook and took out a tiny notepad and a small pencil. She held out both to me. "Would you . . . ?"

I smiled, took the pad and pencil, wrote my name, phone number, and address, then hesitated before handing it back to her.

"Oh my goodness, you live in New York City?"

"Well, I've been here for eight months, but yeah, that's my legal address, I guess . . . I don't know."

"Oh dear, you should come visit me on the farm. It'll balance out your city livin'."

I smiled.

"I mean it." She grew serious. "I would love for you to come for a visit. I would . . . really appreciate the opportunity to get to know you."

"Oh." It was all I could manage. Her offer was touching, but it also felt like too much.

"My husband, Crocker, passed away, and it's just me on the farm now. So . . ."

She didn't press further, perhaps seeing that I wasn't sure how to respond. Maybe she figured I'd never agree to have anything more to do with her than this cordial, if surprising, encounter. A sadness washed over her countenance, like it was pulled from a deep well.

Grace looked down at the hanky, worked it around her nose, then worried it in her grasp.

"I'd love to be in touch if that was okay with you," she said. "And Alexis too, of course." She sighed and then continued more softly, "I've really missed having family."

"That sounds . . . nice." I gave her a hug. Everything felt like a consolation, but I didn't have anything else to offer.

Grace smiled, tears falling anew. She squeezed me one last time before composing herself. "I'm going to introduce myself to Alexis and pay my respects. You should come to the farm for a visit together."

"Absolutely," I said with a smile.

Knowing that would never happen.

The next morning was filled with sunshine, bright and cheery, the opposite of what the day held.

At the funeral, I sat in the front row three people away from Lexie, who was wearing giant Jackie O sunglasses and a black fitted coat. I stared at the casket, feeling like I was hovering above my body at a remove from everything, like my brain couldn't stay present enough to process what was happening. The priest intoned on. The day was brittle cold, yet sunny. So many contradictions.

Then Lexie got up at the priest's introduction and stood behind Gran's casket. I watched her, not following what was happening. Was I supposed to be there too? But she nodded at the priest as if there was an understanding between the two of them.

Lexie, in a faltering voice, like it was all she could manage, read a short poem that was . . . lovely. She got through a few lines, then stopped for a long pause until she was able to continue. She felt something . . . I saw it with my own eyes, felt it in my bones. Something inside me softened.

The processional out of the church, seeing Gran's casket carried to the plot next to Grandpa at the cemetery, it all felt trippy, like I was in a time warp—there, but not. Twenty minutes could've passed. Twenty days. Who knew.

Afterwards, we went to The Cake Shoppe, because as Lexie had announced to everyone who came to the cemetery, Gran loved cake. She did—Lexie had at least remembered that much.

"Hello." Lexie tapped on her champagne glass with her ring finger to get the room's attention. "I just wanted to thank you all for coming to honor our dear gran. Gran was like our mother. We are the people we are because of who she was . . . and we can only hope to live up to every example she set for us." She paused, then raised her glass. "To Annabelle."

Every glass in the room was lifted high. The day felt both interminable and unstoppable. I could slink out of The Cake Shoppe amidst this sea of raised arms, noticed by no one, and end this day.

"Come, dear." Mama P's hand on my back was steadying. "Let's have some cake."

I swallowed, nodded, and let her lead me to a table where Faye and Jack were already seated.

I had a slice of Gran's favorite—three-layer chocolate with vanilla buttercream frosting. We reminisced, laughed about how Gran was so picky with her buttercream—"Not too sweet," she'd admonish.

"This is your gran, Belle," Mama P said. She ate a bite of cake and then shimmied her shoulders back and forth. "Good, good, good!"

Her pitch-perfect impression made us all laugh. And then I cried. Everyone teared up at how jarring it was to have dear remembrances underscored by such profound loss.

We sat silent until Faye, hands circled around a cup of tea, spoke. "Do you know what I truly treasured about your gran? She didn't care a fig about how much money someone had or what their background was, or anything." Her eyes glistened. "She met people where they were and valued them for who they were—not for what they were wearing, or how much jewelry they had on . . ." Her voice gathered steam. "Or the car they drove, or the pocketbook they carried, or the country club they belonged to. She had no time for any of that nonsense. She had a pure heart that was enormous and ever-expanding to let another into her embrace."

Faye's chin quivered. "Oh . . . goodness." She pressed a manicured finger to the corner of one eye. "I'm going to miss her."

Mama P took Faye's hand and held it.

Simon, who was sitting at another table with his parents, Nate, Jenny, Jeremy, and Sydney, got up and approached our table.

"Hey." His eyes were full of understanding, his voice gentle. "Hi, everyone." He put a hand on my shoulder and knelt down to speak to me. "I just wanted to say again how sorry I am. When you're ready for some company, or just want someone to sit quietly with, know I'm here, okay?"

My eyes welled. I nodded.

His smile was soft. He kissed my cheek and stood up, said goodbye to everyone, and walked over to his family's table. My gaze fell to my lap. I didn't have the energy for more.

Later, after Mama P, Faye, and Jack had left, after Simon had ambled out with his parents and his brother's family, after Sydney had left to catch a ride back to school, I sat alone at a table, watching Lexie make her way around the room, speaking to everyone. Hers was a relaxed saunter as she moved from one cluster of Gran's friends to another. Seeing her carry herself with ease, seemingly comfortable no matter who she was talking with, left me feeling hollow, less than. I wished I had more poise in the moment, that I was more polished and together instead of sitting by myself. When she came closer, I overheard the priest telling Lexie what a beautiful job she had done with the poem, with her toast, with everything. He went on, lavishing praise upon her, the way people did.

"You know, I just wanted to say some heartfelt words for my gran . . . She was our world."

"You were obviously a dear granddaughter to her."

"Well, we do the best we can, right?" She flashed a winning smile. "We were lucky to have her."

Any tenderness I'd felt toward Lexie when she read that poem in the church evaporated. Her performance was smug. She was enjoying the spotlight far too much, at what was supposed to be a celebration of Gran's life. Lexie's actions while Gran was alive came nowhere near her laudatory words that prompted everyone listening to wipe their eyes, to nod in agreement, to think, *What a treasure this granddaughter was to Annabelle.*

I didn't have further appetite for my sister. Without making eye contact with anyone, I left. On the sidewalk, I stood holding my coat, wanting to feel the cold, have that brisk slap of different that would put my insides right. I was met with only frigid air.

In that murky swirl of being disappointed by my own shortcomings—how had I not said anything about Gran?—and angry about Lexie's disingenuous display of well-spoken grief and tribute, I felt the gulf between my sister and me grow wider, unbridgeable. The aloneness hollowed me out.

I didn't remember walking to Gran's car or getting in. But there I was sobbing over the steering wheel. Long and loud. At some point my cries were exhausted. I started the car and drove back to Gran's, at a remove from the car, from the day, from everything.

I'd been on the couch in my pajamas since leaving The Cake Shoppe. It was now dark outside. I stared into the fire. Parched. Numb.

A knock at the front door startled me.

I ignored it.

More knocking.

I got up, peeked through the curtains, and saw Lexie. One hand was shoved in her coat pocket, the other, ungloved, knocked again.

I paused, tried to feel something beyond the anger that had bricked itself high over the years. I stared at the walnut door. Lexie was so near I could hear her shuffling to keep warm.

I turned off the porch light.

Locked the dead bolt.

And went to bed.

Chapter 8

The days after Gran's burial bled one into the next. The weeks did. Most of March did.

The emptiness that followed a crying jag was both unnerving and a relief—relief because if I was empty, I couldn't sob. For a moment I'd be held aloft, teetering on the apex of emotional extremes. I wanted to stay there as long as possible because it was the closest thing I had to peace. My roller-coaster days withered me. Grief knew every escape route.

The doorbell chimed.

After a few minutes, I cracked the door open.

A casserole covered with tinfoil rested on a dish towel. Mama P.

I brought the dish in and immediately smelled her baked ziti. She'd been leaving me food every fourth day. Faye left takeout from The Cardinal every second day.

I walked the still-warm ziti to the kitchen and made room in the fridge among the plastic containers and CorningWare. Maybe later I'd get hungry. Every day I thought that. It hadn't happened yet.

Grief was eating through me, leaving behind the bones.

One morning, I shuffled into Target wearing running recovery sandals. Wintry slush slopped through, soaking my wool socks. At least my sunglasses would hide the state of me.

I needed half-and-half, but instead of heading straight to the refrigerated section, I shambled up and down the aisles. Stickers that Gran would've bought when I was young snagged a tender thread inside me. She would've loved this pretty pot holder. And this crocheted rug—she would've mused about getting that for in front of the kitchen sink. *God*, houseplants—she would've wanted all of these. Everything in this big-box store felt intensely personal. Normal everyday things at a normal everyday store. But there was no more normal. Not anymore.

I turned down the snack aisle and sobbed into a display. Family-sized bags crunched as my body gave its weight to a tower of Cool Ranch Doritos. While the rest of the world moved forward, grief gurgled me lower, digested me anew.

Heaving for air, wet socks squishing in my sandals, I ran out of Target without buying half-and-half, my sunglasses concealing nothing.

The doorbell chimed.

People knocked.

The phone rang.

This went on. I answered none of them. Food was left on the front stoop. Saucy casseroles from Mama P, pricey takeout from Faye, boxes of chocolate from Jeremy's nana and pop pop. Jack left a vase of flowers. The people in the village who loved Gran showered me with support, but I couldn't face any of them. I just couldn't.

Just wanted to say that I'm thinking of you.

From Simon.

I know this is a difficult time (understatement) . . . I am here for you.

Simon again.

"Hello, Belle . . . it's Grace. I've been thinking about you. I wanted to say that when you feel like talking to someone, even if you feel like crying and want someone on the other end of the line, I'm here."

She'd left a voicemail. I hadn't called back.

Drinks this week?

The Herpocalypse. I hadn't even let them know Gran had passed away. Basic social graces, accepted ways of behaving . . . it all felt too hard. Without Gran, I was all alone. This anguish, first experienced as a child, was familiar but now felt even more expansive and withering.

I finally forced myself to respond to everyone—to thank them for being there or to let people know that Gran had passed away and I would be offline for a while. I didn't have anything more in me.

One night I padded through the darkened house, the floors creaking how they always did in familiar spots: right before the kitchen, in the hallway outside the bedrooms, places that had been walked over by my mom, by Gran, by Lexie and me . . . and now just me.

I made my way to the back door and stepped into the inky night. The atmosphere did its wicked tap dance between snow and rain. The air hung heavy and thick. I sat on the back step. Let my eyes focus on the shadowy shapes in Gran's yard. The splayed hydrangea branches, the rounded shoulders of the boxwoods. The moonlight brightened as my eyes adjusted to the dark.

The cold, which invigorated at first, now chilled. My nightshirt only reached mid-thigh. The daylilies lining the gravel walkway were now snarled mounds of desiccated fronds. Gran would leave them until they were good and dead, as she liked to say, in case some animal wanted cover, or one last nibble. Same with the hydrangeas—she never deadheaded them until the spring because birds loved to tuck themselves beneath the papery flowers in the winter. Tall ornamental grasses, now brown and feathery, shivered in the breeze.

I hugged myself to keep warm and stretched my legs into the lily bed. My heels plowed grooves through the dirt. Thick clouds rolled in, blotting out the moonlight, but I could still make out the limp, tangled daylily fronds.

This was the time of year Gran would start planning for spring. The thought landed hard.

I ran my fingers through a mound of lily fronds like it was hair. Then pulled until it released from the plant's center with a satisfying snap. My fingers grazed rubbery nubs hidden beneath the hairy mass.

"What . . . ?" I ran my hand along the ground. "Oh my gosh."

I scrambled to pull the dead fronds off the next lily clump, raked my palm against the ground. Little nubs, again—about an inch long, flexible yet sturdy. New shoots were already growing. As icy rain pelted down, a small laugh escaped me.

I worked my way down the line of plants, pulling the old hair free so new nubs could be welcomed into spring. Everything felt poetic in my mind. The action. The import. The larger circle-of-life of it all. I tore through all the lily hair, stray fronds clinging to my nightshirt, my arms and legs. My movement frantic as I went from mound to mound.

"Welcome to spring!" I heard how unnatural my voice sounded, how shrill and forced. My words hung in the darkness, artificially inflated with joy. I grasped dead fronds, tore them from the earth, and beckoned the lilies to this season of confusion in Northeast Ohio, of rain and snow and a calendar page that denoted spring. "Welcome to spring!"

I wiped a lock of hair from my face with muddy hands. Grasp. Rip. "Welcome to spring, my beauties!" I elaborated on my soliloquy. "Oh, you're going to be so beautiful! Just so beautiful. Welcome to spring!"

I knelt on the sharp edge of a stone and could tell I was bleeding but kept moving from lily to lily. Forcing happy into this weird nighttime task I'd set upon. I chirped out falsetto sentences to green shoots I felt but could barely see. I bordered on breathless. "Welcome to spring!"

At the end of the path, dead fronds clutched in my fists, I felt the wave rolling closer, closer, closer. I couldn't stop it, couldn't outrun it, couldn't conceal the pain with a futile gardening gesture in the middle of the night.

The wave crashed, gripped me tight in its churn. I turned my face to the sky, freezing rain pelting me, and gasped, hungry for air. Grief was chewing my flesh, crunching bones, disappearing me down its esophagus into its spiky belly. The unrelenting maw grinding through me anew. This was it. I was done.

And then, without warning or lead-up, there was breath.

Somehow, a mercy door had swung open. My lungs filled. My pulse slowed. There was stillness.

A light went on in the house next door.

Something emerged over the fence. Onto the large weatherproof cushion caddy. Then to the ground.

Someone gathered me into an embrace, her head close to mine, "Come on, let's go inside."

Faye.

She led me into the house.

"Sit down."

I slumped in a chair. My hair dripped on the kitchen table.

Faye draped a blanket around my shoulders, gently rubbed my head with a towel, then wrapped my hair in it.

She put the kettle on, made two cups of tea, and set a mug in front of me. She stirred in a dripping teaspoonful of honey and sat down.

I sipped my tea. The sweetness went down easily. I leaned back, hands cupping the mug.

"You're now a card-carrying member of the Grief Legion." Faye's voice was soft. She tilted her head in a way that seemed empathetic, different than I'd ever seen her. "It's devastating. I'm here to tell you that you're not alone. This journey you're on now, it's different for everyone, but there's an underlying commonality to it. Only those who have experienced the awful and profound loss of a loved one can truly understand what you're going through." She held my eyes, spoke slowly. "There's a togetherness to be shared if you open yourself up to it. There are shoulders waiting, my dear, arms available to hug you, words ready to offer if not comfort, then at least understanding." She reached over and squeezed my hand. "There's no guide, no one can tell you how to grieve. Time helps walk you through it slowly. Slower than we'd like, but that's the nature of it. Grief takes its time. And the more you love, the more you grieve."

She sipped her tea.

"The last thing I'll say is don't listen to anyone who tells you you'll get over it, because they're lying," she said. "What you do . . . is carry grief with you. Always and forever. You'll find the weight becomes less onerous to bear . . . but it will stay with you. With time, what will happen is happy memories will come to the fore more readily and help lighten grief's load. It seems impossible now, but mark my words, it will get easier. What you have to do is let the people who adore you love you. This isn't a walk you take alone. You have an entire legion beside you. Let us help you walk back into your life."

I stared at the table, barely eked out a whisper. "What life?"

Faye placed a hand atop mine but didn't rush to counter me.

Which was a mercy. Maybe she realized I couldn't absorb anything more. I was full. Her words settled around me as we sat quietly. My thoughts did a sharp rewind to a random thought—maybe self-preservation had kicked in, my brain forcing me to focus on something else, something absurd, a non sequitur of a notion. "Did you . . . climb over the fence?"

Faye nodded. "I was a gymnast. 1960 Olympics. Some things you never lose."

"You've been dodging my calls."

Reva, my friend from college who I'd sublet my apartment to, had left several messages, and I finally texted her the news about Gran. She called immediately.

"I'm dodging everyone's calls."

She told me how sorry she was about Gran's passing. Then noted how many calls I hadn't returned. "Belle . . . don't take this the wrong way, but I think you're languishing there."

My eyes watered.

"You're grieving . . . I get it." She paused. "But I think a change of venue might do you some good."

I wiped my cheeks. "I don't know."

"Just for a bit. Try it on for size."

I didn't say anything.

She sighed. "Look. I have to be in Europe for the next six months—this entire project has taken a turn and now it's far larger in scope. I need to be there to take meetings, see operations in person. Why don't you come back to your apartment? Try and reestablish yourself here? The rent's all paid through September, so are the bills, just come."

"I don't know."

"Belle . . . at some point, you have to start saying yes." She exhaled. I was exhausting. I knew it. "If nothing else, just go sit on your own couch in your own place."

I demurred.

She talked some more.

I half listened while nestling deeper into Gran's couch.

We ended the call with nothing decided.

A breeze carrying the faintest whisper of warmth marked the morning two weeks later as I locked Gran's front door behind me. I looked at the bare flower boxes before walking to the waiting car, vowing to plant geraniums in them when I returned.

Every corner of this house I loved, this charming town where I had roots, the entire city of Cleveland, it all was saturated in Gran, her bass drum of a heartbeat, her laughter that could chase away rain, her smile that sang and sang. Every bit was entwined with her. And now, it all screamed of a loss so profound it unmoored me.

I didn't want to hide from Gran's remembrance, but I also couldn't handle any more feeling. I didn't know anything anymore. So, on a whim, as Reva suggested, I said yes.

Mama P and Faye walked outside, giving themselves away that they'd been watching the house. They met me on the sidewalk as I dragged my suitcase through Gran's front gate.

Faye tucked a lock of hair behind my ear, as if to say she understood.

Mama P's brow furrowed. "You're going?"

I hugged her. "Just for a bit."

"How long is a bit?"

My eyes watered.

"Oh . . . okay." Mama P grabbed my hands, but then didn't seem to know what to do with them or what to say.

Faye, her voice assured, put a hand on top of her friend's. "She'll be back."

Mama P screwed her mouth to one side, then nodded. Squeezed my hands and let them go. Didn't say anything to dissuade me.

Faye held my eyes. "You take your time."

Sweet

Part 4

A crunchy cookie is an insult to taste buds.

Chapter 9

I landed at LaGuardia and got swept up in the frenzy—it felt familiar, sent a zip through me. Maybe this was right, coming back.

That fleeting thrill faded in the stop-and-go traffic to Manhattan. The cab's stutter nauseated me. The vinyl seats filled the back seat with a chemical tang. Greasy fingerprints smudged the window. The tether of belonging I'd hoped for didn't assert itself. It was stupid to think this would help, that a plane ride would ease my sorrow. I felt more lost in the back of this cab than I had in Gates Mills.

I looked at the cars around me—businesswomen in the backs of taxis talking on cell phones, women driving families, or themselves. Everyone with such purpose.

Watching these strangers, it hit me that living with Gran had let me regain my footing, but I'd also been hiding. She'd cautioned against that, saying it only once, as was her way. I might've drummed up some freelance work . . . but being back here now, I couldn't ignore how little I'd really done.

The shadow I had carried to Gates Mills in July had followed me back to the city in April. Not only was I still without direction or a steady job, I was bobbing in this grief ectoplasm, unable to pull myself out.

The ribbon of roadway that edged the east side of Manhattan unfurled like a welcome mat. The East River to my left, towering buildings to my right, the bright, sunny turns of the road, the darkened underpasses, it all felt familiar. Which was equal parts comforting and bizarre, considering how long I'd been gone, how profoundly my world had changed, and how much my life needed fixing.

The cab pulled up to my building. I yanked my suitcase from the trunk and stood on the sidewalk, taking in my corner of East Thirty-Seventh Street. Trees on my block were budding. It must've rained that morning because everything was wet and caught the sunlight in such a perfect way, the way it did as warmer weather found its footing. The air smelled watery. Clean. Spring had tiptoed in and given the city a bath.

I climbed the front steps to my building, rode the elevator to the twelfth floor, unlocked both locks to my studio, and walked in.

It had a different smell. Reva must've spritzed some perfume before catching her flight, and without anyone here to open the door or a window, the scent lingered. I turned on the lights. My apartment was just big enough for a twenty-year-old Jennifer Convertibles couch, a storage trunk that I used as a coffee table, a small armoire that held an ancient cathode-ray tube TV, and an unremarkable dining set near a window that framed a breathtaking view of the Chrysler Building's shiny crown. There was a narrow galley kitchen, a full bathroom, and a sleeping loft. In all, the 250 square feet felt like more because the ceilings were so high and the walls were painted white. Illusion went a long way here. This studio had been my sanctuary for more than a decade. Now I didn't know how I felt about it.

Maybe I did need to be here? Maybe it was a little right, getting a break from the constant reminders of Gran's passing—in every corner of her house, her beloved yard, the quaint town of Gates Mills, everything that had always been ours. I hadn't thought that distance could offer any help. But now, nearly five hundred miles away from Gran's, maybe I felt the tiniest bit settled in a way that was both a small relief and a fresh heartbreak.

I was wrong.

Being here was wrong, all wrong.

The following morning gifted me a two-second respite from all feeling when I awoke, a merciful dream-induced ignorance, forgetting what had happened, where I was, who I was without.

But then remembrance crushed me.

I peered down from my sleeping loft.

What was I doing here?

How had I been convinced that returning was the right thing to do? I felt more bereft being away from Gran's beloved home. How could leaving my only tangible link to her ever help? I loved knowing she'd walked the floors that I walked, that she'd sat at the kitchen table where I sat. I loved knowing that the basket next to the squishy couch held her knitting, that she used to put her feet up on the tufted stool, or polka around the dining room. I knew that it was my memories and all that ethereal stuff where true meaning was lodged, that her house might be considered a collection of inanimate objects to anyone else, but to me . . . to me it was all so precious. That was the last place we had been together. I felt close to her there. It was all I had. And now here I was, cracked open in a city that felt not at all mine.

It was also Tuesday, the day of the week we used to have dinner together. Gran always wanted to know what I was eating. One time it was popcorn, which appalled her. "Popcorn is not dinner. It's an after-dinner snack." She put her meal in the oven until my takeout—chicken lo mein—was delivered. We were dinner companions seated at a five-hundred-mile-long table. No matter where I was, Gran had been my home.

The morning was emotional.

By noon, I sat on the couch, staring off into space, withered anew.

At three o'clock, I was still on the couch.

Languishing overtook me in a whole-body way. Everything felt so heavy, like there was no point in moving. Maybe this was depression. It couldn't be normal. Maybe I was coming undone. Are people aware of themselves unraveling? Or is the nature of your inner glue melting something that you can't ever identify? I held my head in my hands, hunched over, and sobbed.

The jag eventually subsided.

The quiet grew brittle. Shattered me. There I was again, in a thousand pieces, some so small they were dust, easily blown under the couch, into the corners. Each time this happened, more and more of me went missing. I was becoming a zombie.

I wiped my face on my shirt that was now too wet to wear comfortably and forced myself to get up. The blood whooshed through my head like it was shocked by the change. I put on a clean shirt and yesterday's fleece. Slipped on a pair of running recovery sandals, patted down my front pockets to make sure I had my keys, and walked out the door.

It felt strange in the hallway, strange in the elevator, strange in the lobby.

I stepped outside. The shift was jarring, like I'd landed on the moon. But there was the sun, such a pretty bright gold, shining down. I tilted my face upward, felt the warmth on my cheeks. Tears found their way out. I wiped my face. Next time I'd remember sunglasses.

I walked down the block. My muscles felt weak, my insides noodly. A snail's pace was all I could manage. Right, left, right, left . . . I told myself to just focus on that. Right, left, right, left.

That was all. At the moment, it was everything.

People raced by, sidestepped me. One woman in a tailored gray suit huffed in annoyance at my sluggishness and brushed by. I exhaled a steadying breath. Right, left, right, left. I made it to the end of the block at Third Avenue. Crossing it was more than I could muster. But maybe I could walk around the block.

I turned toward Thirty-Sixth Street. Right, left, right, left. Got to the end of the block. Turned. Right, left, right, left. Turned again. All the way back to my corner.

When I got upstairs, I took a shower. Put on clean clothes. Picked up the tissues I'd tossed on the floor, on the couch, the ones I'd left in my bed, and threw them away.

The phone ringing startled me. I hadn't answered it in so long—I didn't even remember turning it on. I looked at the caller ID.

"Hi, Faye."

"I wanted to make sure you got there safe and sound."

I choked up.

"It's okay," she said. "I know it's not easy."

"I don't think I want to be here." My voice wobbled. "It doesn't feel right being away from Gran's house. I want to come back."

"I understand how that would be your first inkling." She paused. "And you can come back, of course. Anytime. But . . . before you do, I would encourage you to stay a bit longer. I think being there, as hard as it might feel right now, could actually be helpful."

"I don't see how. My place isn't here anymore."

"That might be true." Her voice was preternaturally calm. She paused. Inhaled. Then exhaled.

"Are you smoking?"

"Don't change the subject," she said. "What I'll say is this: People do, in fact, outgrow that city. Maybe you have. I know I did. But you won't—"

"What do you mean, you did?"

Long exhale. "I lived there in my early twenties—did some modeling."

"Wait, what?" My mind whirled, trying to slot this information into its proper place. "This was . . . after you were an Olympic gymnast?"

Long exhale. "Yes, Belle. People have lots of chapters to their lives. You won't have any idea if there are clues to what your next one is, or where it's supposed to be, until you spend more than twenty-four hours there." Exhale. "Give yourself time before you make a decision. It doesn't have to be a lot. Think of this as a visit, nothing more." She paused. "Take it all in, see if something sparks within you. Maybe it's something to do, someplace to visit—I don't know. All I'm saying is time away from our sleepy village isn't going to tarnish anything for you. If anything, it'll help you stand taller. Trust me on this."

I bit my cheek to hold it together. "Okay."

"And don't you dare breathe a word of this cigarette to Mama P."

That made me chuckle. We talked a bit more, then said goodbye.

I stared out the window. I knew what I agreed to, but it felt so wrong being here, like I'd been ripped from my proper place. A deep blue was rolling into the skyline. I'd forgotten how dramatic the evenings could be.

It was time.

I gathered everything from the kitchen. Set the table with a napkin, a fork, and the salt and pepper shakers Gran had given me. I used to have a glass of wine or a beer when we'd dine, but both felt like too much tonight.

I poured a glass of water, made buttered noodles, and sat down to dinner with the Chrysler Building.

In the days that followed, I kept things gentle, went on a lot of slow walks. First just around the neighborhood, right, left, right, left, reacquainting myself with everything. Returning to these streets was emotional in a way I hadn't expected. Footing was hard to come by.

One day I returned home to a message on my cell. The sight jolted me. I played it.

"Hello, Belle, this is Grace . . . your grandmother's sister." She sighed. "I wanted to see how you're doing. I understand these are difficult days . . . know that I'm thinking about you." I thought that was the end of the message, but then her voice came back on. "We might not know each other real well, but . . . my heart goes out to you. Call me when you can. Okay now. Bye."

Kind of Grace to call.

I didn't have it in me to call back.

After a week, I ventured farther afield to Central Park. Keeping my feet physically moving forward seemed to help. I didn't know why, but walking soothed parts of me that felt bruised and wrung out. The city's stimuli helped distract my mind. Right, left, right, left.

Moving so slowly, I appreciated small delights more—the way the sunlight cut through a leafy bough on a block lined with brownstones, the way tiny dogs marched down the sidewalk like they were big dogs, and how big dogs bowed down to touch noses with small dogs. Walking wasn't the hyperkinetic action it had been some years back. It felt tender. I found myself able to pause and have a bit more understanding about things that would've annoyed me before: a slow checkout line, stepping in an ankle-deep puddle. Things that would've gotten under my skin before now rolled right off. Going through something that was so much worse, carrying an unbearable heaviness, tiny piques hardly registered. Grief softened you.

And yet there was the nagging thought of how much I had to figure out. Squaring my shoulders to reality, finding a job, being able to pay bills and save money like every other functioning adult seemed like enormous undertakings. I was just learning how to walk.

One day, I retrieved my mail and flipped through the stack in the elevator. Restaurant menu, a credit card offer, another credit card offer.

The handwriting on a padded envelope froze me.

Cursive script at an elegant slant.

I'd know that writing anywhere.

And the postmark: Gates Mills.

I lost all breath, transfixed by this envelope. This impossibility.

Instead of getting out when the elevator stopped on my floor, the doors closed with me still inside, shocked. The creaky metal box shuddered when it reached the lobby. I hit the 12 button again.

How was this possible? It couldn't be. It wasn't until the elevator jerked to a stop again on my floor that I realized I'd been holding my breath.

I unlocked the apartment, tossed the rest of the mail on the table, and carried the envelope to the couch. My legs couldn't hold me anymore. I held the envelope on my lap, confusion engulfing me.

I exhaled, drew my legs up underneath me, and opened the seal. Inside, there was a small booklet tied with a delicate pink ribbon. Beneath the ribbon was an envelope with my name on it. Seeing my name in Gran's handwriting tightened my throat. I gently tugged one tail of the bow and opened the envelope.

> My dollies,
>
> You're reading this because I've gone on to my next adventure.
>
> I know this must be a surprise, getting a letter from me now. But let it remind you that I'll always be with you. You'll feel me in the breeze on your cheeks, the warmth from a fire in the hearth, the aroma of freshly baked cookies. I'll be in the cardinal's chirp, a doe's slow mosey, and even those wily raccoons that somehow manage to get into the bird feeder. I haven't left you, and I know we'll all be together again.
>
> Until that day, what I want is for the two of you to be there for one another, to love each other as you did when you were children. Everything is harder when you get older. But it doesn't have to be. Not if you have one another.
>
> It's my last wish that you read this together. Allow yourselves to return to someplace familiar. Let it take you someplace new. Most of all, may it bring you together. Do this for me.
>
> Since I'm not around anymore to say what I want to say . . . or do what I want to do, I've left you letters, which you'll be receiving. You'll both read the

same words, but I've enclosed different photographs with each.

First steps can be difficult, I know. And so, I'd like you to start with what we used to have in the mornings, the one Lexie always wanted more sugar on, the one Belle mashed up because she liked how the colors looked when they swirled.

Know that every day you were my joys. You both made me so proud. I love you and will love you for all eternity. You need only look for me, pay close attention, and you'll feel me there beside you.

All my love,
Gran

I buried my face in my hands, careful not to cry on Gran's letter or the booklet it had been bundled with.

When the wave passed and the waters inside felt calmer, I blew my nose. Then sat, still like a statue, flooded with thoughts. Gran had been acutely aware of her own mortality, yet never so much as hinted at it. How she had protected me—and Lexie—from dwelling in this heartache for even a moment made me tear up again. Had she prepared this while I was there with her? Or was this something she'd planned long ago? When I realized her last wishes, her last words, were saved for us and only us, I teared up again. Gran's graciousness, her mothering, hadn't ceased. Just like the day of our mother's wake so many decades ago, Gran's first thought was of us, her daughter's daughters.

Who had sent this? Gran had obviously entrusted someone to do this for her. My gosh, the planning. I wiped my eyes. It had to be either Faye or Mama P. But the truth was, I didn't care. Gran had found me here in the city. I was greedy for this letter, for all of it.

I ran my thumb over the worn fabric cover of the small book. Faded roses lined the spine. I opened the cover and a whiff of aged paper wafted up. The pages, bound with a thick threaded stitch, had a cottony softness to them. I traced a finger along the single word neatly printed on the first page: *Cookbook*.

I slowly turned the pages, each one filled with neat handwriting, precise pen strokes, as if the words were special, deserving of attention. They were recipes—pages upon pages of recipes. I savored each one, examined the steps. Steps that, surprisingly, were without much detail. Practically no detail. It seemed odd.

There was a recipe for cabbage rolls, another for chicken steak—cut up round steak that was floured and seasoned, then seared until golden. Apple pie. Savory tomato jam. I turned the page. Oh my goodness, *Gran's chicken soup*. I sighed at the memory—carrot coins and bite-sized pieces of chicken bobbing about in a silky broth so flavorful it ruined all other chicken soup for me. These tastes from my childhood summoned some of the happiest memories of my life: Lexie and I working alongside Gran in her sunny kitchen that always smelled faintly of brown sugar, or caramelized onions. We were tiny sous-chefs. A threesome. Precisely the memories I didn't dwell upon the older I got.

Something else peeking out of the envelope caught my eye. I pulled out an old snapshot of Lexie and me kneeling on chairs at the kitchen table, grinning behind a whole raw chicken. Seeing us together as kids, so far away from where we were now, hit dead center in my chest. My gosh . . . the trips to the butcher.

We used to go to the butcher with Gran after Grandpa passed away. I remembered how the bell at the top of the door would jingle when we walked in.

"Gimme an old bird, Johnny," Gran would say.

Johnny, who was Gran's age, would wipe his hands on his stained apron and pull one out from the cooler.

"That's not old." Gran would wave a hand at the offending bird. "I need older."

He'd bring out another one.

"This bird's no good for me—"

"Annabelle, she's old!" Johnny would protest.

"I need one older!" Gran would insist.

It would go on and on like this, the two of them bickering over chicken carcasses. When all was said and done, Johnny would've hauled out upward of eight different chickens for Gran to inspect until she found the right one for her soup. An old bird. That was her secret. She never bought more than one, which meant that Gran and Johnny would have this chicken tête-à-tête every other week.

Thinking back now, maybe Gran had looked forward to that small interaction. Grandpa had passed away a year before my mom. I remembered that he smiled easily, how he laughed with Gran, but beyond that . . . my memory pool of him was shallow. Maybe these trips to the butcher afforded Gran a sliver of normalcy that kept her moving forward, a reminder that life went on after her beloved husband's passing, that tethers to others, or at least a routine, were vital. But I also remembered how Johnny used to smile at Gran, a little knowing twinkle that he'd let show—and it dawned on me that maybe he looked forward to seeing her too.

I stared at the picture, at Lexie and me, so young and chummy, happy to have had a chicken adventure . . . it was all easy then. We were easy. Maybe it was Gran who made it easy. The thought, painful and throbbing, nestled in my center: This was how we began.

It hadn't been going well for a long time.

I returned to the cookbook. What I kept circling back to as I turned the pages were snippets of memories with Gran, of her, Lexie, and me as this threesome. These precious memories that felt so immediate decades later. Pulses still resonated of being together. Secure. Home. All of it tied to cooking. Remembering it with such clarity unsettled me. There was a reason I didn't think about Lexie and me as kids.

I rubbed my eyes. The past flooding the present ran into my abiding disappointment in Lexie. Her standoffishness with Gran all those years. With me. Her reluctance to hold on to any kind of substantive bond with either of us. A kernel of anger glowed red deep inside my chest.

I sat holding the cookbook, deep in thought.

Gran was forcing the issue. I shook my head, unable to believe it.

She was ensuring I would call Lexie.

Calling her was literally the last thing I wanted to do. For obvious reasons. But on top of all that, after Gran's funeral, when I finally went through the contents of the folder Faye had given me, the one detailing all of Gran's affairs, I'd emailed Lex about it. Granted, I kept it all business, no pleasantries, but still. *I emailed.* I explained everything Gran had left us, the numbers Lex would need to call for her portion of Gran's modest brokerage account, how the house would need to be sold eventually but I wasn't dealing with that now. Fortunately, there was enough in Gran's checking account to cover nine months of the house's bills. I was fully transparent and expected to hear back from her. Despite the fact that I had refused to open the door when she showed up after Gran's funeral, I should've heard from her. This involved money, and money was Lexie's favorite thing. She never called, never emailed, never texted.

And now three-year-old Lexie looked up at me from the photo. She was quite possibly the most adorable toddler ever to walk the planet. How she'd grown to be a monster was beyond me.

I dreaded what I had to do. Gran had left us something precious, and Lexie was the only one I could talk to about it. The one person I had to talk to.

I exhaled a big breath and dialed her number. The call rang. My pulse pounded.

The line rang some more.

Voicemail picked up. I cleared my throat.

"Hey, it's Belle." Absurd that I felt the need to clarify this, that she wouldn't know my voice, that I couldn't just say *Hey, it's me* to my sister. "I wanted to see if you got the envelope . . ." It felt so strange saying it aloud. "The envelope from Gran. Call me back."

It wasn't the best message.

I didn't care.

The next day I called Faye. She answered on the third ring.

"Belle, hello. How's it going there?"

"I'm . . . I don't even know what to call how I'm feeling."

"Mmm . . . yes, it can be that way. Just . . . stick with it for the moment, is my advice."

I told her I would, asked how she was, and how Mama P was. Good, good, all good. "So . . . I have a question: Did you send Lexie and me letters from Gran?"

"Letters? From your grandmother? Whatever do you mean?"

I told her about the letter, cookbook, and photo. "You don't know anything about it?"

"No . . . I'm sorry," she said. "I don't know how you got that. You say it's your grandmother's handwriting?"

"Yes. I just . . . I want to know who sent it. Could it have been Mama P?"

"No, she can't keep a secret. She would've told me." Faye didn't say anything for a moment. "I really can't think who would've sent you that. Did you talk to the estate attorney who drew up your grandmother's will?"

"I already emailed her—she said it wasn't her."

"I'm sorry, I'm at a loss." She paused. "We miss you here, but like I told you, it's important to take the time you need for yourself there."

It was funny to hear her officious voice say such tender words. "Thank you. I was going to change my ticket and come back, but I'll take your advice and stay longer. My friend who's subletting gets back from Europe in September, but I'll definitely be back way before then." I paused. "To be honest, I don't have any more idea of what I'm doing here than what I was doing there."

"That might be." She stayed silent for a moment. "But this is also an opportunity." Her words had a backbone to them. "Remember, you're a visitor. Don't squander the time."

We said goodbye.

I chewed my cheek. Then dialed Lexie's number again.

On the fourth ring she picked up. "I know I owe you a call. I've been busy."

No greeting. Her voice curt. Everything I expected. She made me want to scream.

I thought of Gran, paced my studio.

"Did you get the envelope . . . the one from Gran?"

"Yeah." She didn't say anything for a beat. "I don't really understand."

"There's no way you don't understand." I fought to keep the edge out of my voice, but honestly, Lexie was too smart to feign ignorance. She went to Princeton. Georgetown Law. "Gran was clear: She wanted us to read this cookbook together."

"I mean—" Lexie exhaled dramatically. "First of all, who sent this?"

"I have no idea."

"And what is this thing? I just . . ." Another exhale. "I don't have time to cook, all right?"

"Listen." I kept my voice measured, resolute. "Gran didn't ask anything of us our entire lives. She only gave. This is her one request, the only thing she's ever asked." I swallowed, forced myself to stay composed. "We should read this cookbook together like she wanted."

Silence unrolled from the other end of the line. It lasted so long that I looked to see if the call was still connected.

Then, her voice nearly a whisper, "Okay."

Her answer surprised me. Us having any sort of exchange caught me flat-footed. What would this mean, reading something together? I hadn't considered the specifics of what Gran was asking.

"So . . . maybe we email each other after we've made a recipe?" The reality of having to engage with Lexie was already weighing.

"Sure." She sounded like our conversation had drained her.

"'Kay."

I too was spent. This suddenly felt bigger than I had the capacity to handle. And maybe it did for her too. We didn't have much more to say to each other.

When I hung up, it felt like something had been set in motion that I wanted to immediately undo.

The next morning, I made Gran's berries and cream, the first recipe she'd hinted we make together. Not that it was difficult, but Gran had set a shallow dish in front of me so many times over the years with this simple breakfast treat that it was an innate part of me. The instructions were bare bones, as what else could they be? But I didn't need them to make it just like Gran. What I wasn't prepared for, making it on my own in my tight galley kitchen, was how it tugged at a memory that felt excruciatingly tender.

Later, I sat down to email Lexie about the recipe and stared blankly at the screen. I hadn't written her anything of substance in years. The gulf that formed between us in high school yawned wider in college. I went to a state school in New York where I'd gotten a scholastic scholarship, where I ate ramen from a hot pot and drank dollar beers, while Lexie was accepted into a renowned eating club at Princeton and rubbed elbows with a wealthy clique. Her orbit fully spun away from mine in law school when she met Jeffrey and his friends, all monied, all accomplished. Reaching out to her now felt foreign. I glanced at the snapshot of the two of us that I'd tucked into the corner of the windowpane. It easily could've been a picture of two other children—that was how little connective tissue was left after all these years.

I started typing.

To: Lexie
From: Belle
Subject: Berries & Cream
Remember when Gran used to make this? I have vivid memories of us when we were small, in our

nightgowns, sitting at the kitchen table. Your hair would be smushed up on one side of your head because you slept so hard and Gran would gather it all into a ponytail while you ate. You always grinned when she did that—you loved having your hair pulled back off your face. The back door was open because it was so hot in the summer. The sun streaming in through the kitchen windows, there was a palpable cheeriness to it that set the tone for everything. And Gran woke up happy every day, remember that? She was always so happy.

Anyway, this tasted delicious, and was . . . I don't know, kind of emotional to make on my own. Not kind of, definitely. I don't know why I'm couching that. Everything about Gran conjures up so much sorrow still.

Belle

I felt like I'd shared a lot, but what I didn't write was that I still remembered the happiness. I hadn't let myself think about it in years, but that photo brought it all back. Even though sorrow stormed to the front of late, as did anger at Lex . . . happy was there. Lurking. I did remember us three so happy.

My eyes watered as I reread the email, hovered over the Send button, debating.

Then sent it.

I tried to be okay with what I had written, not jangly. Not like I'd given in.

Maybe it didn't matter.

Before I went to bed, I checked my email, scrolling through so much marketing nonsense jamming my inbox.

My pulse quickened as soon as I saw it. My smile couldn't be helped. I clicked on the message.

To: Belle
From: Lexie
Subject: RE: Berries & Cream
Made it. Easy. Good as usual -Lex

I closed my laptop and shoved it away from me.

Chapter 10

I awoke to a robin's-egg sky, sunshine shimmering off the Chrysler Building's crown. The day, exquisite in its beauty, loomed large and long. My minuscule freelance work only occupied so much of my time. It was the first Saturday in May. I'd been floating in this apartment for weeks.

I needed to be a person who did things today. I threw on leggings and a sweater and headed to the lobby for the mail. My stomach flipped when I pulled Gran's second letter from the mailbox.

In my apartment, I held the envelope, pulse thudding, staring at Gran's exquisite cursive handwriting, feeling the cosmic confluence of time, how it was twisting back to greet me here on my couch. I didn't know how long I stayed cradled in the moment. The light had shifted. A tiny piece of Gran was inside this envelope. I slipped a finger under the corner of the flap and teased it open so it didn't rip.

> Dear Belle and Lexie,
> For your next recipe, make what I always kept in a dish on the coffee table, the nibbles that were a little salty, a little sweet, and sometimes even spicy. They were a lot like people, come to think of it . . . maybe a lot like each of us.
>
> All my love,
> Gran

I couldn't help but smile—she was talking about her spiced nuts.

A single black-and-white photo of Lexie as a newborn slid from the envelope. Her mop of dark brown hair was absurd. It looked like she was born wearing a wig. She had the chubbiest cheeks. I lost myself staring at her, contemplating the dimensions of our past, how we began, and where we were now. I wondered if Gran had sent Lexie a baby photo of me.

But something deeper needled at my thoughts, Lexie's daughters. When she was scheduled to give birth to her first, Lexie emailed Gran and me to tell us not to bother coming because her mother-in-law had hired the best baby nurse on the East Coast, as was the way in Jeffrey's family. Gran and I went anyway. We got to say hello to Lexie and briefly hold baby Violet before Jeffrey's family and their posh friends crowded into Lexie's hospital room. They nudged Gran and me aside, then pushed us farther into a corner, ever farther from Lexie and her firstborn.

When Lexie had her second daughter, Gwen, I didn't even bother going. No way would I subject myself to that again. But Gran still went to be by Lexie's side. She always gave Lex the benefit of the doubt. It was more than I was capable of any longer. Lexie called me several times after Gran's visit. I didn't bother picking up.

Memories . . . sometimes they were sweet. Other times, salty.

I went to the store, spent more money than I ever had on nuts and spices, then set to making the recipe. I propped the cookbook up on the counter, and only then realized how pointless that was. The recipes didn't have measurements, just ingredients. I'd never made these with Gran. But I'd eaten her spiced nuts all my life.

I looked up some recipes for a few pointers, learned to whisk the egg white with water, coat the nuts, then add the sugar, salt, and spices. I added proportions that made sense, dumped everything on a cookie sheet, and baked them for a half hour.

A spicy aroma enveloped the kitchen when I pulled the nuts from the oven. They needed to cool—I at least knew that much. So, I washed the measuring spoons and cups, the bowl, and every utensil I'd used. It felt good to tidy up. Here I was, a person cleaning. Things had been messy for so long.

Finally, the nuts were cool. To scoop them off the sheet, I used a spoon, but it just skidded across the hardened mass. The sugar had adhered the nuts to the baking sheet like cement.

I banged on them with a bigger spoon. Stabbed them with a knife.

Unmovable.

The step that had been so obvious to Gran but was lost on me was to line the baking sheet with parchment, or at least oil it. I'd managed neither.

Using a chef's knife and all my weight, I cracked some nuts free to taste one. I closed my eyes in anticipation of being transported back to Gran's living room and ate the nut shard.

Big punches of salt and cayenne hit me first. A middling sweetness and odd spicy plume tilted the entire mouthful into nauseating. I gagged and spat it into the sink.

That wasn't Gran's recipe.

Deep disappointment found me. I'd thought making this would be easy. But of course, the trick with spices was harmonious measurements, balance. Nuts, people . . . same difference. I shoved the cookie sheet into the sink, ran hot water over it, and left it there.

What to email Lexie?

After feeling like I'd overshared in my last message to her, I wasn't sure what to write. In the photo Gran had sent, Lexie held her tiny fists under her chin. Fists that still seemed raised today.

To: Lexie
From: Belle
Subject: Spiced nuts
Hi,
I made Gran's spiced nuts, only they tasted nothing like hers. They were awful. And glued to the cookie

sheet. I'm really disappointed . . . I was looking forward to having them again.

I did get a cute picture of you as a baby though, and that made me smile.

Belle

About an hour later, I got a reply.

To: Belle

From: Lexie

Subject: RE: Spiced nuts

Hey,

I just used sugar and cinnamon on mine because I didn't know what measurements to use with any of the spices. They were fine, but not Gran's.

I got a baby picture of you, which was nice.

Lexie

Nice.

A word that barely skirted the surface of meaning. A word that meant so little.

I laced up my sneakers, grabbed my cross-body bag, and headed out before I could get mired in my emotional stew. I walked south on Park Avenue, got a coffee, and continued downtown. Before I knew it, I was at Twenty-Third Street. That was when it hit me where to go.

I walked to Union Square and from a block away saw the canopied vendor stands lining the northern horseshoe to form the crown jewel of the city's greenmarkets.

It was nearly noon, and the place was packed. People came for early spring produce, farm-fresh eggs, and humanely raised meat, for seedlings in plug pots that they'd set on a windowsill or maybe transplant to a balcony planter. They came for fresh milk and yogurt, for homemade pretzels and local bread, for honey bottled upstate and microgreens. People carried reusable totes. They walked dogs or pushed them in pup strollers the way city dwellers did.

The happy bustle of the crowd, the bounty of farm-fresh goods, the whole scene carried a lightness. One stand displayed an array of tangerine-colored marigolds, just like the ones Gran and I had planted together. I bought two and carried the proud, sturdy blooms through the market. I accepted a sample from the pretzel vendor, a cube of Havarti cheese from an upstate dairy farm, then a cube of cheddar, another of Colby. I couldn't, in good conscience, accept another sample without buying something. So, I bought a small block of cheddar and a wedge of Colby. Then had one last sample. Actually, two.

A handwritten cardboard sign at the next stand stopped me: "Little Rabbit Farm. Help Wanted."

"You need some bread to go with that cheese."

I looked up. A tall man behind the sign smiled. Deep crinkles around his eyes said he was someone who smiled easily. He wore a flannel over a couple of shirts, obvious from the bulk, heavy canvas pants, and boots.

I swallowed my mouthful of cheese. "I'd agree, but I seem to be puttin' this cheese down with no problem."

He laughed. "All the same. You're too skinny, look like you could use this." He cut into a loaf of bread and handed me a hunk.

"Never tell a woman she's too skinny, Bun." A short woman with curly gray hair sticking out from under her knit hat thwacked the man on the butt with a bunch of ramps. Then, to me, "Sorry, he was raised by wolves."

"It's true," he deadpanned. "I was." He slung his arm around the woman's shoulders.

She bumped him with her hip, then leaned her head into him and smiled in such a contented way I couldn't tear my eyes from them. They looked like a bowling ball and a pin next to one another, two opposites who were undeniably a pair.

"You guys could take your act on the road." I pushed my sunglasses onto my head to see them better.

"See, Bunny?!" He turned to the woman. "I've been telling you we've got a chance at real vaudeville success!"

She patted his chest in a good-humored way.

"That's my cue," he said to me, then a scrim of seriousness came down over his cheery demeanor. "I truly meant no offense by saying you looked skinny."

"No worries at all," I said. "And your bread is delicious."

He tipped his hat, then walked back to a truck parked behind the stand where several boxes were stacked.

"Can I help you with anything today?" The woman glanced at me as she filled a bin with pea shoots.

What I wanted to say made me nervous—maybe because it meant taking a step forward—but something was pushing up, a strange and surprising impetus.

"Dearie?"

I met her gaze and held it, unsure. Her eyes softened. She cocked her head ever so slightly as if understanding.

I cleared my throat, pointed at the handwritten sign. "I wanted to ask about . . . um . . ."

"What help we want at Little Rabbit Farm?" She smiled at the relief in my face.

"Sorry, that shouldn't have been so hard to say."

She looked at me with tenderness. "How is it you come to our farm stand?"

Her question, so gentle, closed my throat. What I thought I'd escaped walking to the greenmarket had found me again all too easily.

The woman reached across the table and gave my arm a reassuring squeeze. "We've all been where you are. I might not know the particulars, but I have enough years under this big old belt to know there's commonality to emotion, my dear. To whatever you're going through."

"Can I pay for this?" A woman in black cat sunglasses and Lululemon everything shook a bunch of arugula to draw attention to herself.

The woman called over her shoulder. "Bun, need you up here."

"Comin'!"

"Let's step to the side." She led me to the end of the table and thrust out her hand. "I'm Petunia. Everyone calls me Pet, except my husband, who calls me Bunny."

I shook her hand. "I'm Annabelle, but everyone calls me Belle."

She put both hands on her hips and grinned. "Belle, if I knew you better, I'd pinch your cheeks." Then she laughed.

My eyes welled.

"Oh, my dear, come here, now." Pet took everything I was holding and set it atop a pile of romaine lettuce and drew me into a hug. "It's okay . . . it's okay."

Tears erupted out of nowhere and I couldn't stop them. Pet held me close, this stranger who I knew in name only.

"I'm sorry." I calmed down and eased out of her embrace. "I don't even know you . . . . I'm so sorry."

Pet smiled in a knowing way. "We know each other now." She squeezed my arm. "Okay? We know each other just fine."

I managed a smile. "It's good to know you."

"Would you like to come work with us? It's only temporary, some part-time summer work a couple days a week at the stand here."

I wiped my nose on my shirt, couldn't help but laugh at the absurdity of the situation. "You don't know anything about me."

She waved a hand dismissively. "I know everything I need to know."

I nodded. "I would, yes."

"Good. This is kismet! Now, why don't you come back and meet the girls, I'll introduce you to the husband properly, and we can tell you about the job. Here." She reached under the table, then handed me a fistful of tissues. "Come with me. I know I just hired you"—she raised both hands, her eyes wide—"but it's not official unless the girls approve."

She led me to a nook at the rear of the stand. "Here they are."

Two teacup shih tzus looked up from their blanketed den and came trotting over.

"They're so cute!"

"Meet Flopsy and Mopsy, CEO and COO of Little Rabbit Farm. Their big brother Cottontail is back home."

"Would he be CFO?"

Pet laughed. "That's right."

I bent down, and the pups stood on their hind legs to say hello. I pushed my face close. One licked my cheek and the other tried to lick my eyeball.

"Not the eyes, Mopsy!" Pet said. "Well, you're hired. That's the final approval at this outfit."

The shih tzus trotted alongside us like they were in charge of the place, while the Rabbits explained the job. The days would vary and involved helping Pet and her husband, Harold, with the stand, particularly the crucial unloading and loading of the truck. Pet looked hale, but she walked with a slight limp. The way she moved seemed creaky and uncertain.

"Cranky hips, cranky back, everything's cranky!" She laughed. "But it's a good day . . . a good day indeed."

I hung out with them for the next hour, then walked back uptown, the time spent with the Rabbits replaying in my head. Did I feel steadied by what I'd committed to? At Twenty-Third Street, I thought so. By the time I got to Thirty-Fourth Street, my insides felt wobbly. The sunshine that felt so warm on my face reminded me of Gran, and that singular, beautiful thought skidded headlong into me never seeing her again, us never sitting in the backyard again, never doing anything together.

Grieving was hard enough, but trying to walk back into life, forcing yourself to open back up, possibly turn toward something new . . .

this was painfully difficult. No one ever told you how bruising sadness would whiplash after a moment of happiness, or how hard it was to come by any happy—or how when you happened to, you felt guilty. Because a moment of fleeting joy felt like you were moving on from someone you loved dearly, leaving them behind. And so, you remained dizzy, twirling in grief's centrifuge, nauseous from the loss.

By Fortieth Street, every emotion had snowballed into something unfathomably heavy. My pace slowed at a staircase fronting a steel and glass office building. I strode up the steps, my legs weighing tons, and sat down with my head in my hands. Felt everything there in midtown until I was empty.

"I've been calling you."

Shame washed over me.

Of all the calls that had gone unreturned, it was Gran's sister who I should've gotten back to. Even if that still felt odd, considering how Gran never spoke of her, how she never breathed a word of their rift.

"I know . . . I'm sorry." I sighed. "I've been so bad about staying in touch, but I should've called you. I really am sorry."

"It's okay." Her voice was matter of fact. "I know what it's like to try to regain your footing after your world collapses . . . I know."

I didn't say anything for a minute. Then decided to drop all pretense of presenting a polished me to this woman who was a stranger. "I don't know why simple things feel so difficult, but they do."

"Everything is difficult now, and it's understandable." She paused. "Hold on to the fact that it won't always be this way. Trust your old great-aunt on this."

Her claiming me as a grandniece landed oddly. She hadn't been a part of my life at all. But her plain way of speaking tinged with humor softened my hackles. "You're not old."

"Old as the hills." She let out a laugh, then sighed. "But that's okay because you get wisdom with the years. So, tell me: How is Alexis doing?"

"I think . . . okay?"

Grace paused. "Well, she's my next phone call."

I didn't have anything to say to that.

"All right, dear." Her voice grew fainter, like she had pulled the phone away from her mouth. She spoke to someone. "Okay, I need to go. The mower is here, and I need to direct him." Someone said something in the background. "Oh, you bet, I need to give you direction. You're what? Twenty years old?" In the background: "Twenty-five." "Oh, twenty-five! Come along, you. I'm gonna teach you everything you need to know, and then some." Back to me: "You take care of yourself, Belle. We'll talk soon."

I said goodbye, marveling at her energy. She was three years younger than Gran, which made her eighty-four. And she was about to give some young man an earful of advice that would probably take her up and down the fields on her farm.

I rolled the phone over in my hand, thinking about Grace, how direct she was. And wondered if I'd been making everything with Lexie more difficult than it needed to be.

Gran's next letter arrived the Tuesday before Memorial Day weekend. My heart pounded as I rode the elevator to my floor, holding the letter in both hands.

> My dear Belle and Lexie,
> This letter will be short and sweet . . . the way you were together as children. For the next recipe, I'd like you to make the sweetest one in the cookbook, the one we'd whip up whenever we wanted something to

satisfy our collective sweet tooth . . . or put in our pocket. This isn't a fancy recipe for holidays, it's the one we'd make any day, any season.

I love you both.

Gran

And there was another Instamatic photo enclosed: a picture of Lexie and me in front of Gran's house. Neither of us were smiling.

I remembered the exact morning that photo was taken.

We'd moved into Gran's a few weeks earlier. Dad traveled to Florida a lot—he said for work, but we discovered that he'd met someone down there and preferred being in the sun with her to being in the gray with us. We would live with Gran in Gates Mills from now on. She had told us this as she packed up all our clothes and toys while Dad chain-smoked Winstons in the kitchen, biding his time until he could say goodbye and be free of the obligation.

It was the first day of kindergarten for me and preschool for Lexie. Mom had been gone a couple months and the world felt tilted, like we might slide right off. I still expected Mom to pick us up from Gran's. Lexie usually found her way to my side, quietly, but her need for security screamed. And now we were going to school, facing something else that was new. Being apart, in different rooms all day, was another shock that Lexie had a hard time coping with.

As Gran positioned us on the front step, Lexie started to whimper, the way she would before she cried. I took her hand and held it. Gran snapped the picture just as the bus pulled up.

Lexie gripped my hand as we climbed the stairs, nervously looked around for a free seat, and sat down. Gran waved from the front yard as the bus drove away.

I remembered Lexie looking up at me with her big brown eyes. Tears welled in them, threatened to flood the bus. Her tiny brows knit together.

"The day is going to fly by," I told her in a voice so soft only she could hear. "Gran told me we're making special cookies when we get back home."

She swallowed. "Yeah?"

"We have to do school first though, and then . . . we get to bake with Gran."

Lexie thought about this. Wiped her eyes and nodded. Then faced forward, as if to steel herself. Or detach. I wasn't sure.

I sat on my couch thinking about that tender moment, then looked down at Gran's letter. We'd made her peanut butter cookies when I first got to her house back in July. The memory pricked the corners of my eyes. I ran my finger lightly down the list of ingredients and steps. Instead of falling apart, I was struck with the simplicity of this cookie, its magic written down so concisely. Gran had always made her cookies from memory. She preferred them underbaked, and she passed that love along to us. *A crunchy cookie is an insult to taste buds.* I smiled, remembering what she used to say. We were raised with high expectations for cookies: a tiny amount of crispiness on the outside and a warm cakey inside that was just the smallest step above raw dough.

The next day I made peanut butter cookies in the morning. Ate two for breakfast. The centers were perfect. Gran would've been proud. I stared at the baking sheet and knew what she would've said. They should be shared.

So, I put five on a plate and knocked on my neighbor's door.

Melody opened up, holding an artist's palette dolloped with moody grays and clutching a paint brush between her teeth. Her hair was poker straight, blond. Her white tank was paint splattered, like her black leggings and the tops of her feet. She had a nose ring, rings on every finger, tattoos up and down one arm, a string of delicate blue doves flying beneath her clavicle, and two halves of a burgundy heart resting on either side of a keloid scar that ran down the center of her chest. The scar was dusted with sparkly powder.

As soon as Mel saw me, she took the paintbrush out of her mouth and held it high.

"Finally!" She looked in my eyes and softened her exuberance. "I know, I know . . . you've been dealing with so much. Come in! Come in! Okay, those look delicious, set them down right now." She opened the door wide. We both put everything down and she pulled me into a hug.

Melody was tall and skinny, but freakishly muscular. She crushed when she hugged. We'd been neighbors for fifteen years.

"I was wondering when you'd come back. I've missed you! And I'm so, so sorry about your grandmother—your friend who's staying at your place told me. I'm just so sorry." She pulled away and held my face. "You will get through this. Listen to me: You will. Don't you for one minute think you won't—I mean, I know that's exactly what you think during times like this, but I promise you that you'll get through it. Okay?"

She used both thumbs to wipe my tears.

"I cry all the time."

"You should," she said. "There's no other way through. Come sit down. Ugh, hang on." She shoved a pile of laundry onto the floor. "I'll fold that later."

We sat on her couch. Melody put her hands on my leg.

"Are you holding up? Are you eating? Sleeping? Drinking water?" She sighed. "Tell me everything about how you are."

I chuckled and cried. "I don't know what this is—laughing and crying." I looked up at the ceiling and blew out a breath. "I'm a mess a lot of the time."

"Yes. You're doing it right, then."

"You think?"

"For sure." She waved her hands in an exaggerated way near me. "You're a disaster!"

I barked out a laugh.

She laughed along with me. "No, really, you're a grieving train wreck, I see it!"

"Perfect."

She grew serious. "Lovie, that's what you're supposed to be, a certifiable mess. I wouldn't mislead you here. You need to be a mess. You have to burn up with tears before you can rise like a phoenix."

My chin quivered. "I don't know if I have a phoenix within me."

Melody put both hands together like she was going to pray, held them at her lips. "I know you do."

She reached over, rummaged in a cup beside her easel, and pulled out a fine paintbrush. Brought her palette over and set it on her lap. Pulled down my T-shirt, placed her hand on my chest. "She's here."

She swirled the brush in a slate gray. The paint felt cool on my skin. The brush's tiny licks tickled. Mel hummed quietly while she painted. I said nothing, only breathed. Her studio felt solemn.

Melody leaned back, cocked her head slightly, and stopped humming. A serene smile reached her eyes. She held up a hand mirror. "There she is."

The reflection made me tear up. A slate-blue phoenix with luscious plumes stood proudly in the middle of my chest.

"She's waiting . . . but she's there." Melody gently blew on the paint, then stretched out the collar of my shirt so it wouldn't mar the glorious creature. "Now . . . tell me what you baked. Because I smell peanut butter."

"Cookies." I retrieved the plate from where I set it down. "It's my gran's recipe."

Mel picked one up, bent it in two, and gave me the other half. "Stop," she said with her mouth full. "These are outrageous!"

I grinned. Because I knew. Of course I knew.

Melody took another one. "I mean, you've told me about your grandmother, and she sounded like such a superb lady, but damn, she's cookie royalty!"

I hung out at Mel's apartment and we caught up. I was a person. A person who had a good friend close by who I appreciated. One whose friendship I hadn't watered in quite some time, but who was still there, flourishing beside me as if a day hadn't passed. It filled me with a sense of peace.

Later, I went back to my apartment, my tiny phoenix leading the way.

I thought about what to email Lexie. Beyond the actual cookies, the fact was that I felt alone in the world without Gran. This cookbook, while a gift, also opened up a wound. In the deepest recesses of my heart, I still clung to the time when Lex and I were children knitted to one other. Now Gran was gone. So was our threesome, which as a kid I'd assumed would be permanent—obviously, a childlike notion, considering there was no escaping mortality. But Lexie . . . I guess if I were honest about what spring fed my most difficult emotions, it was this: I'd never expected to lose her, and certainly never expected her to abandon Gran the way she did.

That should've kept me from engaging with her at all. It had for years. You'd think I would've wanted to show her how cruel she'd been. Punish her. And yeah, maybe I'd felt all that when Gran was still with us. But receiving this cookbook, the power behind Gran's words, this prompting from the great beyond that she'd orchestrated . . . it was changing something inside me. Or maybe grief was squeezing shut pathways that used to firehose self-righteousness. Now, a palpable fragility and, if I were honest, a little desperation had colored my worldview. Sorrow shoved a lot to the back burner. Maybe I was too washed out to fight anymore.

I sat there thinking about everything, my hand resting on Gran's cookbook. A fat beam of light flooded through the window, the way it never did, warming the wooden floor to a honey tone. Appreciation for the sliver of beauty overwhelmed me. A softening that felt different than sadness, more like a relaxing, nestled inside. And I thought maybe relinquishing my furious ground might not be such a bad thing.

To: Lexie
From: Belle
Subject: Peanut butter cookies
Hey there,
Remember how you ended up covered in flour whenever Gran made these? How was it you were always dusted with flour? You were like a flour fairy. Gran started putting a smock on you whenever we baked. And there was a pocket on it—remember? I'll never forget that day after everything was cleared from the table, the cookies were baked, Gran had moved them to a cooling rack, then she turned back to you, stared for a beat, and asked what was in your pocket. And with the straightest face possible, you said, "That's my pocket cookie." And then you reached up to the cooling rack on the counter, and explained, as if any explanation was needed, "I get the cookies from here, and then I put them in my pocket." You were so serious! Like it was your job, putting cookies in your pocket. Gran couldn't stop laughing about it all day. For years, remembering that story delighted her.

Anyway, this took me down memory lane a bit. Also, I think you were onto something back then: Maybe what we all need are more pocket cookies.
Xo

To: Belle
From: Lexie
Subject: RE: Peanut butter cookies
OMG, my pocket cookie—I'd forgotten all about that!

I don't know what I did wrong, but these were tasteless. No peanut butter flavor at all. I threw them all out.
Baking: not for me.

To: Lexie
From: Belle
Subject: RE: Peanut butter cookies
So, the secret is to use dark-roasted peanut butter. Otherwise, they won't taste like peanut butter. Try them again with the right PB—they really do taste exactly like the ones Gran used to make. It'll take you back.

To: Belle
From: Lexie
Subject: RE: Peanut butter cookies
How'd you know to use dark-roasted PB? It didn't say in the recipe.

To: Lexie
From: Belle
Subject: RE: Peanut butter cookies
The last time I made these cookies with Gran, she told me that's the secret.

I didn't get a response back. We'd had a pretty quick turnaround on the cookie emails, about a half hour or so in between each, until my last one. And then, crickets.

The days passed, and I wondered if Lexie was smarting because I knew the peanut butter secret and she didn't. I dashed off that last email without thinking of how it would land. Should I have put it differently? Not said anything at all?

I was spending entirely too much time thinking about how peanut butter affected Lex.

Enough.

Chapter 11

I left my apartment early the Saturday of Memorial Day weekend so I had time to walk down to Union Square.

Pet saw me approaching and waved. Flopsy and Mopsy, on long leashes so they could meander within the confines of the farm stand, trotted as far as they could to me.

"I've never showed up to a job and had anyone greet me like this." I squatted down on my haunches, and the shih tzus put their front paws on my lap. "A girl could get used to this."

Pet beamed. "The C-suite appreciates you!"

Harold carried a box over to the table. "Mornin', Belle."

"Good morning." I stood, and the pups marched behind the tables that were already arranged in a large U shape. "What can I help with first? Do you want me to unload the truck?"

"I'll bring the boxes over—you can help Pet unpack and arrange everything. She says I don't present things nicely on the table."

"You dump everything out and it looks a mess!" she said.

"One man's mess is another—"

"Is another woman's headache." She laughed. "You do the arugula," she said to me. "I'll get started on these green onions."

The morning was crisp, but it was bright and sunny. The trees around the park were flowering. It was clear from the crowd that a lot of folks had left town for the holiday weekend, but those who stopped at the stand were relaxed and quick to strike up a chat.

Around three o'clock, a lull in traffic set in. I pulled up a seat next to Pet.

She patted my knee. "Feels good to sit down, doesn't it?"

"Oh, yes." I stretched out my legs.

"Being on your feet all day is real work," she said. "When you can, be sure to sit for a bit. It'll revive you."

I assured her that I would.

"What did you do before coming to us?"

Pet posed the question gently, but all the same, it scratched at my sorrow and career failure. Mostly my sorrow.

"I left the city for a bit to live with my grandmother in Cleveland." I swallowed. "She . . . passed away in February."

"Oh, Belle." Pet rested her hand on my arm. "I am so sorry for your loss."

"Thank you." I stared straight ahead, willed the greenmarket's bustle to steady me.

"Your grandmother was obviously beloved."

I nodded and wiped my cheeks. "My face leaks a lot now."

Pet smiled. "Oh, yes . . . I know that faulty plumbing." She paused. "A little unsolicited advice? Your loss is excruciatingly fresh. The best thing you can do right now is walk through life gently . . . very, very gently. Let yourself heal. There's no other way. Time is your friend."

When the day ended, I helped load the truck, waved goodbye to Pet and Harold, then started my walk home. The city was summoning its evening hum, relaxing into that gauzy time between late afternoon and evening. The streets held a holiday weekend sense of quiet—you could tell when throngs decamped to the Hamptons or Hudson Valley. The weekend that kicked off summer gifted those who stayed in the city with a sense of urban relaxation. Fewer cars choked the streets, fewer horns honked in annoyance. The din was dialed down. Sidewalks yawned open. I soaked up the relative ease.

My phone vibrated as I crossed Thirty-Fourth Street.

The caller ID stopped me. I answered after two more rings.

"Hey, Belle, it's Simon."

Even though I knew it was him, it still took a moment to orient hearing here in the city the voice I'd only known in Gates Mills. Gran had always been my tether to home. Now he was a new one. Like an old computer, my brain was slow to process a simple greeting . . . and feelings that complicated pretty much everything.

"Simon . . . hello." My stomach twisted in shame. How had I let his kindness die on the vine? "I'm really sorry to not have texted . . . or called." Everything coming out of my mouth sounded woefully inadequate. "It's been a bit of a roller coaster, and I've been . . . off."

"I can imagine."

I swallowed. "How've you been?"

"Good, thanks. I didn't want to crowd you, but . . . you've been on my mind. I heard you'd gone back to New York and was wondering how you're doing."

"My gosh, you're dear. I'm . . . I guess doing my best, which doesn't feel like much, to be honest." I cleared my throat. "How are your parents? And Nate, Jenny, and Jeremy?"

"Everyone's good."

I could tell he'd noticed my abrupt subject shift.

"Good." Why couldn't I do anything like a normal person anymore? The conversation was stalling.

"Look, I'm going to be in town on business next month and wanted to see if I could take you to dinner," he said. "Just think about it, no need to commit now. I know things must feel overwhelming."

I bit my cheek, trying to untangle the emotions knotting within me.

"I'm hoping after a think you'll say yes," he said, his voice dropping to an intimate timbre.

My breath caught. He had a way of surprising me. A curlicue of longing unspooled in my center. I was no longer on the verge of tears. Another surprise.

"All right, I'll leave it there," he said after I said nothing. "I have to jump on another call, but I'm glad I caught you and hope you'll consider dinner next month."

"Okay . . . thank you. It was really nice talking to you."

"Be well, Belle."

We ended the call.

I pinched the bridge of my nose, lamenting not just how socially awkward I'd become, but also how my actions—or inaction—had slighted people I was truly fond of. I didn't deserve a phone call from Simon, and yet . . .

And yet.

Gran's next letter arrived the second week of June.

> Dear Lexie and Belle,
>
> For your next recipe, I want you to make the one that's a whole meal. We'd have this in the fall and the winter, when something good and roasted for dinner made us all feel warmer. Lexie, you liked the carrots. Belle, you liked the potatoes. And me, I always thought the onions were best.
>
> You need all three for this dish to taste perfect.
>
> All my love,
>
> Gran

The photo tucked into the letter showed Lexie and me wearing bright red softball shirts. It was the team we'd played for the summer after fourth grade, which meant Lexie had just finished second grade. Our baseball caps were entirely too big for our heads. Our mitts looked gigantic at the end of our skinny arms. But the two of us . . . the two of us fit together perfectly.

I couldn't help but smile at our ease standing side by side, how it conveyed so much connection and comfort. It made perfect sense that Gran wanted us to make her roasted chicken over vegetables—it was the ultimate comfort meal.

This was something else I'd never made with Gran but had watched her make all my life. I went to the grocery store in the afternoon, and when the evening light had softened, set to making dinner.

I cut the onions, carrots, and potatoes into wedges like Gran used to, then scattered them on a baking sheet and went to drizzle everything with olive oil—but only a trickle was left in the bottle. I didn't have any other oil, or butter (Gran would be mortified). So, the trickle would have to do. I dabbed the chicken breasts and thighs with paper towels, smeared what little oil I could on the skin, then set the chicken on the vegetables. I sprinkled salt and pepper over everything and slid the baking sheet into the oven.

After forty-five minutes, I pulled out the sheet to add the kale so it would wilt.

Everything inside me sagged.

Nothing on the baking sheet resembled the dish I remembered so fondly. The chicken wasn't golden and crispy, the vegetables weren't roasted and plump. The pan juices had sizzled away without imbuing any lusciousness at all. I cut a potato in half—the inside was so dry it looked cobwebby. Without enough oil to coat the veggies and chicken, the oven had sucked every ounce of moisture from what was supposed to be a comfort meal.

I stared at the desiccated chicken and withered vegetables—a metaphor for so much between Lexie and me.

Later that night, after throwing away the mess I'd baked to oblivion, after eating cold pizza for dinner, I emailed her.

To: Lexie
From: Belle
Subject: Roasted Chicken Over Vegetables

Hi,
This was an unmitigated oven disaster of my own making because I ran out of oil. I'm wishing it had gone better . . . I guess like so much of late.
Belle

To: Belle
From: Lexie
Subject: RE: Roasted Chicken Over Vegetables
Hi,
Mine was great, just like Gran's.
How do you not have oil?
Lexie

To: Lexie
From: Belle
Subject: RE: Roasted Chicken Over Vegetables
You'd be surprised what my kitchen routinely lacks. Oil, butter, bread . . . and, on days when the plumbing isn't working, water.

I got down to Union Square early the following week. The sun was already steaming the pavement, priming the concrete for an afternoon cook.

Little Rabbit Farm's usual spot was empty. And the truck wasn't there. Normally, Pet and Harold would've been parked behind their designated market spot. Today, nothing.

I checked my phone—no messages. Maybe they'd hit traffic. I watched trucks from different farms jockey for parking. If the Rabbits didn't arrive soon, they wouldn't get a good spot, and the rhythm of the day would be upset. Everything would take longer to unload and replenish, then load back onto the truck at the market's close. A lumbering truck from one farm snared a spot next to where the Rabbits usually parked. Another truck was stopped at the corner of Union Square. If I didn't do something, the Rabbits would lose their spot, so I stood in the road directly behind their stand. The truck slowed, put its blinker on, and veered into me. The driver extended his arm out the window in a WTF gesture.

"You gonna move?" Mirrored aviators hid the man's eyes.

"I'm actually saving this spot, so maybe try parking somewhere else, thanks."

The guy, who looked a few years older than me, took off his trucker hat, tossed it on the passenger seat, and ran a hand through a mess of brown hair. "I'm assuming you're saving it for me, so move."

"I'm saving it for Petunia and Harold Rabbit," I shot back. "Are you Petunia or Harold Rabbit? Have you undergone massive reconstruction surgery in the past week and now are completely healed and look totally different, not to mention decades younger? I don't think so. Move along."

The driver took off his sunglasses and leaned out the window. His eyes, a vivid blue that would've been arresting if they didn't look pissed, stared me down. "I'm Peter, Pet and Harold's son. So. How 'bout it. Want to move?"

I squinted in disbelief. "Your name's Peter Rabbit?"

He shook his head, put his sunglasses back on.

"Okay." Heat rose to my cheeks. "Yeah . . . sorry."

I stood aside as he maneuvered the truck, feeling both disappointed I'd apologized for trying to do something kind and ashamed at how quickly I'd gotten snarky with this stranger.

He parked the truck, shut off the engine, and walked around to the back. Unlocked the padlocked roller door and yanked it open.

"Where's Pet and Harold?"

He hopped up into the truck, undid the bungee cords holding everything in place, then started sliding boxes toward the opening.

"My mom's not feeling well. My dad stayed home with her." He hopped down from the truck and slid a table out to the edge. "Get the other end."

I grabbed it. "What's wrong with her?"

He didn't answer immediately. "Just not feeling well."

Peter Rabbit had none of the charm of a beloved storybook character.

We set up the tables. I unloaded a box from the truck. Went back for another. Repeated that six times in silence.

"I'm really sorry your mom's under the weather," I said. "Did something happen or . . . ?"

My sentence trailed off unfinished because, being new, it didn't exactly feel right to ask for such personal details. But I was concerned and genuinely interested. Pet was such a lovely woman.

"Farm life is hard life," he mumbled.

"I know."

"You can't possibly." He opened a box of green onions and began stacking them on the table. "This is a novelty to you, to all you city people. But it's our livelihood."

I stood chagrined, then opened a box of my own. The aroma of Harold's freshly baked bread wafted up. I started arranging golden boules on the other end of the table in a neat pyramid.

"Let me guess, you're fed up with city life, you want something simpler." Peter tossed the empty box behind him and opened another. Started mounding arugula in a haphazard pile next to the sloppily laid scallions. "And you figured farming's easy, right?" He shook his head. "You have no idea about this life."

I rearranged the loaves, keeping my gaze downward to tamp down the end-of-my-rope feeling that Peter's words had stirred up. The steel I'd summoned so easily protecting a parking spot was gone. A weird emotional whiplash had left me fragile.

"You really don't know anything about me," I said softly, then looked at him. "The happiest times of my life were with my gran doing yard work and planting . . . I think you're rather lucky to do what you do with your family."

He stopped stacking the greens, seemed to shrink as if I'd chastised him when all I'd said was how lucky he was. I couldn't manage any other defense of myself.

There was nothing more to say, and he was silent, so I took my empty box, picked up the one Peter had discarded, and carried both to the back of the truck. I hauled out another box. Stacked parsley in silence. Then chives. Baby spinach. We didn't say anything else the rest of the day aside from interactions with customers.

At six o'clock, Peter retrieved a stack of empty boxes from the back of the truck and started packing up what hadn't sold. Wordlessly, I did the same. We stowed all the unsold produce back in the truck, then the tables, the canopy, and the folding chairs. He yanked down the truck's roller door and padlocked it.

It was bizarre how we'd spent this day, working around one another for hours without interacting in any meaningful way. Peter was standoffish, imperious, and had a massive chip on his shoulder. He couldn't be any more different from his parents. This was where I was working now, so it was up to one of us to reset the tone—and it was abundantly clear that he didn't care if our time was spent in uncomfortable silence.

"I'm Belle." I put out my hand. "I'll see you on Monday. Please give your parents my best."

He shook my hand. His palm was calloused, his grip firm. When I tried to pull my hand away, he held it for an extra beat. "Thanks for your help today."

Then he let go.

I nodded and turned to start the long walk uptown, relieved to finally be leaving him.

Gran's next letter arrived the following week.

> Dearest Lexie & Belle,
> For your next recipe, I want you to make the one that served as base for so many meals. It requires a long simmer and the occasional loving stir. This recipe is proof that from something heated to a boil, a perfect harmony of flavors will ultimately emerge.
> I love you both.
> Gran

Baby soup, that's what we used to call it.

This name for vegetable stock delighted us. Gran said that it was the starter needed for almost every delicious bowl of soup we ate. White bean soup started with baby soup. Veggie soup started with baby soup. Roasted vegetable stewp (Gran's cross between stew and soup) started with baby soup.

The photo enclosed with this letter captured the chaos that reigned when it was being made. Pure, joyous, messy chaos. "No way," I murmured.

Lexie and I stood on chairs at the kitchen sink. I knew that a giant bowl and a footed strainer sat inside the sink out of view, that Gran had just poured cooled broth with all the veggie chunks and tangled herbs into the strainer. Squished bits of vegetables covered the counters. Broth slopped on the chairs, on the floor, on the fronts of our aprons. Our hands were covered in vegetable mash that we'd squeezed through our fingers to extract every last drop of savory broth. Rivulets ran down our arms.

Lexie, in mid-guffaw, had one hand on her head, the other held high. The pose had squished a massive blob of carrot in her bangs, which made her laugh harder. I'll never forget what she did after Gran snapped that picture: She put her other hand on top of her head, rubbed potato, onion, and celery into her hair, and nearly fell off the chair laughing.

I smiled at Lexie's grinning face. Focused on her mouth, open wide, happiness pouring from her, her eyes closed in mischievous joy . . . where had she gone? When was the last time I saw her laugh like this? Or be such easy, silly company?

Hard to believe that Gran had let us make such a mess. Although, really, it wasn't hard to imagine at all.

The Sunday after I got that letter, the weather was dreary. I hauled out the biggest pot I had, washed the vegetables and herbs, peeled the carrots, cut the onion, every bit of it harkening back to when Gran and I had made this together. The recollection didn't summon tears. Rather, it imbued a kind of reverence to my movements. Remembering it all, carrying it forward for myself. Had Gran intended that when we cooked together while I was living with her? I stopped moving the knife, lost in thought. Gran had done more than walk me back into my life—she'd given me presents every day. I looked down at the chunky cuts of carrot and potato. Gran had given this gift of knowing how to make baby soup, and in doing so, she had shared an indelible part of herself that I would now be able to summon and hold close.

I set the knife down and let the emotions come. Heaved out the bruising sadness that lurked, always lurked, the emptiness that still echoed.

This would happen: Grief would roll up unannounced, enormous and inescapable. I'd think I was holding it together, then end up like this.

Eventually, my breath steadied. My mind fuzzed, no longer focusing on the sharp edges of loss.

What I felt instead left me in awe: the full, expansive measure of Gran's grace. Everything she had done during our last months together, thoughtfulness I was only beginning to realize the depth of, landed on me with exquisite poignancy. And for the first time since she'd passed, I felt like there was no one in this world luckier than me.

To: Lexie
From: Belle
Subject: Vegetable stock
I've never made vegetable stock on my own—to be clear, any kind of stock. But you probably knew that, or maybe not. I don't know. That wasn't to say that you should know that about me—I don't mean that to sound accusatory or anything. Sorry . . . I am really all over the place here, feeling scattered. I just finished straining out the veggies and savory bits from the stock. I poured it into containers and now I'm on the couch trying to figure out what to say to you. Making a real jumble of it, I know. But what I keep coming back to is how making Gran's veggie stock was emotional . . . it brought up a lot. More than I'm going to try to put into words, seeing as how I can't manage the simple ones. My chances of putting together thoughtfully nuanced sentences and paragraphs explaining the shades of feeling, all of it, any part of it, frankly, are not good. So, I guess this is . . . I don't know, me sharing as best I can at the moment. And maybe that's better than no words at all.
xo

To: Belle
From: Lexie
Subject: RE: Vegetable stock
Mine tasted like dishwater. Or feet water. One of the two. I threw it out.
I don't understand how yours turned out perfectly and mine tasted like something found in a dingy bath.

I inspected my left eyelashes, which I'd just wanded mascara through.

The normalcy got to me. The bridging of two worlds got to me. The fragility of doing something different got to me. Feeling like I wasn't ready for this got to me.

The last time I'd gotten dressed up for a night out was the Gates Mills holiday party.

I willed myself to keep it together. I'd committed to this. I didn't want to be that flaky person who backed out. I looked up until my pulse slowed.

"I'm going out, Gran." My voice sounded so loud in the bathroom, echoing off the tiled walls. Strange. "And I'm thinking about the last time we did."

The memory of walking to the holiday dance plucked a chord of happy.

"You know who I'm seeing . . . so . . . I know you're glad."

I took a steadying breath, then mascaraed my right eye.

"Okay." I stared into the mirror. "Be honest. Does my eye makeup say *elegant lady* or *tired clown*? Elegant lady, right?"

Talking out loud to Gran made me smile.

"I'm going for elegant lady," I murmured. "So, fingers crossed." I swirled a fluffy brush in a compact, blew on it, and swiped it across my cheeks. "Too much? I need a little color. I've gotten washed out." I waited for my center to hold, then applied some sheer lip gloss, whispered, "But makeup can fix all that, right?" I blew out a calming breath. "You betcha."

The restaurant wasn't far, so I started off on my walk. The evening was warm, summery. Friday imbued the city with a relaxed feel, like it knew the weekend had arrived. The breeze that drifted across the streets, down the avenues, carried an ease that felt different than it did the rest of the week.

Twenty minutes later, I arrived at an elegant Greek restaurant in Rockefeller Center with low lighting and wondered if the sundress and sandals I was wearing were a little too simple. Simon waved from the bar.

"Hi." He met me at the hostess stand with arms outstretched, then seemed to rethink his enthusiasm, and instead took my hands and kissed me on the cheek. "It's good to see you."

He wore a dark suit and looked like he'd recently gotten a haircut. The spicy scent of his cologne scrambled my brain. I gurgled some words, how it was good to see him, and was grateful for the hostess showing us to our table because my tongue had tied itself in a way I hadn't expected.

We were seated in an intimate corner banquette. The silverware polished to a high shine, the crystal votive with a tea light, the elegant stemware, everything sparkled.

Simon leaned closer, his face warmed by the candlelight. "You look beautiful."

"Thank you." I smiled. "It really is so good to see you . . . I mean it, especially after I fell off the radar. I was surprised to get your call."

"Why? I told you back in Gates Mills that I wanted to take you to dinner." He paused. "I'm sorry we weren't able to after the holidays." He held my eyes. "Obviously, I'm even sorrier about your gran . . . How are you doing?"

I swallowed. "It . . . kind of depends on the day. Or the hour, really."

The server came to the table, asked our water preference, and took our drink orders.

"Grief is a hard road to travel," Simon said after the server left.

Something in his face made me say, "Sounds like you know from personal experience."

He nodded. "My college roommate—he was hit by a drunk driver over summer break after freshman year."

And that was what I realized his eyes had, a depth of experience, an empathy gained from something painful and personal.

"I'm so sorry," I said. "My gosh, that must've been hard."

"Yeah. Kids . . . well, they don't have the tools to process that kind of loss." Simon looked up as the server approached with our drinks.

We ordered, the server collected our menus and left.

Simon raised his martini, and I lifted my wine glass to meet it.

"To seeing you again," he said. "I've been looking forward to this trip."

We clinked cheers.

"I'm really happy you're here," I said.

We sipped our drinks.

"So, how did you get through losing your roommate?"

"My mom encouraged me to speak to a bereavement counselor at school, which really helped." The server set down an amuse-bouche, a petite crab cake drizzled with lemon aioli, and Simon thanked her. "What I learned is that everyone gets through it differently, but no one gets through it alone." He smiled at the plates just set before us. "And good food helps."

"You sound like my gran."

"I think we both benefited from similar influences," he said. "What aspirin couldn't fix, food could."

We devoured the tiny crab cakes, raved about the taste. I sipped my wine.

"So . . . speaking of generational influences . . . this is going to sound kind of out there, but I've been getting letters from my gran."

Simon's eyes went wide. "What?"

"Yeah—my sister and me, the both of us." Hearing it said aloud felt like an intense reveal. I'd been holding this knowledge close. Releasing it even a tiny bit made me feel weak. Was it because it made it feel less like mine? "I've . . . I haven't told anyone, well, except Faye because I thought she might be sending them." I answered his question before he got it out. "She's not."

"Wow."

"I know."

In the quiet that followed, I wondered if I shouldn't have shared this.

"I'm speechless . . . what an unexpected gift for you and your sister." He reached across the table and took my hand. "I hope it feels like that. I mean . . . wow!"

I relaxed. Simon understood the enormity and preciousness of it. "It has . . . it's also, I guess, reframing a lot for me."

"In terms of?"

"In terms of my relationship with Lexie." I thought about how to put it. "We haven't been close in a long time for a number of reasons. But . . . I guess I don't know what I'm trying to say."

Simon waited for me to continue.

I hadn't put any order in my head to what I was feeling and didn't have the proper distance or perspective to declare anything. So, my words hung there unfinished.

"It sounds like these letters are both meaningful . . . and powerful." He held my eyes. "Honor them. Your gran sent them for a reason."

I loved that he got the complexity of it. "You are a wise man."

"Well"—he shrugged, his smile self-deprecating—"half a martini makes anyone a philosopher."

The server set down our appetizers.

We smeared tzatziki on pieces of pita.

I shook my head in disbelief. "This is delicious."

"I heard this place was good."

"It's not just that." I was overcome with the sense that I was on the outside of my body, observing the scene, noting how strangely normal this was to be at dinner, talking—laughing even. Being a person, like people did every single day. Sitting there was both familiar and deeply foreign, which left me a little wobbly, but carrying on. "I honestly can't remember the last time I was out to a nice dinner." I looked into his eyes. "Thank you for this. It's really special."

"You've been dealt a lot." He dabbed his mouth with the napkin. "Take my word: Time helps everything."

His eyes were so kind. I really did want to believe him.

Simon was a link to home that I had the strange urge to hold close and keep at arm's length simultaneously. It was such an odd emotional dichotomy. Eventually, the conversation wound its way to life there. He told me about his parents, how they were doing well, how Jeremy was still dating the young woman he'd brought to the village holiday party, that he'd seen Faye and Mama P last weekend when he visited his parents. How they were talking over their respective fences, across Gran's yard, as if she were still there. Hearing about everyone, invoking Gates Mills in all its specialness, tugged at me in a way that comforted, and made me feel out of place here in the middle of Manhattan.

We finished dessert and Simon paid the check.

"Can I give you a lift home?" he asked.

"I was going to walk, actually."

"Care for some company?"

I smiled.

He took my hand.

The night still clung to the day's warmth. Everything twinkled: the gilded Prometheus statue overlooking Rockefeller Plaza, windowed storefront displays, headlights on passing taxis. Everyday bits of the city shimmered.

"So . . ." Simon didn't say anything for a moment. "Do you have an idea of what your plans are?"

"Meaning?"

"Meaning are you back in New York for good or . . . ?" His sentence trailed off.

We turned down a street that held every shadow Fifth Avenue lacked.

The tug of home was undeniable, but I didn't know how to build a lasting bridge from here to there. I couldn't go hide in Gates Mills again. But I wasn't sure if I had a place here in the city either. I needed something to sustain me, to feed my soul—and to pay the bills. The what and where of all that were unclear.

"I honestly don't know what I'm doing." There was no simpler way to put it. "There's a lot I need to figure out . . . and fast. My friend who's subletting my apartment will be back in September." I mustered a smile that felt so meek it could hardly be called a smile.

Simon seemed to take my nonanswer to his question in stride, or a kind of stride. He was quiet for a bit, but then our conversation picked up and we chatted while wending our way to my neighborhood, finally to my block.

I stopped in front of my building. "This is me."

"Nice." He craned his neck up. "Now I know where to picture you."

I smiled at him envisioning where I was.

"I know what it's like in the months after you lose someone, so I don't want to overstep." He faced me, took both of my hands in his. "I'll say good night here like a proper gentleman. But please make no mistake: I meant what I said. I really loved seeing you."

Simon held my eyes. A whoosh of heat engulfed me.

His kiss on my cheek lingered. The intimacy imparted in such a chaste good night stole my breath.

Chapter 12

I'd worked side by side with Peter at the farm stand for a thousand years. How the calendar only said July, I didn't understand. The time clocked was interminable.

He'd made it clear he wasn't there for conversation, so I kept my head down and worked, talking to customers, but to him, not at all. At least not conversationally—he'd relay information about the stand, restocking, or answer questions, but kept it all business. Which was fine. I wasn't there for anything else but to work.

Peter coming in his parents' stead was the new normal. I always asked how Pet was. "Better," he would say, sharing nothing else about this woman I'd become so fond of in such a short amount of time.

On Wednesday, I set out extra early to Union Square. I liked the long walk before and after work. It helped balance . . . everything: sorrow for Gran, my mood, the ability to put one foot in front of the other and be a person doing person things. The more I walked, the less wobbly I felt. I got home exhausted after work, but the fatigue nestled in my bones solidly, like I'd done something virtuous with my day.

I talked to Gran on my walks. The treks downtown and the conversation, albeit one sided, helped me feel less alone. Not that it made any sense, but I wasn't questioning anything that helped.

When I turned the corner at Seventeenth Street, I saw the Rabbits' van. My insides sank. I really thought I'd beat Peter here today. I didn't want to give him another reason to be annoyed with me, so I jogged the rest of the way.

"Hey, sorry, I thought I'd get here before you."

He was inside the back of the truck, sliding boxes toward the door. "It's cool—go ahead and take these over."

His tone was different. I picked up the first box, turned, and nearly dropped it. "Pet!"

She was sitting in a chair by the table, putting handfuls of green beans into a large bin. She turned when I yelled her name, grinned, and stood slowly.

"It's so good to see you!" She opened her arms for a hug. I set the box on the ground and ran over.

"I missed you!" I said. "Are you okay? What was wrong?"

"Oh, don't you worry about me," she said. "When you get to be my age, the aches and pains can lay you up for a spell, but nothing to worry about. I'm fit as a fiddle."

Peter set two boxes on the table. "She insisted on coming today."

"I missed being here," she said. "This is the heart of our work, you know that."

Peter smiled, headed back to the truck.

"I've never seen him smile," I murmured to Pet.

Pet looked amused, then raised her voice. "Peter can be verrrrry serious."

"Someone has to be." His voice was singsongy—and surprisingly, soaked in kindness.

He stacked two more boxes near me, then turned to get more. He even moved differently, like the chip on his shoulder had fallen off.

"He's too serious," Pet mock whispered.

"I can hear you," Peter called from behind us.

His mother laughed. "I'm joshin'. He's a good egg, my boy."

I didn't doubt he was to her. But he didn't emit that energy to the rest of the world. Working beside him for the last thousand years, all he'd exuded was prickliness and sullen detachment. And not just to me—to customers too. Which, fine. I was there to work and wasn't about to hold anyone's mood against them. People have so much percolating under the surface, more than anyone would imagine. So, I bore Peter no ill will. It was more that I wondered how deep his prickly pool ran . . . and why.

The sun rose high and bright in the sky. Every customer who came to the stand was chatty—no one was surly at the greenmarket. With rare exception, the mood among farmers and patrons was reliably upbeat. But underpinning this work I enjoyed, interacting with customers, was the simple truth that spending the day with Pet filled me up.

At a lull in the afternoon, Pet put her hand on my arm. "Come to dinner on Sunday."

I chuckled, started to demur.

"I mean it." She patted my arm. "It's a day off. We'll have a nice dinner. You can spend the night so you don't have to make the trip back home in the dark. We've got a spare bedroom. And then you can drive down with us Monday morning."

"Oh, that's really kind—"

"I mean it," she said. "I've missed seeing you. Come, let me cook for you. You can relax, breathe some fresh air, walk barefoot in the grass, get a good night's sleep—even sleep with the windows open!" She chuckled. "But I know you're a busy young woman with a social life, so I understand if that doesn't work."

I was not young, nor did I have a social life.

"You know what?" I smiled. "That sounds really nice."

"Oh!" Pet shook her pudgy fists near her face in excitement. "Wonderful!"

"But only if I can bring something to help with dinner," I said.

"Fair enough. Tell you what: I'm going to make pork chops and some sort of vegetable, maybe green beans. You bring something that would go with that. Good?"

I told her it was perfect, that I was looking forward to coming.

What was most surprising—part of me really meant it.

I walked home that evening, appreciating the rosy tint of the sky and the tiny bit of calm that accompanied me.

I checked my mail before heading up to my apartment.

Another of Gran's letters had arrived.

My pulse raced as I rode the elevator, as I opened the door, kicked off my shoes, and plopped on the couch. I wiggled a finger under the seal, slowly . . . carefully so as not to tear the envelope.

> Dearest Lexie & Belle,
>
> For your next recipe, I want you to make the dish that we had every Thanksgiving and Christmas. It always dressed the table, was just as good cold out of the fridge as it was hot out of the oven, and there was never enough of it. This one you need to start the day before you want to serve it.
>
> I love you both.
>
> Gran

I slipped the Instamatic photo from the envelope. Lexie and I in bathing suits, our hair wet, standing in our old living room by the piano. My arm is slung around her neck. I'm grinning. My eyes are closed, crinkled in happy. Lexie's laughing, her arms held wide. She's exuberant.

My breath caught.

I remembered the day this was taken. Seemed impossible that I should, considering how young I was, but I did. It was right before lunch. The day was a scorcher. Lexie and I had played outside all morning in the sprinkler, and moments earlier had been on the living room floor in our wet bathing suits arguing about who'd play with the Tuesday Taylor doll and who'd drive the dump truck. Our mother had been adamant that we didn't just play with dolls. "Girls," she said, "should play with everything."

Mom was in the kitchen making lunch. Oscar Mayer bologna sandwiches with yellow mustard. She'd toast white bread and then cut each slice through the middle from the top of the crust to the bottom, revealing a nubby interior, hot and steamy from the toaster. She'd slather one wafer-thin crisp with mustard, then layer two slices of bologna and nestle the other half slice of toast on top. Cut the whole thing diagonally. It was the most delicious sandwich in the world.

Just when Lexie and I were yelling loudest, Mom strolled in. She wore a long off-the-shoulder sundress striped in big blocks of bold color: magenta, deep purple, and pink. It billowed when she moved.

Mom sat down at the piano, glancing at Lexie and me. "C'mere, my dollies."

Before we even got up, Mom's left hand jammed a big-feeling bass chord, that energetic, porky lead-in to Captain & Tennille's "Love Will Keep Us Together," the one that she'd played since I was born (she'd said, anyway). The one that got us amped. By the time she dragged her right thumb down the other side of the piano in a joyous cascade, Lexie and I had flanked her. I must've been five, because I had just learned to snap. Lexie, three, clapped along, her chubby hands making tiny slapping noises. We both danced.

As she sang, Mom moved her shoulders and swayed from side to side, her strong fingers unwrapping this present of a song from the piano in the corner. She never used sheet music. Self-taught, she listened to a song and figured out how to play it for us.

Lexie and I joined in, sang along, our antics getting wilder and wilder.

Mom had a movie star's wide smile—perfect teeth, lips that didn't disappear when stretched in happiness—and eyes that shone vibrant and joyous. They were deep brown like both of ours, and full of emotion.

This was a thing Mom did. We never knew when she'd sit down and play something. That was the fun of it. She'd break up the day with music and cheer, thread some zippiness into a difficult moment. It tightened the bond between the three of us.

We all sang at the top of our lungs. The song usually ended with Lexie and me jumping around, with Mom laughing. Afterwards, Lexie and I insisted on playing something, which resulted in a cacophony. Mom would finish lunch, listening to us bang on the piano and, I like to think now, delighting in how much happier we sounded.

Normally, this remembrance found me in my dreams. Sleep had a way of dissolving that veil between memory and consciousness, beckoning sweet recollections forth. I'd awake remembering how loved Lexie and I were, how joyous Mom made our days, the way she turned toward the happy. Sometimes I woke up with tears rolling down my cheeks, emotion leaking out without my knowing. As the last tendrils of the dream faded, I'd feel her fingerprints on my soul and psyche.

As I got older and was better able to pluck out thorns that sorrow inevitably stuck you with (the *whys* and *it's not fairs* that can bleed away so much life), I understood how lucky Lexie and I were to have had Mom for the time we did, because, God, she was special. Every bit of her mothering was underpinned with love, verve, and song. Not everyone got that. But now I was tearing up with the enormity of Mom's loss. Her absence was profound. The wound had always been there, but now that Gran was gone, it had ripped open anew.

I wiped my eyes and stared at the picture, realized our ages and the time of year it must've been. Was that one of the last times Mom played for us? If she had been in the photograph, would her shoulders, which I remembered as sun kissed and rounded, actually have been pale and bony? Her arms, sinewy? Her dress, such a celebration of a garment, would it have hung off her withered frame? Her teeth gray because cancer had leeched life out of her enamel? Would her eyes be circled with the dark that foretold what was to come?

These were things we hadn't seen as children, changes we never registered. I remembered her head thrown back in happiness, captured forever, joyous in the song. Because that was what you kept track of, love. Cheer. Happiness. And cancer never stole any of that from our mom. Lexie and I had the myopia of all children: toys, songs, our mother's love. But my mom . . . her worldview must've included the world beyond.

I propped the photo on the coffee table where I could look at it, still holding Gran's letter. I reread it.

Stuffing.

Gran was talking about her stuffing.

She used to joke that stuffing was our mother's favorite food group. I mustered a small smile. It really was the most perfect dish of baked savory bread bits. All other stuffing was cringingly bad by comparison, leaden and tasteless as soggy cardboard. But Gran's . . . it was transcendent, each bite a perfect ratio of onions, celery, seasoning, and bread. The top, crisped and caramelized, yielded to a pillow-soft interior. She never varied the recipe, never added fruit or nuts—seasonal novelty had no place in Gran's stuffing.

I felt the gentle tug, a whisper of urging. This is what I'd take to the Rabbits' for dinner.

Every year, Gran made it for Thanksgiving and Christmas. Now, if I ever wanted to savor her stuffing again, I'd have to make it myself. The words in the letter blurred as I realized that Gran had prepared me for when she wouldn't be here any longer. She'd walked me through each step at Thanksgiving—crucially, explaining how all the components should taste at every stage. The way she told me to keep trying it so I could remember all the tastes. The perfect sprinkle of sage over the pulled nubs of bread. The ideal balance of herb and salt sautéed with onions and celery, so the whole mess caramelized sweetly with a hint of savory earthiness. How much chicken stock to mix in to ensure the uncooked stuffing was moist enough, but not too wet that it emerged from the oven soggy. How to dot butter on top so it would turn the crown golden and craggy in the oven. She'd given me this. All these gifts.

I folded the letter and headed to the grocery store with special purpose.

The next night, I pinched the loaf of white bread, just as Gran had taught me, making sure not to use any of the shiny crust tops. Seasoned it with salt and dried sage, tasting as I went. I took my time, fluffing the bread bits, toggling between adding another dusting of sage, a bit more salt. And then, finally, I struck upon the exact taste I remembered. A heady mix of pride and gratitude flooded me.

The melancholy that followed close behind left me exhausted.

An emptiness ballooned—not a cold void, but a space that felt almost hallowed. A numbed-out peace set in. I stared off, focused on nothing—not exactly content, but strangely, not feeling unmoored. For the moment, complete. Was it normal to feel this much blankness? I was at a point in my life where I should know the answer to that, to all of this: what was normal, what to expect. So many books were written about what to expect when expecting a baby. But what about when you lost the most precious person in the world to you? The two most precious people? When the marrow inside your bones screamed at their absence? Where was that book?

While I'd never pick up a book in a preemptive attempt to prepare myself for someone's eventual passing, my gosh, I'd love a manual on how to put myself back together. Everyone needed putting back together at one point or another in their lives.

The next day, I chopped onions and celery into slivers, sautéed them just as Gran had taught me, then mixed the savory sauté with the seasoned pinched bread. I checked it so many times while it baked, I worried I'd messed up the oven temperature by opening the door. But forty-five minutes later, the baking dish I pulled from the oven was undeniably Gran's stuffing, right down to the craggy top. I wiggled off the tiniest golden nub where it wouldn't be noticed and ate it. I closed my eyes in happy relief, in such a sense of centeredness. Gran had guided me when we'd made this for Thanksgiving, and here in my galley kitchen, I swear, she had done so again.

Before bed, I sat down to email Lexie. So much had come up making the stuffing, and the more everything rolled around my head, I wasn't clear on what I felt comfortable sharing with Lex. The emotion, the feeling after tasting it and knowing Gran had helped me recreate some of her magic . . . it all seemed beyond what my and Lexie's interaction had been with one another. Like it was too personal, the feelings too intimate.

I tried to put something into words.

To: Lexie
From: Belle
Subject: Stuffing
Hi,
I made Gran's stuffing.
That simple sentence is really loaded. The truth is, I've been struggling with what to write you. For a variety of reasons. But I want to keep this simple. And so . . . The stuffing was delicious, just like Gran's. It felt like a real achievement. But more than that, because making it was really emotional. It caught me by surprise, to be honest. I got to make this with Gran while I was living with her, so she shared all the tips that I swear helped me make it in my own kitchen. And so, every step of the recipe brought me back to when Gran was here and vibrant and . . . and while I'm so grateful for the time I had with her, there's no getting around the pain of missing her so much. Her stuffing was a gift, something else I'd never attempted to make on my own before. Probably because it's so special, you know? I mean, it's special because it's Gran's, but I think there's more to the feeling. Was it because we only had it during the holidays? Or how it perfumed the entire house when it was baking in the oven? Or was it because whenever we had it, we were always together? I don't know. Maybe it's a combination of all that. I guess what I'm trying to say is this dish means a lot to me. It always has, but I

don't think I fully appreciated how meaningful it was until making it on my own. I know I'm sharing a lot here . . . and to be really honest, it feels strange, almost too revealing. But I think what I'm trying to get at is that for everything making Gran's stuffing made me feel, I really hope you felt something too. In fact, I wish that more than anything.

xo

Because that was the crux of it all, right? Lexie feeling something close to what I'd felt or connecting in some way with Gran's memory—with the three of us. I'd gone so long wishing Lex would hold our relationship with Gran, our relationship with one another, in high regard, that she'd make time for us, give us high priority in her busy life. And so, yes, that was precisely what I'd hoped would come of us cooking from Gran's cookbook. After thinking about what I couldn't articulate to Simon, the bigger picture of it all, I finally had it: I wanted reading this cookbook together to not just be a tether, but a complete reparative experience for Lexie and me, healing years of sourness and disconnect.

But the nagging thought I had was that this was the same dreamer impulse that had kept me in the city far longer than I'd had any business staying . . . because Lexie didn't email back.

Chapter 13

The train pulled into the station right on time.

With an overnight bag slung across one shoulder, I carried the dish of stuffing in both hands as I disembarked. The platform was small, and the sky . . . vast. Far from the city, the quiet felt different. Special.

A small parking lot was next to the station. Peter waved as he got out of a truck and walked toward me.

I waved back. "Hey, thanks for picking me up."

"My pleasure." He lifted the bag off my shoulder, careful not to jostle the dish I held. "What did you bring?"

"Stuffing—I thought it might go with what your mom was making."

"Stuffing goes with everything." He set my bag in the back seat. "Do you want to put that dish on the floor back here so it doesn't move around? I've got a clean box you can set it in."

He couldn't have known how important this stuffing was to me. Him treating it with such care was touching. I set it where he suggested and climbed into the front passenger seat. Peter navigated the truck onto the main road. A warm breeze rushed through the open windows.

"It's so pretty up here," I murmured.

"Yeah, God's country. Nothing like it."

We passed fields. Wound our way through tree-lined country roads. The view was so enchanting that it was several miles before I realized we were driving in comfortable silence.

A split rail fence lined one side of the road for a good stretch until it ended at a wide cinder drive. The wooden sign posted at the drive's entrance read "The Farm at Hill Creek." Beyond a copse flanking the mouth of the drive, the verdant land that expanded behind the fence stole my breath.

"That's some farm."

"It's a training farm. Good folks there."

"What do you mean, 'training'?"

"Just that." He put his blinker on, then hung a left and continued down another long road through open fields. "It's a working farm, and the family runs an apprenticeship program for anyone who wants to learn about farming from the ground up. You get free room and board—and an education in everything farm—in exchange for hard work."

"That's incredible."

"It's part of a grant program the state offers to cultivate interest in New York's farming industry. The hope is that it'll ensure agriculture in the region thrives with successive generations."

I loved that. It also got me thinking.

But before I could dive too deeply into any contemplation, Peter turned onto a long dirt drive that meandered past a front field and up a hill. He stopped the truck far from the farmhouse and threw it into park. "Be warned: The welcoming committee has been set loose."

I looked ahead. Flopsy and Mopsy came tearing down the porch steps. They galloped toward the truck with their tongues out, ears flapping up and down, tiny thoroughbreds on a mission.

"Go on," Peter said. "I'll get your stuff."

"Oh my gosh, they're hilarious!" I hopped out of the truck and knelt down. "Come here, my girls!"

They plowed me over and licked my face. Smothered me with their tiny scramblings.

"Okay, you two." Peter scooped up the pups and extended a hand to help me to my feet.

I laughed. "They're really committed to greeting guests."

"All shock and awe." He hoisted me up. "Which isn't so bad as long as you don't mind rolling around on the ground with them."

After Peter retrieved my bag and the stuffing, we headed toward the house while Flopsy and Mopsy chased each other across the yard.

"There she is!"

I heard Pet's voice before she pushed open the screen door and came out on the porch waving both hands in the air.

I called hello, then said to Peter, "Your mom is the personification of joy."

"Yeah, she's special that way."

"Come here right now, you!" Pet walked toward me, arms outstretched, the slightest waddle to her step. She wore a blue cotton A-line dress and slip-on shoes and had an apron tied around her waist.

"You know, she always wanted a daughter," Peter said to me, then called to his mother, "You can't keep her, Mama."

"Oh, shush, you." She grinned. "Did he tell you I always wanted a daughter?"

"He did."

Pet put her hands on her hips and leaned forward. "It's true! Ha!" She saw the dish Peter was holding. "Oh my, what do we have here?"

"I made some stuffing . . . it's my gran's recipe."

Pet clasped her hands in reverence, then lifted a corner of the tinfoil to peek at the stuffing. "This looks delicious. How special . . . thank you, my dear."

She drew me to her and rocked me from side to side, like we hadn't seen each other in years. Like maybe she knew I needed a hug that big.

"Come on in." Pet waved a hand at the ground. "Don't mind these sad beds—I'm still figuring out what to plant here!"

I looked at the sky to see where the sun was and noticed the beds had some shade to them. "So, this is north facing, right? Some hostas or coral bells or . . . bleeding hearts would grow really well there."

Pet turned and considered me a moment. "I didn't realize you knew plants."

"Just what I picked up from my gran—we did a lot in her yard."

Her smile was sly. "Well, aren't you a surprise."

"I know enough to know how much I don't know."

Pet chuckled. "That's a sign of an open intellect." She looped an arm through mine, and we headed inside. "Let me show you around. Peter!"

"I got her things," he said. "Don't worry."

A honey-colored golden retriever loped into the kitchen.

"This must be Cottontail." I knelt down to say hello. The pup nosed my cheek.

"He's a big love bug who has infinite patience for his two tiny sisters." Pet rubbed the dog's side. "C'mon, boy, let's show Belle around."

The home was cheery. Windows funneled sunlight through the rooms, amplifying the warmth of the woodwork and plaster walls the color of sweet cream. Woven rugs adorned dark hardwood floors. A sofa with plump, mismatched pillows in bright oranges and yellows anchored the living room. The Rabbits' farmhouse wasn't just lived in, it felt loved.

"Your room's back here," Pet said as we turned down a hallway. "We put this addition on some years back so folks could stay overnight comfortably instead of being cramped on a couch and have one of us clodhopping past before dawn, making noise in the kitchen."

The ceilings were higher here, the walls painted a marshmallow color. A dark wood chair rail ran the length of the hall.

Pet waved a hand. "Peter's at the far end there." She stopped at the first room on the right and flicked on the light switch. "Here we go."

The room had a four-poster king-size bed with a poofy yellow comforter and fluffed pillows. A dresser, vanity table, and upholstered chair with a reading lamp next to it made the room positively cozy.

"And here"—Pet walked over to a door and opened it—"is your bathroom. I think it's nice to have your own when you're at someone's house."

"This is beautiful, your entire home is." I cast my eye over the sweet touches, the crocheted doily atop the dresser, the brass lamp with a milk glass shade beside the bed. It all hit someplace deep, someplace tender. "Thank you for having me."

Pet held my eyes and rubbed my arm. "I'm glad you're here."

She couldn't have known that this was my first time being a guest somewhere since Gran had passed. No way could she have known. And yet, somehow, she must've sensed it.

Pet made a feast for dinner: breaded pork chops, green beans slathered with butter and flaky salt, a giant salad with a zippy vinaigrette, and in the center of the dining room table, she'd placed Gran's stuffing, perfectly heated. Maybe it was seeing Gran's stuffing so lovingly positioned, or that this was the first homemade meal I'd shared with anyone since Gran passed . . . maybe it was all the savory aromas that hung enticingly around us, or maybe it was the pork chops.

It was the pork chops.

As my hands served myself and passed dishes clockwise, as my voice answered questions and responded appropriately to the conversation around me, while I was physically in this room with the Rabbits, my mind was yanked back to a time decades earlier when Lexie and I were kids.

We'd gone with Gran to the grocery store. Everything we needed for dinner was in the shopping cart, with one exception: pork chops. We made our way to the crowded meat counter, where Gran politely requested three chops. Just as she gave her order, a tall woman wearing an expensive-looking polka-dot dress loudly demanded that the gentleman working the counter give her six pork chops. The woman's nails were fire-engine red. A string of marble-sized pearls graced her neck. She glanced at Gran, eyed her plain slacks, sensible shoes, and worn pocketbook, then looked away—as if she'd seen nothing of consequence.

The meat man handed the bossy woman six chops, then sheepishly turned to Gran to say he only had two to give her. Gran firmly but politely reminded the man that she'd placed her order before the other woman and requested that her order be filled accordingly. Gran stood with dignity as the snooty woman complained loudly. She didn't react to the woman's biting words as the man took back the woman's six chops—despite her protestations—to give us our three. When we were in the checkout line, Gran turned to us and said, "I want you to remember this: You need to speak up and be strong for yourselves, especially when it's hardest."

"The summer we had that drought," Pet said. "Oh my."

"But Mother Nature, nothing gets by her," Harold added. "That winter, we got more snow than we'd ever had."

My own chuckle brought me fully back to the table. I treasured all my memories, but returning from them, being reminded of where I was and who I was without, left me off kilter.

After dinner, Pet announced, "The menfolk are going to do the dishes while we ladies retire to the porch."

"I'll help too," I said.

Pet shook her head. "Dishes are men's work. You go on out and get comfy. I'll be right there."

I headed to the porch, like Pet instructed. The light was mellow. Chittering from unseen insects was soft, barely perceptible. Soon it would be a cacophony. It only took a tiny pause, a moment of reflection. The somber wobble returned.

No one tells you how hard it is stepping even an inch outside profound loss. Being immersed in Gran's absence at least kept me close to her. I was somehow still in her bubble, however ephemeral, still cradling all the love I had for her, uninterrupted by the noise of the world, by the demands of reality. And so, the muscles and instincts that carried me away from that bubble felt like a betrayal. Every time I'd been away from the bubble for too long, or for an unexpected time, the repercussions hit me later. Grief would reassert itself with a vengeance. It would not lose me. But at some point, would I start to make sense of the sorrow? Find a place for it that would allow me to walk around in the world and be a person? I wondered if my cells were morphing to accommodate sorrow, if I was being reshuffled at a molecular level. And if so, what would I be left with? Because some moments I felt like a desiccated husk. No flesh, no meat to contain the happy.

The screen door opened, and Pet walked out with two cups of tea.

"Here, love." The scent of peppermint wafted off the mug she handed me. Pet settled into a chair.

"Thank you."

She cupped her own mug and looked off into the twilight. I appreciated that she sat silently, enjoying the quiet, like she knew there was something deeper going on inside me, something that roiled and bubbled, threatened this facade I'd managed all evening.

There it was.

I wiped my eyes. Blew out a long quiet breath to steady myself and fished a napkin out of my pocket. "I really can't be counted on to be normal these days."

"Eh . . ." Pet's voice was quiet. She blew on her tea. "What's normal, anyway?"

"Whatever it is, I don't have it." I stayed silent for a bit. "Sometimes I feel like I'm on a roller coaster. I can be normal for a stretch, but then a memory catches me unaware, or me realizing that I'm being normal trips me up. It doesn't mesh with what 99 percent of my insides are feeling."

Dusk descended.

"I wonder . . . if it's ever going to be any different. Or if this is how I walk through the world now." I wiped my eyes. Everything felt darker.

We sat silently.

"Grief is all of that, and unfortunately, there are no shortcuts," Pet said gently. "Grieving is . . . well, I would call it sacred. Here we are on earth with this profound, heartbreaking tether to someone who's passed on, who's maybe looking down on us, watching over us, sending signs to let us know they're there in the ether. I believe in that . . . I do. And what's more sacred than that? At some point, and it's different for everyone, but at some point, your muscles will carry sorrow with grace as you move through your life *living*. Living and doing." She paused. "You've got two hands. You carry grief in one and gratitude in the other. That's the secret." She patted my arm. "It will get easier, I promise you. But it takes time."

We talked a bit more until Peter came out waving a dish towel above his head. "Done!"

Pet grinned. "See, he does dishes too!"

"Subtle, Mom."

She chuckled, got herself up out of the chair. "Okay, time for us old folks to settle in and do old folks things. You two carry on." She looked tenderly at me. "I hope you sleep well."

I thanked her. Peter sat in her chair. We started talking about the night, the calm of the farm . . . a lot and nothing at the same time.

"Did you ever want to do anything else besides farm?" I asked him.

"I mean, I grew up on the farm doing things, but I uh . . . I've actually only been in the family business for a relatively short time, just a few years."

This surprised me. "What were you doing before this?"

"I was an investment banker. Did that for what felt like eons." He stretched his legs and leaned back into the chair. "The job was five parts adrenaline rush and ten parts unfathomable exhaustion and stress." He shook his head as if ridding himself of a disturbing memory, or maybe a way of life. "I was of the mindset that I'd get in, make a ton of money, and get out as fast as I could." He shrugged. "But . . . despite the toll that it takes on your body, your relationships, your health, your everything, really, the money keeps you in far longer than you intended—and definitely longer than is good. The whole thing . . . it changes you. And not for the better, let's just say. There's a ruthlessness that you develop. A coldness. It's . . . unfortunate." He rubbed the stubble on his chin, stayed quiet for a bit. "Anyway, I did that a long time but was able to retire when I finally left."

"Hang on, you were an i-banker and you lectured *me* about how farm life was hard life?"

He winced, which made me laugh.

"You know, that day . . . I was worried about everything, especially my mom." He looked at his boots. "And I behaved poorly . . . I apologize for that."

His vulnerability took me aback. "It's okay."

"My mom told me about your grandmother's passing . . . I'm really sorry."

"Thank you."

"How are you doing?"

I exhaled. "I am so tired of myself. I left New York off kilter, and I returned to it grieving. I'm literally the saddest sack you've ever met. I'm exhausted of being gutted all the time . . . but I also can't help it. And so . . . I'm just deeply and profoundly sick of myself." I shook my head. "Your family has been mind-blowingly kind. And understanding." I smirked. "Well, not you."

He laughed. "I had that coming. Fair enough."

I smiled so he knew it was a playful jab. "Enough about me. Tell me more about you. You live here?"

He nodded. "I'm building a place down the road, staying here until it's finished, which has been nice."

"And your . . . girlfriend? Boyfriend? Significant someone?"

"Ah." Peter scratched the side of his face. "We're going to need beers for that." He stood up. "I'll be right back."

He walked into the house. A moment later a light turned off in an upstairs window. Maybe Pet and Harold's room? Then the sallow porch light went out. The dark stillness of the night flanked me.

Peter came back out cradling two beers in one hand and holding a lighted kerosene lamp in the other.

"Thank you." I took the beer he offered me. "That's a gorgeous lamp."

"She's a beauty, right?" He set the lamp on the small table between us and sat down. "It belonged to my grandparents." He reached his bottle to mine and clinked it.

We both took sips. The lamp flickered a soft glow around us.

"This is truly so peaceful." It reminded me of sitting with Gran in the backyard, watching the fireflies. Taking in the evening air, she called it. I cleared my throat to bring myself back to the moment. "So."

He smirked, picked at the bottle label with his thumb. "So."

"Your significant someone."

He nodded but offered nothing.

"You don't have to get into it. I was just making conversation."

"Nah, it's okay." He scratched his head. "I think it's hard to talk about because the fact of the matter is I have regrets."

"I understand."

"*Reader's Digest* version?"

"Go."

He exhaled. "So, my behavior was hard to reckon with, for obvious reasons. No one likes facing the fact that they were a jerk."

"True."

"But . . ." He took a sip of his beer and sat quiet for a moment before continuing. "I think what was also hard to accept was that the woman I broke up with—and she was wonderful, salt of the earth, so fun and genuine—she's blissfully happy and has the life she wants with a great guy. It made me wonder what happiness I missed out on . . . which is such a selfish response."

"Well . . . the times we're lowest often aren't our proudest moments."

He smirked. "It's a lousy response. Another one. I can face up to it now, all my regrettable behavior. But I appreciate your kind take."

I smiled in sympathy and waited for him to continue. He didn't.

The quiet grew wide.

"Do you ever see her?" I asked.

"I do, actually. At the grocery or hardware store. All over the place. They only live a couple miles away."

"What's that like?"

He shrugged. "Fine. When I broke up with her in my i-banker days, she moved on quickly, probably realized how differently we were hardwired, and found her soulmate who had similar dreams for a life up here together." He looked down at his beer for a moment. "I didn't start thinking about her again until I'd left the rat race some years back and realized my dream of being an investment banker, living a life with all those bells and whistles, was such a hollow victory." He nodded as if affirming something to himself. "And it came at a steep price that I didn't realize—that I had no possibility of seeing—until I was done with that life."

"I'm sorry."

He cleared his throat. "Things work out the way they're supposed to."

Even though his voice signaled that the deep share was complete, something nagged at me.

"You broke up with her a long time ago."

He nodded.

"So . . . like, how long ago?"

"A couple decades, at least," he said.

"What about who you've dated more recently?"

"There really hasn't been anyone noteworthy since her. You know, dates, plenty of those, but nothing meaningful or lasting. I couldn't give that part of my life any time, working a gazillion hours every week."

"And since leaving banking behind to come work on the farm?"

"Well . . . let's just say there still hasn't been much time." He paused. "There's the time thing, yeah, but also . . . I'm in my early fifties. I really don't think I want to be a dad at this point. And the truth of it is I don't want to be a dad to anyone else's kids. It's a . . . I guess a funny time of life to be out there dating. I don't know. Okay, I've shared more than enough!" His chuckle lightened the mood.

"I understand." I sipped my beer. "It's worth mentioning that not every woman has kids or wants kids. You get out there, you might be pleasantly surprised by who you meet."

His smile was easy. "What about you? Significant other–wise?"

Simon flashed in my mind.

"Aha, you paused," Peter said. "There is someone."

"No," I blurted. "No significant other at the moment." I swallowed. "And no real stories in my dating life that are noteworthy."

He looked pointedly at me. "Everyone has a story, and because yours is yours, it's noteworthy."

His voice, gravelly from the beer, landed on me in a curious way.

I sighed. "Things . . . were drastically different some years ago." I thought back to the woman I was then. The very way I carried myself—I wouldn't even recognize that person today. "I had a job. I went out, dated."

"New York is a fun place to be dating."

"Definitely." I stared at the murkiness beyond the porch. "But . . . I don't know . . . things change."

My vagueness glossed over deep pools of insecurity and shame, along with loads more that pressed in close and uncomfortable. No one tells you how easy it is to veer off course in life. Or how grieving someone further knocks you beyond the sidelines. Or how the game keeps playing around you. Or how when you start to tiptoe back into the going and doing of the everyday, you feel off, like you've lost the rhythm for how this thing called living is done. You're more tentative, far more contemplative. You lose a gear. Nothing gets done quickly. No snap decisions are made. The threshold for all of it, for everything, is so low you wonder if you'll ever get to be a real person again, someone with vibrancy and drive, purpose and achievement. A paleness overwhelms. You feel like a washed-out version of yourself. Slower. Wan. Joyless. I just couldn't muster saying any of that to Peter. It isn't a thing other people can readily make sense of.

"I get it." He left it at that.

The silence that surrounded us felt companionable. I was grateful he didn't ask anything else.

"I think . . ." He paused. I looked over. His face was stony. "We're officially a knitting circle now."

I laughed.

"What? I'm serious." His chuckle held a happy resonance. The grimace and sullen dismissiveness when we first met at the greenmarket had fallen away, like a mask had finally been shed. "Hey, I'm good with it. I could do worse than be a modern man in a knitting circle."

"Should we widen our knitting circle?"

He sucked in air between his teeth, a mock wince. "This is a highly selective group. People are going to have to earn a spot."

"Not even your mom?"

He guffawed. "Just try to keep that woman out of a knitting circle!"

I laughed, then grew thoughtful. "You sure are lucky to have her."

The hilarity left him, but even in the dim kerosene light, the warmth in his eyes came through.

"I know," he said gently, then caught my gaze. "Trust me, I know."

We finished our beers, and it felt like a good time to wrap up the night.

"I think I might head to bed," I said.

"I'm not far behind you." He smiled. "Sleep well."

"Thanks, you too." I crossed the porch to the door, my footsteps creaking on the old boards in a satisfying way.

When my hand was on the screen handle, Peter said, "This was nice."

I turned back to him.

"Talking . . . you know. Knitting circle." He swallowed. "Just . . . it was nice. Thanks."

"It was . . . yeah." I smiled. "Good night, Peter Rabbit."

I rinsed my bottle in the sink and found the bin where they put recyclables. As I walked through the dimly lit house to my room, my pulse thudded in my ears. What had that been, Peter drawing out the moment, highlighting its virtue before I left the porch? A nervousness or an insecurity crackled off him. It caught me by surprise but also delighted me. I didn't know what was jacking up my pulse, causing that flutter in my middle, making everything in this dark house seem like some special nighttime lurk.

That wasn't true.

I knew exactly what it was.

The new hallway at the back of the house was softly lit by brass wall sconces. I closed my bedroom door behind me and leaned against it, feeling buzzy.

I heard footsteps in the hallway. Only Peter would be coming down here now. He walked with purpose, then slowed in front of my door.

And stopped.

I swallowed. Didn't so much as breathe. Could he sense me on the other side of the door?

Did I want him to?

His footsteps continued down the hallway, then his bedroom door softly closed.

Chapter 14

Lexie never emailed back after the stuffing recipe. Now, here it was the end of July, and Gran's latest letter had arrived:

> My dear Belle and Lexie,
> Do you remember those times we went fishing on Lake Erie? Casting off from the pier, Lexie's hook always catching on something, or that time Belle caught a fish and nearly fell into the water she was so excited. How we'd only catch what we could eat, and anything else Lexie would kiss and toss back into the water. Then, after we got home, baking up our catch with that crunchy topping. This is your next recipe . . . but not your last. Never your last.
> I love you both.
> Gran

In the Instamatic included with this letter, I was in middle school and Lexie was still in grade school. The confidence struck me. The happiness. In a few years, I'd lose both. Lexie arrived at high school brimming with extroverted self-assurance and flourished among the popular crowd, while introverted me had already been relegated to the odd-duck lunch table. People didn't even think we were related.

But before that cleaving, we used to go fishing all the time with Gran. We'd fish anywhere: off the pier at Lake Erie, from the banks of various rivers near where we lived. If it was bigger than a puddle, we would fish it.

Using kid-sized fishing rods, standing on the riverbank—Lexie in her glitter *Disco Disco Disco* shirt and me in my faded Cleveland Browns sweatshirt—we'd pluck out thick earthworms from a plastic container and bait our own hooks. Actually, I baited Lexie's and mine—she was too grossed out by the worms, the moving tangle of them in the container and the juicy puncture the hook made when it pierced their bodies.

The amazing thing wasn't that we caught fish—it was that there wasn't ever a question we could, or fear that we wouldn't. It wasn't until later in life that fear and doubt started eroding away self-assurance. Childhood pluck waned with age as larger concerns pressed down with their weight. Thinking back, I envied the kid I was then, standing on the riverbank, secure in my Keds, confidently fishing.

In the photo Gran had sent, I couldn't have been more than twelve. We stood on a rocky pier—maybe it was the lake—and squinted into the sun. I grinned at the camera, a fishing pole in one hand and my other arm slung around Lexie's shoulders. She held both arms outstretched, her mouth open in a full-throated laugh. Her silly confidence made me smile. She could be such a ham.

I thought back to the different photos Gran had sent. Lexie fighting back tears she was so scared to go to school. Arms outstretched in a cheeky pose near Mom's piano. Joyous because she'd mashed vegetables in her hair. Laughing in delight because we'd caught a fish that afternoon. They all left me feeling quite tender—about us . . . about everything.

They also made me wonder what photos she'd received with her letters.

Outside of our mom passing away so young, it amazed me, looking back, how much I remembered everything feeling so joyous. What a feat Gran pulled off, giving us a happy childhood despite weathering the most heartbreaking loss a mother and two young daughters could bear.

And all these happy memories came with tastes. We'd made Gran's fish so much growing up, the recipe was baked into my DNA. Maybe it helped that it was simple—her dishes were easy and earthy, but spectacularly flavorful.

Gran always cleaned the fish we caught, tasking us with the topping. She put Ritz crackers in a baggie, which we'd break up with a rolling pin. The craggy shards would soak up the butter and bake to a golden crust atop the fillets.

I made the fish from memory: broke up the crackers, stirred in melted butter. I couldn't find walleye at the fish market, so I got haddock. I nestled two fillets I'd seasoned with salt and pepper into an oiled baking dish. I spread the cracker mixture on top and put the fish in the oven to bake.

Fifteen minutes later, the cracker topping on the fillets was golden. I forked up a bite straight from the baking dish. Buttery tender fish, crunchy topping—it might not have been walleye, but it all took me back to a time that felt gentler.

Adulthood really did complicate everything.

To: Lexie

From: Belle

Subject: Walleye

Hi,

I haven't heard from you in a while . . . I hope everything is okay. Just wanted to let you know that I made Gran's walleye recipe with haddock. It was as good as I remember, even with a different fish. It actually got me thinking about those days when we'd go fishing and how much I loved us all being together. Right now, I'm thinking about what a special time that was. I don't know if I realized how precious those years were when we were in them . . . I guess that isn't something you ever contemplate as a child. But now . . . I don't know. Everything lands with a contemplative force.

Gran sent me a picture of the two of us fishing off a pier. I remembered it . . . or did the photo conjure up a feeling that's in my bones? The exact shape and outline of the memory, the specifics of that day, the way the sun made us squint into the camera, the slate hue of the water . . . does the feeling compensate for what my brain can't quite fully recall? Memory is a mystery. But the feelings threaded through our time growing up with Gran feel like magic. No mystery there.

What pictures have you received? I'm curious . . . and hoping you're well.

Xoxo

Belle

I woke up early on Sunday, brewed a pot of coffee, and sat on the couch with my laptop. As usual, the first thing I did was check my email—my lease renewal had arrived. The management company was offering a one-year renewal at the same price instead of the typical two-year renewal that came with a modest raise. I had until September to return it to them signed. I left it marked unread, so I'd remember to respond in time.

There was no email from Lexie.

But my phone had a text.

Hey, just wanted to say good morning.

Simon.

Butterflies took flight in my middle.

Good morning to you!

I kicked myself for sending that too soon. I hadn't written anything else for him to respond to.

Can I call you?

My pulse hammered at my throat.

Of course.

I answered my phone before the second ring. "Hello there."

"I could've kept texting," he said, "but I wanted to hear your voice."

A heat rose to my face. "Well, now you've caught me flat-footed."

He chuckled. "What are you up to this morning?"

Suddenly, I felt shy about my intentions . . . or, guilty? Or was it all more nuanced than that? I cleared my throat. "I'm . . . just trying to figure out my life."

"Heady stuff for a Sunday."

"Tell me about it."

We laughed.

"How's everything at home?" I asked.

"It's good . . . I like how you call this home."

I didn't say anything. My entire life, I'd referred to Gates Mills as home. I'd actually lived in New York longer than I'd lived in Ohio. But still . . . I never called the city home. "You know what they say: You can take the girl out of Gates Mills . . . but you can't take Gates Mills out of the girl."

He laughed. "That's a thing they say, is it?"

"Fairly certain I saw it on a bumper sticker in Times Square."

We talked for a while. He told me about how he was volunteering at a STEM camp for kids who didn't have access to strong STEM curricula during the school year. I told him about my work at the greenmarket. Our conversation was easy. We jumped from topic to topic like popcorn popping. Excitement underpinned our phone call. Heat.

Eventually, we said goodbye, and I sat, insides buzzing, smiling to myself.

I hit a key to wake up my laptop. The screen saver transfixed me: It was a close-up of a hydrangea in bloom, taken years ago in Gran's backyard. I lost myself in the cluster of blue petals, my thoughts circling back to Simon. I had to force myself to concentrate. It wasn't easy. He was an earworm. More like a soulworm.

I eventually did manage to focus and spent the rest of the morning researching and writing down names and contact numbers of places in the Hudson Valley. Maybe Gran was right when she told me this was an opportunity to reinvent myself. At the very least, I wanted to keep doing something I enjoyed. I wasn't afraid of hard work or long hours. I simply wanted to enjoy what I did. And so, I set to exploring what my future might look like. I even wrote a mission statement for myself.

My pulse quickened as I scanned the description of a "young farmers" internship, similar to the one near the Rabbits' farm. A working farm upstate offered room and board in exchange for offseason labor and lessons around the farm. The education learned from veteran farmhands and hard work sounded ideal.

Until I read this: "Applicants between the ages of 25 and 35 encouraged to apply."

I was too old to even be considered. But how was it that at forty-five, I was completely dismissed from the conversation? Deemed irrelevant and useless. My life wasn't over. I was aching to restart. But society's celebration of youth culture, of all things having to do with young people—who, by the way, probably barely had any real living under their belt—these were the precious souls who mattered. Everyone else should stay outside circles of opportunity and vitality because, obviously, they were close to dead. And we don't want to taint the vivacious young with the olds, the near dead.

I was spinning myself up, I felt it. But this was galling. I thought back to the Fourth of July, going home to Gran's. Gran—who was eighty-seven—and her dear friends helped me stand taller, actually breathe freer than I had in years. After she passed away, Faye and Mama P tended to me, with Faye steadying me enough to return to the city. Both were in their eighties. Then I thought about Pet, how she'd embraced me—literally—when I landed, floundering, at her farm stand, trying as best I could to put one foot in front of the other. Pet was in her seventies. These weren't women to be shunted aside in favor of a younger set with vibrant social media presences but not so much as an ounce of hard-earned wisdom. The women who were wholehearted and empathetic enough to share their life experience with me during the most difficult time in my life, who literally tossed me life preservers time and time again? I'd choose these septuagenarians and octogenarians any day of the week over some young woman whose response to literally everything was to say, *Yasssssssss, slay, queen, slay all day,* and then resume scrolling the feed on her phone.

I should never email when I'm pissed off.

But I did.

Then I sent my missive to the head of the farm internship program. I did not give a frog's fractional fart how it was received. Obviously, this wasn't the place for me, but they needed to know that their advertised ageism, one of the last socially acceptable forms of bias and discrimination, was Mach 5 lousy. Was it my job to tell them this? No. Did I do it anyway? Yup. Was the twentysomething reading my missive going to care one iota about the impassioned points I made? No.

I hit Send anyway.

That was that.

I continued researching, made some calls, and set up appointments.

My phone vibrated.

It was the Herpocalypse text string. The latest, from Bridgette, read:

How are we on the back end of July? How is that possible? Rest assured I've filed a missing persons report on summer. All I want to do is cocktail, dine, and catch up like normal people do—outside with a modicum of quiet and an elevated river view—before summer turns into fall and fall turns into winter. Next Thursday—yes, it'll be August then, so tick tock let's do this. 7 pm. Riverpark. Who's in?

Yeses from Julianne and Lannie came through quickly.

I bit my thumbnail, hesitated, then wrote,

I'd love to join you if you'll have me.

Who's this? Bridgette texted.

My heart sank.

Just kidding. About time.

In the days that followed, I did several Zoom interviews. They all seemed to go fine, but it was hard to judge if they went well enough to land anything. I hadn't left a single Zoom room feeling strongly about anything. Maybe it was the nature of interviewing remotely? The fact that I didn't have good lighting? Who was to say.

It wasn't the most auspicious of beginnings, but I reminded myself that few ever were. I'd keep at it.

Something would unfold. If I kept putting myself out there, I'd land something.

At least I hoped.

Time was ticking.

Before I knew it, it was Thursday.

Nerves kept me home too long, rethinking my outfit—black pants, black slingbacks, sleeveless black top. Black. The color of summer. I was both jumping out of my skin and reluctant to walk out the door. None of it made any sense. Finally, I hailed a cab. I'd waited entirely too long to take the subway or to walk, so now it would be a bigger expense. It was seven o'clock. I didn't have a lot of discretionary income for dinner. But this was one of those times that felt like it wasn't only worth it, but necessary.

The cab pulled up to the restaurant at 7:15 p.m. I put the fare on my credit card and headed inside. They'd already be there, making my late arrival even more of a spectacle.

And there they were, standing near the bar. My insides felt fluttery, like maybe I didn't have the wherewithal to see these old friends, to show up as who I was now, someone who I still wasn't quite clear on myself.

Julianne saw me first. She smiled warmly, didn't say anything to the others, rather, just held my eyes and nodded. Then she waved and beckoned me over.

She said something, which made Bridgette and Lannie look my way. Lannie scrunched her nose the way she did when something tickled her. Bridgette's smile seemed standoffish, like she was reserving judgment on whether to embrace me fully.

I walked toward them. My nerve endings pinged with fear and excitement. These were my women. Or they were at one time, anyway. A long time ago. Were they still? Did we mesh? Would I fit with them anymore? Or were the four women of the Herpocalypse no more?

"Hey." My voice was barely a whisper. I cleared my throat. "It's good to see you."

Julianne held her arms wide. "Oh, I've missed you!" Her hug was tight and long. She rubbed my back. "It's been too long . . . I'm so glad to see you. So glad!"

"Okay, okay, let the Southern lady in, please. Hi!" Lannie bear-hugged me next. "Where you been, girl?"

My throat closed. Every word I might've offered got stuck.

"It's okay . . . it's okay," she said. "You're here now and back. All is right."

Our embrace ended and I looked to Bridgette. Raised a hand like a stranger, which I immediately regretted. "Hi."

She shook her head. "I'd just about given up on you, you know."

This made me tear up. "Really?"

"No, come here, you." She pulled me into a massive embrace, whispered into my hair, "Don't you pull that shit again."

I nodded my head into hers.

Bridgette was still the prickliest, but she also still had that Cadbury egg filling. It might take a beat for her to warm up to me again. That was okay. I had time.

"Do you still like a good sauvignon blanc?" Julianne handed me a glass.

"I do." I was touched that she'd ordered me my favorite summer drink. "You remembered. Thank you."

"Of course we remembered," she said.

We.

I took a sip to settle myself. Then the hostess walked up to tell us our table was ready. It was a relief to catch my breath.

She led us outside to a spot with a view of the East River and the garden area. As we sat down, we marveled at how we were tucked away from the city's din. The waiter came by to explain the specials. We talked about the menu, what each of us was considering. All the menu talk helped me relax a bit. The waiter took our orders, scooped up the menus, and left us.

I was drinking my glass of wine quickly.

"It's wonderful to see you," Julianne said to me. "I can't tell you how happy I am you said yes to tonight." Her face was open and accepting. Julianne was Julianne.

"Thank you for inviting me." I swallowed. "It's really good to see you guys."

"Not seeing you hasn't been easy," Lannie said.

"It was like a wheel came off the car." Bridgette sounded hurt. "And you made it perfectly clear you didn't want to be contacted." Then imperious. Lannie and Julianne shot her a look. "What? She didn't! She was quite clear about that."

I finished my wine, mind racing with what to say.

"I figured you needed space." Julianne held understanding in her voice. "It's been a really weird time . . . just incredibly challenging."

"I thought you were mad at me." Lannie spoke softly, as if tiptoeing up to the admission.

I felt awful. "My gosh, why would you think that?"

Lannie sighed. "I don't know. I rewound every interaction in my head. I wondered if you were upset about something I said, a joke maybe. Honestly, I couldn't put a finger on anything. But . . . I've been in my own head too much. For a while, life felt . . . really insular."

I groaned. "I handled this so badly, and I'm sorry . . . truly, I am." I paused. "The truth is I was embarrassed at how badly things were going for me. I got laid off."

"Along with so many other people," Julianne said.

"Yeah, well, then all the freelance business I'd managed to drum up, that dried up, so I was . . . I guess, really lost, feeling scared, and alone."

As soon as the words left my mouth, a lightness took hold, like a heavy weight had slinked off my shoulders. I'd shed a shame. Such a simple path to some peace. How hard I'd fought this thing that seemed too monumental and beyond me: honesty.

Julianne reached over and squeezed my hand. "Never think you're alone again, okay?"

My chin quivered, but I kept my emotions in check. I nodded, smiled a small smile of thanks.

"We're not temporary." Lannie shrugged. "You're stuck with us."

"Yeah . . . so don't be a twit and disappear again," Bridgette blurted, which made us all laugh.

And suddenly the conversation flowed. I didn't feel jammed up. Bridgette sounded welcoming and cheery, poked fun at herself for being that proverbial one-percenter tart—her words—who was looking to buy real estate and capitalize on low prices. "Pretty sure it doesn't get worse than that!"

"Or . . . does that just make you a New Yorker?" Only Lannie's drawl could make that line sound so funny.

"I think you're practically a New Yorker too at this point, Lannie," Julianne said.

"Oh, no, I'm just a simple girl from Georgia."

"Right." Bridgette laughed. "Who started her own marketing firm that nets millions upon millions in profits every year catering to Fortune 500 companies."

Her smile was sly. "I keep tellin' y'all, I'm just a simple girl from Georgia."

Dinner was a feast. The food, seasonal and fresh, was simply prepared yet felt decadent. But the evening's overall feel had nothing to do with the cuisine. The meal, two hours long, felt like twenty minutes.

Afterwards, we strolled to First Avenue and hugged one another goodbye. Bridgette, Julianne, and Lannie got into separate cabs. I turned down their repeated offers to drop me off and waved as each one drove off.

More than anything, I wanted to walk home, savor the evening, replay our conversation, bask in the connective glow that lingered. It was warm, one of those sultry summer nights that hits just right. The city was still abuzz. Outdoor seating opened up restaurant revelry onto the sidewalks. Block after block, Manhattan felt cheery, hopeful.

I turned onto my street and felt like a different woman returning home. I'd raced out earlier feeling jangly, so certain I'd endure a meal mired in shame. As I unlocked my door, it occurred to me: The only thing that I felt foolish about was keeping my dearest friends at arm's length for so long.

The following morning, Lannie texted,

We have some openings you'd be perfect for. Any interest?

My breath caught. She was offering me a lifeline. A way to get back on track. And not just any track, a proper track with a salary and benefits, one that would allow me to stay in my apartment, pay my bills, and even, hopefully, save money. Be a proper person. What Lannie held was nothing short of a reentry into adulthood.

I broke out in a sweat at the prospect. My reply took no thought at all.

YES.

Chapter 15

The next day, I received another letter from Gran.

Dearest Lexie and Belle,

> For your next recipe, I want you to make the treats we'd make every Christmas, the ones resembling tiny pies. You'd both take turns showering these with powdered sugar. You got so excited the way it would snow in the kitchen, your little footprints all over the floor because more powdered sugar ended up there than dusted on the treats.
>
> I love you both.
>
> Gran

The photo she'd sent was of Lexie and me bundled in snowsuits in the backyard of our old house, our faces pink with cold. I stared at our young skin, Lexie's chubby cheeks. I remembered that day because Gran constantly regaled us with the story, how special it was. It was the first big snow of the year—a bona fide blizzard—so there was no preschool for me. The snowflakes were oversized and dramatic, like someone had plucked feathers off a giant white boa and scattered them from the heavens.

When we woke up, Lexie and I scrambled downstairs, yelling about the snow. Mom had leaned the metal saucer sled against the kitchen door, like an invitation. She put our snowsuits on over our pajamas.

Outside, on the top of the small hill in the back, Mom made sure our scarves were tucked in, that our jackets were zipped up all the way. Gran was waiting at the bottom of the hill to catch us.

"Now, Belle, you have to hold on to Lexie, okay?" Mom plopped my sister in front of me on the saucer. Lexie leaned back into me like I was a puffy chair. "Bellie, did you hear me?"

"Yeah, I will." I wrapped my arms around Lexie.

Mom rested her hands on my shoulders. "Ready?"

"Go! Go!" Lexie yelled, her tiny body tense with excitement.

Mom laughed and gave us a gentle nudge down the hill. Snowflakes hit us in the face like icy darts. The wind wormed its way beneath our hoods, muffling Mom's encouraging hoots from atop the hill. We giggled as the saucer, cold and slippery beneath us, started to spin as we slid down the hill. I held on to Lexie tighter as we picked up speed, faster and faster, until we came to a stop at the bottom and toppled over in a fit of laughter at Gran's feet.

Lexie angled her face up toward mine. Fat snowflakes were caught in her thick brown eyelashes—like she'd put on snow makeup for the occasion. Her cheeks were chapped from the cold air, and her smile was full of joy as she said, "You didn't let go."

The memory was so tender. How had I forgotten so much about us?

But of course, I hadn't . . . I hadn't at all.

Gran was simply reminding me.

The vibration of my phone pulled me from my thoughts. I looked at the screen. Lexie was calling, something she hadn't done since . . . I couldn't remember the last time she'd called. It wasn't too long ago that I would've avoided picking up, but now, a current of happy flowed through me. "Hey there!"

"Hi, look . . ." She sighed. "I just . . . I can't do this anymore. I don't have the bandwidth."

"You can't do what?"

"This cooking thing. I . . . I don't have time to devote to this anymore, okay? Between my job, my kids, and every other thing that's my responsibility, I have nothing else to give. Literally not a spare second. Not to think. Not to do. So, look, I've done what I can. I feel like I've held up my end of the bargain, and I'm tapping out."

"A bargain? Seriously?" A heat engulfed my entire head, set me aflame. "My God, this entire time I thought we were doing something thoughtful together to honor Gran, reading her cookbook as she asked us—the one thing she ever asked of us, mind you!—and here you were thinking that this was a bargain you had to grind out some duty for?"

"That's right, take it to the most dramatic place possible," she said. "Naturally."

"You're . . ." A helpless frustration crept in. No matter how much I wanted Lexie and me to be bonded again, it was never going to happen. "God, cold! And it's one more bullshit excuse—who doesn't have time to make a recipe? But I shouldn't be surprised. You were the one who abandoned Gran years ago. You were the one who stopped visiting, who stopped calling her—"

"I called!"

"Oh, please, you might've called occasionally, but you mailed in those conversations—like you were crossing something off an annoying to-do list." My chest tightened thinking back to that time Gran left a message for Lexie, how downcast I caught her looking after. "You were completely checked out. But what's even worse is that you thought she wouldn't notice how disconnected you were. Like just because she was old, she wouldn't pick up on the fact that you'd drifted from her life. But guess what? She did know! How do you think that made her feel? After everything she did for us? After all the love she'd wrapped us in our entire lives?" I fought to steady my voice. "So, yeah, this, what you're doing now, being your usual callous self. Stands to reason. You've been self-centered and icy for years. Years!"

Lexie hung up.

I threw my phone on the couch. Paced the apartment.

Every word of that needed to be said.

How many times had she behaved hurtfully without any check on her actions? Without anyone daring to call her out? I'd had it. I was done with her. Her frostiness, her painful indifference to me, to Gran, to everything we all were to one another. Done. I'd tried so hard to find a way back to her, but we were two different people who obviously could no longer walk side by side. Or, more to the point, where Lexie was concerned, *didn't want to*. Unfortunate, but there it was.

Everything smashed together—it was too compressed, too hard to tease out what was important. Moments ago, I'd been thinking about Lexie and me spinning on a saucer down a snowy hill, delighted. I'd held on to her, hadn't let go. And it hit me right then: Despite my anger at her treatment of Gran, of her dissecting us from her life, over the years I'd still been holding on in some regard. Backstopping all my outrage was hurt.

And now here we were, in this angry, unfixable place.

My fury burned hot for three days.

But then I had to stop stewing because I had an interview for a mid-level copywriter position in a division of Lannie's company—not an unreasonable job for me, but also something I probably wouldn't have been considered for given my thin resume of late. I was grateful to Lannie for placing her thumb on the scale in my favor.

I needed to tend to my life. Soon Reva would be back from Europe, and I had to get my act together. I needed a steady income. A plan.

The morning was bright. The sky, an optimistic blue. I stood in front of the office building where Lannie's company was headquartered and inhaled to steady myself before entering the lobby. I hadn't been to an office since before the pandemic, but walking through revolving doors, giving my name in the lobby, felt familiar—also, strange, like something my body was doing but the rest of me wasn't on board with.

I took the elevator to the twentieth floor and a woman at least ten years younger than me brought me back to an office. I sat down, nervous with anticipation. But then that same young woman sat on the other side of the desk. She wasn't simply ferrying me from one part of the office to another—she would be my boss if I got the job. My innards sagged as I wondered if I was old enough to be her mother. But I kept talking, answering her questions. I stayed lively and forced every ounce of enthusiasm and youth I had into my voice.

And I'm glad I did because I left not just feeling like I'd nailed it but knowing I had. I walked home—maybe I floated—with a sense of standing on the precipice of something meaningful.

A few days later, I checked my email, scrolled through the usual marketing nonsense.

There.

My fingers pulled up from the trackpad. I froze—didn't click on the email. Everything was still possible right now at this moment. Unknowing allowed for hope.

I blew out a big breath. Tapped the email to open it.

My eyes grew wide as I read.

Oh my gosh.

Then I saw the second email. And a third. My pulse jacked higher as I realized the bigger picture of what was falling into place, exactly what these emails would allow to unfold. Choice.

It was all hard to believe. I'd been in career limbo for so long that this, a position with direction and security, made me giddy. I had some time before my start date, which was good. I wanted to be able to give Pet ample notice. The last thing I wanted to do was leave her in the lurch. Thinking of Pet plucked a tender chord. It had felt like years since I'd inquired about the Rabbits' "Help Wanted" sign.

I sat with the memory, fondly. Then reread the emails. My insides fluttered all over again. First: I had to respond. Second: Get in touch with the management company about my lease renewal. Third: Call

Lannie. I needed to have a conversation with her to express my heartfelt gratitude—also, to explain.

My walk to the greenmarket on Saturday was different than any other. I went over and over what I would say to Pet, how to explain what I'd been offered, and how it meant that I only had a short amount of time left to work at the greenmarket. None of the words sounded right. I tripped over them in my head as a cloudless blue sky cracked me open with its beauty.

I rounded the corner, saw the Little Rabbit Farm tent, and willed my feet to keep walking toward it.

As soon as Pet saw my approach, she waved, then turned back to stacking kale. Her smile gutted me, made me question what I was about to do. My chest cinched in a familiar way, and I stopped.

No, this was right. I forced myself to breathe in long steady breaths. Even though it hurt, it was still right.

"Good morning!" Pet trilled when I neared. She turned around. "Girls, here she is!"

Flopsy and Mopsy emerged from under one of the tables, curious, then ran full force at me as I entered the stand. I bent down so they could climb onto my lap and lick my face. "Oh, thank you for kisses . . . yes, thank you for kisses!"

"All right, all right, you two, let Belle up." Pet hoisted them off me and set them on the ground. "They've really fallen for you!"

"It's mutual." I stood there like it was my first time at the farm stand. I felt like an interloper, like someone who didn't have a right to be there anymore. A jangly fragility took hold. There was no way this conversation could wait until the end of the day. "Could we talk for a minute? I have . . . something to tell you."

Pet saw my face, really took it in, and her eyes softened. "C'mon. Let's sit down."

We sat in the chairs where we usually sat when taking a break. It felt so odd sitting at this point in the morning. Everything in me stiffened.

Pet put her hand on my arm. "Tell me."

I inhaled. Then told her everything. How I'd been trying to figure out my life—literally, my entire life—the things I'd researched, the interviews I'd had, and, finally, what I'd been offered.

"I . . ." There was no stopping me from getting emotional. "I cannot thank you enough for taking a chance on me, and for letting me come and help you at a time . . . my gosh, when I was just barely hanging on." I wiped my cheeks. "I mean it . . . You helped me walk back into my life."

"Oh, my dear." She took my hand and held it. "You have been a ray of sunshine, even when you didn't feel like you were." Compassionate understanding rolled off her, and I basked in the comfort. "I knew we were only going to have you a short while, which is why I treasured it." She squeezed my hand. "But don't you for one minute think this is goodbye. We're not doing a goodbye."

We talked some more. Pet shared some really good advice, which I appreciated.

"What's going on over here?" Peter gave a nod hello.

"Oh, I was just telling Belle that I'm keeping her." Pet squeezed my hand one more time, then got up out of the chair.

"You can't keep her, Mama," Peter said. "We've discussed this."

"I'm keeping her!"

I stood and reached for the box of cherry tomatoes that Peter was holding.

He handed it over. "You're always crying."

His poking fun made me laugh. "I know!"

"Hang on." Peter touched my waist so I didn't move. "Jeez." He locked eyes with me. The moment swallowed every sip of air.

He patted his pockets and pulled out a tissue. Slowly, as if not to startle a skittish animal, he dabbed my cheeks. I felt the barest brush of cotton against my skin. A calm overcame me. A warmth. My eyes involuntarily closed as I inhaled long and deep, air suddenly abundant. When I opened them, he murmured, "Better."

Peter tucked the tissue in his pocket and walked back to the truck.

I made my way to the leftmost table, set down the box, and leaned over it to catch my breath.

Focus. I arranged the tiny cardboard containers just so. Cherry tomatoes toppled left, right. Every which way a tomato could roll, it rolled. This simple task felt like herding cats. I fiddled, stacked and restacked, made ruby red pyramids with the delicate fruit. When done, I stood, gripping the empty box.

The following week, I was surprised to find a letter from Gran in my mailbox. It seemed too soon.

I'd just gotten her letter telling us to make tassies together. I hadn't gotten a chance to make them yet, which I'd be doing on my own. And now, another letter. I wondered why all the way up to my apartment.

> Dearest Belle and Lexie,
> This is the final letter you'll be receiving from me. The rest of the recipes are yours to make together. I trust that you will.
>
> I have one last request of you both: I'd like you to get in touch with my sister, Grace, and find time to see her. I know my mentioning her is a surprise. This is important. Please do as I ask.
>
> While you won't receive any more letters from me, know that I'll always be with you. I love you both dearly and have faith that this is not goodbye forever . . . just for now. For we will all be together again.
>
> Until then, love one another.
>
> Gran

I gripped the letter. Looked in the envelope, but it was empty. There wasn't a photo.

That was it?

No no no no.

Gran needed to keep speaking to me. I needed this tether on a visceral level.

Make the recipes together? Lexie and I should make them together? There was no more together.

The room wobbled. I slumped on the couch. This connection with Gran I'd been gifted through these letters, it was necessary the same way air was. My need was innate. I leaned back and closed my eyes, pulse clobbering at my temples.

With no idea who'd sent these letters, I'd allowed myself to be carried along in ignorance. Why would I question such a thing? And they did carry me . . . I didn't know how, but they underpinned whatever inkling of forward momentum I had managed to muster since returning to the city. Gran had kept mailing me a critical throughline for my life. Or whoever had mailed these letters. Again, I didn't care. I just wanted more. I wanted to keep opening my mailbox and pulling out envelopes with her precise cursive handwriting, with her words, for the rest of my life. For all my remaining days, I needed this.

I was just getting my footing, and barely just. I couldn't do this without her.

Suddenly, it was the morning I'd found her. It was the excruciating silence after her funeral. It was days spent aimlessly shuffling through her house. It was me here in the city unmoored. Without her, I was utterly alone.

The pain pierced as sharply as it had five months ago. Like no time had passed. Like not a single part of me had healed.

I cried myself out. The numbness set in. I stared at the blank wall.

Alone.

Ever so slightly, the blankness shifted.

Alone?

I got up, legs weak, and riffled through a basket of scrap paper I'd scribbled things on until I found it. I wiped my face and blew my nose. Forced down a glass of water. Then made the call.

She answered on the fourth ring.

"Hello, Grace, it's Belle—" I was about to explain who I was when she cut me off.

"Belle, how nice of you to call. How are you?"

"I'm . . . okay." I couldn't remember the last time I had told anyone I was good or well or anything that indicated I was close to okay. It had been so long. And honestly, was I? No. But saying *I'm tender and feeling really fragile because I've been getting letters from my gran for the past four months and I just got the last one and I feel like I'm trying to get my footing in quicksand, oh, and also, my sister and I had a massive fight that feels like a rift that will never be mended* is a lot to dump on a person. Instead, I glossed over myself and asked how she was.

"I'm old," she deadpanned. "Listen, there's something I need to tell you."

I gave her room to speak.

"Your grandmother, God rest her soul, entrusted me with something precious. Something she wanted me to give to you. I'd come give it to you myself, but I'm too old to travel to that big city where you live."

"Oh . . . I see." I waited for her to say something else.

She didn't.

"Can it be mailed?"

"No," she said. "Can you come here to the farm? And . . . oh, I'll be honest with you: I'd love to have a bit of help too. There's some things here that need doin', and . . . well, I'm just not as spry as I used to be. Maybe you could come for a weekend and help an old lady out?"

I thought about the obligations I had to Pet and the farm stand, as well as this new chapter I was embarking upon. But this was Gran's sister, and if she had something that Gran intended for me, I needed to go. I chewed my cheek.

Pet would understand. Maybe I could go before my new job started.

"Yes, I'll come."

"Good! When? Maybe next weekend?"

Her bluntness caught me flat-footed. That was the weekend before Labor Day weekend. Pet would understand. I hoped, anyway. "Sure, I think that'll work."

"Oh, that would be good! You got a pen?"

I wrote down all the information she rattled off: her address and the nearest airport. We spoke a little more before hanging up. It was only then that I thought of how exorbitant plane fare would be on short notice, how renting a car was so expensive. I rubbed my eyes. There was no getting around this. Gran's sister had something for me, and she also needed help. Gran would want me to go. This was what a credit card was for.

The next day, I arrived at the farm stand to no one. The truck was there. But Pet wasn't, Harold wasn't. I tossed my cross-body bag on one of the chairs and jogged over to the truck.

Peter was inside, moving boxes so they'd be easy to reach.

"Hey," I said. "What's going on?"

He held up both hands to stop my panic. "My mom is fine, everyone is fine. My parents had lunch plans with neighbors that have been on the calendar forever. That's why they're not here."

Every tensed muscle relaxed. "Okay. Oh my goodness, my heart!" I grabbed a box and walked over to one of the tables.

Peter followed with a box of his own. "Sorry to hear you're leaving us."

"I know . . . I'm torn up about it."

"Don't be. This was just a summer gig."

I looked at him. "This was so much more than that to me."

His smile reached his eyes. He pushed his floppy hair off his forehead and focused on the onions tumbling out of the box into a plastic container on the stand. "You definitely brightened things up around this stand of ours."

I glanced at him. Was he blushing? It was hard to tell. I fussed with arranging eggplant into a neat pile. "I'd love to stay in touch." I kept looking at the deep purple vegetables, as if they held the meaning of life. Now I was brushing invisible dirt off them to avoid what I'd put out there.

"Oh, please."

My insides sank at his response. Us staying in touch was absurd. I should've known.

"Belle!"

I looked at him.

"We're in a knitting circle! We're bonded for life." Amusement danced behind his eyes. He ran a hand through his hair, grabbed my box, and carried it to the truck.

Heat rushed to my face. I looked down at the eggplant and grinned.

I headed to the truck, where he handed me another box and carried two himself. We unloaded the boxes next to one another.

"So, I have something that I need to tend to that will mean my not being here for a few days."

"Typical," he said. "Give notice and ask for time off."

When I didn't say anything, he chuckled. "C'mon, I'm kidding! Don't worry about it."

"Thanks."

"Is it something good you're tending to, or . . . no?"

"I don't know." I thought about where to begin. "I talked to my great-aunt last night—this is my grandmother's sister who she was estranged from. She needs my help on her farm." I rested my hands on the edges of the box, rubbed a thumb across the waterworn side. "But . . ."

The sentence dangled unfinished as I tried to untangle the emotions that came along with Grace's request.

"But what?"

"I don't even know where to begin." I headed to the truck for another box, returned to the other end of the table to unpack basil.

"I guess it's complicated, like . . . the kind of complicated that spans generations." I explained Gran and Grace's estrangement that no one knew the reason behind, and how I felt compelled to help this woman I had only met five months ago. "Maybe because she's a tether to my grandmother, however imperfect it might be . . . it's something."

My hands were wet from the basil, and it was so hot. I rubbed the water on my arms to cool off. A woman walked past wheeling a grocery trolley to the compost bins.

"You should definitely go to your great-aunt's."

I looked at him stacking green onions. He'd heard more than I said. He had a way of doing that, I realized.

"You think?"

"I do." Peter gathered the empty boxes and walked them back to the truck. He strode back carrying two more. "There's a reason you feel drawn to going." He shrugged. "Sometimes you can't put your finger on the why of something, but that doesn't make it any less important to follow through on. Maybe you won't know until you're there. Here."

I took the box he handed me. Green peppers with taut, glossy skin. I started nestling them together in a pyramid next to the eggplant.

"Don't worry about the stand," he continued. "And if you are, think of it this way: It's the end of summer—most of the city is out of town. I can handle it. Go for as long as you need."

"It'll just be for a few days."

"No problem," he said. "I got you."

Savory

Part 5

A circle, of sorts.

Chapter 16

A footbridge stretched across a rocky creek, the only way to reach Grace's farm. Weatherworn boards groaned beneath my weight. The suspension cables gently swayed. I stepped off on the other side, and a Southern Ohio breeze stirred up a pungent barnyard scent. With a weekend bag hitched over my shoulder, I followed a tractor path to a gray barn. Several cows chewed their cud in the late afternoon sun.

I rested my foot on the split rail fence. A brown cow meandered over.

"Hey there, pretty girl." I reached in to let her smell my hand. She snorted warm puffs of air. The cow chewed slowly while watching me with big brown eyes. "Are you having a little snack?"

"You gonna stand around talking to cows all day?" Grace smiled as she loped toward me in boots and overalls.

I chuckled, waved hello.

"Good to see you." She stretched her arms wide and pulled me into a hug. She was in her eighties but felt as solid as someone two decades younger. She patted my back. "I'm grateful you could come."

"It's nice to be here."

"C'mon up to the house," she said. "I have dinner waiting for us. We eat early here because we get up early."

We walked past a sliver of rolling field and up a gentle hill to a white two-story farmhouse that was weatherworn but proud. My step slowed as I took in the house where Gran had grown up: the strong roofline, an oversized porch that wrapped around the front. Here was the keeper of Gran's childhood.

"Your home is beautiful," I murmured.

"Been here my whole life. Let's go in through the kitchen." She opened the screen door for us. "Your grandmother and I were both born here."

She kicked off her shoes and left them outside. I followed her lead. Aromas of dinner enveloped me as soon as I walked in: caramelized onions, browned meat, and something ethereally bready. I inhaled deeply.

Grace led me through the dining room and up a staircase to the second floor, which had three bedrooms. The room she showed me to was simply decorated: a full-size bed neatly made with a patchwork quilt, a small nightstand holding a porcelain lamp, and a heavy wooden dresser with a crocheted doily stretched across the top.

"Better open this so you don't swelter tonight." Grace parted the lace curtains and shoved the window open. "There." She pointed at the bed. "You'll be plenty comfortable sleeping, lots of feathers in there."

"I can tell—it looks wonderful. Thank you."

"Aw, dearie, thank *you* for coming. C'mon, let's have something to eat."

At the kitchen table, Grace served a hearty dinner of meat loaf, mashed potatoes, sautéed string beans, and buttermilk biscuits. While we ate, she told me how the snow formed dramatic drifts alongside the barn in the winter, how the creek flooded in the spring, and how the summer brought a bumper crop of berries. When my plate was clean, I leaned back, falling into the pleasant anecdotes of farm life that connected a person to the land.

We talked about the drive in from the airport over dinner, about the weather that had passed through, safe topics that didn't delve deep. So much lurked beneath the surface.

We finished dinner, cleared the table, and Grace brewed a pot of coffee on the stovetop, an old glass percolator just like Gran used. Seeing that got me in a tender place.

Grace reset the table with cups and saucers.

There was a knock at the door.

"Looks like we're all here now." She turned the burner off and opened the door.

Lexie stepped over the threshold.

My insides seized.

Cheer drained from my sister's face when she saw me.

She stood, stunned, in the doorway. The doorjamb's chipped yellow paint revealed a sallow dinginess. It framed Lexie in blinding-white cropped jeans, a billowy navy blouse, and open-toed sandals. Her toenails were painted a plummy burgundy.

Despite her put-together outfit, Lexie looked tired, not like the monster woman who stalked my thoughts.

Her gaze skittered across the dimly lit kitchen. "What's going on?"

"Why don't you come in and sit down?" Grace let the screen door go. The hinges whined as it slapped shut.

Lexie stayed just inside the doorway, clutching her Louis Vuitton duffel.

I wouldn't have minded if she'd turned heel, stormed right out, walked over the rickety footbridge, down the gravel road, and kept going. This felt like an ambush.

"Come on!" Grace waved Lexie away from the door. "Shoes off first."

"What?"

"Your shoes." Grace pointed at Lexie's sandals. "This is a farm. No shoes ever come in the house. Dirt and muck stay outside."

Mindlessly, Lexie slid her feet out of her shoes.

"You can put those outside."

She looked at Grace. "Are you serious?"

"Do I look serious?" Grace shot back. "Shoes stay outside."

"These are custom-made Italian leather slip-ons from Sorrento." She dropped her bag to emphasize this point with both hands. "They are kept in satin slipcovers, not on a doorstep."

Grace leaned one hip against the sink, wiped her hands on the threadbare apron tied around her waist. She smiled slowly. "You got special booty covers . . . for shoes?"

Lexie's face reddened.

"Well, you feel free to pamper those babies as you see fit." Grace got another cup and saucer down from the cupboard. "Now, how 'bout you come sit down at the table with us? I just brewed a pot of coffee."

Not waiting for Lex, Grace took the coffee off the stove, ambled over to the table, and sat across from me. "Take cream and sugar?"

She set to pouring three cups of coffee. I added cream to mine. Grace added cream and two teaspoons of sugar to hers. "I like a sweet cup," she said to me with a grin.

Lexie stayed by the door, watching. I could sense she was fighting to make a point, take a stand against being here, which I got. I didn't want to be with her any more than she wanted to be with me.

But Grace's carrying on as if everything were normal had this weird effect that circumvented any bluster or defiance from either one of us. So, I sipped my coffee. Eventually, Lexie set her sandals outside and padded over to the table.

Grace held out the porcelain creamer to Lexie.

"Black is fine." Lexie perched on the edge of the wooden chair, stiff, on guard.

"Relax," I murmured. "It's just coffee."

The muscle on Lexie's cheekbone tensed. I knew she was clenching her teeth. She inhaled, slid back into her seat, and turned on Grace. "Want to explain yourself?"

Grace's cup rattled softly when she set it on the saucer. "Explain what?"

"You said my grandmother entrusted you with something precious to give me," she said.

I looked at Grace. Gran had left something for both of us? Something inside me sagged. Here I'd thought I was special, remembered in a way that Lexie hadn't been. And right then, despite how I felt about Lex, a wave of shame washed over me.

Grace's face was placid. "That I do." She folded her hands across her belly. "That I do."

Lexie shook her head in irritation. "Well?"

"You were both kind enough to help an old woman out, thank you," Grace said. "I'll give you what your grandmother asked of me at the end of the weekend."

"What's to stop me from leaving now?" Lexie shot back.

Grace looked at her squarely. "Not a thing. Except your word. Surely that counts for something." She paused. "But if it doesn't, you can take the keys to the truck and drive yourself home for all I care."

Grace drank back the last of her coffee.

"Alexis, you'll stay in the bedroom next to Belle." Grace put both hands on the kitchen table to steady herself as she stood up. "Belle, show your sister around. It's late for me." She walked around the table. "We get up early around here. That bit about you helping on the farm? That part was true. Good night."

Grace's slippers made soft thwacking noises as she shuffled out.

Discomfort flip-flopped in my chest as the kitchen's silence engulfed us. A headache ground its way closer.

"It's been a really long day." Lexie pinched the bridge of her nose and closed her eyes. "Can you just show me where I'll be sleeping?"

I'd expected venom, loud and splashy, counted on words so sharp they'd wound. Instead, they came out like a plea.

She got up from the table and retrieved her bag from the door, then stood in the middle of the kitchen, waiting. She left her precious sandals outside.

"This way." I led her upstairs. "It's the middle door on the right."

She walked right past me. "And the bathroom?"

"Last door on the right."

Lexie walked into her bedroom and shut the door without uttering another word.

I walked back down to the kitchen feeling a fraction of myself and stood wondering why I'd come back in here. This wasn't my house. And yet, I felt a vague responsibility to leave the kitchen tidy. Maybe it was simply wanting to be a good guest. But it felt like something deeper.

I gathered the coffee cups, spoons, and creamer from the table. I stoppered the sink, made warm soapy dishwater, and carefully set each dish into the suds. The water soothed my hands, and warmth radiated up my arms to my center. Taking care to wash everything helped settle me. My bare feet felt the worn grooves in the hardwood floor where Gran had likely stood when she was young, looking out this same window into the inky night. Two small sconces with faded plaid shades filtered the light softly over the sink. I wondered what Gran and Grace had washed away within themselves while doing the dishes, perhaps side by side. The power of a gentle, monotonous task that improved the appearance of something was surprising. By the time I'd rinsed the suds from the last teacup and set it on the drying rack, my breathing had calmed. My chest had stopped flip-flopping. And my legs felt sturdier.

It didn't solve anything. Lexie was ensconced in her room, angry and alone. I didn't want to deal with her. Some things couldn't be undone or repaired. I wiped down the kitchen table, folded the dish towel, and draped it over the edge of the sink. At the doorway, I turned back, tried so hard to summon some grand feeling of generational connectedness, of life-altering import with Lexie and me being here in the house where Gran and Grace had grown up together. But the tsunami of emotion that I cast around for . . . it just wasn't to be found.

I took one last look around the kitchen. I'd help Grace with what she wanted and would be civil to Lexie despite my anger and the years of hurt. I could do that. I would keep the peace. But that was all. Some things you couldn't come back from. Sometimes it was impossible to rewind the clock. No matter how much I'd wanted us to reconnect at one point, my sister and I were strangers to one another. Finally, I'd accepted that.

I flicked off the kitchen light and went to bed.

Banging. Metal clanging. Scraping against grates? More banging.

I peeled my eyes open. The recollection of where I was, and who else was here, flooded back. A heaviness took root in my chest.

I rolled over. Just five more minutes. Sleep hadn't come easily last night. The room was hot, and I tossed and turned, but it was the ruminating that wouldn't let me fall asleep. I probably drifted off around three thirty in the morning. Just five more minutes.

The door rattled with a sharp knocking. Then it opened.

"Breakfast is ready," Grace said. "Time to get up."

She closed the door. I heard her footsteps to Lexie's room. Same knocking, opening, and admonishment to get out of bed.

I stared at the ceiling. The day felt like it was going to be a lot. More than I had to give.

But I was here to help. I had promised myself I would. Really, by coming here, I'd promised Gran.

I rubbed my eyes and got out of bed. Ambled to the bathroom, then back to my room to change. When I walked into the kitchen, Grace was nestling sausage links next to fluffy mounds of scrambled eggs on three plates. A pitcher of juice and the coffeepot flanked a basket with slices of buttered toast. My stomach rumbled.

"Good morning," Grace said. "Have a seat, dig in, we've got a big day ahead of us."

"Thank you for this beautiful breakfast." I smoothed a napkin in my lap and poured some coffee. "Can I pour you a cup?"

"Please." Grace set the skillet on the stove, then joined me at the table.

Lexie padded in wearing khaki shorts and a pink sleeveless top. Her hair was pulled into a messy bun that looked chic. She had makeup on. I hadn't even washed my face. "Good morning."

"Mornin'." Grace smiled as she slid the coffee closer so Lex could reach it. "How'd you sleep?"

"Good, thanks." Lexie stared intently at the cup she was pouring herself. Didn't so much as glance my way. She took a sip, then became transfixed with her plate. "These eggs are so yellow."

"That's because they're farm eggs," Grace said. "Hens run free here and only eat things they're meant to." She chewed a moment, swallowed, then waved her fork to underscore her point. "None of that factory farm garbage. Only good eggs here."

Lexie ate a small forkful. "Delicious." She sat back and drank her coffee.

The three of us ate in silence. Really, only Grace and I ate. Lexie sipped her coffee.

"You better put more in your belly than that sorry forkful of eggs," Grace said to Lex. "You need fuel for your day. Trust me on this."

"I don't normally eat breakfast." Lexie looked wearily at her plate. "Never any time."

She said it almost to herself, then picked up her fork and ate.

Grace watched her for a bit. "You do your body a favor by eating a good breakfast."

I braced for Lexie to spit something back.

Instead, she smiled softly and took a piece of toast. "This is a treat . . . thank you."

Grace nodded, then looked down at her plate and finished eating. She wiped her mouth and scooted her chair back from the table. "Well, before we get started, we're going to need to get you some proper farmin' clothes."

Lexie's brows knit together. "What do you mean?"

Grace got up. "What I mean is, you're going to be scratched like an angry cat got to ya dressed like that. And burned by the sun. Hang on."

She strode out of the kitchen.

Lexie kept her eyes down as she forked up the last of her eggs, then cut a sausage link into small pieces as if a child were eating it. She proceeded to eat each piece one at a time. All the while focusing her gaze anywhere but on me.

"Are you literally not even going to look at me?" I blurted.

"Why?" She turned to me. "Do we have anything to say to one another? We don't. So . . . why?"

"Okay, this should do you nicely." Grace strode back in with an armful of clothes. "These will keep your legs covered." She handed Lexie a pair of faded denim overalls, shapeless and worn. "And here's a good shirt. It's long sleeved, but not heavy. You need sleeves." She held out a white long-underwear shirt with frayed cuffs and a stretched-out neckline. "And these, in case you don't have long socks, because you'll need to wear boots. There's a pair outside that should be your size."

Lexie blanched.

I grinned, leaned back in my chair, and ate another piece of toast. This was better than watching TV.

Grace turned to me. "You'll need something too. Wait here."

Lexie smirked.

A moment later Grace came back holding more clothes. She handed me the pile. "There we go."

"Anyone home?" An older man opened the kitchen door and leaned over the threshold, careful to keep his feet outside. He removed his trucker hat to reveal closely cut salt-and-pepper hair—mostly salt—and a ruddy face like he spent his life working outside. "G'mornin', Grace. We're getting ready out here."

"Mornin', Bo," she said over her shoulder as she washed her hands. "Have you eaten?"

"Yes, ma'am. These the girls?"

"Sure are. Meet my grandnieces, Belle and Alexis."

"Pleasure, ladies." He gave a polite nod, then said to Grace, "We're going to need a little more time before we can get started."

"That's just fine." She wiped her hands on a dish towel. "I have something for them to do first."

Bo put his hat back on, tipped the brim, and walked out.

"So, you *do* have a crew to help you with all this," Lexie said.

A smile crept over Grace's face. "Of course I have a crew. You know how big this farm is?"

Lexie smirked and walked out with the armful of clothes.

"You better change too," Grace said to me.

It was like she knew I didn't want to follow Lexie too closely. I went to change, and when I got back down to the kitchen, Grace had already cleared the table. Lexie came in a moment later.

"You look like proper farmers now," Grace said. "Let's go."

We followed her outside, wiggled our feet into boots after shaking them to make sure no critters had crawled in overnight. The morning was already heavy with humidity.

"You have to get work done early in the summer because, come midday, the heat will cook ya. Weather can be tricky this time of year, but today, we got heat."

She stopped at a small outbuilding that looked like a shanty, went inside, and came out carrying two big pallets filled with small plastic baskets. "You two take these."

Lexie and I each took one, and the three of us hiked up a hill to a sunny clearing that was overgrown with a massive bramble of blackberry bushes.

"Oh, wow." I stared at the dense tangle of branches and berry clusters poking through the leaves. They were freakishly tall, formidable, and deserving of respect, like we were visiting a family of berry giants who lived on the hill. The bushes loomed over us, their rounded shoulders questioning the intrusion. "Is this a normal size for these bushes?"

Grace smiled. "These are special." She walked closer, inspected a branch, and picked a berry that was an inch long, its skin taut and glossy. "Yes, these are ready." She bit into the berry. "Good, good, good."

My breath caught. Grace hadn't just uttered the words Gran always used to say. She sounded just like her. The moment folded in on itself, bent time. It all tripped me up, standing on this ground that Gran used to stand on beside her sister, who shared Gran's cadence, her word choice, her very DNA. Origins held power. Grace craned her neck to look at different parts of the bramble, silently losing herself in berry inspection. And just like that, it felt strange being here with her. There were origins, yes, but there were secrets as well.

Grace showed us the other half of the berry. "See that color? How deep it is? These are ready to be picked. Okay, I'm gonna leave you to this while Bo gets things ready."

"What do you mean?" Lexie said as Grace started down the hill. "Where do we start?"

"You're smart," Grace called without looking back. "You'll figure it out." She raised her arm in a casual wave.

We watched her stride down the hill. She'd left us alone.

Lexie and I moved to opposite ends of the bramble and started picking. Before I knew it, thinking switched off, and I lost myself to the task at hand. Over and over, I plucked berries off thorny branches and nestled them in a basket.

I ate one—couldn't help it. Tangy juiciness flooded my mouth, overwhelmed my taste buds. I looked around, started to say something, then remembered . . . everything.

So, I said nothing to Lex, just kept picking. The branches were heavy with fruit. It didn't take long before I'd filled a basket and gotten another one. Soon that one was filled. The sun was beating down. Time passed. I filled basket after basket. The back of my neck was damp with sweat. The bramble had a subtle sweet scent to it—berries being baked ever so gently by Mother Nature. I eased my way through the thicket to get another basket.

Lexie was standing over the ones I'd already done, hands on her hips. "You should fill those all the way to the top."

I shook my head and headed back into the bramble with an empty container.

"You're wasting a ton of space."

I closed my eyes and bit my cheek. The basket's grid imprinted itself in my grip. The sun blazed down, cooking all of me.

"I'm just saying—" Lexie started.

"Oh my lord." I stomped out of the bramble. "You're seriously critiquing how I'm filling a berry basket? Of course you are. Everything in your world is perfect and this"—I tossed an empty basket on the ground—"this isn't perfect."

"Girls!" Grace called from the barn, waving us toward her. "Come here!"

I waved back and glanced at Lexie.

Her face was placid. "Everything isn't always what it seems."

She turned and headed down the hill.

I stood a moment watching her, then followed a few steps behind.

Grace waved us over. Bo and his crew had set up a massive plank that went from an opening at the top of the barn to the ground.

"What's that?" I pointed at the metal contraption.

"That's a conveyor to get the hay bales to the loft so we can store them," Grace said.

Lexie shaded her eyes as she craned her head up, taking in the mechanics of it all, then turned to Grace. "What are we doing, then?"

"Well, see all that hay out there?" She pointed to the field, where neat mounds of hay lined the grass. "Bo is going to do a pass—here he comes now." She nodded at the tractor in the distance driving toward us with a contraption attached to the rear. "See how he drives so the baler behind the tractor is positioned over a row of mounded hay? That's so the rakes can pull the hay into the baler. That arm that keeps poking up in the middle? It's compacting the hay into a bundle, then when the bundle's the right size, the machine ties it all up with twine and kicks it out onto the ground. Watch—it's about to happen."

Sure enough, a neatly packed rectangular hay bale inched out of the back.

"So, that's haying?" Lexie said. "Driving a tractor?"

"These days it is." Grace beamed.

The three of us watched Bo drive toward us, then turn the haying assembly so it faced the field for another pass. He idled the motor and hopped off, adjusting his hat. "Ready?"

"They sure are." Grace nodded, hands on her hips.

"Wait." I looked around, panicked. "We're driving the tractor?"

"Sure," Grace said.

"But . . . we've watched Bo drive it for two minutes," I said. "How does that make us ready?"

"On a farm, dear, you've just gotta do, you can't stand around studyin' and analyzin', worrying about the outcome of things," she said. "You gotta just get out there and get it done."

"Exactly," Lexie said, then turned to Bo. "I'll go first."

The two of them walked over to the tractor and Bo talked to Lexie for a moment, with her nodding every now and again. Then she climbed aboard, moved the gear shift, and drove off.

I squinted to see the caravan more clearly as it trundled down the field. "She's actually doing it."

"Of course she is." Grace chuckled. "And so will you."

We watched Lexie steer the baler rakes over the hay. Tight hay rectangles got spit out onto the ground. She drove to the end of the field, then all the way back. Back and forth. Back and forth. We stood under the hot sun watching Lexie. After a while, Bo waved to her, and she idled the tractor near us.

"That was impressive," I mumbled.

"It was." Grace patted my back. "Now, your turn."

Bo helped Lexie off the tractor. I walked toward them.

Bo cranked a thumb toward Lexie. "She did great. You ready?"

Lexie passed me without making eye contact.

"Belle, ready?" Bo made a motion to follow him.

"Yeah . . . sorry, all set."

He helped me into the tractor seat and explained how to control everything. How to drive, how to position the baler rakes. I tried to absorb what he was saying.

"Got it all?" Bo looked at me carefully.

I nodded. "I think."

Starting the tractor, I drove off, thrilled that the linked convoy was staying straight. Then I realized that the rakes weren't over the mounded lines of hay. I glanced over my shoulder. Instead of the mounds being sucked up neatly, they'd been flattened by the tractor wheels.

I turned the steering wheel—too much and too quickly, which jammed up the convoy and caused it to buckle briefly before I cranked the wheel in the opposite direction to compensate. *I'm going to break something.* Sweat dripped down my back as I looked over my shoulder again. More mashed hay. A depressed zigzag pattern.

I neared the turning point, the spot where Lexie had maneuvered the tractor in a tight turn. I spun the wheel. *No, too fast! Too fast!* I pulled out of the turn, making a wide arc that only mashed more hay.

I slowed the tractor down to a crawl, debating what to do. Follow the arc into a random row in the middle of the field, or cut back over to the area where Lexie had left off? Everything was starting to feel untenable and pointless. I looked across the field. Grace, Bo, and Lexie stood watching with their hands shading their eyes.

Backtracking seemed the least humiliating option. I again tried to position the baler, and looked over my shoulder to make sure the rakes were combing up the hay. They weren't. I turned the wheel, overshot the row, then cranked the wheel back. *Why can't I do this?* I continued until the convoy was back at the starting point, not having baled a single bale of hay. I turned off the engine and slumped in the seat.

The tractor exhaust settled. I climbed down and trudged toward the disappointed threesome.

"It can take a couple tries to get the feel of it," Bo said.

Lexie's face soured with mockery. "Excellent crop circles."

A pool of childish emotions irrationally welled up. "Shut up, Lex."

She laughed.

I hurried over to the water pump, worked the arm up and down until spring water pushed forth. I cupped my hand under the stream and shakily brought the water to my mouth.

"You know—" Lexie said, behind me.

"No!" I spun around to face her. "Just . . . back off. You don't think I feel foolish enough? And not just here?" So much was behind the words that bubbled up. "Go ahead, tell me how I'm falling short, or what I'm doing wrong. Go on!"

Lexie pulled back slightly. Uncertainty flashed in her eyes.

"Well, go on!" I said. "Do you know what kills me? You've barely spoken to me in years! But whenever you did, you led with judgment and condescension. So go ahead, lay it on me. Tell me all the things I should be doing, every step I took wrong in my life." I walked away from her. "That's literally the only time you talk to me!"

I paced back and forth near a tree, like an agitated bull. I'd dropped reason somewhere out on the hay field. Then driven over it with heavy farm equipment.

"That's right, play the victim card, run out your 'poor me' routine!" Lexie narrowed her eyes as she stormed my way. "You are *so* good at that—you've really perfected it after all these years. Did you ever think of *trying* something?" She shook her head quickly, marveling at her words. "Just try something! Stop playing it safe and staying somewhere where you're unhappy—every lousy job you've held, every crappy situation you've found yourself in. Why didn't you *ever* try to help yourself? It's pathetic! Maybe if you did that every now and again, you wouldn't feel like the world was judging you."

Out of the corner of my eye, I saw Grace sit down on an old tree stump, working a long strand of sweet hay between her teeth. She stayed in the background, simply watching, like she was at the movies. I didn't care who saw this meltdown. I was so past caring.

"Not the world, Lex! You!" Something between a laugh and sob escaped my throat. "You're so superior! And dismissive! You don't think I try? Do you think it's been easy growing up in your shadow?" I paused, rubbing my forehead, and saw Grace get up from the stump and walk over to the water pump, still watching us. "How easy do you think that's been? When you're *younger* than me?!"

"Like I said." Lexie took a step closer so she was right in my face, then whispered, "*Pathetic*."

"You're mean, you know that? And here—" My voice hitched, but then the anger stormed back. "Here I actually thought we might be getting closer again. And if that makes me pathetic for having that hope, then fine, I'm pathetic . . . but you know what? You've grown into someone hard and bitter and mean—not the sister I grew up with. I'm done with you! Do you hear me? Done!"

Then a shocking, icy whoosh of frigid water landed on us.

"Holy Christ!" Lexie looked around like a wild animal.

We were both soaked, our hair dripping cold streamlets of water.

Grace stood a couple of feet away, calmly holding an empty bucket, hay strand still in her mouth. She looked slowly between the two of us, then said, "It's gettin' hot. Time for lunch."

We ate outside in the sun.

Lexie and I sat on a log to dry off. The surprise dousing, the shrill moment that had played out too long and too wrong, left us silent. Grace and Bo ate at a small picnic table in the shade, chatting within earshot, while Lexie and I ate in damp clothes, plates balanced on our laps like children who weren't well behaved enough to sit at the grown-up table.

Bo chuckled. "They got a fire in them. Those girls come by it honestly, that's for sure." He nodded slightly. "God rest her soul."

Grace took a bite of her chicken. "That they do." She chewed thoughtfully. "We were so young, just like these two." She sighed. "And so stupid."

"Eh." Bo shrugged. "If people knew then what they know now, we'd have a planet of geniuses on our hands." He wiped his mouth. "And who'd want that?"

The rest of the afternoon was uneventful, spent collecting sticks for kindling and picking berries under the sun. I worked side by side with Lexie, feeling foolish about my outburst and somewhat lost. An uncomfortable cloud hung between us.

Silently tending to farm chores in such close proximity made our rift feel even larger. As the day wore on, regrets piled up in my head. Grace stopped work to bathe and start dinner, while Lexie and I finished bringing the last of the berries down from the hill. When the sun hung low in the sky, we headed back to the house.

I cleared my throat, which felt thick from not talking all afternoon. "Do you want to wash up first?" It was my first direct remark to Lexie since our outburst.

She glanced over at me as we walked, took several steps before saying, her voice quiet, "No, that's okay. You go first."

With only the sound of our footsteps between us, we made our way down from the field just as the sun started to tuck itself behind the hills.

Chapter 17

Dinner was a feast: juicy pot roast with potatoes, carrots, and onions. I ate three buttermilk biscuits, sopped up every drop of gravy. Grace invited Bo to join us, and it wasn't until the middle of the meal when I caught him looking at her that I realized he was someone special in her life. Not so much farmhand as elderly romantic lead. Together, they seemed decades younger.

"That was delicious." Lexie looked satisfied, like after Thanksgiving dinner when you sit back with a full belly and simply enjoy the act of breathing.

I agreed.

"Grace here, she can cook up a storm." Bo gently placed his hand on hers and they shared a smile. "Now, if you ladies will excuse me." He scooted his chair back and strode out of the dining room.

I started to rise. "We should help clean up."

"After the work you two did today?" Grace said. "I'll manage that."

Bo walked back in and nodded to Grace, who smiled at him.

"Bo made you girls a fire, so don't let it burn alone."

"Better mind her," he said with a wink. "She's a feisty gal. Besides, cleanup is my job."

"Tonight, it's mine." Grace gave him a knowing look.

"Right." He smiled. "I'll take my leave. You ladies have a good night."

We said goodbye to Bo and followed Grace into the kitchen, carrying the dishes.

"After a day of work and a good dinner, it's nice to relax outside in the evening air," Grace said. "Alexis—get those blankets from the back of the couch. There's a cold front supposed to move through here tonight. Belle, you warm up this cider." Grace took down three heavy mugs from the cupboard and put a cinnamon stick in each. "When it's nice and hot, pour it into the mugs but leave a good inch at the top. Don't fill them all the way."

"Okay."

Grace walked outside.

I heard Lexie talking on the phone to her kids in the other room, but then the tenor changed completely, like a steel-toed boot stomped on the chirpy happiness.

The cider came to a simmer, and I turned off the burner, straining to hear what Lexie was saying. I didn't have to, though, because I knew. She was complaining about me to Jeffrey. Maybe it was better that I couldn't hear her catalog of grievances. I poured the cider into the mugs, then picked them up and headed for the door.

Grace came back in, the scent of woodsmoke trailing her. "Whoa, hang on. Put those back down."

I did.

Grace pulled a bottle from a cupboard. "They need a little topper." She poured an inch of brandy in each and stirred them with the cinnamon sticks. "There we go."

I raised my eyebrows. "I didn't think you drank."

"Oh, I like a nip every now and again. My favorite is after working outside—"

"A cold beer."

She put a hand on her hip. "Now how in the world did you know that?"

"Gran . . . she loved that too."

Grace's eyes watered, seemed full of happiness and heartbreak. "That was our favorite thing after a full day of work." She lost herself in a memory. "After our mother passed away, Annabelle and I did all the farmwork. And a beer after, when the sun was hanging low . . . it just put the day right." She turned and headed outside.

I picked up the mugs and followed.

The fire Bo had built within a circle of stones glowed magnificently in the darkness. Four weathered Adirondack chairs sat around the fire.

"This is wonderful," I said.

Grace sat down. "Sure is nice to have someone to enjoy it with." She smiled as I handed her a mug. I set one mug on the wide arm of the chair to Grace's left for Lexie, then sat down beside her.

The flames danced and twisted. Logs popped every now and again. I looked up at the sky plastered with stars.

I sipped my cider and coughed. "Oh boy. Got a little kick, huh?"

Grace smiled. "That kick'll keep you warm."

"Where did you and Gran get the idea to have beers after working outside?"

Grace leaned her head back. "Our mama." Her smile grew wide. "Her favorite thing after working all day, in the barn, in the fields, all over this farm, was to have a cold beer. She'd hold it with two fingers, dangling it, and walk barefoot in the grass. She'd do this kind of lazy, happy stroll with her beer, looking out upon everything she'd done all day." Grace stared off into the darkness, as if watching her mom. "She'd only have one. 'You have *a* beer, you don't fall into beer,' she'd say. We knew some folks who fell into the bottle. It was just . . . real sad." She sighed. "We lost her so young . . . too, too young."

I knew that lament. "How old were you and Gran when your mom passed away?"

"Just teenagers—I was fifteen and Annabelle was eighteen." She turned her head toward me, a pained look on her face. "I'm so sorry that you lost your mom as young as you did. When I read that it broke my heart."

"What do you mean 'read it'?"

Grace sipped her cider. Before she could answer, Lexie marched over, arms full of blankets.

"Sorry—was talking to my kids." She handed us each a blanket and sat down.

I nestled the green wool throw over my lap and immediately felt warmer. Grace was right about the cold front.

"I want to thank you both for helping out today," Grace said. "I know it wasn't an easy thing to come here, us not knowing one another and all. You both took a leap for me, and I'm . . . Well, I'm just real appreciative."

I basked in the glow of Grace's gratitude.

"Why don't we know you?" Lexie blurted.

I stared at her. "Lex, stop it."

"I think it's a fair question," she shot back.

"Why do you always have to be so difficult?" I said. "You rub up against people like sandpaper. I do not understand it."

Lexie put up a hand in a blasé dismissal. "Okay."

"It's not an unfair ask." Grace sat still for a bit. "We've worked next to each other, we've had dinner . . . but we haven't really talked. So, now we're gonna talk. And the first thing I'm going to say is: You walk a mile in my shoes before you come at me with that indignant tone. I don't need to know you well to know that you could do with a little empathy when you address folks. Those are just manners. You're old enough to have 'em."

Lexie sank back into her chair. No one ever talked to her like that. I held my breath, eyes wide.

"You hear me?" Grace said.

Lexie swallowed. "Yes, ma'am."

The three of us sat in silence for a minute that felt like an hour.

"So . . ." I ventured, "you were the one who sent the letters."

"I didn't send any letters," Grace said.

"You didn't send letters telling us what to make in the cookbook?" Lexie said.

Grace turned toward her. "*What* cookbook?"

"We were each sent a handwritten cookbook of all the things Gran used to make," I said.

Grace let out a shaky breath. Her hand had a frail shake to it as she wiped her eyes.

I looked at Lexie, who shrugged.

The silence grew fat around us.

Grace let out an anguished sigh. She leaned back, stared at the sky studded with bright stars. "I made those cookbooks—and gave one to Annabelle before she moved up to Cleveland. It was . . . sentimental." A tear rolled down her cheek. "We didn't need a cookbook to tell us anything our mama made. We'd learned it all at her knee." She shook her head, lost in a memory. "I think it was just my way of saying how much I'd miss her."

"How did Gran have both of them?" I said. "Because we each got one with a series of letters."

Grace's smile was soft, admiring. "Wow . . . wow." She sat for a moment. "Oh my goodness, she was special." And then a guttural sob born from deep hurt let loose.

Lexie and I sat motionless, unsure. Grace didn't seem the type to want to be comforted.

The fire crackled. We let Grace take her time to cry it out. Eventually, she calmed. Fished out a hanky from her pocket and blew her nose.

"I got so angry at my sister that I mailed my copy of the cookbook to her."

"When was this?" I asked.

Grace blew out a breath. "More than sixty years ago."

"Why?" Lexie asked. "What happened?"

Grace sat silent, then sighed. "After Annabelle moved away, after I'd gotten married, I was approached by strip miners who wanted to buy the farm and tear it up for coal. A big seam runs underneath this area. A rich seam." She fell quiet again. "This company was trying to buy the farms all around here and was gunnin' for our land. But I wouldn't sell." She shook her head. "They tried all sorts of things—lying, saying everyone else had sold, threatening me and Crocker, harassing us. It was awful . . . just awful."

We agreed.

"And Annabelle—she didn't . . . she didn't know the whole of it, all the ugly—she wanted me to sell, kept writing me letters when I wouldn't answer the phone anymore." She wiped her nose. "I was pregnant . . . and the company's harassment, the threats, the stress of it all, I lost my baby."

"I'm so sorry." Lexie's sincerity was unmistakable.

I echoed her sentiment. "I can't even imagine that heartache."

"No one can until they go through it," Grace said. "I thought I knew grief when my mama died and then my papa—but I didn't know from grief . . . Oh, I didn't know."

She wiped her cheeks, and sat, shaking her head. The fire crackled, filling up the yawning silence.

"And in that grief-stricken place," she continued, her voice soft, "I blamed my sister because she'd wanted me to sell too. I told her never to contact me, then sent her my cookbook." She wept quietly. "I said the most terrible things."

Grace shuddered as a fresh sob overtook her. Then, stillness.

She cleared her throat, wiped her nose with a hanky, and stared into the fire. "I never spoke to her again."

Grace held so much hurt, just as Gran must have. I ached for her and Gran's loss.

"At the time, and for years and years after, I thought she'd lost all connection to this land, this . . . this wonderful place where we grew up, and I was mighty angry about that." Grace got quiet. "But . . . she only wanted what she thought would be best for me. She didn't want me to work myself to an early death like our mama." She exhaled. "Our mama died young, too young. And . . . I see what Annabelle's intentions were now . . . I do." She stared into the fire. "But I considered our time together growing up on the farm to be the happiest time of my life—I only wanted to hold on to that, to recreate that with my own family, with my own girls." She wiped her eyes. "After my miscarriage . . . it simply wasn't meant to be. I couldn't have children after. And that made me blame her even more."

The fire's flames didn't lick as high now. Gone was the brightness. A deep orange enveloped the three of us.

"No matter what Annabelle said or wrote, I was incapable of hearing any different than the worst." Grace sat silent, then, her voice full of emotion, "I turned my back on the most important relationship of my life and went more than sixty years angry . . . feeling like there was a hole in me. Like I didn't have family."

Tears streamed down her face. "I'm sure this sounds like a flimsy reason for so many years of ill will to fester. But let me tell you, that's exactly how it starts."

Gran would've been carrying this same heartbreak—silently, stoically, or maybe even angrily. Every now and again, I saw glimpses of their rift's enormity, but only that. Because whenever Gran alluded to it, she'd quickly reel it back in and lock it away again. Thinking of this heaviness living inside her . . . it pierced me.

Something nagged at me as well. I waited until it seemed Grace wasn't going to say anything more.

"But you called Gran's house out of the blue."

"I did . . . I was too late, but I did."

I treaded carefully, kept my voice gentle. "Why?"

Grace smoothed the blanket on her lap. "Because Annabelle wrote me one last time, right before—" She took a moment. "Right before she passed away . . . I called the day I got her letter, but it was too late."

She wiped her nose. "She knew her time was near and she . . . she wanted to talk to me before . . ." She choked up, the hardest part left unsaid.

Her and Gran's history, heavy and tragic, left a dent in my center.

Thoughts pancaked on top of one another, thick and weighty. They left me weak with awe.

I had never had any idea Gran's time was close—or even that she'd had a foreboding sense of her own mortality—or that she'd wanted to speak with Grace before, as she put it, she went on to her next adventure. She was just so happy and vibrant all the time. What my mother had done for Lexie and me, shielding us from a greedy disease and her impending death, so Gran had done.

"She wrote me about the two of you." Grace pointed a finger back and forth between us, steel returning to her voice.

Which immediately got Lexie's back up. "Meaning?"

Grace's face hardened, as if to say, *Now, we talked about tone.*

"I just meant . . ." Lexie softened. "What did she say?"

Grace gave a nod, as if she approved of Lexie's correction.

"She told me that you'd drifted apart, that you used to be inseparable as children but were now like strangers."

I kept my eyes on the fire, the weak shadows it cast.

"And seeing as how neither of you can look my way, I gather there's some static between you two. Couple stubborn mules, the both of you."

Neither of us said anything.

"In her letter, my sister asked me to bring you both here six months after she passed. I don't know why that was her time frame, but it was."

My breath went thin thinking of everything Gran had set in motion. The preparation. What she'd shouldered. The care she'd taken.

"And so here we all are." Grace sat placid. "I sit here with more regret than you'll ever know." Her head slowly shook no to whatever was looping through her mind. "If your grandmother and I had made the effort to speak with one another, to try to understand each other instead of talking past or hollerin' at one another, we would've saved our relationship and grown old together—spending holidays, getting to know you. I could've known . . ." She stayed silent for a long moment. Then choked out, "My niece before she passed." Grace shoved the blanket from her lap, downed the last of her cider, and scooched herself to the edge of the Adirondack chair. "It's easy when you're young to dismiss people and hold on to anger and resentment. But in the end, that just ends up stealing a good life right from under your nose. And you two have a story of your own, I know you do. You're in a place where you can change the direction of your story—of your whole relationship. This is what I wanted you to hear . . . sitting in this place where your grandmother and I began. And yes, I'm on a soapbox. But I'm an old lady, so I get to do this. I speak bluntly, and I might not know you well, but because you're Annabelle's granddaughters, this comes from a place of love. Don't end up like your grandmother and me. There's nothing I regret more than the decades I lost with my sister. And if you conduct yourselves the way we did, the blame will fall on both your shoulders equally because you've been warned. What you do with that knowledge is up to you."

We sat silent for what seemed forever.

I felt like a fool.

Lexie kept her eyes down.

"Well, shit." Grace sighed. "I wanted to get up and walk into the house, really make something of my exit . . . but I need help out of this damn chair."

I smiled and got up immediately to help. Lexie was there by my side.

"Come on, Auntie." Lexie smirked as she reached for her. "You're not that old."

"Speak for yourself," Grace retorted. "You'll understand when you're two hundred, like me."

Lexie and I held Grace's arms—but she stood with no assistance from either of us.

Then strode toward the house easily.

"You're such a faker!" I called after her.

Grace threw her head back and laughed. Waved a hand in the air. "Good night! There are beers in the fridge!"

We watched Grace head inside. The light went off.

We sat back down.

"I like the sound of a beer," Lexie eventually said. "You?"

"Sure."

She went in, then came back out, handed me one, and sat down.

Quiet enveloped us.

My thoughts were still wrapped in Grace's story. It should've lightened the moment, made this—us—easier, but a heaviness overwhelmed. Like deep down I knew we were unfixable.

"I feel like we should be able to . . . talk." Lexie held her beer with both hands. "Or something."

I swallowed. "Should we?"

She stared at me across the fire.

"I'm not saying that to be difficult, I wonder if it's just the truth of where we are." My voice was quiet. "We've been different for a long time."

"Why does it matter that we're different?" She paused. "Peanut butter and chocolate are different. They're still great together."

I couldn't help but smile a little, but thoughts of the past crowded my head. "There's no getting around that we've grown apart . . . you chose the people you wanted to surround yourself with years and years ago." I met her eyes. "Gran and I didn't make the cut."

"What are you talking about?"

"Literally every rich friend you've made since college, Jeffrey's entire family . . . I mean, you cleaved yourself from Gran and me and attached yourself to them and their world." I swallowed. "And it was clear what they thought of us: I was a pathetic underachiever and Gran was too simple. But what's worse is that you adopted their entire worldview . . . and that really hurt, okay? It hurt."

Lexie stayed silent.

"You . . . haven't been there in any way, really. For a long time. Years. Not for me, not for Gran. Ever since you started running in those well-heeled crowds, ever since you met Jeffrey, you've distanced yourself from us." I shook my head in resignation. "Connections fray."

Lexie stared at the fire. "You've got me all figured out."

"It's not that complicated."

"Right." She ran a hand through her hair and looked up at the sky. "Because you're the only one who feels . . . the only one who's ever going through anything."

Her voice lacked its usual punchiness.

"Right?" She focused on me, a small sad smile on her face. "I'm the one with the perfect life, the one on top of the world." She gazed heavenward once more, a singsong lilt to her voice. "The one that everything works out for."

We sat in silence.

"Is . . . something going on?"

Lexie took a swig of her beer and, in the flickering firelight, looked drained, like the vibrancy had leaked right out of her. She spoke slowly. "Yes . . . something is going on."

I waited for her to elaborate, but when she didn't, a bead of worry formed in my stomach. Which led to confusion because things didn't happen to Lexie, and I certainly never worried about her. Everything tilted. "Do you want to tell me about it?"

"Jeffrey is having an affair."

"Oh, Lex . . . no."

"Oh, yes. With—wait for it—a woman who has a coffee kiosk in the lobby of his building." She drank deeply from her beer. "Who's got to be twenty years younger than me."

I didn't know what to say. Lexie had an enviable life, the ideal marriage. Nothing ever didn't go her way. Her day-to-day existence was marked by polish and accomplishment. It had been our entire adult lives. "I'm so sorry."

Lexie didn't say anything.

"No . . ." When she continued, her voice was so soft. "I'm the one who's sorry." She looked up at the sky, searching. "You're not wrong. I got swept up in a lot, I know I did. The fancy lifestyle that was so different from how we grew up . . . all of it." She rubbed her eyes. "I think . . . I think I lost myself a bit." She sat silently with that admission. "And then for years I was trying to do everything in my power to stabilize my marriage, which, I don't know . . . maybe it never seemed secure. And, yeah, I canceled a lot of trips home. I pretzeled myself so we'd only do the things he wanted with the family and friends he wanted . . . and for what?" She shrugged.

The shock of hearing Lexie regret anything kept me silent.

"Do you know what I feel? Gutted . . . and so foolish." She rubbed the edge of the bottle label with her thumb. "On some level, you're right . . . I did get mean, or hard, I don't know which. Maybe both. I'm really sorry . . . for all of it. For all of me, I should say." She stayed quiet in her doleful reverie, then lifted her eyes to meet mine. "By my own hand I lost so much."

Lexie's gaze was filled with a remorse that she obviously struggled to fully attach words to, but the painful facets were clear. I felt the full dimension of her regret. And right then, I knew I didn't need to go on any further. She understood it all.

Lexie's eyes welled, and she blinked to contain the emotion. Cleared her throat. "On top of it all, I'm the trashiest cliché ever."

"No, you're not."

She looked pointedly at me. "My husband was so unhappy that he soothed himself at a *coffee kiosk*. With a two-bit lobby barista. Who makes crappy cappuccinos."

We drank in silence.

I wasn't sure what to say. But even after all these years, I still knew when Lexie wasn't in the sentimental end of the pool, when she was wading in angry depths and needed to be reset. I knew that much.

"It's a . . . real art," I ventured. "Knowing most of a cappuccino should be froth."

She chuckled.

"Like, don't try to cover up your inadequacy as a barista by dumping in a bunch of hot milk." I ran with it. "Stop that. Stop that right now."

"Amateur."

Her momentary cheer faded. She grew quiet.

"I really am sorry," I said.

She nodded thanks, shrugged. “What are you going to do?”

No way was she this blasé about her husband of fifteen years, the father of her daughters, cheating on her. “You don’t have to put on a front. It’s okay.”

“I’m not.” She sat silent, staring into the fire. “Like I said, this didn’t come out of the blue . . . things haven’t been good for a long time. Years. And yeah . . . that Christmas four years ago when I canceled last minute . . .” She sighed. “It was really getting bad then. I knew something was wrong but . . . I had no idea it was an affair.” She shook her head. “He was also pissy because we were going to Gates Mills. He could be that way—anything with his family was great, but mine?” She shrugged again and stayed quiet. “A lot has gone on . . . it’s been all-consuming for a long time. So much of what I thought our marriage was, who he was, just . . . wasn’t. Honestly, it’s too much to get into.” She shook her head. “And now . . . I’m just exhausted. Hurt and outrage . . . are unbelievably exhausting. And when I’m not feeling aggrieved or . . . oh my God, so furious, this weird numbness overtakes me.” She held the cold bottle to her temple, let out a shuddering sigh. “And the truth of it is, I feel utterly alone now.”

My breath caught.

“I don’t even cry about it anymore.” She took a swig of her beer. “I’m . . . empty.”

I wanted to circle back to her feeling alone but couldn’t figure out how to bridge it . . . or us. So, I asked, “When did you, or how—”

“Find out about the affair? Right after Gran passed away.” Her head shook wearily. “That monster. I was so upset—and he knew how upset I was.”

“Wait, about Gran?”

A sour incredulity radiated off her. “Of course about Gran, what’s wrong with you?”

“I just . . . didn’t think—”

"What? That I didn't grieve her? Because the only way I could possibly have felt anything was if I crumbled like a grief cookie? That would've proved how devastated I was?" She choked up, looked like she was about to explode. "Or showed I regretted that I didn't make the effort to spend more time with Gran? That I didn't prioritize her when I had the chance? Me feeling like I had to put my kids and family and home life first meant one of the most important relationships in my life suffered. You don't think I look back now and have bone-crushing guilt about my choices? Regrets that I cannot even delve into because it's too painful?" She rubbed her eyes. "What am I supposed to do with that now? Knowing that I didn't have the strength to shoulder my lousy husband's temporary disappointment so I could've had more time with Gran?"

I was wrong. Lexie had the words.

She stared into the fire for a long time.

"Who's the rich one here?" Her voice caught. "Huh? Who? You have the bulk of the memories, the special moments with Gran, all the nuances of how she—I don't know, seasoned stuffing sauté!" She shook her head, eyes watering, then inhaled a raspy breath. "I mean, my girls barely knew her."

Lexie hunched over and covered her eyes. Her back heaved as she cried into her hands. Then she sat up, face red, hair every which way.

"You have a treasure trove of experiences that bolster you," she murmured. She gazed into the fire again, eyes glassy, far off. "What do I have?" Her face screwed in distaste. She spit out, "Pointless, nothing . . . frequent flier miles. Who cares about frequent flier miles? Who?!" She barked out a wild laugh, then fell silent, bunched the sleeve of her blouse and wiped her nose with it. "I do. Right?" She nodded, tears staining her silk blouse. "I know. Me."

Silence fattened around us again. The fire sent dusty orange cinders into the night.

"Did you ever think that I might not be the cold automaton you've painted me as?" Lexie said. "That maybe I struggle but in different ways than you? I get that you can't understand. Fine! But the difference between you and me is that I never nailed you to a cross because you couldn't see things from my perspective."

I was at a loss. "I didn't—"

"You didn't think, Belle," she cut me off. "As usual, you didn't think past yourself. I've got plenty of feelings and opinions, and a lot of them are . . ." She inhaled, eyes closed, and stayed silent for a moment, as if holding in something bigger than herself. "They're really difficult to reconcile in any way at all." She paused, then let out an exasperated breath. "I mean, jeez, Belle, you're older than me! Where's your maturity? I literally don't understand. How'd you become this weird lost child person?"

I sat stunned by the depth of complication within her . . . but also by hearing what she honestly thought of me. It all left a mark. I thought back to her clipped response in that initial email about the first recipe we'd made and how bitter and angry I was. Never did I think that maybe she was so depleted about something in her own life that she didn't have anything else to give. That she'd shown up as best she could. I'd never considered anything beyond judgment and derision when it came to my sister, never given her the benefit of the doubt, the one person who I craved a connection with most of all. Who had I become? I sank back into the chair, withered by the honesty that had firehosed out of Lexie hot and strong.

The logs popped and snapped, filled the silence between us.

"I think . . . I've gotten knocked off my path a bit," I murmured. "Kind of beaten down."

Lexie stretched her feet out in front of her. "That's relatable, happens to everyone, including me." Her voice had lost its sharpness. "After Gwen was born—you weren't there so you couldn't have known—I had a really hard time. Postpartum depression." She opened her mouth to continue, but emotion choked off her words. Eventually, she said, "It was bad. I called you. A few times. But you never called me back . . . So, I understand what it's like to go through something." She sat silently for a moment. "But the difference is I don't have my mail sent to some beaten-down place. I keep moving forward. I think you need to work harder to try and do the same. If for no other reason than for Gran . . . no one loved life more than her. Is shutting down any way to honor her?" She paused. "I know you don't need me to answer that."

That got me. Of course it got me. I looked up at the sky studded with stars, let the tears roll down my face. For so much. Gran, obviously. But also for how ashamed I felt for only considering the me of everything, how I felt about Lexie's actions or inaction, how I was affected, never thinking about what she might be going through, how she might be feeling. I'd relegated her to a cold kingdom of unfeeling and couldn't see anything else . . . or maybe wouldn't, because that bolstered my hurt, my victim worldview. Lexie had really struggled at one point . . . and I hadn't taken the time to consider that or to help.

I covered my eyes, so ashamed.

Lexie let me feel what was coming up, didn't try to corral it or downplay it, which I appreciated.

And then in the long quiet that followed, something she'd said in that torrent of words made me smile. "I'm not weird."

"What?"

"You said I'm weird . . . I'm not weird."

She sniffed a laugh and looked at me tenderly. Then seemed to make a calculated decision. "Well, your shoes certainly are. What's with these weird slip-ons you've taken to wearing?"

"They're recovery sandals, designed to realign your feet after you run."

"Okay, you ran not five yards today, so those are officially an odd fashion statement," she said. "Either that or you've completely given up trying at the most basic of levels. You're wearing slide-in shoes. With socks . . . and shorts!"

All I could do was laugh. She went on and on until we were both laughing so hard, trying to catch our breath, that the tears came again, but this time from humor, and for the first time in years, a sense of togetherness.

Eventually, silence returned, but this one, more peaceable. The dark was so deep here without a streetlight or a building anywhere within eyeshot. Sitting in the inky night I felt a part of it, not separate. Such a strange connective feeling.

"Do you know what gets me?"

I asked what.

"I was always the one who compromised when it came to our careers."

"What are you talking about? You're so successful."

"But my career took a back seat to Jeffrey's. Didn't matter that I achieved just as much as he did, my goals, things I wanted to do to further myself . . ." She shook her head, lost in thought. "If it didn't mesh with whatever he wanted, it wasn't going to happen."

"Jeez . . . I'm sorry."

"I mean, for me to get to the next level in my career, I would've had to take jobs that were bigger and more complex, ones that would've had me in New York for extended periods of time, maybe even relocating there." Lexie plowed on. "The kids were young enough that moving would've been a nonevent. But he didn't want to move, refused to even look into relocating and transferring to another office." She drank deeply from her beer and sat silent for a bit. "And now where am I? At a place where I can't uproot my kids—I mean, I could, but why would I inflict that disruption on them?"

"I see what you mean."

"And you know, maybe I'm to blame too, because as much as I would've liked to have done that when they were younger, we also had this fabulous life. Things were easy." She stared into the fire. "The choices we make, right?"

I added a fresh log to the fire and used a stick to nestle it in, then sat back down. Lexie looked lost in thought.

"Who's to say you can't make some changes now?" I put it gently, unsure of what was unspooling in her head.

She blew out a big breath. "Oh, there'll be changes all right." She looked at her bottle and got up. "I'll get us another."

The kitchen door slapped shut as Lexie came out with two open beers. She handed me one and held the bottom of hers out. I clinked it with the top of mine.

"It's ironic, this fancy neighborhood that I wanted to maintain for so long . . . now all I want to do is get out of it." She slumped in her chair. "Start somewhere fresh. But now that we're looking at shared custody, that's impossible."

"Oh."

"Yeah. I filed for divorce." She wiped her cheek. "I have no idea why saying that makes me emotional, because there's no other way. I don't have it in me to get past what he's done. He's tainted everything . . . us, our family. I'm done."

"It doesn't mean it's not still hard."

She bit her cheek, didn't say anything. "Beyond all the things you feel when you're in this situation, it's staring down a life that looks completely different from the one you're familiar with that really gets me—and I'm not talking about a house or a fancy part of town, I'm talking about a feel. Maybe it's the predictability of your days . . . the rhythm." She ran a hand through her hair. "I don't know if I'm making any sense. But I think what it comes down to, when I get past the hurt, the betrayal, I'm left with this life that's in a lot of ways foreign to me . . ." Her voice wavered before she fell silent. "I just really feel alone."

I stared, didn't even know how to react.

"And . . . I can't forgive myself for not seeing Gran more." The pain on Lexie's face was pure and sharp.

It gutted me. I pushed the blanket off my lap and went over to her, wrapped my arms around her. "Gran never saw your not being there as something that had to be forgiven. She just loved you."

Lexie's body shook as she cried silently into me. I held her as she sobbed out what she'd been carrying around for so long. For the first time since we were kids, I was the big sister providing comfort, like decades earlier when we sat in a hot car in a funeral home parking lot, waiting to say goodbye to our mother.

I held Lexie until she calmed down and sighed, flashing a small smile to indicate she was okay. For the first time in ages, I was filled with wholehearted empathy for my sister. She needed help to sounder footing, but in a way that only she'd respond to.

A little laugh erupted out of me. "I didn't even think you had tear ducts!"

"Is that what these are?" She smiled at her own deadpan. "I'm going to get a tissue."

Lexie went inside—she seemed sturdier as she walked away, more herself, which pleased me. I put another log on the fire and sat back down, falling into my thoughts. Something still wasn't fitting right about all of this.

Lexie came back and blew her nose.

"So . . . let me ask you: Who sent us the cookbooks and letters, if it wasn't Grace?" I said. "The only other people I could think of were Faye and Mama P, and they weren't sending us things."

"You asked them?"

"Yeah."

"When?"

"Right when I first got everything." I thought back. "I didn't understand how we could be getting letters from Gran."

Lexie sat silent.

"Call Faye." She held up a finger. "My money's on her."

"You think?" I looked at my watch—it probably wasn't too late to call. "I have to get my phone."

"Here." Lexie handed me hers. "Use mine."

I dialed. Faye answered.

"Hi, Faye, it's Belle—I'm using Lexie's phone. I hope it's not too late to call."

"Not at all," she said. "How are you?"

"I'm . . . well, I'm feeling . . . sturdier, I guess."

"I'm so pleased to hear that."

"So . . . this is kind of random and I know I asked you this some months back, but are you the one who sent Lexie and me the cookbooks and letters?"

"Yes."

My eyes grew wide. Lexie laughed and pointed at me. "I told you!" Then, more loudly, "I knew it was you, Faye, you sneaky minx!"

Faye laughed. "You got me."

"But I asked you point-blank when we first got everything—I specifically asked if it was you who sent it and you denied it!"

"Correct."

"So, you lied."

"Yes, I did."

I laughed. "I'm putting you on speaker. I don't get it—why?"

"Because your gran didn't want either of you to know who was mailing them until all the letters had been sent," Faye said. "I think she thought that the mystery of it all might keep you engaged. Her dream was that you two would be drawn back together. I didn't know what was in the envelopes, or anything about a cookbook. And I'm perfectly fine lying for a greater good. I would do and will do anything for your grandmother. Including lie."

My eyes pricked with emotion.

"Are the two of you on the farm?"

"We are. You knew about us going to the farm?"

"The whole goal was to get you two there together. I did know that." Faye paused. "How is Grace?"

"Good. She gave us an earful tonight."

Faye laughed. "Just as she was supposed to. Excellent."

"Wait." My mind raced. "Have you two talked?"

"Oh, countless times. She introduced herself to me at the wake and then after the funeral I had her over for lunch and we reminisced about your gran and talked about everything she'd left for us to do. We were in the dark about all the details, what was in the letters and all that. But we were two puppeteers who needed to work together. Turns out, I quite like her."

"She's neat." The fractured relationships cascading through the years hit me, and the tears came. "I would've loved Gran to be here tonight."

"She's there with you." Faye's voice felt like a caress. "She is."

I appreciated the assurance. Perhaps in time I'd be able to bend more easily to this notion of Gran being with me in the special moments—or even just a mundane, quiet moment—her invisible hand letting me know she was still present in some ethereal way. I hoped so.

We wrapped up the conversation and said goodbye. I handed the phone back to Lexie.

"Mystery solved," she said.

I smiled, lost myself looking at the fire. "Hey . . . what pictures did Gran send you?"

"Do you know, I actually brought them with me?" Lexie's voice was quiet, a little sad. "I thought I'd show them to Grace."

I looked at her. "I brought mine too."

Her face softened. "Really?"

"C'mon, let's go get 'em."

We spent the rest of the evening until our eyes grew heavy not delving into details about what had happened with her and Jeffrey, not exchanging rote questions and responses about work or the kids. Rather, we reminisced. The pictures Gran had sent sparked a trip down memory lane. But our common experiences beyond the photos became rarer the older we got, so we started sharing what we'd each gone through separately. Each of us only had half a story and together we'd have one that was complete.

It wasn't until we really started sharing that I realized how little we'd interacted over the years. So much time had passed; too many years had been squandered.

It felt good—more than that, it felt right—to finally start kneading our stories together like a crumbly dough that suddenly comes together in a supple, unified whole.

But it was undeniably bittersweet.

Chapter 18

The following morning, Lexie and I worked like veteran farmhands alongside Grace, Bo, and his crew. When the air still had a slight chill to it and dew sat heavy on the grass, we picked more blackberries, filling two more flats of containers. When the sun hung high in the sky, warming our foreheads and cheeks, we dug up rows of potatoes from the garden, then put them in the root cellar to store. And when fluffy clouds rolled in, we took turns driving the baler across the field. By my second pass, I'd found my groove maneuvering it over the rows of hay, so I stayed on the tractor while Bo's crew hauled the bales into the barn. By late afternoon, Lexie and I were spent. The sweetest kind of exhaustion had found me.

"C'mere." Grace waved Lexie and me over from the water pump, where we were gulping down spring water.

A couple of guys from Bo's crew set a hay bale beside the barn. Grace nodded thanks as they walked off.

"I want you two to sit here so I can take your picture." She pointed to the bale and waved a Polaroid camera.

We did as she asked.

"Ready?" Grace closed one eye and looked through the viewfinder. "Say cheese."

I wrapped my arm around Lexie, giving her a squeeze, and the two of us smiled squinty smiles. With a click of the camera, my heart lightened. As the still-undeveloped picture ejected from the front—three times, because Grace wanted to give a snapshot to each of us and keep one for herself—I thought about how long Lexie and I had gone without creating a single happy memory together. And today, we were inking them as quickly as a camera shutter could open and close.

"Good!" Grace beamed.

Lexie and I watched the snapshots develop in our hands. Our faces smiled up at us. Happy. Secure. Like we'd never stopped holding on to one another like that.

Looking up from the photo, my thoughts thick, I managed, "Thank you."

"Oh, you're welcome, now." Grace nodded as if to seal the emotional acknowledgment. "I better get cleaned up, there's dinner to make."

"What if . . ." Lexie pursed her lips. "What would you think if Belle and I made some dessert?"

"That'd be real nice," Grace said.

I looked at Lexie but didn't say what I was thinking.

"Yeah." She nodded. "Gran's tassies."

I smiled, my throat tight with emotion.

"Do you mind if I check the kitchen to see if I need to get anything?" Lexie asked. "I think I saw a general store in town, right?"

"Sure did." Grace waved an arm toward the house. "Help yourself—take the truck if you need to."

I watched Lexie walk with purpose toward the kitchen door and thought about all of us here together on the farm. Lexie was headstrong, so similar to Grace—and in other ways, so much like Gran. My sister and I lived hundreds of miles from where our family line first pounded its genealogical stake into the ground, but there was no escaping certain familial traits. There would always be those characteristics—for better and, sometimes, worse—that followed us, no matter where we were.

"You know, I've been thinking . . . I want to give your copy of the cookbook back."

Grace shook her head. "Oh, no, Belle."

"Really. It's yours. I think Gran would want you to have it."

She touched my face tenderly. "I appreciate what you're sayin', but my sister knew what she was doin' when she gave them to you and Lexie, and she was right. That cookbook is my past. I don't need it anymore." She dropped her eyes for the briefest of moments. "It belongs to you and your sister now to remind you of your future."

Grace pounded chicken cutlets until they were thin, then dredged them in flour, egg, and breadcrumbs. Since she knew the tassie recipe by heart, she also guided us in all the ingredient measurements. Lexie made the dough while I mixed the brown sugar filling.

The two of us worked silently side by side. I hadn't cooked with my sister in years—and the last time we'd done it without animus was when we were kids. Us here in this farm kitchen was new terrain. But we were doing it, even if it felt stiff. And definitely quiet. Maybe just doing it together in any way at all was something.

"I forgot to preheat the oven," Lexie said.

"Already did," Grace said.

Lexie looked sheepish. "I forgot you know this recipe better than either of us."

Grace's smile was gracious. "I'll tell you what: I haven't made my mama's tassies in a long time . . . I'm really looking forward to them."

Grace set the plate of prepped cutlets in the fridge. While chopping the pecans, I glanced back and saw her watching from the doorway, her smile tender, like it was underpinned with melancholy. She caught my eye. Two generations, divided by decades, had dovetailed. She gave a tiny nod and walked out.

Lexie was rolling the dough into little balls. I forced myself to focus and grabbed a knob. The dough was supple—the mixture of cream cheese, butter, and flour mixed up silkily.

"The dough came out nice," I said.

"Yeah."

We kept rolling.

When we accumulated enough for two tins, we smooshed the balls into the mini muffin cups, ensuring the sides were of even thickness, that there were no holes in any of the tassie bases. I sprinkled pecans into each doughy cup. Lexie gave the sugary filling a stir, then carefully poured just the right amount over each pecan bed.

We were doing it. But it was like working on an important project with a coworker who you didn't know very well. We were cordial, but color and warmth didn't find us. It was all black-and-white adherence to process.

We slid the pans into the oven, and I set my phone's timer.

"If you want, I can watch these." I waved my hand toward the oven. "If you need to call the kids . . . or anything."

Lexie wiped her hands on a dish towel, mustered a smile. "Yeah . . . thanks."

I wanted to think I was being considerate and not just wanting space so the disappointment didn't feel so thick.

After dinner, Grace, Bo, Lexie, and I sat outside around the fire, sipping apple brandy in delicate glasses. The temperature had turned cool again and the fire felt good and warming. Our conversation wound its way from the curious mannerisms that cows had (Grace and Bo) to how funny Gran was (me), to how strange it was to raise children (Lexie).

"Whenever I use logic with my kids, I feel so stupid," Lexie said. "One night, we're eating dinner, and Gwen was in a chair that you attach to the table—she was one—and Violet, who was three, was next to her on a booster seat. They're eating, everything is fine. I turn my back for, I swear, not thirty seconds to get something from the fridge and I come back to the table and there's Violet using both hands to mound a pile of mashed potatoes on Gwen's head. I'm like, 'Violet, what are you doing?' And she says, 'I'm putting a mashed potato hat on Gwennie,' like this is something one does. Meanwhile, Gwen is looking at me with these wide eyes, just going along with things, not understanding. And so I say to Violet, literally the only thing I could think of was 'If Gwennie had wanted a mashed potato hat, she would've put it on herself!'"

She had us in stitches.

"I would love for you to bring them to the farm," Grace said.

"They would love it here!" Lexie turned to me. "We should figure out a time to come back with the kids."

I smiled. "Absolutely." Knowing we would make it happen.

Grace's look of obvious contentment reminded me of Gran when something worked out just the way she'd hoped. "I think this is a good time . . . I have something for you girls." She shifted in her seat and pulled a photo from her coat pocket. I assumed it was one of the pictures she'd taken earlier, but as she walked toward us, I saw it had scalloped edges. Lexie leaned over as Grace handed me a black-and-white picture, then sat back down next to Bo.

What I held in my hand was the beginning: two young girls in smock dresses and old-timey shoes sitting on a bale of hay, just as Lexie and I had earlier. Gran and Grace. Their arms were linked and their grins, toothy, happy in the sunshine of the moment. It was long before paths would be chosen and decisions would be made separating them in a way they never would've imagined—not on that summer day when they were young and together, smiling easily into a camera before heading off back into the fields.

Gran was so young, just a girl. They hadn't even lived their lives yet. My eyes welled. Lexie wrapped an arm around me. Just like Grace, she didn't say anything—no words were needed.

"Now, I only got one of those to give you." Grace wiped her nose with a hanky and tucked it into her pocket. "So, watch over it."

Nodding, I looked at her and flashed a teary smile. "Don't worry, we will."

After a moment of respectful silence, Bo spoke. "Well, ladies, I have to say, tonight was a pleasure." He looked at Lexie and me. "And it was an honor spending the weekend with you both . . . a real honor. But it's time for this old man to get some shut-eye, so I'll take my leave of you all."

Lexie and I hugged Bo goodbye. Grace held his hands when she bid him farewell, as if thanking him with her eyes.

Night had settled in, enveloping the fields, the trees, and even the fire with a deep and restful calm.

With a yawn, Grace announced it was past her bedtime. She hugged us good night and headed in to bed.

Lexie and I sat in companionable silence. The fire crackled. The sky brightened with stars.

"Are you . . . seeing anybody?" Lexie posed the question gently, which felt kind.

"Um . . . no. Not formally, like you know . . . something declared."

"Something declared." Amusement played across her face. "So, you haven't planted a flag in someone. Named a special somebody your country of relationship?"

I laughed.

"Or maybe there have been territory talks?"

"Stop it!"

"Are you blushing?"

"You can't possibly tell that in the dark. But yes, I am."

Lexie got up, did a funny little sashay over to me, topped off my brandy, then sat back down. "So?"

"It's not that I'm being cagey. I just don't know where to begin." I thought for a moment. "Probably because I haven't sorted anything out for myself, really. Or, I don't know, maybe I have. For the moment, at least."

"You're using a lot of words to say nothing. Let me know when you're going to say something. Anything at all."

I exhaled. "Remember Simon from back home?"

"You mean Nate's brother? Who decamped to the West Coast forever ago? Of course I remember him! I don't understand—how'd you reconnect with him of all people?"

I told her about meeting him at the village holiday dance and feeling like something was starting between us. I told her about going to dinner in the city, about how sweet he'd been. Then I told her about Peter, about the handful of moments where it felt like something was budding, and how it was both nothing and something at the same time, which, ultimately, was really just confusing.

"You're dating," Lexie said. "People date around all the time."

But that wasn't it at all.

This tiny thing I was trying to carve out for myself in this world, doing something I loved, I was protective of it. I needed to guard it. And that was why I hadn't been more engaged with Simon or encouraged Peter in the least. It would be easy to get into a relationship and let myself get swept up into a guy's life, but then I wouldn't create anything of my own. And I desperately wanted my own thing. If I was destined to spend time with someone special, they'd be there when the time was right. Right now, I needed to show up for me.

"I've got some other things going on and . . . in time I'll have space for a relationship. But now I guess I want to take this time to focus on myself."

"All right."

I debated whether to share the rest with Lexie.

"What are these other things going on?" she prodded.

"I sold all my furniture—there wasn't much, really," I blurted. "Donated a bunch of things . . . things that didn't even have any meaning, but I just kept for, I don't know . . . security? And put the rest in storage."

"Okayyyy . . . why?"

"I'm leaving the city, giving up my lease."

"Where are you going to live?"

"On a farm cooperative."

Lexie's face fell. "You've renounced your possessions and are moving to a"—here she bent her fingers in air quotes—"cooperative . . . Okay, this is a cult. You've joined a cult. I won't let you do this."

"It's not a cult. It's a farm that you have to apply to and everything. It's a six-month program. You get room and board in exchange for offseason work and learning to be a farmer. It's designed to help foster interest in New York farming. They have a grant from the state and everything—it's totally legit. There was an age requirement that I surpassed in a major way, so I wrote them this outraged email . . . and they agreed with me. I got a spot."

"You want to . . . farm." She cocked her head. "You want to farm?" She didn't let me answer. "No, no, no. You do not want to farm."

"I think—"

"Stop this right now."

"Would you just listen?"

Lexie slugged back the rest of her apple brandy and stood up. "Nope." She thrust the snifter toward me. "Here—I want you to drink until you sober up."

I held her eyes, didn't move. She dangled the bottle. Then flashed a resigned smile and sat back down with it.

Lexie refilled her glass and took a slow sip. Looked at the sky, exhaled, then focused on me. "All right. Tell me everything."

Everything was a lot. Everything was definitely more than I knew myself. But I wanted to shift my life in this sweeping way, and right now, knowing that was enough for me. Whether it would do for Lexie . . . It wasn't that I didn't want it to do for her, but for once, I wasn't cowed by the shadow of her disapproval. I wasn't even sure why this gumption had found me now. The only thing I could think of was that maybe for the first time in years, I was pursuing something I believed in. And that kernel of inner strength, so long latent, wasn't just enough, it was more powerful than I ever expected.

I cleared my throat. "I think—no, I know—I haven't been happy in a long time. For years." Lexie's face softened at this, which made me tear up. "I know . . . It's embarrassing how long I didn't do anything about it, just . . . I don't know, slid lower and lower trying to get by, slogging my way through the days." I thought back to all the months that felt largely gray. The friends that I let slip from my orbit. A stab of regret pierced me. "I think unhappiness whittled me down until I was kind of a shell. I'd lost my job, and the life I'd thought for years that I wanted—the one I stayed frozen in lackluster jobs for—it . . . well, I guess it didn't have the same shine." I sipped my brandy. "But I was so beaten down, really by my own actions or inaction, that I didn't know how to pull myself up, if that makes any sense."

"It does . . . sure." Her voice held a level of empathy that was new.

"And so I went to Gran's, as you know." I bit my cheek. Thinking about my time with Gran and how precious it was, how lucky I'd been . . . it was hard. When I thought back to weeding the flower beds, watching birds together, I just assumed there would always be time. I was too focused on my own issues, just as Lexie had said, which dismayed me. The reflexive wondering that regularly kicked in laid me out. Had I appreciated each moment as fully as I could have? My chin quivered. "How did I not realize how little time I had with her? How was I so oblivious?"

"If you had known, you wouldn't have had all the wonderful moments you shared." Lexie's voice was tender. "You would have been disengaged, so focused on the clock ticking, and in no way present. You would've been observing and worrying, not fully enjoying Gran."

I wiped my cheeks, murmured "Thanks," even though I wasn't sure she was right.

"Really, I mean it," she said. "Be grateful. You got honest, pristine time together, not something marred by worry, or the thought of time slipping away."

I managed a small smile, but that was all. I might never reconcile that.

"So . . . then you went back to the city, I take it?"

"Yeah." I wiped my nose. "I don't know why. When I got there, it just felt so wrong. Any footing I ever had there was totally gone. So . . . I started doing things that interested me. I got a job at a farm stand at the greenmarket."

Lexie smiled—not in a condescending way, in a "that tickles me" kind of way. "Really?"

"Yeah. And then Gran's letters started arriving." My eyes watered. "And it all kind of snowballed from there. The woman who runs the farm with her husband has been really—" I choked up thinking about Pet, who had showered me with kindness and compassion from the moment we'd met, and who offered gentle guidance to help me see what I wanted for myself. "She's been wonderful, just really supportive." I nodded to keep it together. "Anyway, she helped me see that it's actually garden and landscape design that I love. Like . . . what Gran and I used to do together. Creating beautiful spaces in nature really intrigues me. So, I'm doing this farm internship, yes. But I'm also apprenticing at a landscape design firm in the Hudson Valley—it's really respected, and business is booming because so much money has moved into the area. So, I'll get a modest stipend from them while I apprentice for six months."

"Oh, wow, okay."

"Yeah, and so my hope is that I'll learn about building gardens, soil management, planting, and all that on the farm, with my room and board paid for . . . and then with my apprenticeship at the design firm, I'll earn a little money to put away. Then, after six months, I should be able to afford something modest up there to rent while I work at the design firm. The apprenticeship is the first step to getting a salaried position there. Or . . . I don't know. I mean, who knows where I'll decide to live."

Lexie stared like she was waiting for me to say something more, after I'd said everything, shared more with her than I ever had as an adult. The silence ballooned and I felt a lingering ache, like I'd pressed an old bruise that hadn't fully healed.

"You've put thought into this—something beyond thought, really." She smiled, finally, but it was tenuous, like she was struggling to find the proper position for me in her head now. "It sounds like you're excited about this, which—" She paused. "Which seems like an important change." Her smile widened. "I'm happy for you. Really."

I tried to speak but emotion flooded my throat, breached the dam, and the tears fell. "Yeah?" Then I laughed. It was such a relief to gain a smidge of approval from my younger sister, which felt foolish, like something a child would hope for. I'd been a child for so long.

"So, you think you might live someplace else besides New York at some point?"

I shrugged.

"You're thinking about Gates Mills."

"I don't know what I'm thinking," I said. "For starters, I don't have any money to be considering anything past my immediate paycheck. So . . ." I shook my head. Lexie had touched something that was too tender.

"Okay . . . I understand." She sat silent for a bit. "You know . . . we do need to talk about Gran's house . . . about how we want to handle it."

She spoke gently, with real consideration, but the thought of saying goodbye to our beloved home with Gran was like having to say goodbye to her all over again. I looked up at the inky sky. I couldn't fathom selling her home that held so much precious past. Couldn't imagine going through her belongings, the smocks she wore to garden in, all the pretty porcelain dishes in the kitchen larder . . . the sewing room. Giving away anything of Gran's was unthinkable. I didn't want to let go of anything. Not even the scraps of material she lovingly kept. Tears rolled down my cheeks. I didn't want to talk about this. I didn't even want to think about it.

"And I know that's really difficult." Lexie paused. "Which is why I think we should keep the house and everything as is for at least a couple years before we even start talking about what we want to do."

I shook my head and looked at her. “It costs money to keep a house. Taxes, bills, it’s not insignificant . . . I can’t even pay rent. And then the upkeep of a house . . . I don’t see how that would work.”

She held up both hands as if to calm. “I can handle the financial part of keeping the house. It’s . . . the least I can do. And I hope you’ll let me do this for the two of us. We can decide everything when it feels right. Until then, Sydney can check in on the house. She comes home from OSU once a month and I’ll pay her to keep tabs on things. I already talked to her about this.”

I thought back to seeing them speaking at Gran’s wake, dreading what Lexie was saying to Sydney. Something else I’d obviously misjudged.

Lexie nodded, willing me to understand. “Having time to breathe without more upset wouldn’t be bad. Besides, who knows—you might want to go back to Gates Mills.”

I really hadn’t thought that far ahead, but a lightness settled in my chest. Not having to say goodbye to Gran’s house brought tears to my eyes. “Really? You would do that? Are you sure?”

“Yeah. This is going to sound funny coming from me, but sometimes doing nothing is the absolute right thing to do. I’m certain this is one of those moments. And, I have to say again, I’d really like to do this for us.”

I nodded like a bobblehead, so full of gratitude. “Thank you.”

Lexie’s smile in the flickering light, radiating from a deep pool of happy, reminded me so much of our mom’s smile right then.

“So, when does your farm thing and landscape design apprenticeship start?”

“October first. Actually, it starts on the fifth, but my apartment lease ends on October second, so I’m moving up there on the first.”

Lexie bit the side of her cheek. “Would you . . . be willing to go somewhere with me? Like in a couple weeks?”

"Really?" Her question touched me. "I'd love to." Then I remembered my reality. "But I have no money, so as long as it's cheap. Like a movie?"

"Not a movie . . . and money isn't the issue." She grew serious. "It's whether you can take the time, given all these new things you're venturing into."

She'd never before extended that kind of consideration to me, or anything I'd done. I was touched. "I'd love to."

We talked until the fire no longer licked the dark sky, until its embers no longer glowed hot orange. Lexie and I poked out the last of the flames with sticks, then went inside and climbed the stairs to sit on my bed and talk a little more, making our time together last as long as possible.

I woke up in the middle of the night to find Lexie sleeping soundly next to me—we must have fallen asleep in my bed while talking. I peered more closely at her and, even in my sleepy state, couldn't help but smile. When we were kids, she'd slept with both her arms above her head, as if someone in her dreams had arrested her. That remained true to this day.

It was dark and still—the kind of stillness that descended on a house when it was way too late to go to bed and way too early to wake up. A chill hung in the air, so I carefully pulled up the comforter that was folded neatly at the foot of the bed and tucked both of us in.

The time with Lexie during this trip was so different from every other one of our thorny interactions in previous years. Like a bone that had been set after splintering, things between us still felt fragile. But bones have a way of mending.

And then it dawned on me: Just when Lexie and I were growing close again, geographic realities loomed large. For years, the miles between DC and New York had seemed a blessing. Not so much anymore.

I turned my head to see Lexie, breathing quietly, looking serene in her slumber. As a kid, I had never thought it possible there'd be a day we wouldn't play together. Time then had passed with a lazy ticktock of hide-and-seek. As adults, time had raced bitterly by.

Amazingly, by Gran's invisible hand, Lexie and I had found our way back to that comfortable cocoon of childhood companionship—that easy take-for-granted togetherness. I smiled to myself in the dark and nestled deeper into my pillow.

The sweetness, it was still there . . . and every ounce of it, still ours.

Fat

Part 6

Allow yourselves to return to someplace familiar.
Let it take you someplace new.

Chapter 19

I'd sat on more than my share of benches over the years. Growing up in Gates Mills, they were usually attached to picnic tables. When I was older, living in New York, more often than not, they were in Central Park. But I'd never had the exquisite pleasure of sitting on a bench overlooking lush olive groves in Tuscany—until now.

The spark of conversation at Grace's farm had ignited a trip here to a Tuscan palazzo—a prominent noble family's home at one time, now a luxurious cooking retreat where Lexie and I would be for the next five days.

It was still early, and tendrils of mist hovered close to the ground. I'd taken my morning espresso outside while Lexie stayed behind to email her nanny about my nieces. Today was our first day of cooking, but it wouldn't start until after everyone had a chance to sleep in and enjoy a full Italian breakfast. Little here, we'd discovered, was rushed.

I took in the quiet vista, my head full of memories. Since Gran passed away, the shattering grief had felt like I was losing myself bit by dusty bit. I thought about those bits of me blowing away . . . and wondered . . . maybe I hadn't lost anything at all. Maybe all my memories were puffing up, asserting themselves, becoming an indelible part of me, actually fusing with my cells so I could hold them closer, walk every step with them, breathe with them in my lungs. Maybe I was becoming more complete, more fully myself with every memory of Gran, of my mom, of Lexie, inflating me—stabilizing me, blowing away the detritus and making me more whole than I'd ever been before. Which was both a bizarre and heartbreaking thing to contemplate. Who would ever think themselves more whole after someone beloved passed away? After two of the most beloved people in your life died? But if I'd never had them, or my memories of them to buoy me, how tragic would that have been? Perhaps this was Gran's final gift. Reminding me of all the love I'd been surrounded with—and showing me how to carry it. Not to move on from any of it . . . but to move forward *with* it all. Maybe the secret was to hold them close—Gran, my mom, my childhood with Lexie—and let them fortify me . . . let their transcendent importance make me into someone new. Someone who understood the gift of time, the precious and stabilizing force of love. Someone who carried all the pain but had it alleviated by the joyous buoyancy of memories, and in doing so, became a more whole version of herself, something new. No longer a husk of a person. Not every day, anyway.

Grief . . . in a trippy way, could make us whole, in an elevated sense of the word. Whole with memories, with the love that still warmed us, with experiences that made us more complete versions of ourselves. As little sense as that made, grief put us on another plane of understanding and living.

"Wow, this is beautiful." Lexie sat down next to me, holding a cup of cappuccino. "So, of the countless reasons why I love Italy, do you know what one of the top ones is?"

"Tell me."

"They serve balsamic vinegar at breakfast." She sipped her coffee and sighed contentedly. "We may never leave this place."

We sat side by side, basking in the serene view.

"Thank you again," I said. "This is amazing . . . and it's incredibly gracious of you."

"Thanks for coming." Her smile was thoughtful. "I wanted to give us something special."

I murmured that it really was. And then summoned to get out what I'd been wanting to say to her for weeks. "You know, back at the farm?"

I'd thought about this so much and now struggled with how to word it. "You were telling me about everything . . . and said that you felt alone."

Lexie stared out over the trees for a beat, then, her voice soft, said, "I remember."

"I wanted to say then that you're not . . . you'll never be alone." I swallowed, emotion rising up.

She scrunched her nose up, kept staring out at the horizon. Said nothing.

Which deflated me.

Then a tear rolled down her cheek. She nodded, then took my hand and just smiled. Because she couldn't get the words out. And I had no more of my own. But for the first time in years, we didn't need a single one.

As we walked back to the palazzo, Lexie said, "The morning session is being taught by, and I quote, 'a chef embodying youth and vitality who's groundbreaking in her approach to Italian cuisine.'"

"When do kids graduate from culinary school these days, anyway?"

"Beats me—she's probably too young to drive."

We swung the palazzo's heavy wooden door shut behind us and were greeted by a comforting fire in the main room's hearth. We deposited our coffee cups on a sideboard and made our way to the kitchen. The ceiling curved in dramatic arches, reflecting the exquisite masonry of times long ago. The further we walked into the depths of the building, the more it felt like Lexie and I were being tucked away in time.

Ten of us gathered around a massive wooden island in the center of the room. Conversation crackled about which new chef would be teaching us. The chatter died down when an old woman ambled into the kitchen. She leaned on a cane, slowly shuffled her feet.

"Bene." She smiled at the sight of everyone in the room, laugh lines crinkling and eyes twinkling with delight. Her face reminded me of an ornament that Gran had given our mom the Christmas before cancer took her from us: a Mrs. Claus face made from a dried apple. The ornament had a petite poof of cottony white hair, tiny wire glasses, and a red felt collar. Every year since Mom passed away, we hung Mrs. Claus on the tree, right in the center where she could be seen by everyone. With each passing year, her apple face became drier and more wrinkled—but Mrs. Claus's smile and eyes remained cheery and full of life, like she embodied our mom's happiness.

"Bene, bene," the woman muttered as she made her way to us. Then she spoke with a louder voice. "Buongiorno, class."

Polite, if somewhat puzzled, smiles looked back at her.

She chuckled and propped her cane up against the island. "What? Am I not the embodiment of youth and vitality?"

Everyone laughed.

"Yes, I have a very good press person." She giggled, her shoulders moving up and down. "I am being funny with you, no? I am, and I am not." She raised a finger and became serious. "What people do not realize is that the tastes and techniques these new chefs come up with, they are rooted in traditions that are very old . . . almost as old as me."

She looked around the table, a smile dancing on her lips. "And that, you see, makes me very young. Very young indeed." She touched the arms of the people standing on either side of her. "Yes, you see now? Bene . . . Let us begin. My name is Annabelle."

Shocked to hear Gran's name said aloud, I looked at Lexie. Her eyes were wide and watery, like she'd been enveloped in an unexpected hug. I took her hand in mine. She squeezed it.

"Today you will call me Annabelle." She moved her arms like a conductor, her smile wide. "But by the end of the week, I hope you will call me Nonna, which means 'grandmother' in Italian. That is how special I want this week to be for you."

Heart thumping in my chest, I blinked to contain my emotion.

Lexie shook her head in disbelief, flashed a teary smile, then wrapped her arms around me.

"Bene, bene, we have a dessert here in Tuscany, which we will make today. It's called torta della nonna . . . grandmother's cake."

As Chef Annabelle talked, my head flooded with memories—memories that had been undammed by Gran, the photos, the recipes. Memories of our mom, of us as kids with Gran, running barefoot, kneeling on kitchen chairs, our fingers overlapping in squishy dough, of us playing. So much playing . . . and there it was, a crystalline moment pushed itself to the fore: The two of us dipping plastic wands into bottles of soapy water, then gently blowing a stream of bubbles. Delicate soapy circles that shimmered, had an opalescent rainbow sheen to them. They lifted up, up, up into the cloudless sky, held aloft by happy breath, carrying the air of innocence, connection, and a feeling we didn't yet know as love. When the bubbles burst, we blew more and then more. There were always more bubbles. More delight to be had. The action was simple. Nothing lurked behind our joy.

As an adult, what I'd learned was that the magical soapy mix sometimes had to be shaken. Done right, the bottle held the promise of more.

Standing in the palazzo's kitchen with Lexie, having gone through so much, I now saw the bubbles for what they were: hope.

Epilogue

Dearest Violet & Gwen,

You're probably wondering why I'm giving you the beginning of a cookbook.

This isn't for today, and probably not for many tomorrows, but when you're older and ready, this cookbook will be waiting.

I made four of these—one for each of you, one for your mom, and one for myself.

You see, Gran's last gift to your mom and me was a cookbook with all her recipes. It's precious, an enormous loving present in a tiny book. But the recipes, the ones Gran made us all our life, the very ones she made with Great-Aunt Grace and their mother growing up, they didn't have much detail. No precise quantities of ingredients, little explanation of how to make them. That's because Gran already knew the recipes by heart. She didn't need anything written down.

Well, your mom and I kind of needed those details to ensure we could keep making Gran's delicious dishes. And so, that's what I've done here, written everything down for the ones we've figured out so far—the ingredients, the amounts, the steps, all the tips I realized were important when making these dishes on my own and with your mom, and, importantly, every bit of advice Gran shared with us.

Now we have the specifics of Gran's kitchen magic in one place so we can all keep her traditions going. As your mom and I figure out the rest of the recipes together, we'll add them to our books. I think Gran would love this.

In fact, I can hear her saying, "Good, good, good."

Much love always,

Auntie Belle

Peanut Butter Cookies, a.k.a. Pocket Cookies

The best thing about Gran's peanut butter cookies is that they actually taste like peanut butter. And the secret is using dark-roasted peanut butter as the base. Gran loved the Santa Cruz Dark Roasted organic brand—it gave her cookies a deep, delicious peanut-buttery zing.

But I worried that we might not be able to find that brand all the time, so I tested lots of other peanut butters, and I'm thrilled to say that Smucker's Natural Peanut Butter works perfectly too (I like the chunky version). It produces the exact same deep peanut butter flavor as the Santa Cruz. Bonus: It's available pretty much everywhere! I think Gran would definitely approve.

Gran always said that a perfect cookie has a warm cakey center and a crisp exterior. The key to achieving this cookie bliss is the bake time. And everyone's oven is different, so keep that in mind. What my oven does perfectly at 14 minutes, yours might do ideally at 15 minutes. Have patience with that first sheet and adjust your bake time accordingly.

It's worth noting that these bake up beautifully straight from the freezer. Usually, Gran would bake off a sheet, then portion and shape the remaining dough into cookies and freeze them to bake off later. Having cookies ready to bake is one of the reasons she lacked freezer space, but now I understand what a wonderful problem that is to have.

Ingredients

- 2 Tbsp. butter
- 1 jar (16 oz.) Santa Cruz Dark Roasted Peanut Butter or Smucker's Natural Peanut Butter (neither should have added sugar, salt, or oil)
- 2 c. dark brown sugar
- 2 eggs plus 1 egg yolk
- 2 tsp. vanilla
- 2 Tbsp. half-and-half
- 1 tsp. salt
- 1 tsp. baking soda
- ½ c. bread flour (Gran used bread flour because it makes a chewier cookie)

Preheat the oven to 350 degrees. Line a baking sheet with parchment paper.

What's great is that this is a stir-by-hand recipe. If the peanut butter has separated, make sure to mix it thoroughly in the jar before beginning.

Melt the butter in a bowl and then stir in the entire jar of peanut butter.

Add the dark brown sugar and mix.

In a separate small bowl, whisk together the two eggs, one egg yolk, vanilla, and half-and-half. Add that to the peanut butter mixture.

Stir together the salt, baking soda, and bread flour, then add that to the mixture.

Use a ¼ cup measuring cup to portion cookies. Gran loved a big, chubby cookie, so make them into plump patties. Position the cookies on the baking sheet. Eight typically fit on a sheet pan. Bake for 14 minutes. Allow them to cool for a few minutes on the cookie sheet before transferring them to a cooling rack. Gran used to lift off the entire parchment sheet with the cookies and set it on the rack.

Whatever cookies don't get eaten immediately, store in a plastic bag (or a pocket).

Pecan Tassies, a.k.a. Little Pecan Pies

Gran used to make these during the holidays for everyone she loved. And she had an enormous heart, so come the holidays, her kitchen was overrun with tassies. They truly are tiny pecan pies, as Mama P called them. Two nibbles and you're done, but oh, the taste! Just tiny pie perfection. Gran would nestle the tassies in decorative containers that she'd lined with dessert doilies. To this day, I see a white dessert doily beneath a pastry and I think, *Special.*

Ingredients

Crust:

- 1 c. butter, softened
- 6 oz. cream cheese, softened (Gran always used Philadelphia brand)
- 2 c. flour

Filling:

- 2 Tbsp. butter
- 2 eggs
- 1½ c. light brown sugar

- ¼ tsp. salt
- 1 tsp. vanilla extract
- 1¼ c. pecans, chopped
- Powdered sugar for dusting

To make the crust, combine butter and cream cheese in a bowl and work with a wooden spoon until the mixture is smooth and creamy. Add the flour in fourths, blending thoroughly. Work with fingers into a smooth, blended dough. Refrigerate the dough for a short while so it's easier to shape.

Preheat the oven to 350 degrees.

To make the filling, melt the butter in a bowl and then whisk in the eggs, brown sugar, salt, and vanilla.

Pinch off small pieces of dough. Shape into balls that are about 1¼ inches. The dough will be extremely elastic and easy to handle. Put each ball into the cup of a mini muffin pan. Press the dough against the bottom and sides of each cup. Sprinkle a few pecans in the dough-lined cups.

Spoon the filling over the nuts until the filling nearly reaches the top of the muffin cup. Add a few more nuts.

Bake for 15 to 17 minutes or until the filling is almost set.

Allow them to cool slightly in the pan, then transfer them to a cooling rack. When fully cool, dust with powdered sugar.

Makes 3 to 4 dozen.

Stuffing

Done right, stuffing should make you forget about everything else on your plate. It should make you forget about the turkey, or that meat loaf. You should have no memory of whatever vegetable might've been served alongside. If you're lucky enough to be eating such a scrumptious stuffing, all that matters is . . . stuffing. You could eat nothing but that for the rest of your life, eat it all day, every day. And you'd be so happy. Gran's stuffing, I'm delighted to tell you, is exactly this kind of stuffing.

Ingredients

- 1 loaf white bread (I've found Whole Foods white sandwich bread works great . . . back in the day, Gran used Wonder Bread)
- 3 tsp. dried sage, divided
- 2 tsp. salt, divided
- 4 Tbsp. butter, divided
- Olive oil
- 3 c. finely chopped onion
- 3 c. finely chopped celery
- 1 egg
- 1 Tbsp. half-and-half (splash)
- 1 c. chicken stock, plus additional as needed (anywhere

between 1 Tbsp. to ¼ c.)

The stuffing requires the bread to be pinched the day before you assemble it. Don't use the end pieces of the loaf. Do what Gran did and give those to the raccoons. In a bowl big enough that you can toss and season the bread, pinch pieces from the entire loaf. Do not use the shiny tops of the loaf (the consistency doesn't bake up well). And use a light touch as you pinch—you don't want to squeeze the bread too tightly. Torn pieces should be somewhere between the size of a nickel and a quarter. But there's no set rule—you just don't want them too big because the bread and the savory aromatics should hug one another equally. After the bread is pinched, season it lightly with ½ teaspoon salt and ¾ teaspoon dried sage. You're just doing a little sprinkle throughout. Taste as you go—when you have the tiniest salty taste and the faintest hint of sage, you've seasoned enough. Let the bread sit out uncovered overnight to dry out. Toss the bread pieces every now and again to circulate air around the pinched bits.

If you want to split the recipe up into two days, you can chop the onions and celery and store them in the refrigerator until you're ready to sauté them. Or you can chop up everything, sauté it all, then store it in the refrigerator until the next day when the bread has dried and you're ready to assemble the stuffing. Gran used to do it both ways and it always worked great. She always said to do what's best timewise.

The key with the onions and celery is chopping them finely. For example, Gran would cut a typical celery stalk down the middle at the top where it was thinnest, then into thirds (or even fourths) toward the fatter base before she started chopping. You don't want the bits of onion and celery to be too thick or big because then it throws off the balance of the dish. A fine dice for both is the way to go, Gran always said. It's a lot of chopping, but trust me, it's worth it.

Sauté the celery and onion in batches—either in the same pan, or if you have the pan power and space, multiple pans. Gran always used one pan and typically did it in three batches, using a cup of onions and a cup of celery in each. For every batch, use 1 tablespoon of butter and a light drizzle of olive oil in a large pan over medium-high heat. Add 1 cup each of onions and celery. Add the salt and sage—if you're doing three batches, that's ½ teaspoon salt and ¾ teaspoon sage per batch. Gran used to say it should whisper sage and salty goodness, not scream it.

Preheat the oven to 375 degrees. Butter an 8-inch square baking dish with a scant ½ tablespoon butter.

When the batches of onions and celery are all sautéed and the bread has dried out overnight, it's time to assemble and bake. Combine the sautéed bits and the bread in a large bowl and toss to combine. Gran always did this first so the seasoning from the sauté could really soak into the bread before she added the rest of the ingredients.

In a small dish, whisk together the egg, half-and-half, and 1 cup chicken stock. Pour the wet mixture over the bread mixture a little at a time, mixing thoroughly as you go. When everything is mixed, you may find that you need a little more stock—it all depends on how dry the bread was to begin with. Here, Gran always said you have to use a judicious approach—too much stock and the stuffing will be soggy, whereas too little and the dish won't come together in a cohesive whole because some bread will remain too dry and not flavored through. So, do exactly as Gran did: Examine the raw stuffing, and if some pieces still look dry, add more stock 1 tablespoon at a time. Then mix it again. You really need to eye it—if you see some bread pieces that look dry, more stock is needed. But you don't want to have stock collecting at the bottom of the bowl. The bread should be moistened, that's all.

Put the mixture into the buttered pan and spread it out evenly. Dot the top with ½ tablespoon softened butter, cover with foil, and bake for 25 minutes. Then, uncover the dish and bake for 10 to 15 minutes longer, until the top is golden.

Vegetable Stock, a.k.a. Baby Soup

Baby soup is what Gran called vegetable stock. Now that I make it on my own, the beauty I've found is that it's flexible and forgiving.

Gran always used big quantities of herbs—parsley, dill, thyme, sage, and rosemary—to give the stock a full-bodied taste. Typically, she'd make a big batch in a 10-quart pot and freeze the strained broth in containers ranging in size from one cup to four cups. That way, whenever she needed some good broth, all that was required was a quick thaw.

She'd layer all the veggies and herbs. She never counted herb sprigs, just tossed 'em all in. The more flavor the better, she always said. And when she wanted to use the stock in a recipe, be it soup or maybe a base to cook a grain, and she wanted a less-concentrated flavor, she'd just add water.

A couple of things Gran always stressed in terms of quantities: the carrot, potato, and celery ratio tended to be one-to-one, with the exception of celery, which she always used a lighter hand with. If you use far more carrots than potatoes and celery, the broth tastes really carroty, almost gamey, and one note (which is exactly what Gran really didn't like about boxed broths).

Gran would use her baby soup as the base for her vegetable and white bean soups. I've also used it when I make freekeh, or if I want to make another grain, say quinoa or farro, taste extra special. You can stir in white miso paste to make a super savory broth to sip or even a ramen dish. And if I'm making something that calls for a little water, I use stock and it really elevates all the flavors.

Ingredients

Note: This is what Gran usually used when making baby soup in a 10-quart stockpot. Nothing is chopped finely. Herbs are added intact, stems and all.

- Olive oil
- 3–4 medium yellow onions, cut into quarters (if the papery skins are clean and free of dirt, leave them on, it'll give the stock a rich hue)
- Salt
- 2 garlic heads, cut in half so the cloves are exposed
- 1 big bunch each of parsley, dill, thyme, sage, and rosemary (the parsley, dill, and thyme bunches tend to be bigger than the sage and rosemary)
- 8 carrots, peeled and cut in half or thirds if long
- 5 celery stalks, cut in half or thirds if really long
- 8 potatoes, unpeeled and cut into quarters
- 2 bay leaves
- 10–15 peppercorns
- Water

Start with a stockpot over medium-high heat, coat the bottom of the pot with a good glug of olive oil.

The first layer to go in is the onions. Gran always put them cut side down. Sprinkle a little salt over the top. Add the garlic in here too.

Next layer: All the herbs. It doesn't matter how you nestle them in. Remember, everything is going to be covered with water.

Next layer: Carrots, celery, and potatoes. Pile 'em in.

Add the bay leaves and peppercorns. Pour enough water into the pot to cover everything by 1 to 1½ inches.

Cover the pot with a lid and bring to a boil. Gran always uncovered the pot as soon as it started to boil and lowered the heat to a rapid simmer. Then, she'd tilt the lid so the pot was mostly covered but uncovered enough that the stock didn't boil over.

Cook at a rapid simmer for a good hour. You can't cook it too long, but you need to cook it at least an hour for the flavor to develop. Stir it a couple of times to get all the savory bits moving around. You'll notice the broth will turn a deep gold color if you used some onion skins. Toward the end of the cooking, add some salt to taste. Gran never seasoned her stock fully—that is, she didn't make it as salty as she'd normally like. That's because she wanted the option to season it depending on what she'd make later.

After an hour or so, turn off the burner, cover the pot with the lid, and let it cool completely.

Once cool, strain all the liquid. Gran would use a fine mesh strainer balanced over a large bowl. This is the most time-consuming part of the entire process, but if the stock is cool, it goes quickly enough. Have all your containers clean and ready to be filled. Freeze the extra so you'll always have some baby soup on hand.

Berries & Cream

You know a recipe is simple when its name holds the bulk of the ingredient list. Gran made this for your mom and me all the time growing up. Berries drizzled with cream, then topped with the lightest dusting of sugar . . . It really is a perfect combination of flavors. Kind of like raspberry ice cream when it gets all melty.

Ingredients

- Fresh raspberries
- Half-and-half
- Sugar

Tumble some berries into a bowl. Gran always put this in a pretty, shallow dish with a scalloped edge (it was such a dainty touch). Add a bit of half-and-half—it's not cereal, so you're not pouring a ton in, just a splash. A pinch of sugar over top, however sweet you like, and that's it!

Savory Tomato Jam

This is summer cooked down to its sweet jammy essence. And the beauty of Gran's recipe is in its simplicity. She used cherry tomatoes, heirloom tomatoes, plum tomatoes, or slicing tomatoes. You name the tomato, and she made it into savory jam.

Sometimes Gran would run the cooked-down tomatoes through a food mill, which removed the skins and seeds and processed the jam into a velvety consistency.

Gran would serve savory jam alongside toasted pieces of bread that she'd rubbed with a garlic clove, drizzled with olive oil, and finished with a sprinkle of flaky salt. She served it alongside cooked white beans. I've served it atop yummy grains like farro or freekeh. It's terrific as a smear on a sandwich, or as a condiment on a cheese board. It freezes really well and is a true treat in the middle of winter when you get to thaw out a little taste of summer.

Ingredients

- Olive oil
- 1½–2 lb. tomatoes, chopped (Gran usually cut paste tomatoes into sixths, cherry tomatoes in half—this is just to help them cook down more quickly. Let the size be your guide.)
- Two whole garlic cloves, peeled
- Salt and pepper

Over medium-high heat, coat the bottom of a large stainless-steel pan with olive oil. Add chopped tomatoes and whole garlic cloves. Season with salt and pepper.

Cook the tomatoes, stirring and breaking them up with a wooden spoon. Once the tomatoes start to break down, Gran always lowered the burner to medium and let the heat do the work to reduce everything to a thickened mass. This usually takes about 30 minutes or so.

Serve warm from the pan or reheat at a later time. You can also let the tomato jam cool, then pass through a food mill for a smoother consistency. Tastes like summer either way!

Farm Breakfast

This recipe is many things—savory, yummy, and above all else, infinitely flexible.

Gran often used roasted potatoes from dinner the night before, sometimes roasted veggies, and always whatever greens she had on hand (kale, rainbow chard, spinach, you name it—if it was green, it worked!). If she had roasted onions already made, she usually didn't sauté any more, rather just incorporated those oniony bits that were already cooked.

This is Gran's easy yet hearty breakfast that feels decadent and yummy at the same time.

Ingredients

- Olive oil
- Either 3 green scallions, 2 shallots, or half a small onion, diced (Gran happened to like onions a lot, but if oniony bits aren't your thing, use less)
- Potatoes (you can use leftovers chopped up or use 1–2 small potatoes cut in a small dice so they cook quickly)
- Salt and pepper
- Other add ins: leftover vegetables that have been sautéed or roasted—peppers, zucchini, broccoli, or cauliflower. (Gran would add raw bell peppers, zucchini, or yellow squash early

to the sauté stage.)

- Greens (Gran always said the more the better. Sometimes she'd use an entire bag of spinach or a bunch of kale. The greens really cook down, so toss in a hearty serving, all chopped up.)
- 6 eggs (Figure 2 eggs per person. Gran always made hers with at least 6 eggs, sometimes more, even if nobody else was eating with us. That's because the leftovers save wonderfully in the fridge, and then for the next couple of days, a quick reheat is all that's necessary for a delicious cooked breakfast.)
- Splash of milk or half-and-half, optional
- Sometimes Gran would add her slow-roasted tomatoes, but if she did, she always added them after the eggs were fully cooked.

Start with a large pan over medium-high heat. Coat the bottom with a good glug of oil. Add in chopped onions (scallions, shallots, or onions—whatever you decide to use) and raw diced potatoes, if using, and season with salt and pepper. If you're adding in raw peppers or other veggies, add them here. Cook until softened and a little brown around the edges.

If you have leftover cooked veggies, chop them up and add those next. I usually warm them in the microwave a little before adding just to speed everything up.

Next, add the chopped greens and sauté until wilted and any moisture is evaporated (this is most common with fresh spinach).

Finally, whisk your eggs with a splash of milk or half-and-half (you can use a nondairy milk if you prefer, or omit altogether) and a little salt and pepper, then add to the pan of veggies. Use a wooden spoon to incorporate everything, breaking up the mixture as it cooks.

Cook until the eggs are no longer loose, season to taste with salt and pepper, then serve warm. Maybe even add some feta or cheddar—because, as Gran liked to say, cheese makes everything better! Leftovers can be refrigerated for a later breakfast delight.

Walleye with Cracker Topping

Gran always made this with walleye, but what your mom and I discovered is that if you can't find walleye at the fish market, any mild white fish works wonderfully with this buttery cracker topping.

Ingredients

- 5 crackers, Ritz or similar, per fillet
- 1 Tbsp. butter per fillet
- Olive oil
- Fish fillets (walleye, haddock, tilapia, and sea bass all work beautifully)
- Salt and pepper
- Lemon

Preheat the oven to 350 degrees.

Depending on how many fillets you're making, multiply the amount of crackers and melted butter in the recipe.

In a plastic bag, or with your hands, crush the crackers so there are a few small rough shards remaining. It shouldn't be cracker dust, as Gran used to remind us.

Melt the butter in a bowl. Add the broken crackers and stir to combine.

Lightly oil a baking dish and the fish fillets with just the thinnest coating of oil (the butter in the cracker topping will add lots of richness). Season with salt and pepper. Place in a baking dish. Top each fillet with a layer of buttered cracker crumbs.

Bake for 15 to 20 minutes depending on the type of fish you're using. You'll know it's done when it flakes apart with a fork. Serve immediately with lemon.

Candied Spiced Nuts

Gran always had a bowl of these out on her coffee table. You can make them as spicy as you like—really kicky like Gran did or sweeter without any heat. Both ways are delicious.

Ingredients

- ½ c. plus 2 Tbsp. coconut sugar (you can also use brown sugar, but the coconut sugar seems to meld with the nuts better—it really adds something special)
- 1½ tsp. smoked paprika
- 1 Tbsp. cayenne (you can add less for milder nuts, or more for even spicier nuts)
- 1½ tsp. salt
- ½ tsp. ground cloves
- 2 tsp. cinnamon
- ½ tsp. ground ginger
- 1 egg white
- 1 tsp. water
- 5 c. mixed nuts (Gran used pecans, cashews, walnuts, and almonds)

Preheat the oven to 300 degrees. Line a baking sheet with parchment paper.

In a small bowl, mix together the coconut sugar, smoked paprika, cayenne, salt, ground cloves, cinnamon, and ground ginger. Set aside.

In a large bowl, beat the egg white and 1 teaspoon water until frothy.

Add 5 cups mixed nuts to the egg white froth and stir until coated.

Add the spice mixture to the nuts and stir until the nuts are evenly coated.

Spread nuts in a single layer onto the baking sheet. Bake for about 25 minutes.

The nuts will be soft when they come out of the oven. Allow to cool on the pan for at least five minutes before stirring to break up the nuts into clusters. The nuts will harden as they cool further. Store in the refrigerator.

For candied nuts that aren't spicy, omit the smoked paprika and cayenne, then add an extra ½ teaspoon ground cloves.

Roasted Chicken Over Vegetables

This is an entire meal made on one baking sheet. It was Gran's comfort meal that she'd make when the months got colder. Not only did it warm us, it made the entire house smell delicious.

Ingredients

- 3–4 potatoes, cut into 2-inch pieces
- 6 carrots, cut into 2-inch pieces
- 1 large onion, cut into 2-inch pieces
- Olive oil
- Salt and pepper
- Chicken (Gran often used a whole chicken, but it's easier to use 2 half-chicken portions that are bone-in, skin-on. You can separate the breast from the thigh in each half—kitchen scissors work best—so you have four pieces total, 2 breasts and 2 thighs.)
- 6 stalks kale, de-ribbed and cut crosswise into 2-inch ribbons

Preheat the oven to 400 degrees.

Place cut potatoes, carrots, and onions onto a baking sheet (or in a metal roasting pan). Drizzle with just a tiny bit of olive oil, then season with salt and pepper. You don't need much oil at all, just enough to give the veggies the thinnest coat. The chicken juices will keep everything moist.

Dry the chicken pieces with a paper towel. Coat with a little olive oil and season with salt and pepper. Place atop the vegetables on the baking sheet and roast for 30 minutes.

After 30 minutes, remove baking sheet, move chicken to one side, and stir the vegetables. Spread the vegetables evenly across the sheet again, add the kale on top of the vegetables, and then reposition the chicken on top of the kale.

Bake for another 15 minutes, or until a thermometer stuck in the thickest part of the chicken breast reads 165 degrees.

Let the chicken rest for a few minutes before serving.

Author's Note

I wrote *Recipe for Joy* at a profoundly tender time in my life, after my beloved mother passed away. Devastating loss shatters completely. It leaves you feeling like a husk of yourself, papery and fragile . . . a breath away from dusty obliteration. This was my experience, at least. Everyone grieves differently. There's no one way, and there's certainly no "right" way.

It was during this time, living in the charming village of Gates Mills, Ohio (yes, Gates Mills is a real place on the east side of Cleveland that's truly so lovely—a place that I've celebrated and taken a bit of creative license with in *Recipe for Joy*), when reality felt bewildering, when deep and abiding sorrow whiplashed, that I began putting pen to paper. That in and of itself felt so foreign, even though writing is what I've done my entire life and what I've always known. And at that moment when it felt like I knew absolutely nothing . . . if I could do anything, maybe I could write.

At least, that's what I thought.

But I couldn't use my laptop. (Too emotional—why? No clue.)

So, I wrote longhand (also, it turned out, not easy).

Nevertheless, with our sweet pup, Kona, by my side, I sat on the couch and tried to do this thing that was such a difficult undertaking . . . probably because my mom had always championed my writing. We shared a love of books and good, meaty prose. She always read whatever I wrote. So, I sat there with a notebook, and everything bubbled up

. . . then overflowed, the way it can with grief. But the notebook that I eventually filled contained, if I squinted in just the right way, the vague shape of a story. In time, I transcribed all of it to my laptop and continued working. It was different than any other way I'd ever written anything, but perhaps at that point in my life, different was necessary.

Heartbreakingly, during this time, we had to say goodbye to our beloved Kona, who cuddled with my mom, who always found his way to my side, and who filled our lives with love for more than fourteen years. We also had to say goodbye to the home we all loved in Gates Mills, the home and sweet town that served as a sanctuary for us, that held me through the deepest lows of my life, and that gifted us countless precious memories. Grief followed my husband and me back to New York, where, eventually, I finished my book with our new fur baby, Poirot, beside me.

Shattering loss isn't something that's talked about often. But we all experience it. My mother might be your sister, or your grandmother, or your brother, or your beloved fur baby, or your aunt, or your grandfather. Our stories are unique, yes, but they all echo with that same heartbreaking familiarity.

What struck me in the aftermath of my mom's passing is how the people who recognized that echo showered me with understanding and love. They taught me that from unfathomable loss, beauty and meaning can arise. Transformation can take root. And slowly . . . more slowly than you ever thought possible, life can unfold anew. It's not that we move forward without our loved ones. We move forward with them . . . always with. I strove to capture some of these feelings—the gutting echoes, the tentative steps that couldn't possibly lead anywhere but end up pointing you toward hope—within the pages of *Recipe for Joy*.

The story also serves as a love letter to Gates Mills and to Cleveland, a village and a city that I love dearly and will always hold in my heart. It's a tribute to my grandmother and her culinary influence, to my great-aunt, who comforted me when I needed it most, and to my incredible sister, whose arm was lovingly linked with mine as we endured the unfathomable. But more than anything, this is a heartfelt homage to my sweet mom, whose abundant cheeriness and indefatigable spirit is threaded through many of the characters in the story. I wanted to write a book that is unflinching in its depiction of how grief cracks you open, but also to show that the pieces can nestle back together, perhaps never the same, yet still holding strong with the fortifying gilding of memory. I wanted to convey that while all of this takes time, happiness can indeed be rekindled. Life can continue. And even those places where grief and heartbreak cracked you clean through, a glint of sparkle can emerge.

For more, please visit monicacomas.com.

Acknowledgments

I'm deeply indebted to my agent, Mark Gottlieb at Trident Media Group, for immediately believing in *Recipe for Joy*. Thank you for championing my work, and for always being a thoughtful sounding board for all things story and publishing. Mark knew exactly whose hands to place my book in, those of Chantelle Aimée Osman at Lake Union. Her infectious enthusiasm for my novel on our first call will stay with me forever. But it was the abundantly gracious and talented Carmen Johnson and Emily Freidenrich, with their combined star power, who swooped in with their magic and brought this book to life. Faith Black Ross was instrumental in putting that final sparkle on the story, helping to make it shimmer. In working with these fiercely gifted editors, I immediately knew that I'd found my publishing partners and home. I'm grateful to Sarah Horgan for creating such a joyous cover, and to Valerie Paquin and Carrie Olschner for their keen-eyed copyedit and proofread—I'm in awe of their artistry. Thank you to the entire team at Lake Union for bringing my book baby into the world.

I've been so fortunate on this author journey to walk alongside Marcia Bradley, Traci Higgins, Elizabeth Murray, Ramona Reeves, and my forever friend, Andrea Leskovar—all spectacular writers and even better friends. My weekly writer group with Sheila Miller Bernson, Jackie Goldstein, Joan Hoffman, Ariel Nazryan, and Joan Paylo is precious to me—these women I'm lucky enough to know are sterling writers all, wonderfully witty, and supportive beyond words.

Beyond my writing circle, I'm blessed to have indefatigable cheerleaders in Susan Bates, Wendy Berner, Marc Cianciolo, Katie Coff, Susan DelGenovese, Jennifer Groscup, Alice Groscup, Shaynee Novak, Jenn Patel, Diane Peluso, Wendy Pollack, Cindy Schreiber, and Emma-Jane Skogstad. Simply put, I adore you all.

Every writer benefits from those with more expertise, as I certainly have. I'm thankful for many workshop experiences, particularly the Community of Writers Fiction Workshop and The Writing Institute at Sarah Lawrence College. Leigh Eisenman guided me early in my career, and I'm fortunate to call her a friend today. My favorite teacher, Mr. Stanley Siedlecki, who taught my creative writing class at Mayfield High School, encouraged teenage me to keep writing—little did he know that he was providing a lifetime of inspiration. Or maybe he did . . . great teachers often do. Thank you.

The biggest thank-you to my in-laws, who welcomed me with open arms so many years ago and have treated me like family ever since. When I said "I do" to my husband, little did I know what a loving family he'd bring along with him. Claire Basel and Bill Basel, Claire Comas McIntyre, Lily McIntyre and Charlie McIntyre, Iris Quayle and Dirk Quayle, Caroline Lee, Frank Comas and Candice Wolfson, and the late George Comas, I cherish all of you.

Enormous thanks to my family, the Atwoods, Uncle Lenny Blake, Aunt Sophie Pertlaga, the Blanks, and, importantly, my late grandparents, Anna and Leonard Blake, and my beloved mom, Patty, whom I carry in my heart. My Midwest roots are deeply important to me—they're roots I'm always proud to have showing.

Sweet Kona started this book by my side and Poirot finished it with me. Their pitter-patter paws have infused my days with the most joyful rhythm. I love our shih tzu babies to my core.

About those Atwoods . . . the most special heartfelt thank-you to Annie, Stetson Jr., Stetson Sr., and Cooper, but especially my sister, Kristie. It's difficult to put into words how much Kristie means to me. She's the best gift my mom ever gave me. I won the sister lottery with her and am abundantly grateful for how tightly we're bonded despite the hundreds of miles between our homes. Not everyone gets that in life—believe me, I know how lucky I am, for Kristie's sparkle is rare, indeed. She's the person I can tell everything to and want to cook everything with. She's the one I carry the most history with, and the one I laugh hardest with. Despite never ever being able to keep up with Kristie on a run, I wholeheartedly wish we lived closer because she's indelibly a part of me in a way no one else is. Something to work on in our next chapter. I love you.

Thank you to my beloved mom, Patty. Much like with my sister, it's hard to know where to begin. My mom left us entirely too soon, but of course we carry her with us. I overflow with gratitude for all the gifts my mom bestowed upon me. She gave my sister and me a deep appreciation for nature, for birds and animals, for digging in dirt, and, yes, for cookie dough. She taught us to read, instilled in us a love of books, and ferried us to the library when we were small. As we grew, she poured her enormous, supportive heart into us. She raised us to have morals, to be kind, to stay curious, and to never stop learning. And in her final years, our mom gave what can only be described as a master class in grace. I am the woman I am because of my mother.

Finally, deepest, heartfelt thanks to my husband, John. Everyone should have a partner who insists they believe in you, as John has told me for years. When I doubted myself, he said it even louder . . . and more loudly again and again and again. Then he gave me a room of my own. I love him for this and for so much more it would fill an entire book. When we met (more than two decades ago now), my mom, sister, and friends jokingly referred to him as The Fabulous John Comas, and TFJC has only grown more fabulous with each passing year. In the entirety of what life can throw at you—the joyous, the grief stricken—John has held my hand through it all. I wake up every morning so grateful we get to go on this adventure together, finding the humor whenever possible, turning toward the happy, and holding every cherished memory close. From the bottom of my heart, thank you, my cozy husband. I love, love, love you always and forever.

Book Club Questions

1. Belle flees to her grandmother's house in July of 2022 feeling alone and ashamed because she's lost her job and fallen from her social circle. Is this believable for a forty-five-year-old woman at this particular moment in time? Why or why not? Was it relatable, frustrating, or both? Also, have you ever felt stuck in your life or known someone who has?
2. Belle and her sister, Alexis, are estranged. They're also very different people. How has each, whether due to circumstance, personality, or misunderstanding, fueled the distance between them?
3. What does Gran do for Belle while she's in Gates Mills? What do Gran's friends do for Belle? And how do their actions, both overt and subtle, feed into Belle's resurgence? Discuss how community fills a need of Belle's. Has community ever helped you through a difficult time in your life?
4. When Gran dies, Belle's grief is deep . . . It's also layered. Beyond the passing of her beloved grandmother, what else might have been stirred up by Gran's death? Also, there are countless reasons people grieve. Aside from the loss of a loved one, what are other events in life that can elicit a sorrow response?
5. Grace says to Belle at Gran's wake, "Families come in all shapes now, don't they?" What does this reveal about Grace? And the

fact that she has to say it, what does that reveal about Belle?

6. History repeats itself, or at the very least, rhymes, in this book. What themes span generations in the story? And what role does food play?
7. Belle must regain her footing after Gran passes away. How does she help herself do that? How does she hold herself back? Finally, how do others help, and who, if anyone, in your opinion, is absent from that help?
8. When Belle receives Gran's first letter, she's still grieving deeply. What do the letters offer her? By the last letter, Belle is still mourning, but she has also changed. Describe how.
9. Grace and Gran grew up close, just like Belle and Alexis, but their fracture lasted decades. Discuss how these two sets of siblings, born in different eras, are alike and how they're different.
10. This story falls at the intersection of tricky relationships, food, and memory. Discuss how food is indelibly linked to your own memories or traditions. Do you have any cherished recipes that are meaningful tethers to a time and place or to a person?

About the Author

Photo © 2024 Dorothy Shi Photography

Monica Comas was born and raised in Cleveland, Ohio. She holds a bachelor's degree in English from The Ohio State University and a master's in journalism from New York University. She's worked as a newspaper reporter, a journalist covering stocks and the economy, and a financial editor. But fiction has always been her true love. Monica lives in New York with her husband, John, and their tiny shih tzu, Poirot. For more information, visit www.monicacomas.com.